CW00517061

The Summer Will Come

A novel by
Soulla Christodoulou

***

The front cover has been inspired by the painting of Alexandros Sainidis who lives in Athens, Greece. He is a university student and can be contacted via Instagram @sofosgatos
It has been modified to produce the book cover by Mya Glenister who can be contacted via
Facebook @ArtfulSilver or Instagram @artful_ginger

www.dragonrealmpress.com

*This book is dedicated to my Great Aunt Alexandra
who showed such passion and belief in me when
I told her about the story I was writing.*

*Also to my Grandparents who, without their brave sacrifices,
hard work and commitment, to making a new life in London,
there would be no story to tell.*

It is with huge admiration, love and devotion I thank my mum and dad for sharing their memories with me; the happy, the sad, the joyful and the painful.

Thank you to my creative writing buddies Louise Stevens, Mark Glover, Ian Grant, Judith Crosland and Lee Amoss for your critique and unwavering support for the story I wanted to write and to Lia Seaward, Paula Panayi and Candida Akiki Darling for their beta reader feedback.

I would also like to thank Mr William Mallinson and Dr John Burke for casting their eyes over the historical parts of the book and checking my interpretation and transcript of events for accuracy and credibility. I am indebted to you both.

The title of my novel

The Summer Will Come

has been taken from the poem written by Evagoras Pallikarides.

Poem by Evagoras Pallikarides, hero and poet
(27th February 1938 – 14th March 1957, aged 19)

A day before his trial, and having decided to join the EOKA
fighters in the mountains, Pallikarides broke into his school
and
left a message and poem for his fellow students to read the
following morning:

'Dear school friends, at this time, someone is missing from
among you, someone who has left in search of the fresh air of
Liberty, someone who you might not see alive again. Don't
cry at his graveside. It won't do for you to cry. A few spring
flowers scatter on his grave. This is enough for him…'

I'll take an uphill road
I'll take the paths
To find the stairs
That lead to freedom

I'll leave brothers, sisters
My mother, my father
In the valleys beyond
And the mountainsides

Searching for freedom
I'll have as company
The white snow
Mountains and torrents

Even if it's winter now
The summer will come
Bringing Freedom
To cities and villages

I'll take an uphill road
I'll take the paths
To find the stairs
That lead to freedom

I'll climb the stairs
I'll enter a palace
I know it will be an illusion
I know it won't be real

I'll wander in the palace
Until I find the throne
Only a queen
Sitting on it

Beautiful daughter, I will say,
Open your wings
And take me in your embrace
That's all I ask…'

He signed it Evagoras Pallikarides on 5th December 1955.
(He was to appear in court on 6th December 1955, the
following day)

It has been an honour and an absolute pleasure to connect with
Thoula Bofilatos and her father Andreas Pallikarides who are
directly related to Evagoras Pallikarides and who shared their
memories of him as well as precious personal notes and
information. Much love and gratitude.

Contents

Chapter One

Elena, 1953

ELENA KICKED OFF the threadbare sheet she was entangled in with her tanned, slender legs. She spread her arms out to cool herself but her brother's chubby body, curled into a tight ball, filled all the space next to her on the mattress they shared, leaving the entire left-hand side of the bed empty. She let out a deep sigh, threw her slim arms above her head instead and held onto the solid bars of the iron bedstead. Elena relished the relief of the cool metal in her small fists. She shifted onto her side and one of her arms hung loosely over the bed's edge, almost touching the floor.

A stream of sun bounced off the roughly plastered walls highlighting the dust motes dancing around the small bedroom. The walls were bare other than an icon of the Virgin Mary, holding a baby Jesus in her arms, which hung by the shuttered windows. Below the religious artefact stood a dark oak chest of drawers, which held a small silver hairbrush and mirror set, a sepia photograph of her and her brother at about aged two, her mother, father and grandmother. Elena's only doll with porcelain face and floppy legs was lying next to the photograph, a gift from her *theia*, aunt, in America. Next

1

to the drawers, a pile of school books and two pencils were arranged neatly on a footstool. Two pairs of black lace up shoes lined up on the floor had seen better days.

The familiar squabbling and scratching of the hens in the neighbour's yard, and the braying of the donkey in the scrap of land a hundred yards away, carried faintly in the air. Elena strained her ears. She picked out the sound of heavy steps as her mother moved around the inner courtyard of their stone-built house in the mountain-side village of *Kato Lefkara*. The other sound cheered her more; starlings chittering away in the stunted silvery olive trees, pomegranate and orange trees crowding the outside space. She imagined the protruding roots pushing through the dry, cracking soil as they cooked in the day-long angry sun, desperate for water. The roots reminded her of the bumpy veins on her *yiayia's* translucent hands dotted with purple age spots.

A small smile crossed Elena's face as she thought of her maternal grandmother, whom she was named after. It quickly gave way to a wide yawn and she pushed her brother away from her with her leg. She suddenly felt claustrophobic; the June heat swaddled her like a thick woollen blanket. She sprung to her feet. As she whooshed past the wash stand she blew a kiss at the fading image of her father in the frame. She had no memory of him. This, and his worry beads which adorned the end of the bedstead, were the last tiny fragments she had of him.

'*Kalimera mama*,' she said, scrunching her hazel

eyes against the dazzling sapphire. The sweet smell of honeysuckle kissed her nose and her sweaty bare feet left little ghost footprints across the still cool slabs of the courtyard as she skipped over to her mother. She knew too well that before long, as the sun edged lazily over the slate roof of the house, the garden pavers would be as scalding as a clay oven. Elena delighted in the early morning, the time when she wandered around without her heavy-soled leather shoes hindering her.

'*Kalimera agabi mou*,' her mother said as she tucked Elena's long hair behind her ears before bending to give her two kisses, one on each cheek. '*Ela, psomi, halloumi, tomates...*' she said, pointing to the thick slices of freshly baked bread, already arranged in the bread basket, and the fresh Cypriot cheese and over ripe tomatoes.

The wooden table was ancient, the paint blistered by the burning sun flaked off the legs in fragments leaving what looked like a shower of blue confetti on the slabs. It was bowered by a tangle of vines, weighted low with bunches of green and purple grapes.

'Where's Andreas?' asked her mother, Evangelia. Elena pointed towards the bedroom, pulling her dark straight hair into a high ponytail and securing it with a black hairband almost frayed to breaking point.

'He's still sleeping,' Elena said and she made a loud snoring noise. Her mother laughed.

'It's not funny *mama*,' complained Elena. 'He snores all the time and he takes up all the bed.'

Elena dragged one of the wooden chairs, with the worn raffia-woven seat, over to the table. She reached for a chunk of bread and took a bite out of a tomato, its warm juice ran over her chin. She wiped it with the back of her hand.

'Manoli came to me this morning, bless him. God answered my prayers. He saved me the trouble of going to fetch fresh milk. The rocky stretch is becoming too much. I didn't have the energy today. He's a good man looking out for us,' said her mother.

Elena's mind drifted to Manoli, one of the younger village shepherds and his brown hair and matching dark brown eyes, his face pocked with chicken pox scars. He herded his father's tattered flock of sheep and nimble-footed goats across the rock-strewn mountainside. She often saw him in the distance, on her way to school. He would wave frantically and make her laugh. He spent his days wandering across the ridges, the goats' bells sending a merry jingle into the air, as they hopped and jumped ahead of him, climbing across the bumpy terrain, and meandering through the dusty olive trees and dry earth.

At the end of the day, as the sun dipped behind the rough peaks, Elena sometimes caught another glimpse of his shadowy figure as he made his way back to the patch of land his father owned on the edge of the village, a straggling line of dusty sheep and sprightly goats ahead of him. His piccolo echoed a resounding tinkle of notes as he played the same traditional tune.

4

'Here, have some milk. It's still warm.' Her mother poured her a glass of goats' milk from the battered metal container which she usually kept in the dark coolness of the larder.

Elena broke out of her reverie and chatted away while her mother, tall and slim, her light brown hair catching the rays of the rising sun, stretched to hang the washing on the line. The fraying fisherman's rope stretched from one olive tree to another, secured to a rusty nail which protruded from the outside wall of her mother's and *yiayia's* shared bedroom, directly next to Elena and Andreas' bedroom. The only other rooms were a kitchen not much bigger than a scullery and a tiny square sitting room with an open fire.

The laundry was a daily chore as they did not have other clothes to wear. Hence Elena's mother woke before sunrise to wash the clothes by hand, in the dark stone drinking trough which had been used for watering the donkeys, by her grandparents and their parents before them. She hung them and dried them in the heat of the fiery sun ready for Elena and Andreas to wear to school every day. Most clothes were hand-me-downs from other families in the village.

Elena didn't like it even though many of the children in her class also wore hand-me downs.

'Clothes have always been passed back and forth between families in the village,' one of the teachers said to her when Elena complained about her ill-fitting skirt.

5

'It's a way of helping each other.'

Elena was aware how some items were handed down to the point even her mother, one of the neatest, most experienced seamstresses in the village, according to the women who sewed with her, could not patch the thinning, holey fabrics anymore. And that's what life had been like since Elena's father had left. At least that's what her mother kept saying but never directly to Elena. She would never admit that to her. But Elena would hear her talking in hushed tones with the neighbours; Christalla and Athenoulla and Demitra and sometimes with the priest, *Pater* Vassilios.

Elena gobbled her breakfast, not waiting for Andreas to join her, and ran over to the outdoor bathing area. She washed herself in a colossal stone basin, in the furthest corner of the garden, balanced on top of two rocks. She splashed herself with the lukewarm water which had been heated by the sun as she tugged impatiently at the disused table cloth pegged between two canes, which screened the wash area from the rest of the courtyard. Two more rusty nails, hammered deep into the side of a silvery, bent olive tree, held two threadbare towels. An olive-infused bar of soap sat in a jar on the ground.

She dried herself with force and dropped the towel to the floor. She slipped on her knickers and leaned across to take her blouse and skirt for school. A magenta fabric caught her eye.

'What's this?' asked Elena as she shook out a

dazzling pink garment which lay folded on a bench too rickety to sit on.

'A dress for you and trousers for Andreas,' her mother called over from where she was unpegging some of the already dried clothes from the washing line.

'*Mama*! It's so pretty. I'm going to wear it today.'

'Don't be silly Elena *mou*. The dress is for going to church on Sundays and to wear on Saint Days, special occasions.'

'But *mama*...'

'I said no. That's enough of your answering back.' Then, her voice calmer, she said, 'You can wear it on Sunday to the *panigiri*. The whole village will be celebrating the beautiful British Queen's Coronation with a street party. Your school will be giving out a special mug, with a picture of the Queen on it, to each of you too.'

'I love it,' said Elena holding it against herself. She swayed back and forth pirouetting on the spot. All at once she felt guilty for complaining about the clothes not being new.

'One of *theia* Christalla's cousins passed it on.'

'I will be the prettiest girl at the festival on Sunday!'

'Stop with your vanity, girl.' Elena ignored her mother and went on twirling with the dress in her arms, only in her underwear, casting dancing shadows across the uneven slabs.

'I'm going to look like a queen.'

The next hour seemed to pass in a flash and Elena had to pull her brother by the legs to wake him. They couldn't be late. They had another eight days of rising early before school closed for the summer. It took Elena three vicious tugs before Andreas stirred and finally rose.

Elena dragged him by the arm along the narrow cobbled streets. Her shoes, two sizes too big for her, flip-flopped loudly as the sound bounced off the stone walls of the village houses along the way. Andreas crunched on a fat bread stick sprinkled with sesame seeds, oblivious to the noise they were both making. She thought about the smack of the ruler on their palms, their certain punishment for being tardy, and taking long purposeful strides she tugged with vigour at Andreas' arm, pulling him along the winding street.

The sound of an engine roared and then a car came down the hill at speed towards them. She just managed to dodge it. She pulled Andreas back against the wall, as the car swerved, dangerously close to them. She let go of the school books she was carrying. The high pitched sound of screeching brakes filled the quiet of the village and she let out a cry of horror as the car ran over the books, leaving a shower of white pages flying in the air like hungry seagulls. Elena stared after the tail lights as they disappeared round the bend as the car zoomed out of the village by the main road. One by one she saw the villagers come to their doors.

'What's happened?' called one.

'Goodness! Whatever was that noise?' shouted an old lady.

'Elena! Andreas! Are you hurt?' asked the priest's wife.

Elena huffed and puffed, gesturing after the car, now long gone, in an exaggerated manner, her heart beating so hard she was sure it was going to jump out of her tiny chest. A few minutes passed. Once the shock had worn off and she found her voice and told the gathered crowd all was fine. Elena could hear them sighing with relief. She saw one of them cross herself in thanks to God for keeping them safe from harm.

'I'll let your mother know all is well,' said one and assured the children were unharmed the neighbours went back to whatever they had been doing before the commotion. Andreas and Elena sneaked a peek at each other; they both laughed. Andreas, she saw, had tears tracing down his pudgy cheeks as he chewed on a finger nail.

In the kerfuffle Andreas managed to wriggle free of Elena's loosening grasp. He stopped and bent over, tugging at the laces on his shoes, his bottom pushed back against the bumpy stone wall of the *kafeneion,* which was empty and still. It was far too early in the day for the older men of the village to descend upon the coffee shop.

'*Mama*'s tied these too tight. They huuuurt,' he whined. Elena saw him scrunch his eyes in an effort not to cry. 'My feet are screaming.' But she knew his crying had nothing to do with his shoes.

He jumped over the low wall and sat on one of the coffee shop chairs, knocking over one of the glasses left there from the night before. Water filled the open *tavli* board and the backgammon counters sat drowning.

'Well I can't hear them,' said Elena, 'and they'd be screaming even more if they'd got run over. They're just hot and sweaty.' She climbed over the wall to collect what was left of their school books. They were ruined. The pencils were shattered.

'No they're not! The shoes are too small.'

'Well at least they're not too big like mine!' she said, looking at the 'boats' on her slender feet. 'Some other girl has worn these until her big toes almost pushed through the tips,' she said, pointing to the hated shoes. But Andreas wasn't listening.

'*Ela,* Yioli! *Ela,* Niko!' Andreas called as he tried to race towards two friends strolling past the *kafeneion*. 'Did you see that car? It ran me over, ouch.' Ignoring Andreas' moans Elena's sinewy arm pulled him harder than she knew was necessary while she tightened her free arm, clinging in desperation, onto their now dishevelled, almost pageless books.

'Come on shortie! Stop exaggerating,' she said as he fell in behind her, his legs dragging.

'Be quiet!' Andreas sulked as Elena, tall and willowy in contrast, towered over him.

They caught up with Yioli and Niko who both

wanted to know what had happened. As they walked through the rusty iron gates leading into the yard of their school, Elena, now breathless, filled them in with the confused excitement of what she and Andreas had experienced.

Some boys kicked a semi-deflated ball around the concrete yard, while others huddled in small groups in the shade of the makeshift canvas awning playing *lingri*. Elena watched on as the boys played. Zacharias balanced a piece of wood across two bricks on the ground. Rico then used a twig to flick the piece of wood as far away as possible. Stelio, the marker, marked the spot where Rico's wood had landed and so the boys continued to flick the wood as far away as possible. They took it in turn, whooping and teasing each other's efforts, until a winner was announced by Yiannis who measured the distance the wood had travelled each time. Some girls were perched on the stone steps in the shadow of the school building, talking and laughing, as they watched two of the younger girls playing *vasilea*.

'One, two hop. Three four scotch.' sang Stella at the top of her voice, like a cockerel at dawn.

'Five, six hop. Seven, eight scotch,' repeated Mirianthi as she threw her stone further along the chalked hop scotch ladder. Her curls bounced around, appeared golden in the sun. Elena looked with longing at Mirianthi's blue school shoes with the pretty buckle and how her butterfly print skirt fluttered around her legs as

11

she hopped.

Elena didn't have the energy to play today. The hop-scotch game was too exerting and the morning was hotting up. She was flustered after the near run-in with the car. Elena felt irritated and she still had to explain to their teacher what had happened to their books and why they didn't have their pencils.

The three teachers, *Kiria* Maria, *Kiria* Eva *and Kiria* Anna appeared from inside the building and took their positions. The children waited in line for the Principal to ring the school bell at 7.30. Elena noticed it was *Kiria* Anna holding the brass bell with the smooth wooden handle.

'Can I ring the bell?' asked Elena with a sudden burst of enthusiasm.

'Why yes. Thank you,' said *Kiria* Anna.

'Where's the Principal?' asked Yioli.

'He won't be in today,' replied *Kiria* Maria.

Elena wondered why. The Principal had never had a day off school.

Elena rang the hand bell. Its ding-dong chimed across the school playground.

Sitting in rows behind wooden desks the fourteen children in Elena's class, aged from seven to as old as ten, copied what *Kiria* Maria chalked on the rickety blackboard at the front of the room in large, rounded, even spaced letters. Elena sat in the back row; a head taller than the others even though she was two months shy of her ninth birthday. She smiled, relieved her teacher had replaced the pencils and note books for each of them with no charge. Elena knew her mother couldn't afford to pay for new ones.

I gata troei psari, The cat eats fish
O skilos bezi me to tobi, The dog plays with the ball
To helithoni betaei, The swallow flies

One after the other the children read the sentences out loud as *Kiria* Maria pointed to each word with a long cane and commended them for their clear pronunciation.

The lesson was interrupted by Elena and Andreas' mother who knocked before entering the classroom. She stood respectfully to one side until *Kiria* Maria approached her. Elena stood and walked towards the front of the classroom when she saw her mother. She stopped by the second row of desks when her teacher motioned for her to wait. Elena listened, straining her ears, to the conversation.

'There was an incident this morning, *Kiria* Maria. I wanted to check Elena and Andreas were not hurt. My neighbour came to tell me.'

'They are perfectly fine as you can see,' she said, nodding in Elena's direction and then in Andreas' who was still seated. 'I've given them a new exercise book and pencil each.'

'I'm so relieved. Thank you. You're most kind.' Evangelia gave the children a smile and mouthed she would see them at home and she left.

Kiria Maria continued with the lesson. Elena returned to her desk.

'*Bravo* Niko, *bravo* Yioli, *bravo* Petro, *bravo* Sofia...Andreas?' Andreas clearly hadn't been following. Elena knew he couldn't concentrate in class and wondered whether he'd been more shook up about the car than her. She wondered who it could have been driving out of the village at such a dangerous speed. She hadn't recognised the car.

Andreas struggled to read any of the sentences his teacher pointed at. His face was becoming flushed as his nerves got the better of him. Elena could see he was unable to concentrate on what *Kiria* Maria was saying to him. Andreas stared out of the window, shying away from *Kiria* Maria's piercing stare; a sheen of sweat coated his forehead as he sank deeper into his chair, his sagging posture shrinking him further.

'*Ade* Andreas,' she persevered, her fat upper arms shaking as she tapped the words with her stick. 'Come on, Andreas.'

But after two more failed attempts, her impatience got the better of her and she snapped, her pink rosebud lips opening wide to reveal rows of pearl white teeth crowding her small mouth. The scrape of the metal chair across the floor punctuated the silence as Andreas stood up. He burst into tears, his face congested with embarrassment as he stumbled out of the classroom. Niko

14

shoved his hand, palm facing out, in the general direction of his shamed classmate.

'*Na*,' Niko said out loud. Elena could see the gesture mirrored the thoughts in the majority of pupils' heads. 'He's so stupid.'

The other pupils, some of whom had been sucking in their cheeks with repressed laughter and others who had been whispering to each other, now roared out loud. Elena hesitated for a split second, gave Niko a condescending shrug of her shoulders and then chased after her twin.

But by the time she had got to the main school doors Andreas was already charging through the school gates. She lost sight of him as the road curved behind the village church. Elena slapped the heel of her hand to her forehead. She walked back to the class, puffing and wheezing. She mouthed an apology to *Kiria* Maria who nodded discreetly in acknowledgement. The rest of the day's lessons continued without any further disruptions. *Kiria* Maria kept control with her solemn stare.

***

The evening's winter sun, gentle and watery, dipped behind the red tiled rooftops. Elena straddled an old empty keg and read her spellings out loud. Intermittently she stopped and questioned her mother about the car.

'Apparently it had something to do with the Principal,' said her mother eventually.

'Why was he driving so fast? Where was he going?' asked Elena, her eyes wide with surprise.

'Nobody knows.'

'I rang the school bell because he wasn't there,' said Elena.

Elena enjoyed school and was more excited than usual about the next day when *Kiria* Nitsa, a teacher from Larnaca, a main coastal town, was coming to do art with her class. *Kiria* Nitsa visited once a month bringing with her an array of paper and coloured pencils and crayons. Art was Elena's favourite subject. She often imagined herself sketching and colouring all day but knew she couldn't waste her one pencil on drawing. She would spend hours a day-dreaming about the drawings she would sketch one day, when she had a pencil in every colour of the rainbow.

As the sun dipped behind the uneven rooftop the family sat to have their dinner in the shady canopy of vines, their branches and boughs intertwined and twisted around the makeshift arbour above them. *Yiayia* was there too; her maternal grandmother and Elena moved her chair closer to her so she could smell her familiar sweet aroma of rosewater. Her *yiayia* squeezed her hand.

'You're a good girl,' she said to Elena. Elena beamed from ear to ear. She loved it when her grandmother told her she was a good girl.

Her mother brought out a tarnished metal pot with a lid and put it in the middle of the table, resting it on a wooden board, scarred with knife marks. Elena knew it would be beans or lentils. They rarely had money for meat which she didn't mind, but she knew Andreas loved meat more than anything. The bread basket was already filled. One by one her mother served the *louvi* and *kolokithaki* with a slatted spoon to drain the boiled salted water. The little black-eyed beans and thick slices of courgette sat in a heap on the plates while *yiayia* drizzled generous amounts of olive oil over them. Elena squeezed fresh lemon over them spraying Andreas who was sat opposite her in the process.

'Sorry,' she giggled, as the zest tickled her nose.

'No you're not.' Andreas pulled a face.

'No arguing and say your prayers,' admonished Evangelia, tucking a loose strand of chestnut wavy hair behind her ear. They did swiftly and crossed themselves before they tucked in, soaking the olive oil and lemon dressing with their bread. They ate their meal in silence, their heads lowered over their bowls. The quiet of the evening was intermittently punctuated by the overpowering hum from the cicadas, hidden in the trees. The sky was streaked orange and pink and purple as the sun set low above them and Elena wondered whether everyone in the whole wide world could see the same multi-coloured sky as her. She wished she could paint a sky like it. She thought about her father. She often thought about him. She often had little conversations with him in her head even though she didn't know him.

Andreas remained silent the entire time they ate, which was unusual, because normally he would natter away and be told off for talking with his mouth full.

***

'It doesn't matter,' Elena said to him later on as she got changed for bed. She didn't want him to worry about not being able to read yet.

'It does matter,' he said, a tremor in his voice as the welling threatened to choke him. Even though they were twins, and he was an hour and a few minutes older than her, she was protective of him. Elena knew he was upset and could see him frowning in an effort not to cry. She leant over and ruffled his thick dark curls but he didn't pause from his daily evening chore. He scrubbed at their school shoes, even though they hardly required a clean, before placing them next to each other by the footstool. She waited for him to climb onto the tall bed and then she closed the pale delphinium painted shutters before getting in next to him. They said their prayers together and crossed themselves. Elena pulled the sheet over them both, tucking the edges in around them. She knew their mother would come in later to check on them both. She would hear the creak of the door as she pushed it open, her leather-soled slippers, scraping across the concrete floor, the thin rug slightly muffling the echo of her tardy steps.

The next day at lunch time, which marked the end of the school day, Elena ran to her mother and gave her a big hug proffering her picture of green pastures and lush trees against an azure sky and scattered tufty clouds.

'That's lovely, Elena *mou*,' her mother said, barely glancing away from her embroidery. Elena noticed her mother's eyes were red and sore, as were her fingers from the lace-making she'd been bent over all morning.

'Have you been crying?' Elena asked.

'No.'

'Why are your eyes so red?'

'I'm tired *agabi mou*. It's been a long morning. This sewing is more arduous than ever today.'

'But you're always sewing. Why is it so much harder today?'

'The Principle's daughter has eloped with someone from another village,' said *theia* Athenoulla sitting next to her. 'Apparently she was lying in the back of that car that nearly run you over. Her poor mother, worried sick she is.'

'She's run away?'

'It looks like it,' said her mother.

'And you work too hard Evangelia,' said *theia* Athenoulla.

'She does,' chipped in *theia* Christalla as she pulled her thread through the embroidered table runner she worked on. Elena looked at her mother. She saw how she sat there all day, her chair leaning against the front of their house, facing out onto the narrow street, sewing continuously.

'I know, *mama*,' she said. And she knew exactly how tiring it was because she felt it too when she sewed the whole day long. The idle chatter between the women offered the only other distraction which broke the otherwise mundane quiet. Elena often sat and listened to how they called out to each other and took turns to make the strong Greek coffee, served in demitasse cups, and pass round short glasses of water to each other to stay hydrated.

The lace making was a historical tradition of the village; mothers of mothers and generations before them passed on the delicate craft of the embroidery sewn onto the natural linen using white or brown thread. This is how Evangelia, and the majority of women in *Kato Lefkara,* earned a living and it took hours and hours of delicate hand stitching and pulling to produce a runner or a place mat. She knew she would sew for a living one day too, just as Evangelia had taken the place of her mother now *yiayia* was too old and her sight failing. It was an inevitable fate. But she wasn't complaining. She knew that's how it would be. She didn't expect anything different unless...unless they went to England.

'Is it because of Andreas?' Elena prompted, not convinced with her mother's answer about the Principal's wife.

'Andreas? He's always causing mischief. If I cried

every time he misbehaved, we would be drowning in salt water.' True, thought Elena. It was not the first time Andreas had run out of school and it wouldn't be the last.

Chapter Two

Elena, 1953

THE VILLAGE CELEBRATIONS of the Queen's Coronation brought cheer. The courtyard of the church was decorated with bunting and the usual stall holders added extra decorative trims to their tables and awnings in blue, white and red. Stall holders organised themselves in rows, back to back, along the front of the church entrance and spilled out along the main winding streets which led to the church. The tall wooden flag pole flew the Cyprus and British flags. Both fluttered in the summer breeze, side by side. A flight of swallows passed through the blue sky effortlessly, their long pointed wings spread wide and their deep forked tails like streamers.

Tables for eating and drinking lined two sides of the courtyard with people crammed in around them. The whole village was celebrating. The priest sat amongst them, the Sunday service concluded, his glass of *zivania,* a colourless alcoholic drink made from grapes and pomace, topped up by the men sitting at the same table. People dragged and carried chairs from home too ensuring enough seating for everyone. They sat haphazardly in the muted shade of the tall firs around the perimeter of the church wall. They ate from plates of food on their laps, glasses balanced on upturned crates and empty boxes. A loud hum of talking and singing filled the air. Elena's mother smiled and Elena gladdened to see her happy and relaxed amongst her aunts, cousins and neighbours.

Every horizontal surface staggered under the weight of all the food, crammed with homemade trays of *makaronia tou fournou, kiofdethes and koubebia;* oven macaroni, meatballs and stuffed vine leaves. Colourful bowls of salad swimming in olive oil and freshly squeezed lemon passed back and forth as people filled their plates, black olives peering out like beady eyes at them. Portions of sweets and delicacies and pastries bought from the many stalls were shared amongst everyone generously. Bowls of fresh figs and huge slices of honey melon and water melon brightened the table with purples, yellows and reds.

The villagers, wearing their best outfits, shared what dishes they had with their neighbours and friends. Stray cats and kittens meowed for scraps and children sneakily fed them under the table.

Zivania and red wine flowed, empty bottles stacked under the tables. The village folk were jubilant. Amongst the plates of food, the Coronation Day mugs distributed to the pupils by the Principal, at the end of the morning church service, sat on the table where parents promised to keep them safe for their children. The Principal had not stayed long making his excuses to get to an appointment.

Elena and Andreas mingled amongst the throng, visiting the stalls with their school friends. Evangelia gave them a penny each to buy a treat. Niko, Stella, Yioli and Zacharias each had a leather pouch with coins in it to spend on whatever they liked and envy crept up on Elena. They bought whatever they laid their eyes on, but Elena had to spend her money carefully. She couldn't choose between a portion of *pastelaki* and a portion of *bourekia.* She liked both equally.

The *pastelaki,* a sticky concoction of sesame seeds, almonds and pistachios bound together with honey and cut into bite size chunks, glistened. The *bourekia,* little parcels of deep fried pastry filled with a creamy cinnamon sweetened cheese, were dusted white with icing sugar. Finally, she chose the *pastelaki;* these would last longer and her money, she observed, would buy her seven pieces. But in the end Elena ate two *bourekia* too.

'*Ela,* Elena, b*ourekia*,' Yioli's mum offered as she took one herself.

Elena tucked in delighted, relishing the sweet aroma of the cinnamon.

'What a pretty dress,' Yioli's mum said, running her tongue over her lips.

'I saved it especially for today.'

'Well today is definitely special.'

Elena wandered off for a while on her own, drawn to the art stall. Fascinated by a painting of green hills dotted with sheep, she stood staring at the picture in the centre of the 'Larnaca Art Gallery' stand draped in a British flag and shielded by a red, white and blue striped awning. A brown tabby cat, skinny and scraggy, lay sprawled under the table in the cool shade.

'Do you like this?' asked the lady as she tucked an errant strand of dark hair under her head scarf. Elena noticed her long almond-shaped fingernails painted as red as a cherry and her lips to match.

'It's very green,' said Elena, stroking the soft folds of her colourful berry pink dress.

'Painted by an English woman,' she told Elena as she re-arranged three smaller paintings of the ocean at the front of the table.

'And they're very blue,' said Elena feeling the bumpy layers of paint enhancing the sea waves.

'She sells the paintings so she can carry on living here. She has no husband.'

'Why doesn't she want to go back to England?'

'She likes the sun too much,' laughed the lady, the whites of her bulging eyes staring at Elena like the little white rubber balls sold in the village shop.

'England,' Elena said, dreamily thinking of her father.

***

By late afternoon some families made way for home, having finished eating, seeking the peace and quiet of their courtyards. Others tarried, immersed in their drinking and chatting. A neighbour kindly offered to walk Elena's *yiayia* home. This meant Evangelia could stay longer and the children could also enjoy the rest of the celebrations.

A group of musicians, from the village, arranged themselves in the far corner of the church yard, adjacent to the church ground's gated entrance. The music started and the village audience clapped and cheered.

One man settled on a wooden chair and played the *bouzouki*, its flat front decorated with mother-of-pearl shining softly in the dipping afternoon sunlight. His fingers moved deftly across the strings as he bobbed his head in time with the music, smiling across at the gathering. A young boy drew his bow at right angles across his violin as he tucked it under his chin. An old man, a brown cap tilted across his head at an angle, stood leaning against the back of a chair. He sang out in a croaky voice; traditional words of love, lost and found, happiness and sadness, wars and victories.

Three men leapt from their seats. They cleared a space and danced while those watching crouched on bended knees and clapped in time with the low metallic sound of the *bouzouki* and the higher pitch of the violin notes. The men danced with light steps and springs in their knees. They lent forward towards the ground.

'*Opas! Opas!*' they cried.

Their arms waved and swung low as they touched the

ground with their hands and clicked their fingers to the beat. Everyone cheered as the three men took it in turns to bounce on bended legs, the older man dancing with slower dignified steps. The other two kicked their legs out high in front of them, whirling and slapping their thighs as they continued to move in time to the music.

One of the young boys on the sidelines whistled with his fingers. Elena watched as he made the perfect whistle-hole with his mouth and the shrill cut across the hub-bub of the *panigiri* and the entertainment.

Another member of the band, maybe as old as twenty, thought Elena, played a wooden flute, the high pitched clear sound exquisite. The notes of a traditional women's dance tune struck out on the violin as a fifth musician tapped on his *toumbeleki,* a hand drum. The intense sound sent goose bumps over Elena's arms and the back of her neck.

A number of women, maybe ten or twelve, moved to the space marked out as the dance area. A lady started singing, her voice flowing like a gentle river. The women stood in a circle and took the hand of the woman standing either side of them, holding on at shoulder height. In time with the music, they danced gracefully making steps from left to right, crossing their feet at intervals. They let go of each other's hands and turned.

Facing inwards again, they took the hand of the person on each side of them. They continued, some singing the words of the song as they danced, others smiling at each other as they whirled round the dance area. More women joined in and, as the circle tightened, it created a spiral of women dancing around those now in the inner circles. Elena took part, holding her mother's hand. Yioli and Stella tried to break into the circle and Mirianthi took Stella's hand but Mirianthi couldn't keep pace with the steps and eventually let go, standing to the side to clap as her friends danced on.

The singing and dancing continued. Evangelia, now exhausted from the dancing and the ferocity of the day's blazing sun, persuaded Elena to go home with her at around nine o'clock. Andreas had fallen asleep across two chairs pushed together, curled like a foetus, holding onto a wooden top he bought from one of the stalls. Two women went round the tables lighting candles and the glow of the flames sent orangey shadows bouncing off the church walls as the sky darkened.

Tables were left in disarray and tacky with rosewater cordial spills and empty glasses, splattered with dribbles and food congealed in its oily juices. The women promised to return in the morning and tidy properly. Stray cats lounged around the edge of the church courtyard purring contentedly, fat and swollen with the abundance of food they'd eaten. She wondered if there would be cats in England too.

***

But elsewhere on the island not everyone celebrated. In Paphos, on the western side of the island, the British flag flying high was not received with joy and smiles. As the British Army began singing their national anthem, school children marched upon them throwing sticks and stones. A young, athletic boy by the name of Evagoras Pallikarides, shimmied the flag pole and tore the British flag from it. He threw it to the crowd of students below him and they ripped it, setting the shreds alight. It was a momentous occasion for all the wrong reasons as far as the British were concerned but for all the right reasons as was to become evident over the next few years.

'I've had a lovely time,' said Elena, as she danced and her pink dress shimmered in the otherwise dark, twisting road. She held tightly onto the two mugs and the paper bag with her five remaining pieces of *pastelaki*. 'The best time ever,' she said as the faded moonlight cast shadows in the road and she hummed a tune to herself. 'And I will treasure my mug forever,' she sighed, as she stifled a yawn.

'We're all ready for sleep,' said her mum, wheezing slightly, as she stumbled carrying the sleeping Andreas home in her arms. 'But it was a lovely day,' she said as she hoisted Andreas further onto her hips.

Elena fell asleep and dreamt of green fields and big black and white cows. She saw a grey sky and she stood in the cold rain. She was searching for the sun. When she looked more carefully, through the fat raindrops, she could see a round face with blue eyes looking at her. She woke, her hands frantically wiping the rain from her face and her slender body.

***

'So what do you think my dream means?' asked Elena after recounting her dream in as much detail as she could to Athenoulla after school the next day.

'I don't know,' she said, folding and unfolding her apron as she tried to avoid Elena's intense stare.

'But you know everything about dreams. I've heard you talking about dreams and their meanings with other people. Everyone comes to you.'

'Well, that's different, Elena.' She ushered her away. 'I haven't the time for your silly nonsense. Now get off home. Your mother will be wondering where you've got to.'

She tried to broach the subject with her mother too but her mother had no time for her. 'Questions, questions. Dreams are just muddled pictures of books you read. Your mind putting the words into pictures as you sleep. The dreams mean nothing.'

But Elena hadn't read any books with green fields in them or pictures of cows. She remembered the painting she had seen at the *panigiri* and thought that's where the image had sprung from. Then she remembered her own picture at the bottom of her wardrobe and how *Kiria* Nitsa from Larnaca had commented she had seen the exact same fields when she visited England many years before.

'But it could mean we're going to England. To be with father.'

'Your imagination is running away with you. Enough.'

***

The dream 'of England' continued to enter her sleeping thoughts and filled her waking moments. On her last day of school, she asked *Kiria* Maria. 'Does Paphos or Limassol have green fields with cows?'

But she was met with a curious little expression and dismissed with an impatient wave of her teacher's hand. This confirmed her dream must be 'of England' and she was comforted by the thought of England being close to her. But she didn't say this to her mother. She kept it hidden deep in her heart. It was her happy secret.

***

School closed from the middle of June and Elena worked incessantly over the summer holidays to contribute to the household's income. She pulled out the rickety chair from under the kitchen table and positioned it, under the mass of magenta flowers creeping in abundance across the upper part of the outer wall, facing into the street, where she sewed till sunset. She didn't stop until she had completed nine arms' lengths of *gazi,* a simple embroidery stitch. She received a shilling for each length from the lady in *Pano Lefkara* who exported the lace to Europe.

Elena mostly enjoyed the peace and quiet and although her friends would sometimes pass by and have a natter with her, she secretly wanted them to leave her alone so she could finish her nine arms' lengths as quickly as possible. Her mother had promised her a bar of lavender soap if she earned a shilling every day of the holidays. She worked quickly and her neat stitches could not be differentiated from the work of the other women who had been lace-making for fifteen, twenty and thirty years.

'I'm so proud of you,' her *yiayia* would say each evening at dinner. 'God will reward you one day. He will bring love and joy into your life.'

'Thank you, *yiayia.*'

'Stop it Mother,' Evangelia scolded one evening, her almond shaped eyes dull, dark circles taking the shine out of them. 'Life isn't made of dreams. Life is real. Life is hard. The sooner she realises the better.'

'Nothing wrong with a little dreaming coupled with the right energy,' the old lady retorted, pulling her black scarf over her hoary strands of hair, smiling at Elena, her crooked teeth filling her mouth. 'There's always a way to something better.'

Elena watched as her *yiayia* shuffled over to the orange tree in the courtyard. Curious to see what she was doing, Elena followed her. She watched as her *yiayia* took a handful of rusty, bent nails from her deep dress pockets and stooping poked them in the dry soil around the roots of the tree.

She spoke with watery eyes. 'My father's father always said dreaming is a way of making reality happen. There is always a remedy. Just as this simple trick will help our orange tree's leaves shine gloss green again, as the roots take the iron from the nails, so will your dreaming create the reality you want. Hold onto your belief with every bit of strength Elena *mou*.'

***

It was almost the end of August and Elena had worked every day not once complaining her brother disappeared with his friends most days; playing football in the school yard, collecting prickly pears from the mountainsides, collecting 'magic' rocks which shone with special powers and generally larking around keeping the old men of the village, who sat in the *kafeneion* daily, amused with their capering. She knew too that he would have eaten at least one tiny piece of *loukoumi*; the owner of the *kafeneion* not only knew how much he liked the sweet jelly but also how their mother couldn't afford to buy it.

The women in the village were raised to be passive and accepting of their role in life; to marry well, be respectful wives and loving mothers and to not be feisty. So Elena was happy with her life in the village. She didn't complain too often. She had her dreams but she kept them in her head and in her heart.

Chapter Three

Christaki, 1955

CHRISTAKI THRUST HIMSELF further and further into the salty white waves coming directly at him until he gasped for air. He slowed his pace until his breathing regulated, came less hard. He continued to take in air deep into his lungs until he thought he would burst. His strong, but narrow shoulders and long arms pushed him further out against the crash of the sea as it came directly at him.

The ocean was fresh now and the May sun dipped behind the line where the blue sea met the orange horizon, but he liked the way it felt as it ran over his bronzed body, as it soothed his aching muscles and soaked through his dark wavy hair, cooling his head. He swam out more towards the wave breaker of huge boulders into the azure of the sea. The exercise relaxed him and his mind wandered to a conversation from the night before.

'You have a rare head for numbers. And sequence. And order,' said his accounting teacher at the extra evening classes Christaki had enrolled for.

'Thank you, Sir,' Christaki replied, puffing out his chest with pride, his chin upturned.

'You will be a success whatever you do, my boy. You are hard-working. Diligent. I wish you well

Christaki, yioka mou.'

'Thank you, Sir,' he repeated.

Allowing himself a small smile to spread across his face, as he swam, he recalled the affectionate phrase, 'my son', used by Kirio Melis. He wondered why his teacher had been uncharacteristically emotional. Christaki still had a few months of the course to go and was going to be in class the following week again, as usual.

He swam harder, his shoulders taking the full force of the water. He was anxious about what might happen that evening. He tensed even though the swim normally relaxed him and a sharp pain crossed his upper back as he twisted his tight torso to stay streamlined; to maintain his pace.

Christaki attended high school in Limassol until classes finished at two o'clock. He regularly swam afterwards, even in the cooler autumn months, and then worked until eight o'clock, sometimes later, at the village Co-operative General Store. His family managed this; Christaki worked there from the age of eleven, four years now, to supplement the family's many other sources of income.

This evening he wanted to delay his return to the village where he lived in the Amathus District of Limassol. Ayios Tychonas, built into the coastal hills, sat lazily, the dull murmur and enticing fragrance of the ocean ever present. Many of the village houses built of stone, cream and grey and white, constructed on one level, had an inner courtyard around which the rooms would open onto. Smaller abodes had one room for sleeping and eating in and an outside space with a wood stove and washing area. Homes throughout the village, painted various shades of blue; front doors and window shutters, reflected the village's proximity to the sea.

Many of the villagers herded goats and sheep for a living, spending many hours a day herding the life stock over the hilly, rocky terrain for miles and miles, the coastal air matting their hair daily with the salt it carried from the Mediterranean ocean. Christaki knew only too well about the hard life of the shepherd. Lonely. Physical. One of the oldest inhabitants of the village, Antonis, now nearly crippled with arthritis and unsteady on his feet, continued with his shepherding and tested the endurance of many of the younger, newer shepherds he trained and shared his knowledge with.

'I don't understand how Antonis hikes across those mountains day in day out,' said Christaki, in admiration for Antonis as he chatted with his mother, Anastasia. Christaki went out with the old man when he wanted a bit of company. Antonis was patient, said little but he taught Christaki all he knew about feeding, grooming, clipping and delivering new lambs and kids.

Christaki's family were wealthy and worked hard; the importance of hard work had been instilled in him, being the eldest, from a young age. Loizos, his father, was a forward-thinking man and his main aim was to make a good life for his wife, Anastasia and his three children, Christaki, Pavlo and Melani.

Anastasia, a re-nowned seamstress, had clients from villages as far east as Zygi, Pyrgos, Parekklisha and Moni and as far west as Mouttayiaka, Ayios Athanasios, Ypsonas and Germassoia. She not only excelled as a dressmaker and seamstress but she repaired and made adjustments to garments. Her nimble fingers made her most reliable and she often worked late into the night sewing in the dim light of the oil lamp.

Loizos, a shoemaker, had his own shop on the outskirts of the castle area of Limassol. His clientele consisted of a combination of rich and prosperous families who came and placed orders with him from as far afield as Larnaca, and those who lived locally who required repairs to their shoes over and over again. He was a fair man and well-respected and often carried out repairs for free in exchange for a bottle of olive oil or a basket of figs or fresh fish caught the same morning or support collecting the carob from his abundance of trees during the harvest.

The carob trees, scattered across hectares of land, inherited by Christaki's parents from their parents, provided additional seasonal income for the family; the slow-growing evergreen trees brightening the otherwise dry, infertile, harsh climate. Carob was the "black gold" of Cyprus's export economy alongside copper and the land stretched across the double-peaked mountainside to one of the "secret" caves.

Christaki's family didn't harvest the carob themselves but relied on regular workers from the surrounding villages, who came every season - August to October - and laboured, from the first yellow glow of dawn to the last burnished pink of dusk. Many of them worked for Loizos to repay debts accumulated over the year by their families.

'Carob harvesting…' one of the men explained to Christaki as he paused to splash himself with water from the well at the end of the day. '…is a manual process, unchanged for centuries. Even machinery can never replace the hand-picking. It takes precision, patience.'

'Patience?' asked Christaki.

'Yes patience, care not to damage the flowers. Or next year's crop'll be reduced, even ruined.'

Loizos appeared carrying a tray of little glasses. A stout man, with a purposeful stride, a calm force of energy seemed to surround him and echoed in his movements and facial expressions. His smile touched his eyes which shone with a glint.

'Thank you my friend. What more does a man need than somewhere comfortable to sleep, a meal and zivania amongst friends?' another man said as he took a glass. 'Stin iyeia sas, to your health,' he said as he threw his head back and swallowed it in one gulp.

'Stin iyeia sas,' repeated the other men one by one as they took their glass and drank.

Anastasia, Christaki's mother, slow-cooked lamb or pork in the outdoor stone oven and the smell of the onions, coriander and meat juices permeated the air all day.

'There's kleftiko enough for all and bowls of beans or lentil soup,' she said as she served the men, who were openly grateful for her show of warm hospitality.

'More zivania.' His father generously refilled their glasses and passed hot bread round. The men tore off chunks with their worn, calloused fingers, hunger undoubtedly growling in their stomachs. They slept in the open fields or in the enclosure next to the house, situated in the oldest part of the village, and backing onto open land.

***

'That's it. The donkeys won't carry much more weight,' said one of the men as he loaded the harvested carob pods into huge rattan baskets the following morning. He secured them either side of the donkeys and fastened them with rope, secure round the back and belly of each animal.

Christaki and his father plodded off to sell the tons and tons of carob to an exporter based in the nearby fishing village of Zygi.

'We'll have to make five maybe six journeys' said his father. 'It's been a good harvest. The Russians will be pleased with their cargo when they receive it.'

Christaki crossed the beach, his feet caked in the cooling sand. Careful not to tread on the scattering of pebbles washed over it he stepped over a mound of trawler nets and around a stack of wooden crates. He grabbed the towel he'd left by his leather flip-flops, on top of a boulder, and used it to roughly dry his black wavy hair. He shivered as the ruffling breeze, on the back of the setting sun, kissed his damp skin. His eyes were bleary, stinging from the saltiness of the water and he blinked a few times to clear his cloudy vision. He blew his nose into his hand and wiped them on the towel. Clearing his throat, he spat onto the dry sand.

He pulled on his T-shirt, put on his watch hidden beneath it and slipped on his flip-flops. He felt the warm sand stick to his toes and wriggled them to dislodge some of the grains. Rolling his towel haphazardly lengthways he hung it around his neck and ambled towards his green Vespa, hidden by the brambles and overgrown wilderness which skirted the dirt track leading from the beach to the main road. He picked up his wallet, still on the motorcycle seat where he left it, and re-arranged his college books which protruded from the makeshift storage box he had secured to the back of his moped.

The snap of a broken twig alerted him to someone close by. Christaki strained his eyes in the low light. As he stared across the wilderness, domineered by huge rocks and mounds of debris, a shadowy figure ducked behind one of the overgrown tangled bushes behind a discarded bench.

'Ela,' he called out. 'Who's there?' An involuntary shiver ran along his spine like a slithering grass snake. He knew he was being watched. He felt the hair stand erect on his arms and the back of his neck; he fought against sickening nerves. He walked with a determined stride, in an effort to quash his anxiety, towards the cluster of brambles, and as he got closer tiptoed with caution. From where he stood, he spied two shadows, crouched still. He edged forward towards the hazy light. The humming of whispering drenched the air.

Someone hauled themselves to their feet with a groan. Christaki let out a sigh of relief. He recognised the back of Panteli's head between the sparse zig-zags of the thorny bushes, the distinct bald patch above his left ear a dead giveaway.

'Panteli?' he called out, his voice edgy still, his eyes transfixed. Someone shot off. He saw the back of a girl; a flash of a brown dress, a pale blue scarf over her head and a tan leather satchel over her shoulder. She clambered over the rocks like a wild hare towards the main road. She didn't look back. He waited with bated breath, his heart thumping in his chest, the saline air around him filled with dust.

'Panteli?'

'Yes, it's me,' Panteli said as he revealed himself from his thorny hideaway, clearing his throat and brushing dry earth from his palms and then his knees.

'What are you doing? Christaki asked. 'You frightened the life out of me.'

'Sorry. I was…I was meeting Katerina.' His cheeks reddened.

'Katerina?'

'Yes.'

'Why here? Why are you hiding?'

'It's complicated. Her father doesn't approve of me.'

'Since when?'

'Since I joined EOKA.'

'EOKA?'

Christaki knew about EOKA; Ethniki Organosis Kypriou Agoniston, the National Organisation of Cypriot Fighters. The initials splashed in thick dull red paint tarnished the sides of buildings in Limassol and the crossroads leading into the village. Desolation took hold amongst the people of Cyprus and more recently, in Ayios Tychonas.

He listened to the men talking as they drank their coffee and played tavli at the kafeneion. Conversations were tense but not altogether unfriendly as villagers were divided; their topics focused on the leaders of EOKA, a colonel by the name of George Grivas and Archbishop Makarios. They discussed their conviction to the cause and how surrender would be a grave dishonour.

Christaki knew his father supported AKEL, the communist left-wing party and he would not go against his father and his beliefs. He trusted his father's acumen and insight into the politics of the country. He essentially believed, too, in the rights of the working class people and their right to fair pay and good jobs.

'Yes. I had an interview, an initiation. I'm seventeen next month. I want to play my part,' he said, with undeterred, fierce loyalty. He stamped his foot; a spattering dust rose and pattered back to earth.

'Why do you have to? Why can't we carry on like before? We live in the same town, the same village. Why get involved? And what about Katerina? What's she say?' Christaki gripped his friend's arm. A nerve twitched in Panteli's temple.

'She supports my decision. She…wants to do her bit…'

'What d'you mean?'

'She wants to do something.'

'Like what?'

'Leaflets…pamphlets…'

'For God's sake, Panteli, her dad'll kill you if he finds out!'

'He won't find out. And it's got nothing to do with me.'

'Well, he won't take it like that when he discovers she's been meeting you…and he's sure to find out,' said Christaki, concern in his voice, a deep furrow of anguish etched on his forehead.

'I can't ignore what's going on,' he said. His eyes reflected the red low sun opposite. 'Things are getting worse. People are getting heated more and more, especially since the British have arrested people unfairly. Anyway I've said too much…if anyone asks…you didn't see me.'

As Panteli walked away Christaki noticed Panteli's leg; blood seeping through a makeshift bandage, creating a patch-work map. Christaki wondered what sort of initiation he had gone through and fought against his running imagination.

The sudden rev of an engine over the incessant rumbling of the cars and trucks on the main road, forced Christaki to divert his attention. He recognised Yianni, on his motorcycle, one of his closest friends since elementary school. He was three years older than Christaki and already married to his childhood sweetheart, Despina. Despina was Christaki's cousin. He waved at him with both arms and called out his name but Yianni didn't react or acknowledge Christaki. A flash of blue whizzed by as he passed at speed. He wondered where he was going in the direction of Germassoia village this late in the day. Something bad was coming. He felt it.

Christaki started his moped. It lurched forward seconds before the familiar low humming of the engine kicked in. He revved the motor and drove off and round a bend towards the winding dirt road which took him back into Ayios Tychonas and his home nestled at the foot of the shuddering hills. The nausea in his stomach reminded him of what was inevitably waiting at home: more arguments about EOKA, more disgruntled villagers, more crying women, his own mother sobbing into the night's silence when she thought everyone else slept, deaf to her cries. He flexed around the handle-bars, his knuckles white from his tightening grip, his head banging with overwhelming anxiety and the thundering in his ears. A growing fear coursed through his veins.

He arrived home, submerged in his own taunting, cheerless thoughts, and propped his moped against the side of the olive tree on the narrow lane leading to his house. He walked to the back, the kitchen door stood propped open as usual.

He pushed the beaded curtain aside and walked into the kitchen; the beads knocking against each other.

'Ela mama, ela baba,' he called out for his parents.

No-one was there, but through the open doorway on the other side, he could see the table set for dinner in the courtyard. A carafe of red wine sat proudly in the middle of the table alongside the overflowing bread basket and a plate of lemons cut into quarters. The house was silent, eerie. The familiar queasiness rose within him and he began to sweat and shudder. Where were they? He glanced at his watch; it was gone eight and they habitually ate together at eight. Where were Pavlo and Melani? He tried to push away his growing uneasiness. There had to be a logical explanation. He threw his towel onto the back of a chair and wandered back outside.

He strained against the now near darkness around him and could hear the scuffling and scratching of the rabbits in the hutches some fifty feet away, by the periphery stone wall of their garden plot; an open expanse of flat rocky terrain. As far as he could, he made out the deserted landscape apart from the murky silhouettes of the olive trees and prickly pear plants against the inky, silver-threaded sky. About to turn back towards the house, he saw the weak light of a paraffin lamp bobbing behind one of the hutches.

He remained transfixed, his wide eyes bulbous with fright. Not sure whether to call out or run in the opposite direction. His heart pounded. He took a couple of steps closer, craning his neck. A figure hopped over the low wall, and landed on the uneven, rocky ground. A man. He momentarily lost balance but regained control as he came towards Christaki.

'Ela Christaki mou,' called out his father, 'We've slaughtered two rabbits!'

'Ela baba,' said Christaki, relieved to recognise his father's nearing silhouette. Three other figures behind his father came into view; his mother and Pavlo and Melani. The four figures came closer. Christaki was surprised to see Melani with them. She would usually cower away from killing anything let alone two of her dear rabbits.

'Pater Spyrithon, is coming for a meal this evening.'

That explained the more formal table setting. His tummy rumbled in protest of him not having any lunch.

Dinner wouldn't be until gone half past nine by the time the gentle priest made his way through the village, stopping at the kafeneion along the way, which Loizos usually teased him about.

'I was worried when you weren't home,' blurted out Christaki. The quiver in his voice revealed his fear.

'Why? Has something happened?' asked his mother as she approached, reaching out to stroke his face. He took her hand in his and a deep reluctance to let her go came over him. He adored his mother.

'No nothing,' he lied.

Back in the house his father wasted no time in skinning the rabbits and portioned them ready to cook in the fournaki. His mother roughly chopped onions and scattered bay leaves over the meat. She set the round earthenware dish in the stone oven and secured the iron door.

'How was the sea?' asked Pavlo, who preferred to sit around than to exercise.

'Cool, refreshing.'

'You look agitated,' said Pavlo.

'It's nothing. Nothing for you to worry about.'

'What does that mean?'

'Leave it, Pavlo.'

'The potatoes and the koubebia are cooked if you want to eat now. Pater won't mind. And he prefers the rabbit to the stuffed vine leaves,'said their mother.

'Will he not be offended if we don't eat with him?' asked Christaki, always respectful.

'It's your father he wants to spend time with,' said their mother.

'I'm eating now,' said Melani, 'and then I'm going to Katerina's.'

'What you going to Katerina for?' asked Christaki.

'Nothing. A chat…girl talk,' she said, winking at him.

'Well, I don't think you should. She's a bad influence.'

'What? Where did that come from?'

'Why d'you say that about the girl? She's a good girl,' said Anastasia.

'And polite, respectful,' said his father.

'Yeah,' said Melani, 'so stop being mean. I'm going whether you like it or not. You're always bossing me.'

'That's the way it is,' he retorted.

'In your world maybe, not mine. You're never going to get married. No-one will marry a tyrant like you.'

'Enough,' said Loizos. He stared at them, in turn, with his dark eyes.

That's all he had to say. His reprimand was not to be ignored.

Melani ate dinner in silence, alone, the whole time scowling at Christaki who stood opposite her staring right back. When she finished, she put her plate and cutlery in the butler sink, turning round to stick her tongue out at him. He didn't say anything. She wrapped her shawl around her and shouting bye to no-one in particular, she skipped out the door, her slender hips swaying. She was immature for her age and appeared younger than her fourteen years. Her light brown hair, scooped back into a high pony tail, matched her cinnamon eyes, and her high cheek bones shone out of her face, her lips a rose-bud pink pucker. Christaki had a bad feeling about his sister meeting Katerina.

The priest didn't arrive until after ten o'clock. He rat-a-tat-tatted on the open kitchen door and floated through the bead curtains into the kitchen, across the sitting room and into the courtyard. Loizos, sat at the table, listening to the local news on his old wireless; the volume crackling. He was tall and slim, wearing his simple black cassock. His eyes were dull, with dark circles around them and his cheeks were sallow against his long silvery beard. He greeted them in a cheery voice but his face did not glow as it normally did when he smiled.

'Kalispera, Pater Spyrithon,' said Loizos, rising from his seat, taking the priest's right hand in his and lowering his mouth to kiss the leathery skin, showing reverence to his Apostolic office.

'Good evening my friend,' said the priest. He hesitated for a split second before noticing Christaki and Pavlo. Both had remained seated at the table, even though they had finished eating long before his arrival. They hadn't wanted to offend Pater who had baptised them as babies and watched them grow up by not being present for his visit. They had sat compatibly animatedly talking about everything and anything but not what was surely on their minds. They obediently stood and mirroring their father's gesture, kissed the priest's hand.

The priest took his place at the table and said grace. They each crossed themselves before starting their meal. Anastasia served big hearty helpings for them and his father, mother and the Pater, proceeded to tuck into the stifado. The rabbit with onions, had been baked for two and a half hours in the stone oven which had also been 'warming up' for over an hour so it was the hottest it could be. The meat fell off the bone and smelt delicious; the aroma of onions hung in the air. The two men soaked the thick meat juices with chunks of bread and crunched on fresh spring onions and thick slices of cucumber. They clinked their glasses, merriment in the air, and gulped the red wine while Anastasia sipped at hers deep in thought. Small talk took place around the table, interrupted only by the flies, which they intermittently swatted away. They talked about Christaki's accounting lessons and Pavlo's school lessons; he was a year younger than Christaki.

The solemn, inevitable talk of EOKA commenced once Anastasia had made her excuses and disappeared into the kitchen to wash the pots and pans and prepare the dough for the bread the following morning.

'Our village now has a growing number of EOKA

members. There are fourteen, including two young boys who are joining as soon as they are seventeen,' said the priest. 'I'm not sure who is acting as leader in the village but one of my parishioners told me a plan of attack has been hatched. I am not getting involved but it is hard when many of the villagers want to show the British they are not to be messed with. They want Enosis with Greece and whether we agree or not we have to accept what the majority of our people want.'

'First and foremost we have to protect our men. I will not get involved in this. But if anyone asks you can direct them to the secret cave. They can use it for a lookout and a base, somewhere to hide in case there's a situation…you know, requiring them to go into hiding. I know these men, the old, the young, I cannot let them perish,' said Loizos.

'Are you sure Loizos?' asked the priest.

'Yes. I'm in. I cannot desert them even though I don't agree with the EOKA fight. The cave might be on my land but I'm willing to turn a blind eye.'

'May God protect you and that which is yours.'

'What of the others? Those sitting on the fence so to speak?'

'Some villagers have expressed their lack of support, as you have my friend, and although we have lived here for years together, we must be careful who we speak to.'

'Has it really come to that?' asked Loizos.

'Unfortunately, I think it has. We must err on the side

of caution.'

'I can't ignore my neighbours and friends. We've lived in harmony for so many years,' said Loizos.

'It's hard. It's harder for me as the priest here. I have a duty to all. But your duty is first and foremost to your family. Second your country.'

'I have cousins who are involved. They want Enosis, union with Greece. How can I not speak to them? We live in the same village for God's sake.'

'Be careful, all's I'm saying.'

A silence hung between them for a few minutes as both men contemplated. Christaki shifted his seat and surveyed the rooftops he could see from the elevated position of their house. He wondered how many families were having the same conversations about loyalty and family and dying for their country. He knew of one boy, maybe a couple of years older than him, who bored of life in the village and Enosis provided something exciting for him to focus on. He had only boasted about it the other day, despite Christaki telling him to keep quiet about his beliefs and his involvement.

'Now the business of supplies,' said the priest, stroking his beard which made him resemble one of the saints on the icons in his mother's prayer room. 'We have a pistol…bandages and scissors from a friend who works in the main hospital. We even have a suture kit. I've also hoarded three bottles of zivania although I'm praying no-one will be so badly hurt they have to be inebriated as the only bearable way for their wounds to be treated.'

'And what about the use of code?'

'We have yet to establish this. But given time we will be ready.' The priest lowered his voice. 'Christaki, have you thought about what we discussed last time I was here?' asked the priest, concentrating on Christaki, who until now had not been included in any of the conversation and had simply sat and listened.

Christaki had thought of nothing else, especially since his run in with Panteli. 'Well, I'm not seventeen yet, so I can't officially be recruited into EOKA directly, so no-one can be suspicious of my convictions or beliefs,' he said. But I'm ideally situated in the Co-op to intercept messages possibly being passed back and forth between the village EOKA group and the main planning contingency in Limassol. I won't change my routine so it won't raise any suspicions.'

'You've thought this through well,' said his father. Pater nodded thoughtfully.

'Of course,' Christaki said, surprised at the clear answer he gave. 'Evidently it's a big risk. But if baba believes this is right, then I do too,' Christaki said with more conviction than he felt.

'For God's sake,' burst out Pavlo. He left the table, clumsily pushing his chair across the stone flooring, his long legs banging into the sideboard in the lounge as he rushed past it. Christaki bid the priest good night and chased after his brother.

'I know you're afraid. But I'll be careful. I have to do this. And I'm not actually involved in anything. Just kind of keeping an eye,' he told Pavlo when he caught up with him.

'Please don't do it,' Pavlo begged Christaki with ferocity as he elbowed him away. 'It's like spying. If anyone finds out, you'll be arrested, or worse.'

Christaki left him knowing too well Pavlo was too upset to talk further. Back on the veranda he listened to the priest's parting words to his father.

'That's what we all want, our families to be safe.' The priest checked his watch. 'I must go,' he said as he shook Loizos' hand warmly, but with strength.

He squeezed Christaki's shoulder as he walked over to Anastasia who, busy in the kitchen kneaded dough for the family's weekly supply of bread. She knew she could buy bread from the Co-op but her mother had taught her well and she preferred to make her own. Christaki had heard her say so often enough. Clouds of flour dust rose and clung to her hair and streaked her face as she pulled and stretched the dough with a confident expertise, with great mightiness for a small woman of only five foot two.

'Busy, always, Anastasia mou. Thank you and kalinichta,' the priest said bidding her good night.

'Sto kalo,' she responded, 'Go well. Kalinichta.'

She covered the dough, now ready to proof, in cheesecloth; it would rise by morning and be ready to knead one last time before baking.

'We will talk tomorrow,' Loizos said to his wife and to Christaki.

Christaki stayed awake for another half an hour or so contemplating; the people who were getting involved, dragged into this thing; whatever it might be. But he knew already the ending would not be a good one; good people, innocent people on both sides were going to get hurt, were going to die.

Christaki had heard Melani talking to Anastasia in the kitchen when she had returned not long after the priest's arrival for dinner. He knew his mother had no idea about Katerina's involvement in distributing the anti-British leaflets across the area. He wondered who printed them and where? Could it be someone in the village? Although the leaflets were written in Greek, he knew once they had been scrutinised by the British, they would believe them to be anti-British; a voice against them.

**

Two weeks later, as May's breeze slipped away to let the heat of June in, Christaki spotted Katerina in the wasteland on his way into Limassol to take some extra supplies to his father. He slowed his moped.

'When I say "ready", throw your ammunition,' commanded Katerina as her words carried on the chilly breath of the wind.

Christaki wondered who she was talking to and struggled to catch her words. He couldn't see anyone around, but then in the far distance he saw Melani. He recognised her yellow dress and floppy summer hat she wore to protect her from the morning sun. She looked like an ordinary young girl taking a hike across the hills overlooking the sea. What was she doing? He wondered. She should be at school. Suddenly she waved a blue scarf in the air, waving at someone. Christaki made out a boy on his bike on the road directly below. When Christaki peered back, he caught sight of Melani scrambling over the hillside. She's going to the secret cave, thought Christaki.

The boy pedalled like mad towards Katerina and the others. Christaki could see the sea breeze blowing into his face.

'Please God let this not be what I think it is,' Christaki prayed. He peered back to where Katerina was now half-crouching, and noticed the other children, some as young as nine or ten, but most of them from high school. They too squatted low behind the boulders and rocky crevices of the mountainside. The more he focused, the more children he saw.

Within minutes the boy appeared at the foot of the disused field.

'They're on their way. Melani waved four times,' he said, catching his breath. He threw his bike to the ground and joined his school friends crouched behind an abandoned truck.

'So there are four trucks,' Katerina's distinct voice carried on the wind as she addressed the hiding students.

'There are four trucks,' she called out this time in a half-whisper. 'You know what to do. We've got about five minutes.' There was a commotion as the young people moved into position. Some children hid behind rocks and boulders, others crouched low, camouflaged by bushes and thickets.

Christaki saw the Keo beer delivery truck trundle past and take a right into the road leading to Ayios Tychonas. Two older men on their mopeds whooshed past, sending a billowing cloud of dust into the air. A small convoy of British military vehicles followed.

'Ready?' called out Katerina. 'Now!'

What happened next terrified Christaki and he was unsure what to do. He pushed his moped over and lay low. He scrambled over the rough terrain to where the children were hiding. He caught his elbow on a jagged rock and winced from the pain. Blood seeped through his shirt sleeve. Their action stunned him.

The thuggish children sprang out shouting and screaming. They bombarded the military trucks and jeeps with rocks, bricks, stones and sticks as they drove by. A rock hit the first jeep's windscreen smashing it instantly. It came to a sudden halt. A screech of brakes filled the air as the trucks behind swerved and collided with it.

Christaki, his eyes fixed on the target, saw one skid, its side and windows indented and crushed from the flying rocks. It ended half way in a ditch on the other side of the road. The soldiers rushed out and ducked behind their battered jeeps; both the back tyres blown. There was no movement for a few seconds. Doors clacked open and banged shut as the soldiers got out, shock on their faces. Two showed signs they'd been hurt. One held his arm and grimaced from the pain and the other who wore no beret held his head where an open wound gushed blood.

'British out! British out!' yelled one of the boys and the others joined in with him as they waved their crude home-made banners in the air. A white bed sheet painted blue with the Greek flag, the initials EOKA and the word Enosis painted across it flapped in the air. A smaller flag made from scraps of blue and white silk, sewn together to form a white cross on a blue background, waved high above their heads.

'What the?' yelled an officer, as he grabbed his rifle, blood dripping from his face. He directed the other soldiers to evacuate their vehicles and take cover.

Christaki's heart beat faster and faster.

'EOKA!'

'Enosis! Unity with Greece!'

'Zhto H Ellas! Hail Greece!'

'Eleftheria H Thanatos! Freedom or death!'

The students screamed a barrage of obscenities in Greek and waved their arms in the air. Handfuls of anti-

SOULLA CHRISTODOULOU

British leaflets were thrown into the air. The papers scattered across the rough terrain and into the road, other sheets fluttered in the air like soaring albatrosses.

The officer panicked. Caught unawares. He raised his rifle and shot three times into the air. Silence prevailed.

'This is not the answer! You're putting yourselves in danger!' shouted the officer. 'You are so lucky not to have hurt any of us seriously! This is your one and only warning!'

'Enosis! Unity with Greece!' yelled Melani, as she showed herself. The others joined in until their chanting became deafening.

Christaki panicked. The situation was spiralling out of control. He had to act, fast.

'I will make sure she goes home,' he interjected, grabbing Melani by the arm.

'What do you care? Who are you?' asked one of the officers.

'I don't care about her! She's always stealing our fruit. A stupid twelve-year old!' He knew that mentioning her age would be the only thing that might save her.

'And?'

'And what you do to her won't be as bad as what her father will do when he hears about this!'

The officer tutted and let his arm holding the rifle fall limp by his side.

***

In the privacy of their home, as the sun begun to set at five o'clock, the shutters remained closed to avoid anyone overhearing the family talking.

'How could you be so stupid?' yelled Christaki.

'Why is it stupid? I wanted to do something,' Melani insisted, tilting her chin in defiance, her dark almond-shaped eyes glinting with passion.

'You should have told us what you were doing!'

'Why? So you could try and stop me?'

'No. So we can protect you.'

'Well we had it all planned out. It's taken weeks. And I don't need protection,' she said with defiance.

'And how did you know about the secret cave?'

'I heard baba mention it.'

'For goodness sake!' yelled Christaki.

'And I'm not doing this alone.'

'Katerina helped,' volunteered Christaki before she could say anything else. 'She's involved, she was there this morning,' added Christaki.

'So what?' said Melani.

'So that's what you were planning two weeks ago? You should've told me!'

'Don't shout, baba, pleeeaase.'

'How can I not shout? You're too young to be involved. You're still a girl.'

'Why can't I help? I love our country!' she raised her voice again and shook her long hair, shining golden, back and forth, in defiance.

61

'Melani mou,' her father said. Christaki could tell Melani was pushing his patience. 'You want to be a part of this. I praise your conviction to the EOKA cause even if I disagree. But it's far more complicated. You're putting yourself, and us, in danger.'

Anastasia and Pavlo sat at the old pine table. The mellow grain of the pine, scarred and battered over years of wear and tear, shone in the light of the crescent moon. They both didn't say anything throughout the whole conversation and then right at the end Anastasia said, 'It is time we thought about how this is going to work out. I'm scared Loizos, scared for our family, for our home, the villagers.' She didn't cry, her eyes glinted with a sad determination.

'When the time is right Anastasia, agabi mou, my love, we will have passage to somewhere safe. I promise to make plans for our escape, in case,' said Loizos.

Christaki looked from his mother to his father and then to Melani and Pavlo. He had no idea about this. His heart bursting with love and respect for his father, this man who worked so hard to give them a good life. He turned away from them and walked towards the back of the house. He stared out across the vast blackness of the open land and then at the full moon sitting on the dark vengeful shadows of the mountains. He could hear the quiet scratching of the rabbits in the hutches as they drifted into sleep, the sound of a motorbike revving its engine cutting across the quiet.

He wondered how life was going to unfold and he shivered even though the closeness of the night swaddled him.

Chapter Four

Evangelia, 1956

'WHAT DOES THE letter say? Who sent it? Is it Father?' Elena asked, her voice squeaking as she hopped from one foot to the other with excitement, her arms waving around in an uncoordinated fashion.

'I haven't opened it.'

'Why not?'

'Because I've been busy all day, sewing, cleaning.'

'Where is it?'

Evangelia's heart had fluttered like Sunday best ribbons in spring time as she fingered the creamy white envelope, unable to open it. The letter from England still lay on the bedside table. She had waited so long for this moment, she had almost surrendered all hope, resigned to the real possibility she would live out her days in the village as the woman whose husband emigrated to London and never sent for her; left to raise her children on her own and to live with the daily sympathy of others, the woman whose husband didn't love her enough to be with her.

She thought about all the time she had spent waiting; waiting for a letter, waiting for a call, waiting for money to be sent over, waiting for good news. She smiled as she remembered the many phone calls over the first year, via her neighbour Crystalla three streets away, the only one in the village with a phone. They had been short, but punctuated with hope and promises and declarations of love from her husband. Her heart skipping like a wild hare when she spoke to him and for days after her dreams would be full of him and her, love and passion.

But as the years passed, the phone calls became less frequent and when they did come there were long silences and no answers to her questions. Instead of leaving her joyous and hopeful of the future, and what it might hold, the conversations left her deflated, insecure and unsure of whether there would ever be a life in England for her and the children. So in many ways, Evangelia had resigned herself to being the wife without the husband. Divorce was not an option, living apart was inevitable.

Elena bounced across the courtyard and within seconds returned outside waving the letter in her outstretched hand. 'Go on, *mama*. Open it.'

'Leave it on the table. I'll open it in a minute.' She smoothed out her apron in her lap and her fingers played with the trim. She repeatedly pushed strands of her hair behind her ear.

Moments later Evangelia opened the letter carefully, her hands trembling. She sat heavily in the chair by the table, let out a slow sigh, and then, after fidgeting to get comfortable on the itchy raffia seat, focused on its contents. Elena waited, her hands twisting and untwisting. She was bursting to ask again who the letter was from but Evangelia could see how Elena fought the urge to rush her.

'It's from your aunt, Panayiota. She has a house. She says we can all go and live with her. *Yiayia* too.'

'In England?'

'Yes in England, in London.'

'And Father? Will he be there?'

'I expect he will be there too,' said Evangelia, and then more forcefully, 'Yes, of course.'

Elena threw herself at her mother and hugged her, burying her face into her ample bosom, laughing loudly, out of control.

'I'm so happy,' she sang out as she danced across the courtyard.

'Why are you so happy?' asked Andreas as he sauntered in.

'Ugh, you're all sweaty!' taunted Elena.

'Well I'm not the only one. I was playing football...in the village square with Niko and everyone. We're all sweaty!' he answered back.

'That's what my dream was about. The cows in England and the grey skies!' said Elena ignoring him.

'What?'

'We're going to England!'

'What?' he asked instantly confused. '*Mama*?'

'It won't be yet, probably after Easter next year. Or even the year after. That should give us enough time to get ready. There's a lot to sort out,' said Evangelia.

She could barely remember her husband's touch. He had, after all, left when the twins were almost two years old, to carve out a better life in England and had promised to send for them when he had saved enough money for the crossing and had a home for them to come to. She had believed him with all her heart and soul. The story was repeated many times over and she had grown to love the romance of it initially. But as the months turned to years and she found herself still waiting for him to send for them her fairy tale became entangled with the tale of the *kalikanzari* who lived in the forests of the Troodos mountains; a story of mischief and trickery her own *yiayia* used to tell her as a child.

'Your father wanted more than what life in the village could offer us.' She repeated the same response, word for word, over the years to Elena and sometimes to Andreas, who asked about his father less often.

'But why did he go without us?'

'He had to go alone. He needed to settle, find a job.'

'How long does that take, *mama?*'

'As long as it takes. Now stop all the questions. Go and find something to do. Leave me be.'

But something still rankled her. The letter had come from her older sister Panayiota and not from Kostas. Something told her things would not be well and certainly not as well as she had hoped all these years, as she had prayed for over and over again, but she brushed it aside.

She should have been giving thanks to God her older sister had come to her rescue but instead agitation consumed her.

'Who cares who sent it?' said Andreas in a low voice, as he tugged at the fringing of the blue and white chequered cloth on the table, pulling out strand by single strand. The children had gathered in the courtyard of Elena and Andreas' home after school. Evangelia had promised she would make *eliopites* for them as a treat. As a rule, she did not like baking almost as much as she didn't like cooking, but had been persuaded by Andreas who ate the little olive pastries like they were chunks of chocolate. Evangelia, sat in the shade of the vines and continued her sewing. She sipped at her glass of water and listened to the children's chit-chat.

'What difference does it make?' asked Yioli, slurping the last of her juice out of the baby glass bottle.

'Well it means Father hasn't kept his promise,' said Elena.

'Maybe he can't write. Maybe he told your aunt to write the letter for him,' chipped in Niko.

'Yeah, that's it,' said Andreas, dropping a handful of the loose cotton threads onto the stone floor.

'Maybe, but *mama* doesn't seem excited,' whispered Elena.

'Well, she's got a lot of organising to do all on her own. My mum says she's a saint. Putting up with not having her husband here and being on her own all this time…and…' Yioli coverd her mouth, realising she'd said too much.

'Yes…well…*baba* has been working hard to prepare a better life for us. He's been on his own…completely on his own.' Elena swatted wildly at a fly with the full force of her hand, her lips clamped shut.

'You know what I mean, the main thing is you're going now.'

'Yes. We're going. But I'm going to miss you,' Elena said, her voice softer, full of emotion and with stinging eyes she gave Yioli a tight squeeze.

Evangelia listened to their conversation and realised the children had a point. She wondered what sort of a life she would be taking them to. Would it be to somewhere better? It was the biggest chance she was ever going to take but she knew it was her only chance to see her husband again and she had to take it; for better, for worse. And things here were progressively getting worse with the English.

***

'Where will you be residing?' asked the official. He twiddled with his pen and Evangelia watched a bead of dripping sweat disappear into his hair line.

'In London with my husband and my sister.'

'Who else lives there?'

'My sister's three children and her husband.'

'How big is the accommodation?'

'It's a four storey house. It says so in the letter.' He carried on reading through the letter for what might have been the third time. Evangelia's eyes squinted as she concentrated on his stubby fingers and ridged nails.

'When did the letter come?'

'A week ago. The post mark says September 18th.' Evangelia pointed to the Queen's head on the stamp, smudged by the inky frank mark imprinted across it.

The official stood tall and sashayed towards a part-glass partitioned area behind his desk where Evangelia saw him talking to another man. On the wall behind him hung a picture of HM Queen Elizabeth II and an old map of Cyprus, the glass broken in the bottom corner of the frame. The official paced the small room while the other man leafed through the paperwork.

'Why has it taken you so long to bring the letter in?' the official asked when he eventually came back to the front.

'Because I've been working and I didn't have anyone to mind the children, so I'm finally here. I had to bring them with me.' She felt the pressure mounting aware of the heat and the vast number of people who had now filled the space behind her.

'So you want to travel together with the children and your mother and the Kyriakides Family in April, not next year but the year after…in 1958? In eighteen…nineteen

70

months' time?'

'Yes. I have a lot to organise before then. And I need time to save for the tickets.' Evangelia knew this was an understatement and the undertaking was sure to involve the most tremendous preparations and planning.

'And the Kyriakides?'

'We'd like to travel together. I have all their paperwork here,' she said again wondering why he kept asking the same questions.

'I can't authorise their papers. They have to come here in person.'

'But I said I would...'

'Those are the rules. They are not family. They can come any time with the paperwork.'

'Very well. I will tell them.'

The official stared at her askance and hesitated before taking out a pad in triplicate. He filled out the details painfully slowly. His writing was small, rigid. He held onto the ink pen at an odd angle, dragging the nib across the page leaving tear marks on it. Just like him, thought Evangelia, hard, but inside she thanked God, grateful things were now at long last moving in the right direction even though the mundanity of the process was agonising.

She looked apologetically to the crowd of people behind her, noisily pushing their way towards the three desks at the front. He got up a second time and went to consult with the same man again. A decision has to be imminent, she thought to herself.

'*Ade,* what are we waiting for?' called out the short obese man behind her as he now pushed against her lower back, his big belly as round and as solid as a watermelon. He called out again aggressively. 'I've been waiting for over two hours!'

A couple of other men called out too taking their cue from him and she felt a surge of bodies move forward. People floundered in the heat, tired and dispirited.

Evangelia, her legs aching from standing for more than two hours, was pushed into the heavy oak table. She flinched from the pain in her abdomen. The muggy, oppressive heat strangled her. Her dress stuck to her back, the sweat damp and uncomfortable. She peered over the man's shoulders to Elena and Andreas, chasing each other in the huge square courtyard, the ornate iron gates majestically towering over them. She watched as three other young ones participated and wondered whether it would be as easy for her children to join in with other children in England. She wondered what sort of a life they would have. What was she taking them to?

The ceiling fans barely circulated any air and what breeze they did create was warm, stifling. She tried to reach into her bag for the flask of water she had brought with her but as she did she found herself drifting. The room spun in and out of focus around her. She held onto the desk to support herself but the nausea swaddled her. She slumped onto the tiled floor, darkness engulfing her.

She came to sitting on a metal chair in a room painted alabaster white. A floor to ceiling, blue-framed window opened onto a small yard with a water fountain in the middle; but no water flowed from it. Elena and Andreas were sitting obediently opposite her on a couch covered in a cream crocheted throw.

'*Mama, mama*,' yelled Elena when she saw her conscious.

'Ela, Elena mou. Andreas.'

A lady in a beige uniform and a crest on the shoulder, one of the government officials, offered her a glass of water.

'You fainted,' she said.

'I'm so sorry. I was so hot…'

'Don't apologise. As long as you're alright now…your children were so worried, bless them.' Evangelia tried to stand but still a little unsteady swayed and flopped back into the chair clumsily.

'Take as long as you need.'

Evangelia worried her collapse had stymied the process and as if sensing her anxiety, the woman said, 'Vasili is finalising your paperwork for you.'

Evangelia exhaled in relief, and watched the woman walk out of the narrow doorway, her wavy bouffant a work of art blooming out of the top of her head. She watched her as she entered another office almost identical to the other man's; the same portrait of the Queen adorned the wall and a map of Europe with black arrows in different directions marking out different sea routes hung next to it. She stroked the faces of her children finding solace in their sweet concern. She had to be strong for them. The journey ahead was going to be long and difficult.

An hour later, maybe longer, she pigeon-stepped back towards the same desk she had fainted at; the number of visitors had dwindled considerably. The official had already embossed the paperwork with a large stamp. As Evangelia watched her approach him, she saw him flurry something across the page. It was his signature. The relief overwhelmed her; the paperwork was complete; identities, proof of address and an acceptable bank balance, recorded on the three sheets of paper.

***

The journey back to the village was slow and the backs of her legs sweated, sticking to the plastic seats of the bus. Evangelia hung her head, eyes shut, she whispered a grateful prayer everything was officially sealed.

As the bus trundled along its route she noticed British soldiers stationed along the main road in front of a dilapidated building. One soldier barked orders at another. This scene maddened many passengers on the bus who were talking animatedly about the 'troubles' getting ever more brutal and unpredictable. A couple of older youths, no more than eighteen years old, were talking.

'D'you hear about the house in Larnaca?'

'Yeah, anonymous tip off apparently.'

'The Brits searched for more than five hours...'

'I read they found weapons...ammunition in the sewers, under the house...'

'And phosphorous flares.'

'The house was only 300 feet or so away from *Ayios Nektarios* Church, my dad said. Not that "he" saved the men hiding there...'

'The EOKA rebels caught were beaten, with the butts of rifles, eft standing, no water, no nothing. Passing out from heat exhaustion and dehydration.'

'Bastard British! I heard they forced those men into military trucks. They're all in the detention centre in Nicosia.'

Evangelia continued listening to their account of the story which had been paraphrased with embellishments, differing from what she had read in the newspaper. Snippets of conversation continued to buzz around her ears.

An elderly gentleman and a younger man, perhaps his son guessed Evangelia, spoke of school children in the Larnaca district who had petrol bombed two British military trucks causing injuries to three troops. But it had not stopped there and caused continuous disturbances with school children continuing to strike in an outward demonstration of their allegiance to EOKA.

'Don't you dare do anything like that, d'you hear me?' said the older man.

Evangelia listened to the thrum of conversation and whispered stories. Her head pounded and the stink of sweaty bodies filled the air. She wondered how much of the conversation the children had taken in. She was glad Elena and Andreas were still at the village school and not at the high school where they could have been drawn into the daily fracas. Elena, though, appeared dreamy, pre-occupied, and Evangelia saw sleep pulling Andreas deeper and deeper as his head lolled gently on Elena's shoulder, the bus's monotonous rhythm evidently soothing him.

Finally, at the crossroads with *Pano Lefkara*, Evangelia alighted from the bus with Elena and Andreas. Elena ran off towards their home, eager to stretch her cramped legs, and encouraged by her mother to go off she disappeared. Andreas, still sleepy, walked ahead more slowly, his pace ponderous. Evangelia lagged behind him further still, a little weak from her fainting episode but pleased she would not have to make the journey back to the government offices again. She was lucky to have so many good neighbours, so many people to help her get organised.

She was also relieved Elena appeared happy at the prospect of leaving although she wondered whether her daughter truly understood what that meant; that she was unlikely to return to the village, that any of them would.

As she neared the *kafeneion* at the top of the village she noticed a large group of men, some holding spades and shovels and others hammers.

Her heart missed a beat and the lightness she felt disappeared; she felt the blood pumping through her, echoing in her ears like thunder. Despite her fatigue she ran towards the crowd of men and older youths. As she neared, she caught fragments of frantic conversation as everyone spoke over each other.

'Manoli's been arrested. There's no other explanation.'

'His donkey's been found slaughtered.'

'We must retaliate.'

'This is an invasion of our freedom.'

'He's innocent.'

'We have to prove it.'

Without asking what had happened she realised the repercussions of the EOKA struggle had now tarnished her own beautiful village. It was too much. She uttered Manoli's name under her breath. Sorrow crumpled her face as her worst fears came true.

She didn't stop to talk, to ask questions, embarrassed of the emotions coming at her, wanting to get home, to be safe.

***

A few weeks later, as the first chill of winter hit *Kato Lefkara*, Niko's father, Zeno, drove Evangelia to Limassol on his way to work so she could apply and pay for the first part of the crossing to Italy. He dropped her at the beginning of the port area, promising to meet her at the same spot at 1pm so they could have lunch together at a relative's restaurant before making their journey home.

This was the last step and once those tickets were paid for there was no return but perhaps this was the right time to go. Cyprus didn't feel safe anymore. Four more men from the village had been arrested and their families had no news of them.

She walked briskly, the sea's breeze tugging at her scarf. She took the path towards the harbour office which would take her towards the port as Zeno had told her. She had only visited Limassol a handful of times and she felt conspicuous in the unfamiliar territory so her quickened pace gave her confidence.

She looked across to the rough waves and white spray of the November sea on her left where wooden jetties and short platforms led to where simple, tied fishing boats bobbed in the wild splash of the waves against their sides. In contrast, huge container ships were aligned in the distance. She knew the cargo ships were laden with copper, carobs, wine and timber. The entangled wind carried the sound of clanging chains and scraping metal as their huge hulks were loaded. It boasted a different world to her *Kato Lefkara*. She could see workers, running the length of the platforms, yelling to each other and directing cranes with their heavy loads onto the huge vessels sitting effortlessly on the water like majestic swans.

To her right coffee shops and booths selling newspapers and sweets lined the wide street, towered by tall buildings with Corinthian pillars and peaked stone entranceways; solid wooden doors with black painted ornate ironwork, dotted the wide street. She recognised the distinct building of the Bank of Cyprus with its emblem – an ancient Cyprus coin bearing the inscription '*Koinon Kyprion*' meaning common to all Cypriots – proudly shining out from its façade. The pavements were a moving patchwork of people making their way to work, moving quickly as if to avoid the wintery coat settling around them.

A yellow and cream bus juddered through the slow-moving traffic while mopeds weaved in and out, some drivers shouting obscenities at the speed they were going. The bus was full to bursting with passengers their hot breath leaving misty patches on the windows as they stared vacantly out at the cold sunshine. The rack on its roof, burdened with luggage and suitcases, boxes tied with string and baskets overflowing with dried fruit, groaned under its bulky weight.

A lady pushing a bicycle knocked into Evangelia
'Excuse me,' she apologised.
'Koulla?'

'Yes?'

'Is that really you?'

'Evangelia *mou.* I don't believe my eyes! What are you doing here?' asked her old school friend.

'What are you doing here? I didn't recognise you. Your long hair…' Evangelia stuttered taking in the dark brown, baggy clothes Koulla wore.

'I'm moving to England, a new life. You know,' said Koulla, stroking her short locks, tucked under a brown felt cap, as if remembering the long hair she used to have in her school days.

'Me too. Getting the tickets and boarding passes today,' said Evangelia, disbelief in her voice still as she took in the much altered physical appearance of her friend. She used to be so feminine with her long flowing hair, thought Evangelia, the prettiest in the class by far.

'So we might be travelling together. Oh I am so relieved. I'm travelling alone with my daughter. Leon will follow once he has sold the tailoring business and the house.'

'Well, as far as I know there's only two more crossings via Italy so yes, we could be.'

'And how are you Evangelia? How many children do you have?'

'I have two – they're twins, a boy and a girl.'

'How lovely. How old are they?'

'Just into their thirteenth year in August.'

'I was a bit slower than you. My daughter's going

into her second year next week,' she said.

'I heard you weren't falling. Glad it worked out for you in the end,' Evangelia said, squeezing her friend's arm affectionately and then pulling away embarrassed at her candid show of emotion.

A huge crowd of people waited to be seen by the two staff at the port protected by the booths they worked from. There must have been at least a hundred and fifty people, pushing, shoving for a space, edging forward like a shoal of fish. The two women continued to chat together and found they had lots in common as adults. Koulla sewed all day in her village doing alterations by hand to support her husband's business.

'Look at my finger!' she said as she showed Evangelia the callus on the inner edge of her finger. 'That's from pushing the needle through the heavy suit fabrics. I don't use a thimble.'

'I don't either but sometimes when my finger is so sore I put one on but I can't sew as quickly.'

'What will you do in England?' asked Koulla.

'I'm not sure. My sister takes in piecework, blouses, skirts, trousers and machines from home so I may do the same. Her boss supplies the machine and the cottons so I won't have to buy one.'

'My uncle has a home and business in Blackpool. I will head off there so I can stay with him and my cousins and help out where I can until Leon joins me.'

'Blackpool?'

'It's by the coast, in the North. You'll have to come and see me there.'

'I'd like that though I'm not sure how far it would be from London and…'

Evangelia and Koulla grabbed onto each other as a fracas broke out ahead of them. A man shouted anti-British obscenities.

'Out with the British!'

A group of men were trying to quieten him not wanting any trouble where there were women and children. Out of nowhere came a piercing crack. Panic instantly choked the faces of the people around her as they ran away from the port in all directions. Some tripped and fell over. Others screamed and took cover behind benches and trees. Women scooped sobbing children in their arms and ran towards the main road away from the port, dropping their bags. Others held onto each other as they ran in tandem away from the commotion. Others merely stood there in the middle of the chaos huddled together while others ran into the roads; the drivers honking at them while they ran blindly into the streets.

In the commotion, Evangelia and Koulla became separated. Evangelia ran and took cover behind a lone skeletal lemon tree, her heart thumping so hard she thought it would jump out of her; her teeth chattering from the cold, from the fear curdling inside her.

Confusion screamed at her. She gasped in horror as she tried to scan the area for Koulla.

'May the Lord protect us. May the Lord have mercy upon us.' A man said to no-one in particular, as he crouched with his arms over his children and his wife.

'Joseph! Joseph!' A mother, holding a boy's satchel, stood calling out the name of her son. She frantically searched the melee of faces for him. Her tears splashed the front of the scarf wrapped around her coat as they fell.

'Help!' an old lady called out weakly. Dressed in black from head to foot she had fallen and people were jumping over and around her as they escaped. At the same time, she desperately tried to hang onto her shawl being tugged at by the sea breeze; silvery strands of hair falling across her face. Her wailing ran through Evangelia like the funeral bells in the village. She shuddered and suddenly felt deep despair; a wretchedness so great it gripped her like an invisible demon.

A man ran towards the old woman, showing a respect for the old lady no-one else had.

'*Ela*,' he said and he tried to help her up but couldn't lift her on his own. 'Help!' he called out frantically only to be ignored by those around him who were no doubt too worried for their own safety.

Evangelia ran out to help him and they half carried half dragged the old woman over to a tree, propping her against it. Her leg appeared to be broken, her black tights ripped and her lower leg stuck out at an awkward angle from the knee, the inflammation already deforming the otherwise slender limb.

From her vantage point Evangelia saw a young man, lying with his face towards the ground, a pool of blood staining the pale earth around his head crimson. His head smashed in by a bullet. He was dead. Three British soldiers surrounded him.

There was a man next to him, on his knees; the grief on his face clear; anger, disbelief. 'Move back,' he yelled. 'This is all your fault. All this trouble!' He repeated the man's name over and over through his tears, as they brimmed and sloshed like water spilling over the rim of a glass. He shoved and pushed at the British military with a flailing arm.

The soldiers stared at each other and remained silent. The man took off his jacket and draped it over the lifeless body. A heart-wrenching painful cry came out of him and he tightened his grip on the faded grey cap laying on the ground next to him.

Evangelia crossed herself and raised her eyes to heaven. She prayed silently as she sat crouched next to the old woman waiting for medical assistance. Her whimpering had quietened, her face pale as she sat huddled next to Evangelia, doubled over. She could smell the familiar rose fragrance in her hair which reminded her of her own mother but the sweetness mingled with the bitter smell of death made her nauseous.

As strong as Evangelia was, and reserved, even she

couldn't hold back her outpouring of tears any longer. She felt ashamed weeping in public but she couldn't stop herself. Everything felt too difficult, too big for her. The red letters – EOKA – mocked her from a tall building in the distance. This was the reality now. She had been sheltered from it in the village, but being here she realised how dangerous Cyprus had become. Her mind wandered to Manoli who hadn't been seen for two days in the village. The men had searched for him but found no trace of him across the mountains where he shepherded his straggly herd. The rumours found their way to the women and children, despite the menfolk trying to keep the tales quiet. It remained unverified, but everyone feared he had been arrested and sent to the detention centre in Nicosia to face the plight of the many men now deprived of their liberty.

She felt a heavy darkness shroud her; the wings of a huge black eagle. She wasn't sure how long she stayed with the old lady or how long it took to clear the area and obtain some normality but when she searched for Koulla she couldn't see her. She prayed her friend had escaped unharmed. British soldiers walked around with rifles. They were checking the area around the port and it appeared as if they had possibly detained two men. Other troops it seemed had been deployed from the other check points at the entrance to the old town, the area tightly cordoned off by the local Police.

The medics arrived to take the old woman away.

'I am so sorry I can't come with you. I'm meeting my neighbour to go back to *Kato Lefkara*,' explained Evangelia. Anguish consumed her. She didn't want the old lady to be alone but knew she couldn't miss the rendezvous with Zeno. 'I have to get back for my children.'

She walked towards the meeting point where she had arranged to meet him; there was nothing else she could do, there was no access to the old town and the port ticket offices were closed. She would be obligated to return another day to buy her tickets. She thanked God she was unharmed and wondered again about her friend Koulla. She tried to remember the name of the town she was going to be in but could only remember it began with B. It was eerily quiet.

She waited patiently for Zeno, sitting on one of the wooden benches, her back to the sea, facing the main road. One o'clock came and went and she did not see him. The silence swaddled her and she realised the road must be cordoned off; no traffic passed through. Panic rose within her. How long should she wait? How would she get home?

'Is the road closed?' she asked a passer-by.

'Yes. It should re-open soon, but who knows?'

***

By three o'clock she began to fret and decided to cross the road and walk towards the main junction into the old town. Zeno would be coming from the same direction. She shuddered as the breeze came in from across the azure sea, biting at her nose and ears. She should have worn her hat, she thought, pulling her coat tighter.

As she neared the corner of the street a commotion arose ahead, raised voices, an English accent. She held back, ducking behind a parked car. She peeked out from behind the wheel arch and saw two British troops pull a man from his bicycle, grab his satchel. They pulled what appeared to be papers from inside and threw them into the air, scattering them across the pavement.

Evangelia's heart stopped. She knew what they were, anti-British leaflets and she also knew what the consequences of distributing them were. They both kicked at the bicycle, the sound of the crumpled metal hit her. The man made to run away but one of the soldiers, too quick for him, slapped him across the face, throwing him to the ground. Before he was able to defend himself he was cannoned from all directions by the butts of their rifles; once, twice, three times, on and on.

Evangelia let out a strangled cry which echoed around the almost silent street. She tried to scream but she had no voice. She tried to run towards the man to help him but she found her feet rooted to the ground as if in quicksand. The soldiers didn't so much as glance back after they beat him close to death and walked off, laughing and taunting, calling him a filthy dog. They threw a chair against a shop window which smashed; a mirror image of their state of minds, thought Evangelia. The smell of fear hung in the air and flooded her senses.

Moments later, Evangelia found her voice and ran towards him. The body lay in a crumpled heap. She knelt next to him and turned his bleeding battered head to face her, scared he was dead. She held his head, blood running between her fingers, congealing on her palm. She looked into his eyes.

She stared. It wasn't a man. It was Koulla's face staring back at her. She sobbed silently as she cradled her limp body in her arms; the blood from her friend's wounds seeping into her clothes and smearing her hands and face. She prayed these would not be her final moments, that she was going to make it. The harsh words of the British soldiers echoed in her mind and she sang a long-forgotten lullaby through her dewy tears and her agony poured back into her.

People who sheltered behind the closed doors of the surrounding buildings slowly spilled onto the pavement alerted by Evangelia's cries for help. Two men in suits helped lift Koulla into the chair of a nearby coffee shop, the building an old ramshackle echo of a more fortunate past. Evangelia hastily shrugged off her coat and wrapped it around her friend. She stared at Koulla's wristwatch; it's glass face shattered, time stood still at 3.24pm.

The owner brought over a glass of water. Someone

close by was scribbling on a notepad.

Evangelia lifted it to her mouth. Koulla opened her eyes.

'*Ela,* Koulla *mou,*' she said as Koulla drank thirstily, her lips bruised and bleeding, her face contorting with pain as she swallowed, red spider-veins blotching her cheeks.

A woman appeared with some bandages and warm water. Between them, she and Evangelia dabbed at the cuts on Koulla's head and face. Another woman appeared with a glass of warm milk sweetened with sugar and cinnamon.

'Tell Leon I'm sorry…tell him…'

'You can tell him yourself, Koulla *mou.* You will be okay,' said Evangelia.

***

Out of nowhere, a few minutes later, Zeno appeared.

'Zeno! Thank God you found me.'

'Evangelia!'

'Thank God you found me!' she said again, fighting back the sting behind her eyes, overcome by emotion and exhaustion.

'I recognised your coat. I was delayed at the control point. I was so worried about you…the shooting. Thank God you're safe.'

The relief on his face made Evangelia a little uneasy,

embarrassed. It had been a long time since she had seen such warmth towards her from a man. They held each other's gaze for a split second longer than they should have. Evangelia smiled nervously. Zeno shifted his gaze to the floor but not before Evangelia saw the flush of guilt cross his cheeks.

'We can't leave her here,' said Evangelia breaking his stare.

'Of course not,' said Zeno.

'She lives in the next village to us. Please Zeno…'

'I said yes, Evangelia *mou.* Hear my words. Of course we will take her home.'

One of the suited men helped Zeno settle Koulla on the back seat of Zeno's car. Evangelia wedged a folded blanket under her head. Evangelia covered her with her coat. Instantly, Zeno took off his jacket and draped it over Evangelia's shoulders, who was shaking not only from shock but a drop in temperature.

Evangelia composed herself and got into the front seat next to Zeno. She was already dreading making the inevitable repeat journey to buy the tickets. The wretchedness of both incidents haunted her. But strangely she also felt something else; a warm glow emanated from within her despite feeling cold. A glow she couldn't deny had something to do with Zeno but feelings she knew would remain unexpressed.

She fumbled with the strap of her handbag and peered out of the window, avoiding eye contact with

Zeno. They drove home in silence, Evangelia occasionally turning back to check on her friend who was asleep; a pained, contorted expression crossed her wounded face already smudged with red and purple bruises. The journey home otherwise, thankfully, uneventful.

Chapter Five

Evangelia, 1956

BACK SAFELY IN Kato Lefkara Evangelia thanked Zeno for bringing her and Koulla her friend home. His hand moved to touch hers but Evangelia moved hers away. He let it rest on her arm fleetingly; she felt her pulse race as she fought an overwhelming feeling inside her. She bid him good bye and closed the car door.

She walked towards home, glad to be back among the steep winding cobbled streets familiar to her. As she walked she passed three women who sewed for a living with her. They bid her *kalispera*, their words leaving clouds in the air in front of them. She hurried past, barely making eye contact wanting to be away from prying eyes, the cold biting at her. She wanted to be in the safety of her home and to see the children. The day's events and her emotions, upturned and inside out had discombobulated her.

As she neared her house, she recognised the carefree laughter of Elena and Andreas as it echoed off the stone walls lining the narrow street. Elena caught sight of her the moment she came around the bend and came running to her. Evangelia hugged her tight for a few moments and then peeled her daughter off her.

'I'm tired Elena *mou*. Where's *yiayia?* Is she home?'

'You were gone ages *mama*,' complained Elena.

'And you're cold. Come on get inside. Is *yiayia* home?' she asked impatience creeping into her voice.

'She's made dinner and before you say anything she said we could play until you came.'

'Alright, alright.' She waved across to Andreas and blew him a kiss. He passed a ball to Niko who kicked it against the side of a house. The rhythmic bouncing suddenly made Evangelia weary. She pushed open the gate to the courtyard.

'Why are you so late?' asked *yiayia*.

'Oh, Mother. I'm so glad to be home. There was an attack, a shooting and an old lady got hurt. There was blood. My friend Koulla was attacked.'

'Now, now, you're safe. Sit down. God has sent you home.' *Yiayia* wrapped her arms around her daughter and held her, silently, until Evangelia eventually wiped her eyes, her nose and face with her palm. 'Now tell me everything. From the beginning.'

***

The following day Evangelia woke earlier than usual. She swept the courtyard, boiled eggs, cut bread and cheese ready for breakfast and then sat in the shade of the olive tree drinking her sweetened coffee. Her thoughts going round in her head made her light-headed and the same thoughts had plagued her through the night. How could she have feelings for Zeno? He was her friend's husband, the father of her children's best friend…and she was a married woman.

Her turmoil was made worse with worry for Koulla. How was she going to find out if she was back at home in *Kato Drys*? She had refused to let them take her home last night insisting she walk there alone, despite her injuries.

She would have to make time for the half hour walk to the village to check on her. There was no other way she could get there, unless she asked Zeno to take her in the car. But something told her it would not be a good idea; it would be like dancing with the devil.

She waited until her mother was awake and explained how she was going to take the walk to the next village to check on Koulla. Her mother looked at her, wary, fear in her eyes.

'You go, my child. I understand. I will start on the lace for you this morning. You can't lose any earnings this week.'

'Thank you. And say good morning to the children for me. I will be back as soon as I can. By lunch time.'

'May God go with you.'

Evangelia swallowed the last of her coffee, leaving the sludge at the bottom of the cup, and taking her shawl and handbag she left.

The walk to the next village was a difficult one; the main road leading to it was a narrow dirt track; one side overhanging the steep cut-away of the mountainside and the other closed in by rocky, terraces split open by the roots of carob and olive trees. The dry air was heavy with dust and Evangelia struggled to keep her pace as she pushed her way up the incline. Twice she had to push herself up against the dry stony façade as a car and then a delivery van sidled up the road, chugging loudly, the tyres kicking up dust and debris; each vehicle threatening to conk out as it rumbled up the steep track.

Once in the village Evangelia had to find her bearings, she had only ever come to the village once before yesterday and had no idea where Koulla's house was. She hoped she would come across someone to point her in the right direction. She walked past the small stone church with it's neat front courtyard; she noticed how the gate with the peeling paint looked surreal in the early morning light. As she walked past two decrepit shells of homes, the windows partly boarded and the weeds strangling the dilapidated doorways, she flinched as a starling whooshed past her ear. Her heart thumped in her chest.

Relief flooded her as she saw an old lady walking towards her. Traditionally dressed in black from head to foot she smiled revealing a toothless, gaping mouth yet her eyes shone like diamonds.

'*Kalimera.*'

'*Kalimera sas.* I'm looking for Koulla's house.'

'Who are you?'

'I'm her friend. I walked all the way from *Kato Lefkara*.'

'You're going to be disappointed. She's not here. No-one has seen her for a few days. Her husband's going out of his mind.'

'Can you tell me where she lives?'

'I will take you there.'

Evangelia couldn't refuse the kind gesture and although the old lady walked with the slow pace of a turtle Evangelia found the patience not to rush her.

Eventually, and no more than five minutes later, the old lady pointed to a house with a turquoise door and pink blooms around the adjacent window.

'Thank you. You've been most kind.'

'Go well, my child,' she answered weakly as she began the slow arduous walk back in the direction from which they had both come.

Evangelia knocked on the front door, its frame splintered with flaking paint, and waited. She could hear a child crying inside and wondered whether she should push the door when it swung open. A man in a vest and a face still half covered in shaving soap suds stood looking at her.

'Yes. Can I help you?'

'I'm looking for Koulla. I'm her friend Evangelia.'

'She's not here. I don't know where she is.'

'I saw her in Limassol.' The man's face visibly paled and he pulled her into the house abruptly. Slamming the door behind him.

'Who did you say you are?'

'I'm Evangelia, her friend from *Kato Lefkara*.'

'What do you want with her?'

'To see she's alright.'

'Why wouldn't she be?'

'I'm not here to cause any upset but I saw her in Limassol. She got hurt. I brought her home, back to the village yesterday.'

'So you're in this too?'

'I don't know what you mean. I happened to bump into her by the port in Limassol. There was a shooting. I lost her and then it looked like she was distributing leaflets, anti-British leaflets. She was attacked by two British servicemen.'

'And why are you telling me this?' His eyes darted to the door and out of the window, his voice hushed and grainy.

'I don't know. I'm trying to make sense of it myself. I want to check she's alright. To talk her out of carrying on with this. It's dangerous.'

'Don't you think I've tried? We've got a two-year-old daughter for God's sake.'

'Yes. Of course. Sorry, I didn't mean...'

'I suspected she'd gone off to fight the cause but expected her to change her mind when she saw the dangers. But she won't listen to me. Says she has every right to fight for *Enosis* as any man does. It's not the first time she's disappeared.' He bent and scooped the child who was pulling at his trousers into his arms. He ruffled her hair; a matted and tangled mass of curls.

'Thank you for caring enough to come and check on her but you should go. And be careful. Don't talk to anyone. People may be watching and you could get yourself embroiled in something you can't control.' Evangelia hesitated. 'What is it?'

'An old lady brought me here. I told her I was looking for Koulla.'

'Did she ask you anything?'

'No, but it's unlikely she'll be involved in anything.' But panic rose in her voice.

'I don't know any more. It's a scary situation and one we mustn't underestimate. Go straight home. Talk to no-one.' He patted her arm. 'Thank you Evangelia. I will tell Koulla you came by.'

***

The journey back to *Kato Lefkara* was just as treacherous, if not more so, as she had to steady her pace going downhill. She walked, her feet moving one in front of the other, without focus, her jumbled, fearful thoughts bombarding her, pressing her forward.

The sun high in the sky, reflected off the white grey mountainside. Hotter than ever she felt the sweat clinging to her back and her upper legs chafed as perspiration dampened her inner thighs. Evangelia could think about nothing but the stark reality of the words spoken between her and Koulla's husband. She understood the dangerousness of the situation and still reeled in shock to discover Koulla had been missing for days at a time. She had been stupid to reveal herself to the old lady.

As she approached the crossroads at the top of *Kato Lefkara* she heard the engine of a car sputter to a slow. As it came to a standstill ahead of her she recognised it. It was Zeno. Her heart thumped and suddenly she panicked. She approached the car and Zeno hung his arm out of the open window, smiling at her as he cut the engine.

'Hello Evangelia. I'm glad I've seen you.'

'Zeno. How are you?' she forced herself to ask formally, conscious of her red face and her dress sticking to her.

'I'm well. I'm glad I've seen you.'

'I didn't thank you properly. I was rude.'

'No not at all. You were scared. You were afraid.'

'Well thank you Zeno. I don't know what I would've done without you.'

'I'm going to Limassol day after next if you want to go back and organise those tickets. I'll stay with you this time. The business I need to take care of won't take long so I can do it in the afternoon.'

Evangelia wrestled with the feelings surfacing as she faced him and the need to go back to Limassol which terrified her. She couldn't face going alone. Eventually she sighed and agreed to the trip back together. She declined a lift back into the village and as Zeno sped off in his car she drew in the fresh air of the mountains and continued her walk home.

Something inside of her caused her alarm. Her feelings around Zeno had changed from one of cordial friendship to something more almost overnight and she knew he felt it too; something more affectionate, intimate, and it worried her. Village life was claustrophobic, everyone knew everyone's business and if she wasn't careful someone would discover the change between Zeno and her. She vowed to keep her distance and avoid being alone with him. And Maroulla, after all, was her friend; they sewed daily and had known each other since childhood.

***

Two days later she queued for the tickets to England and she was calmer around Zeno away from the village. Despite the increased police presence, and a cordoned off area to keep the queue more orderly, a notion not normally practiced by the Cypriots, they both chatted amiably; anyone watching them would easily have assumed they were husband and wife.

Zeno, unusually demonstrative for a man, leaned in towards Evangelia on more than one occasion. As he spoke, he brushed his arm against hers, touched her hand, stroked her shoulder. She felt a faint tingle inside her every time he touched her and she wondered whether it was because she had been without a partner for so long. She felt confused. Wondered whether God had sent her the opportunity to go to England; before anything happened between her and Zeno; something she may regret.

After queuing for an hour Evangelia finally had the tickets she needed in her hand. She walked with a bounce in her step back towards the car with Zeno but she noticed how he hung his head and dragged his feet like a chastened school boy.

'What's the matter Zeno?' she asked.

'I don't know. I guess I will miss you and the children when you go. We all will.'

'It's still a long way off so let's not think about our goodbyes now.'

'You're right. I'm sorry. But I can't help it. You know how I feel.' He waited for a reaction but Evangelia said nothing. 'I know you've guessed and I know you feel the same Evangelia *mou*.'

'Zeno, please. You have to stop this talk of feelings. We are both married. Nothing can ever happen between us. Nothing.'

'Please wait here. Let me do what I have to do at the office. Wait for me.' He passed the car keys to her and walked off, his brown leather briefcase in his hand.

Evangelia waited in the car but the heat, and her

building agitation, began to fry her. She got out and leaned against the passenger door; her eyes darting around. Visions of Koulla being battered came to her. Still worried about another outburst of violence her anxiety heightened her senses. Every knock, bang and screech made her jump and the heat felt all the more stifling as her panic grew with every waiting minute.

She noticed a higher police presence on the streets of Limassol too. More British soldiers in full uniform stationed themselves along the main road giving the impression of a town under siege. A check-point further along the road towards the old town stood incongruent against the pretty buildings and the deep cobalt blue of the sea.

She shook off a shiver as she thought about the events of the last time she came to Limassol and fought her emotions. She avoided looking anyone in the eye and lowered her head as anyone walked by not wanting to give away her fear.

Zeno came back to the car within half an hour, which had felt a lot longer and her heart surprised her as it skipped seeing him walking towards her.

'All done. Everything okay while I was gone?'

'Yes. Fine,' she answered, catching her breath as she let out a sigh of relief.

'Right. Let's go and get some lunch. I'm so hungry my stomach has collapsed.'

Evangelia didn't argue wanting a drink more than

anything; her throat scratched like sandpaper as she swallowed and her head ached from the oppressive heat.

They ordered a simple meal; grilled seabass and salad with feta cheese, black olives dripping in olive oil and crushed garlic cloves, chunky locally-baked bread scattered with sesame seeds and aniseed.

'Thank you for your kindness, Zeno.'

'Not at all. I like to help you. I want to help you.'

'Well I appreciate it and without you I don't know if I could've faced coming back here alone. It's a big city and it feels alien to me. I've not left the village for a long time until recently. I've forgotten there's another Cyprus, a fast-moving, changing Cyprus. I'm not sure I like it to be honest. It scares me.'

'Things are changing. And they'll get worse before they get better and mark my words there will be bloodshed, and lost lives and crying women for their husbands, sons, brothers, fathers.'

'Oh don't Zeno, please, I can't bear the thought of…' She let her voice trail off as the waiter interrupted their conversation. He cleared their empty plates and returned to fill their glasses with water from the carafe.

Back at the car Zeno took Evangelia's hand in his and held onto it even as she tugged to pull it from his grasp.

'I understand nothing can happen between us and I respect you too much to persist, to pursue whatever this is between us but I'll always hold you dear in my heart Evangelia.' He locked her eyes with his, holding hers there for a few watery seconds. Then he lent in and gave her the gentlest of kisses, barely brushing her cheek. He stayed there for what felt like an eternity, his warm breath heating her from the inside out, and then he stepped back. 'I won't say anything to you again. I promise. Friends?'

'Good friends,' said Evangelia. He let go of her hand yet she could still feel the imprint of its warmth on her heart.

Chapter Six

Loizos, 1957

MOMENTUM AND SUPPORT for EOKA grew steadily as more and more Cypriots became disillusioned with being under British occupation and took action to support *Enosis*, unity with Greece. The Cypriot newspapers reported stories and accounts about the inhuman treatment of the EOKA rebels arrested. The unrest spread across the whole island, impacting on the communities of Famagusta, Nicosia, Larnaca, Paphos and Limassol.

The particular news on everyone's lips, and at the forefront of their minds, was the tragic story surrounding Evagoras Pallikarides who had joined EOKA as a seventeen-year-old in 1955 and died a hero when hanged in March two years later. He had defiantly and bravely stepped in to support a friend who had been beaten and then tied to an electricity pole by two British soldiers. Pallikarides had set his friend free and as a result of his actions a £5000 reward was put on his head by the British Army. Arrested on the same day, the British detained him until, eventually, they found him guilty of firearms possession. His 'murder' caused huge waves of anger across the island and more and more men of all ages signed up to the underground military organisation;

EOKA was suffused with righteous heroism and although it was not an elitist group those who were recruited had to show a commitment and belief in 'secrecy, privacy and dependability'.

Those initially against getting involved were drawn in, and many men and even women, were involved in fighting for freedom. The men were the ones on the front line. Many British soldiers were killed not only through random attacks, but strategically planned and executed operations, something the British were slow to realise. But women were just as involved and integral to moving things forward. They were the cogs who ensured the coded notes regarding counter-attacks were delivered to the right people and these attacks were planned and synchronised to achieve maximum disruption and lawlessness.

Loizos was proud of his son Christaki who, despite pressure from school friends and villagers, remained neutral. He knew Christaki wouldn't let him down. He would stand his ground. He was steely, not easily agitated, unlike Pavlo who always talked too loudly and Melani who was more easily influenced.

***

When Christaki walked into the Co-op at six o'clock, on the last day of April, ready for the late shift, his father strode in two steps behind him. Loizos watched the purposeful strides of his son, his slim strong shoulders, his arms hanging loosely at his sides as he walked. It was like seeing a mirror image of himself as a young man. They had the same physique. The same gait as they walked.

Christaki bid Anna good evening as he walked through the door, propped open with a crate of *Keo* beers. Loizos had seen them being delivered that morning on route to his shoe shop. Delivered directly by the manufacturing and bottling plant in Limassol, the *Keo* truck driver, a man Loizos had not seen before, had found it difficult navigating the narrow streets to the Co-op and had carried the crates the last few hundred yards to the shop, parking the lorry near the priest's house.

'*Kalispera*,' she replied, already pulling her work overalls over her head and hanging them on the hook outside the store cupboard.

'Busier today?' asked Christaki hopefully. The Co-op had been taking less and less income since the troubles, which affected all those who had a stake in the business. For some it meant no income at all especially now many of the men were spending money on the fighting efforts they believed would free them of the British.

Anna shook her head. 'Loukia's coming in later, something about bread.' Clearly in no mood for talking she left hurriedly murmuring something about her mother-in-law coming over.

Christaki tidied the shelves and re-arranged some of the fruit and vegetables. He liked things neat and tidy and would often complain to his parents the others working there didn't exhibit the same work values.

He served two customers as they walked in one after the other, making polite conversation with each of them as he always did. Finally, after the wife of the retired school Principal, bid them both a good night, having relayed all the aches and pains she ever suffered in her sixty-eight years, Loizos and Christaki were in the shop alone. Loizos paced up and down one of the crowded aisles, agitated, his ears burning red showing his turmoil. He clenched and unclenched his hands in an effort to calm his agitation. Christaki, in contrast, he noted, was calm, normal. *Thank God he doesn't suspect anything, thought Loizos.* Loizos checked his watch. At half past seven and as if on cue Loukia walked in.

'I have a delivery of bread,' she said innocently, 'from my father for Dimitri's family. Father asked me to bring the loaves here.' She strained to lift the huge basket onto the front counter, the weight of which looked like it would snap her. Her stick thin limbs jutted out from her flowery dress like pins, her legs only minimally fatter around her knees.

'Here, let me help you,' offered Christaki.

'I also have a list from my mum,' Loukia chimed a bit too merrily, pushing her dark curly hair away from her face to reveal rosy sweaty cheeks.

'Can you get what she wants together for me? I'll be right back.' She disappeared just as quietly as she had appeared, her skinny frame dancing like a feather on the wind.

The two of them were alone again in the shop. Loizos pulled the door shut and, taking the key from under the counter, he locked it.

'What's going on?' asked Christaki.

'Don't ask questions. There's no time,' answered Loizos as he grabbed a newspaper and spread the pages out on the floor behind the counter. He didn't want to take any risks and the unrest between villagers of opposing opinions meant anyone could be watching. 'Quickly. If anyone sees the Co-op closed it'll be sure to raise suspicions.'

'Why? What do you want with the bread?'

'Not now Christaki. Watch the door.'

Loizos counted the loaves one by one and placed them on the open newspapers. Christaki stood by the door, Loizos aware of his stunned silence. He set to work roughly pulling apart the loaf with no sesame seeds, scattering crumbs everywhere, until his probing fingers found what he hoped for; a folded note as he had suspected. He read it immediately and put it hastily inside his jacket pocket, shaking the errant crumbs off it.

'What is it?'

'It's a coded message. Loukia is unlikely aware she

delivered it but I'm glad we've intercepted it.'

'But Father...'

'Not now Christaki.'

'What's... they'll find out it's you, us,' said Christaki, his voice rising in panic, as he caught a glimpse of someone walking towards the shop door.

'No. They won't.' But Loizos knew only too well the reality of what was happening around them and how listening ears and seeing eyes got wind of everything. They couldn't be too careful, however much of a pacifist he believed himself to be. Pushing back the unlocked door Loizos pretended to be wiping his brow with the handkerchief, his heart still thumping in his chest, as another customer walked in wanting a kilo of potatoes and a kilo of onions.

Loukia came back not five minutes later. She paid for the shopping and went off. A minute or so after she'd left Christaki noticed her headscarf on the floor and rushing out of the shop, his father close behind him, called after her but she had already disappeared around the bend on the lane leading to her house. Loizos watched him as he rolled it into a tight ball and shoved it in his trouser pocket.

'You can drop it off to her later, son.'

As they turned to go back into the shop, a scuffle from the bottom of the road, towards the lane leading to the church, alerted Loizos to something untoward. He stopped in his tracks and listened but no other sound came. He took two paces in the direction of the shop and heard it again. He looked back, a few paces behind Christaki already in the shop, and thought he saw the back of someone cowering in the shadows, behind a stack of mopeds.

The shop remained quiet for the rest of the evening. The time seemed to move deliberately slowly. More slowly than the Sunday Church Service, thought Loizos, the three hours of which he endured only for the sake of Anastasia every week.

Eventually they locked the shop and walked in the direction of Loukia's house. The sky deepened to an inky blue and glittering stars dotted the cloaking canvas. The village screamed eerily quiet. Loizos couldn't shake off a feeling of foreboding; the brilliance of the stars a contrast to the anxiety building within him. He pushed his hands deeper into his trouser pockets and urged his son to increase his pace. As they came round the sharp bend of the lane a battered farm vehicle blocked the road ahead; its headlights on full beam. Loizos, slowed his pace almost to a halt. He averted his eyes from the harsh lights, swallowed and carried on walking nervously towards the lights.

'Can I ask where you're going?' said the taller of the two men standing in front of the open truck. His eyes rested on Loizos' face. He could feel the man's stare under his skin, going right through him. Loizos recognised him. It was Aki, the cousin of Dimitri married to Loizos' sister Irini. He was not much older than Loizos himself. Aki, was left a widower after his wife died giving birth to their seventh child. It was a sad situation. A man left to bring up seven children with no wife. Recently Loizos had heard a rumour Aki had been keeping bad company. He hung around with those in the village who supported EOKA. He was a dangerous man and rumoured to have killed for personal rivalries. But Loizos didn't like to gossip or pass judgement although he had heard the men talking about it at the *kafeneion,* on more than one occasion. His priority remained stoically with his own family and their safety.

'We're returning a scarf to a customer who dropped it,' Loizos said, conscious of sweat beads forming on his forehead.

'Oh yes?'

'Yes, Aki. And how are the children?' asked Loizos clumsily in an effort to bring some normality to the situation.

'Well?' Aki asked, ignoring his question.

'Yes,' said Christaki forcefully, 'Here, if you don't believe us.' He took out the tight ball from his pocket and unravelled the scarf to show him.

'Who said I don't believe you, boy?'

'Sorry. We're both tired and want to get home,' said Loizos, desperate to diffuse the situation. Loizos put out an arm across Christaki to quieten him and waited, holding his breath.

'Then be on your way. We have no quarrel with you.'

'So what's going on?' asked Loizos boldly, after exhaling slowly.

'Nothing to worry about, we're waiting for someone,' Aki said as he resumed the job of rolling a cigarette and lighting it. He passed the cigarette to his companion. Cigarette smoke curled between them as they both took a long puff of the roll-up in turn. The other man avoided eye contact. Something's not right, thought Loizos.

'Well, good night,' said Loizos, putting out his hand which forced Aki to extend his too. Aki shook Loizos' proffered hand.

'We can't miss the slot,' said the second man, Loizos still in earshot. Loizos knew what he meant but didn't react.

Loizos and Christaki walked off, in tandem, towards Loukia's house. They didn't speak to each other for the rest of the five minutes it took to reach her back door.

'What d'you think that was about?' whispered Christaki.

'Well, if it had anything to do with us they would have detained us longer. Don't dwell on it and thank God they were our men and not the British who keep noseying around. Putting curfews on villagers and telling them when and where they can leave their village, their homes. It's keeping them a prisoner that's what it is.'

They left the scarf with Loukia's father, Marko, who

thanked them for returning it. Loizos hid his shock at seeing Marko's unshaven face, grey with fatigue and worry. He wanted to ask how things were but was afraid of the answer; the danger it may put his family in. So he said nothing.

'Thank you,' managed Marko.

'It's not a problem, good night,' said Loizos. He shook Marko's hand, but Markos avoided eye contact. Something clearly wasn't right, thought Loizos.

'Good night,' said Christaki. They both made their way back along the darkened path, careful not to disturb the stray cats lying on the now cool boulders and rocks which edged the route roughly back onto the road again.

The village was pretty at night and they walked home in a companionable silence; the rush of the sea on the wind the only sound and the thud of Loizos' heavy strides as he kept pace with his son. They passed *Pater* Spyrithon who had been visiting one of his parishioners, unwell with a high temperature and swollen glands. The older generation often wanted a visit from the priest and a prayer rather than a visit from the village nurse or doctor. Loizos passed the coded message onto the priest seamlessly as they passed each other in the narrow cobbled street and bid each other a good evening.

At home, they found Anastasia waiting for them. Sitting on the couch, she had finished hemming a customer's dress by hand. She appeared tired and anxious, frown lines etched across her brow, but she didn't say anything. Loizos gave her a nod which indicated the note had been intercepted as planned. Unusual as it was, and dangerous, Loizos didn't want to lie to his wife about anything.

His wife understood exactly why he had elected to scupper the planned EOKA mission.

Melani was bent over her school books, kneeling at the coffee table on a blanket she'd spread across the floor, and Pavlo was out in the courtyard playing backgammon with a school friend. Loizos, felt a stab of relief to see the rest of his family were home and safe. The stories of rival groups, now being identified as Turkish-Cypriot or Greek-Cypriot, turning on each other were too rife. He was aware of the friction between some of the villagers which existed even between brothers and uncles and nephews within the same family. Loizos didn't want his family to be torn apart by the politics of EOKA. He wasn't prepared to risk the lives of his children and wife for *Enosis* with Greece. He was already one step ahead in his plans.

Anastasia immediately served dinner; a simple meal of lentils and fried onions which Loizos and Christaki drizzled with olive oil. They filled themselves with chunks of fresh bread and then ate *halloumi* and water melon cut into big fat juicy slices.

'Did you hear about the incident in Limassol, by the port today?' asked Anastasia, as she sat back down to her sewing, her eyes soft and gentle as they reflected the light of the lamp opposite her.

'Yes, I did. It's unbelievable that such a thing would happen. *O theos na mas voithisei.*' Loizos asked God to protect them.

'And then four men were arrested as they were walking to work by the market. Hauled off like animals.'

'*O theos na mas voithisei,*' repeated Loizos.

'We'll be safe, though won't we?' asked Melani, the sombre conversation distracting her from her studies.

'Yes darling, I hope so,' said Anastasia her eyes full of grief and sorrow. Loizos could see how the troubles were taking their toll on his beautiful wife and his heart was breaking.

***

It was early evening, the June sun had sleepily set across the tops of the mountains setting them alight with fiery reds and hot oranges. Dimitri, a heavy drinker and a mouth to match his big set physique, sat in the shade of the *kafeneion's* awning. Despite his denial it was obvious to all he was a seasoned drinker; the thread veins in his cheeks gave it away.

Despina, Loizos' niece walked by the coffee shop, carrying a basket of figs.

'*Ela,* Despina.' Dimitri called out to her. He sat languidly in his seat, his shirt, stretched taut across his muscular arms and broad shoulders, was untucked and unbuttoned to his naval.

'*Kalispera* Dimitri,' she called back dismissively, too focused on admonishing her boys who ran ahead of her as they threw stones and sticks at each other.

Despina's nineteen-year-old husband, Yianni, and friend of Christaki, had joined EOKA and was one of the men hiding in the mountains. Gone for five weeks, she was seen crying desperately, striving to bring up their two-year-old twin boys alone. It was common knowledge the family had paid what little money they had for ammunition and food supplies for Yianni and the five other men in hiding with him. Despina barely had enough money to buy basics. It was a desperate situation, and although the villagers tried to help, she was a proud woman and refused offers of help, insisting she could cope on her own. It had got to the stage where dishes of food and baskets of fruit were being left outside her door in the hope she would accept the help offered.

'Despina!' his tone was harsh, his words slurred. Loizos and so many of the villagers, Despina included, knew only too well what he was like when he was drunk, having seen him pick fights, brawling in the streets.

'Leave her be,' interjected Michael, Anastasia's younger brother. He was tall and lean with jet black eyes sunk deep in his face. His nose was long but it suited his elongated features which were softened by his mop of dark curly hair. He continued to flick through the newspaper and quietly drank his coffee with Loizos at a table set against the wall under the blue shuttered windows behind him.

'What's it got to do with you?'

'Nothing. I'm just saying.'

'Just saying? Well that's not what I've heard?'

'And what's that supposed to mean?'

'You know! Late night calls. Skulking around where you shouldn't be.'

Michael ignored his ranting and striking a match, lit a cigarette. He inhaled deeply and then slowly exhaled. He let out the thick smoke which trickled upwards before disappearing and leaving behind only the strong odour of the foreign cigarettes in the air.

'Can't speak now can you?'

Michael said nothing.

Dimitri carried on riling him. 'God has given me eyes and I can see well with them!' he spat out.

'Then you can see clearly I'm right here and choose to ignore you. You're drunk.'

The few men left in the village, mainly old and frail, stopped playing cards and backgammon. They looked uncomfortably from one man to the other. No-one spoke, the only sound now not the throwing of dice and the counting of counters and shuffling of cards, but the copper bells jingling round the goats' necks as they were herded from one tangled field to another a few feet behind the coffee shop.

'Drunk am I?' yelled Dimitri at Michael.

'Yes, you are.'

'Enough, Dimitri, Michael' interjected Loizos.

'Wondered when the traitor would speak,' said Dimitri.

'Leave it,' begged Loizos.

'Why? We all know you stole that note. You prevented our attack on those bloody British!'

'Show some respect. You're an embarrassment to your family,' continued Michael.

'Enough,' pleaded Angelo, the owner of the coffee shop, 'Don't rile him,' he hissed at Michael. He cleared one of the tables, piling empty coffee cups and water glasses onto a round metal tray, the *Keo* emblem printed on it. He roughly wiped the table and tucked the chairs which had been left strewn in a mess and threw the damp dish cloth across his shoulder.

'Me an embarrassment? When you won't fight for your country's freedom?'

'And you're making no difference at all. Innocent young boys are getting murdered, leaving their mothers' heartbroken and empty.'

'Who says so?' asked Dimitri, banging his clenched fists on the coffee table and sending the demitasse cup jumping into the air slopping the dregs of his discarded coffee over his trousers.

'Everyone.' Michael's voice came out raspy, barely audible.

Dimitri, his face contorted and red with anger, stood

with such ferocity his chair was thrown across the coffee shop and into the road. He glared at Michael and draining his glass of the last of his *zivania* he stormed off in the direction Despina had taken. A crowd of teenage boys playing football in the otherwise quiet street found the outburst entertaining and jeered at him as he stumbled away, the dust rising from the brittle soil under his feet.

No other known incidents between the two men followed, even though they inevitably crossed paths in the village streets and the altercation was soon forgotten by the village gossipers. At church at the Sunday service, seated two rows from each other, Michael didn't turn towards Dimitri even once. Loizos, however, could feel the animosity between the two men like a shroud of black funeral lace over a coffin.

***

One Monday night, towards the end of the smiling summer, Loizos walked past Despina's house after an emergency meeting to double-check timings and positions of an EOKA planned attack. He was loaning out his farmer's truck in an effort to thwart the attack which risked killing hundreds of men. He noticed her main door was ajar which was unusual so late at night. He checked his watch; it was gone ten o'clock. He slowed his pace. He walked closer peering through the gap in the doorway. He listened and began to walk away when raised voices coming from inside stopped him in his tracks. He stepped back, pushed the creaking door further open, the sound of its old iron hinges squeaking achingly against his eardrums. He took a few steps into the courtyard.

'Despina? Despina?' he called out to her. He continued walking towards the voices and then saw the familiar pose of Dimitri. He was stood over Despina shouting. She was cowering, her two children crying as they held onto her legs. She was repeatedly saying no.

'What's going on?'

'Well, well, well…that's exactly what I want to find out,' said Dimitri.

'What's going on Dimitri? Despina?'

'Nothing. He just burst in here,' answered Despina, her voice high-pitched, terror in her eyes.

'Keep out of it,' yelled Dimitri.

'Come on Dimitri. Let's not fight. The children are scared,' said Loizos, a sweat breaking out on his forehead. He took a few more paces closer, his hands in front of him, palms facing up indicating he meant no harm.

Dimitri calmed for a few seconds and Despina made to walk away towards one of the bedrooms, ushering the children to hurry.

'*Boutana*!' he suddenly yelled at Despina. 'I know what's going on! The whole village knows, you whore!' He took two wide strides and stood behind her. She stopped in her tracks but didn't turn round. His breathing was heavy, coming in loud shafts. He pulled her by the arm and twisted her round to face him.

'Go to hell,' she said, her eyes burning with red like fire.

He slapped her across the face sending her flying back and knocking her head against the stone basin outside the bedroom. Blood instantly appeared, soaking the side of her head and filling her ear. The boys were suddenly deadly quiet but the tears left smudgy track marks across their pudgy cheeks. Their eyes protruded as if on stalks, their expression one of horror and fear.

'Enough!' demanded Michael. He appeared out of no-where and grabbed Dimitri by the hair. Swinging him round Michael punched him straight in the middle of the face. His nose audibly cracked and the blood poured out. Dimitri taken by surprise was dazed by the blow. He tried to shake his head to bring back his focus but Michael was too quick punching him twice in the tummy. Dimitri doubled over, his hands clutching his stomach. The blood from his nose continued to pour as he shook his head in disbelief.

And then there were four other men, brawnier, bigger. Loizos didn't see them come in but had surely been waiting nearby. The four of them grabbed Michael and pushed him to the ground.

'Stop!' yelled Loizos. He grabbed a broom and held it up to protect himself while trying to keep them away from Michael at the same time. 'There's too much blood shed already. Stop. Think about what you're doing!'

'We know exactly what we're doing. She's a whore and he's been sleeping with her!'

They moved in closer to Michael who was still dazed on the cold stone floor, each kick they threw sent a dull thud around the courtyard and an agonising cry from Michael. They beat him in succession, crazed expressions on their faces, their fists hitting out viciously not caring where their punches landed. Loizos waded in and cracked the wooden broom handle over the back of one of the men. The man collapsed, whimpering like a snared fox. Now who's the tough one, thought Loizos.

What happened next was unreal. It unfolded in front of Loizos' eyes in slow motion yet he could not react. One of the men, Savva, his eyes glinting like a madman, shook out a hidden penknife from his sleeve. He brandished the pen knife wildly, waving it around like an agitated huntsman towards Michael.

'I'm unarmed,' Michael said, his eyes begging, panic in his voice.

Savva continued waving the penknife. Loizos moved closer and could smell the alcohol on his breath. He'd been drinking.

'For God's sake,' shouted Dimitri, 'Have you gone mad?' but his words fell on deaf ears.

As Michael straightened himself up he struck out with his arm, a sudden jerky movement, uncoordinated. The penknife made contact with Michael in the chest and there was a sickening slithering wet sound as Savva pulled the knife out of him. He had a crazed expression. His lips curved into a twisted smile. Michael sunk to the ground. Blood soaked through his shirt and spread across the dusty floor, leaving a pool of puce liquid. The men shocked by the outcome of events ran off in a panic, spinning away as the realisation of what had happened hit them; one of them stuttering on his words while another opened his mouth but no words formed. Dimitri's mouth fell open, but no words came out.

He mouthed the words 'sorry' at Despina and then at Loizos before running off behind the others. Despina remained rooted, unable to move, her chin trembled, the colour drained from her usually olive-rose face. She held onto her boys; their faces hidden in the folds of her dress.

He died instantly. His eyes wide open but lifeless. After a few seconds, maybe minutes, she let out a piercing cry which rang across the sleepy village.

She gently untangled the boys from her and leant over Michael, cupping his face in her hands. She kissed him gently on the lips. They were already cold.

Chapter Seven

Loizos, 1957

THE ATROCITIES CONTINUED and the village was not left unscathed either as relations and friends settled in neighbouring villages were arrested or killed during the troubles. Police brutality was rife, and although the women were not the ones hiding in the mountain caves or involved in meticulous planning and execution of the continuous barrage of attacks on the British patrols, they were beginning to feel the brunt of the conflict in their own streets. School children continued to become increasingly violent in their retaliation, and the British troops did not hesitate to beat women and children.

As a result of these clashes, the newspapers highlighted the despicable treatment of civilians who openly opposed the British troops. It was reported a group of women and some older men in a village not fifty kilometres from *Ayios Tychonas* had been shot dead because one of the women's boys, twelve or thirteen years old, and an old man, refused to rub off the EOKA slogan from a *kafeneion* wall. The incident left carnage and a promise that revenge would be taken. Three days later the British troops – all eight of them – were ambushed while on patrol, and shot dead. Five days later another clash between EOKA rebels hiding in the mountains resulted in one Cypriot dead but over a hundred British troops either dead or injured. It was a victorious day for EOKA and for those who supported the cause.

But there were also losses on the Cypriot side. One group hiding in the mountains were caught from two different directions and trapped in the middle, with nowhere to escape to. One rebel threw himself off the snowy, rocky mountainside, than be captured and tortured by the British. The rest of them, twelve men and one woman, already frost-bitten from the freezing temperatures they had endured for weeks, were arrested and beaten. They were trundled off to the prison camp in Nicosia where it was rumoured the torture of all the prisoners was inhuman. Even the two mules were not spared. The British troops shot the animals in front of them in a menacingly cruel show of power and barbarism.

***

The funeral, known in the Greek Orthodox religion as the Office of the Burial of the Dead, took place two days later. Wednesday's temperature had already reached thirty-two degrees by ten o'clock despite being early September.

The coffin, which seemed small despite him being a tall man, was carried by Loizos, Christaki, Pavlo and three other close friends of the family. Their mother and father followed the coffin with heavy steps through the village streets from their house to the church, the bells ringing loudly across the village bringing the mourners together. Both frail and entirely lost in their grief they held out their hands as mourners passed on their *silibitiria*; their condolences. Anastasia, her face shaded by a piece of black lace, and the three children walked alongside them, the rest of the family fell in line behind them with at least another thousand mourners.

The church, heavily decorated with icons of numerous shapes and sizes and ages, was already bursting with mourners, dressed in black from head to toe. Some were talking in small groups, others were lighting candles and placing them in the sandbox by the entrance of the church. There was a line of bereaved kissing the main icon of Jesus on the iconostasis, which partitioned the nave from the sanctuary, at the front of the church and crossing themselves. A hush ascended on and spread across the church as the family approached through the main doors and the mourners parted to make way for the casket and the family at the front.

'Blessed is our Lord God, always; both now and ever, and to the ages and ages,' sang out the priest in a soft but monotone humming drone. The priest said prayers and swung the delicate, brass openwork censer from its four chains. The four chains represented the four evangelists; Matthew, Mark, Luke and John. The church was stifling and made all the more unbearable as the smell of incense filled the oppressive air. Loizos found himself counting the four chains over and over in his head as the overpowering waft of frankincense filled his nostrils.

The added heat from the still lit but guttered candles made it even hotter and a number of bereaved were helped out of the church as they dropped, fainting. Anastasia did not cry once at the funeral, but she wasn't entirely focused on the service. Loizos took in her lowness of spirit, her exhaustion and missed already her usually smooth, clear skin, her perfume. Her hands gripped tightly onto her black handbag.

'Let us pray to the Lord. Lord have mercy. For you are the Resurrection, the Life, and the Repose of Your servant Michael, O Christ our God; and to You do we send up glory, with Your Eternal Father, and Your All-Holy, good and Life-creating Spirit, both now and ever, and to the ages and ages. Amen.' The priest continued in his low sing-song voice and the mourners crossed themselves three times and repeated amen.

The service continued for a full hour and Anastasia joined in intermittently with the hymns and listened to the readings and the prayers. She held her head high, sending out the message her brother had died an innocent man. Despina sat between her two children towards the back of the church. Catching a glimpse of Despina through the melee, Anastasia's expression remained stoic, proud.

The casket, facing east with the feet towards the altar,

was left open for mourners to pay their last respects after the parents and immediate family. Many of the family kissed him; The Kiss of Peace and Anointing. At the end of the funeral, mourners passed by the casket again and placed a flower on top.

The old cemetery, a piece of land furthest away from the church towards the most central part of the village, was edged by a stone wall no taller than two feet. A second cemetery had since been sectioned off towards the outskirts of the village but the family had wanted Michael buried here where most of their ancestors were buried. The sun peeked from behind the palest white trickle of clouds, giving the whole event a surreal atmosphere. The old grave stones, mostly crosses, were higgledy-piggledy, some so old, covered in lichen and moss, you could barely read the inscriptions on the stone. Others were toppled over, the roots of the olive trees protruding through the dry earth, matted brown with the dead pine needles of the ancient fir trees. The sun's rays peaked through the waxy leaf canopy above. It was peaceful despite the obvious heart ache and cries the place had witnessed.

The priest completed The Trisagion Service, the service at the wake, which took no more than ten minutes in duration.

'Holy God, Holy Mighty, Holy Immortal, have mercy on us,' he repeated the prayer three times. The mourners crossed themselves and some repeated the prayer out loud while others mumbled the words inaudibly to themselves. *Pater* swung the incense-infused thurible filling the air with the musky familiar smell of church and the soft gentle sound of the clinking chains. In the near distance the snorting and grumbling of the goats on the mountainside could be heard faintly and the braying of a donkey. He sealed the casket with holy oil and sand before it was lowered into the ground, again facing east, onto the decomposed casket of his uncle who had been buried there three years before.

With the service ended, the wake, by the graveside spilled out onto the quiet dirt path alongside it. The rest of the day was one of chatter and remembering the man who had been snatched away so cruelly. The mourners who remained drank red wine and *paximathia*, crunchy dry-baked bread sticks, halloumi and black olives. The children, many who were too young to discern what was happening, enjoyed the day off school and ran around the small cemetery playing chase. By seven o'clock the last of the mourners drifted away leaving Anastasia and the immediate family by the graveside.

Loizos saw her relax slightly, she's at peace at last, he thought recognising the change the funeral had instilled in her. Her features looked lighter, brighter and her shoulders were less tense. She looked softer and more relaxed despite the harsh black of her clothes shadowing her of light like the wings of a crow.

He put his arm around her and led her away, whispering her name. He was not a demonstrative man and yet the funeral had brought out in him the deep love and respect he had for his beautiful wife and he uncharacteristically told her he loved her. She looked at him, her eyes wide and the tears fell openly.

***

There were no other incidences of death or casualties in *Ayios Tychonas* since the murder of Michael. Loizos hoped, as the days turned into weeks and the weeks into months, Anastasia and the children would move on from the horrific incident. But he was wrong. They were inconsolable.

Anastasia had sought out Savva and Dimitri the day before they were caught and arrested in an abandoned house in *Germassoia*. She still wore the traditional black of mourning from head to toe and both men almost didn't recognise her, so altered did she appear from her usual self. She had aged overnight, her pained expression one of a woman in her seventies, of a woman who had seen so much of death it had seeped into her and become a familiar part of her demeanour.

'If this was his fault, then it serves him right. But if it wasn't his fault, then may the ones to blame not see forty days after him.' She faced them straight on, her stare unflinching as she clearly said the words she came to say.

Dimitri died within twenty-nine days of her curse, in prison, and Marko was shot dead trying to escape thirty-four days later. Anastasia cried till she had nothing more to release. She desperately missed her brother and devastation encompassed her as well as the belief he had died in vain.

'He was innocent,' she insisted. She could barely speak from her sobbing, choosing to hide away in the semi-darkness of her bedroom most of the day; her eyes red and sore. Neighbours, friends and family visited her but she withdrew from the affections of everyone away wanting to bury herself in her grief; wanting to mourn the loss of her brother in peace. She remembered how the children loved the way Michael used to tell silly jokes and make up stories about the people he worked with in the *bandoboulion,* the market place in Limassol. As she recalled his wonderful tales she cried harder and Loizos could do nothing to ease her suffering; all he could do was wait.

Listening to her silent crying every night, unable to take her pain away Loizos could not stop the guilt from eating him either; he had been unable to save Michael.

Eventually Anastasia returned to her life again, but she was only half in it. She took on dressmaking work and put what little energy she could muster into making money. She knew this was the only way out for them now. If they had money they could escape.

She didn't talk about her feelings with Loizos but now and again she spilled her heart to him and begged him to take them away from the village. She couldn't face passing Despina's house, knowing her brother had passed his final moments, on that cold floor. She couldn't bear seeing Despina either nor Loizos' sister Irini who was now struggling to keep the family together and living with the shame of what Dimitri had been involved in. She wanted to leave the village and the bad memories it now held for her. Even though the men had been arrested she was broken.

***

Loizos and Christaki continued to pass coded messages back and forth. Both had evaded swearing the oath to support EOKA, and in his heart Loizos knew he would flee to England before putting his family in danger. He was pulled in one direction by his beliefs in AKEL, yet sympathised with the EOKA cause and the men and young boys already deeply entrenched in what had become to be known as the Cyprus Emergency.

He needed to put a plan in place. He had some letters sent over from family in England recently. He was going to use them as a ploy to get his family out before it was too late.

'So how are you all?' asked a neighbour while they were playing *tavli* at the *kafeneion* one evening.

'We are all well, but we've had a letter to say Anastasia's sister in England is poorly.'

'Sorry to hear that. I'm sure she will improve.'

'With God's will, yes.'

Over the next few weeks when someone asked after his family he mentioned Anastasia's sister was unwell in England and was begging to see Anastasia and her family one last time. People were kind and offered their blessings which played on his conscience as he fought to hold onto his resolution that this was the right decision. He could not choose conflict over the love for his family and his duty to protect them.

'*Na daxo ston Ayio Fanourio*,' said one kind lady, offering to bake a *fanouropita*. This was a traditional sweet-bread baked in the name of Saint Fanourios and many baked it either in the hope of finding something they had lost or a cure would be found for the ailment being suffered by the sick person they had baked the cake in aid of. The *fanouropita* was offered in church on Sundays where it was blessed by the priest and shared among the congregation in the hope their prayers would be answered.

'*Efharisto*,' he would say, thanking them all and in the meantime bought tickets for all the members of his family one by one so as not to arouse suspicion they may all be leaving on the same day. The tickets were open tickets which meant they would be checked on board but their accommodation would not be allocated until the actual day of boarding. This meant he would need cash on him to pay for whatever was available.

Christaki continued to receive notes from Loukia and

passed them onto his father who would pass notes back. This worked well. There were no questions, and in particular no discussions, especially since part of the EOKA oath taken was 'I will never reveal any of the instructions given me even to my comrades' and 'If I renege on my oath, I will be worthy of every punishment as a traitor and may eternal contempt be with me'.

***

September passed and it was already October. The beginning of the forty day fast for Christmas was soon to start and Loizos talked about his commitment to his business and his customers at such a busy time. His reason for not going with his family seemed convincing enough and no-one questioned it.

On the 6th December after the church service, the family gathered in their main sitting room, the fire roared and spat as Loizos stoked it with more firewood. Everyone, including aunts, uncles and cousins, had crammed into the only heated room in the house to observe the traditional *vasilopita* cutting.

'And here it is. The beautiful cake,' said Anastasia. Children chorused their enthusiasm with oohs and ahhs of joy; excitement in the room building as Anastasis counted the total number of family present. Carefully she scored the top of the cake into the correct number of pieces; one for each person present. The cake, particularly special, because a hidden coin was buried inside it, was cut piece by piece. The tradition brought laughter and joy into the house and the lucky winner of the piece which held the coin was said to have good fortune and success all year through.

One by one they each took a piece from the platter. Some took a bite straight into it others turned their piece this way and that to see if the coin was wedged into their slice.

'I've found the coin!' yelled Christaki at the top of his voice.

'Luck will be yours all year through, *agabi mou*,' said Anastasia.

'It would be you!' sulked Melani.

'I've won it for all of us,' said Christaki pulling Melani towards him and giving her a bear hug.

'Come here,' coaxed Loizos recognising the disappointment of the younger children. Take this and spend it wisely. He handed them all a silver coin each. They soon forgot about not winning the *vasilopita* treasure.

All the family members cheered and for a short while Loizos forgot the heartache that lay ahead. The coin falling within Christaki's piece of cake was surely a good sign; it was a sign of hope for the future, at least for his family.

***

As his family readied to leave the village ten days later they were forbidden to say the fond goodbyes they wanted to on the pretext they would be returning after their two week stay. The papers were authorised for their passage and signed by the appropriate government officials and stamped.

'How can I leave Loukia and Katerina?' complained Melani.

'It won't be for long,' insisted Anastasia.

'But I need to be here.'

'Family is more important Melani. You remember that,' admonished Loizos.

'Well I still don't see why I have to come.'

'Because I said so,' said Loizos, his eyes a gritty black.

They continued to argue right up to the day they were leaving. The boys, displayed their disapproval through what they didn't say than what they did. But again no-one spoke of the real reason they were leaving.

Chapter Eight

Christaki, 1957

THE PORT THRUMMED with activity as their bus pulled into the harbour. The ocean shone a brilliant blue in contrast to the crashing sea spray and the chill of the early January air filled Christaki's lungs. They made their way to the main boarding point for the passenger liner that would take them to England and to freedom.

'Here, let me help you,' offered a young man, as Malanie's case burst open, spilling half her belongings as she dragged her luggage to the main entry point.

She was about to thank him when Christaki interrupted. 'That's okay. I've got it,' he said and the young man walked away.

'What's with you? He was only helping.'

'Well I can help you. Don't start, okay?' said Christaki.

He let go of his own case and together with Melani gathered her clothes and clipped the clasps back together.

They re-joined the others who had walked ahead so as not to attract any attention. They each had their own tickets and were to board via the check-point at different times so as not to arouse suspicion.

'Don't forget what *baba* said. Families leaving the

country are finding it difficult to do so, even with the correct papers. The British, as well as EOKA nationalists, are on the look-out for possible EOKA traitors. Don't talk to anyone, Melani.' Melani looked at him, her features strained and tired.

Christaki put on a smile, as he walked, in an effort to look relaxed. He knew his friends Panteli and Yianni had been involved in serious action against the British patrols and had both been detained in the prison in Nicosia. He had made the trip to the prison to see them one last time before he left but the guards had not allowed him to speak to them. From behind the barbed wire fence he thought he had seen Panteli, recognised the back of his head but he hadn't seen Yianni at all. Christaki had left with a heavy, desperate heart that day. He forced the tears back until he finally arrived home where he had collapsed in his mother's arms. He shuddered as he thought of his friends in that hell hole, that place not even fit for animals.

Once on board, Christaki felt the tension begin to fade. Anastasia's strained features and the tightness across her shoulders softened. She unpacked the suitcases and placed items in the cupboards and drawers. Pavlo appeared carefree; as he lay across the bunk beds in the cabin they were sharing. Through the open cabin door, he could hear Melani slurping her lemonade while she chatted to another girl in the narrow corridor outside.

Christaki took a stroll around the upper deck of the

ship while he left his mother to unpack and Pavlo lounging. He was relieved to be on their way yet anxious about having to leave his father behind, but he remembered his father's last words to him, 'Freedom is in the air. Breathe it in deeply son.'

Even though the cold air was biting at the back of his throat he thought he could taste freedom already as he peered across the gleaming ocean back to the island of love but a love which was now muddied and destroyed and there was no going back.

Chapter Nine

Elena, 1958

THE NEW YEAR came with a flurry of fresh snowflakes and freezing temperatures brooded over the villages at the legs of the mountains. In the distance the flour-white peaked Troodos mountains resembled thickly iced *kourabiethes*: rich, golden domed crumbly cookies covered in layers of icing sugar traditionally served at weddings and on Feast days.

As she made her way to school with Andreas, Elena could see the dark foliage of the fir-covered mountain sides and across to the olive groves set into the knotted hills. She wore two pairs of wool socks over her knees to keep her long legs warm and a berry red hat which covered her ears. She had no scarf; her brother had it and a pair of orange gloves. They bundled against the whisper-light flakes whirling towards them and Elena secretly hoped the snow would settle. Their tones were ecstatic as they tried to catch them in their hands and stuck out their tongues to lick them. By the time they got to the school yard the snow was falling fast, unusual for it to reach *Kato Lefkara*, nestled into the mountain, and the children were jumping with joy as the flakes continued to dance around their smiling but frozen faces, blushed from the nipping cold.

It was the day of *Kiria* Nitsa's visit from Larnaca and Elena was relieved to see she had still made it to the village despite the weather. She came into their class with a bundle of rolled sheets tied with string. She bid them good morning as she placed it with her bag of art materials on *Kiria* Maria's desk. The children were thrilled to see her, especially Elena.

'*Ela,*' she addressed the class. 'Over the holidays my cousin in England sent me some photographs.' She pulled the knot on the string and released the bundle which unrolled, unravelling the photographs across the desk.

When the children saw the pictures of Big Ben and Buckingham Palace they were all in awe of the magnificent buildings. Elena took in the detail of each one. She was enthralled by the wide river and the clouds drifting in the sky. She looked in wonder at the tall cylindrical upright boxes.

'What are they?' she asked.

'These are letter boxes for posting mail. Like our little yellow boxes. These are telephone boxes, like our green ones, with a phone fixed in them so you can make a call using coins. They're also painted red.'

'What's the big clock?'

'That's called Big Ben, it's a part of Westminster where the government resides and has meetings,' explained *Kiria* Maria. 'And this is where the Queen lives with her family when she is in London. This is Buckingham Palace, but she has many palaces to call home.'

The noise level in the room suddenly rose a few decibels as the children threw themselves into animated conversation and fired questions at her.

Kiria Maria stepped forward from behind her desk and glared at them all. Immediately they quietened and muttered their apologies, heads bent in obedience.

Desks were scraped across the floor as they were pushed together in fours to make room to accommodate the big pictures and painting sheets. The children settled into a quiet hum as *Kiria* Nitsa handed out pencils, paints and paint brushes. *Kiria* Maria gave a sheet of paper to each pupil.

'That's where we're going to live,' said Andreas to Niko, pointing to the picture of Buckingham Palace.

'Don't be silly. You can't live with the Queen,' chuckled Niko.

'Not there with her. I mean in London.'

'And that's where you can post me a letter,' said Niko, 'if you learn to write,' he sniggered.

Andreas shoved him in the side with his elbow. 'I'll be writing in English so you'd better learn to read!' he shot back.

The boys eventually settled into a quiet harmony roughly replicating the buildings onto their sheets of paper and then, filling their brushes with too much paint, making a mess of their painting.

'I'll be able to telephone you from London,' said Elena to Yioli.

'You better,' said Yioli.

'Oh I will most definitely. We will have more money too so I'll be able to telephone you every day if I want.'

'You'll be too busy with homework and new friends to remember me.'

'No I won't. And if I am I'll telephone you when I finish. They don't lock the telephone boxes at night!' said Elena, leaning into her friend and hugging her tight.

Most of the morning was spent painting and drawing and Elena allowed herself to be lost in her thoughts. Her mind was full of the images she had seen that morning but more so that she would be moving to England within the next few weeks. She furrowed her forehead in concentration and drew her lines carefully with a gentle sweep of the pencil and then shaded in using the array of colours lined up in the metal box. She combined the paints and pencil colours together and *Kiria* Nitsa was delighted with her efforts.

At the end of the session, as the church bells rang one o'clock across the village, the children formed a row at the front of the class and the Principal came in to judge the paintings and award a special prize. He walked back and forth along the line, taking his role most seriously, twirling his thick moustache, which jiggled under his nose like a black hairy caterpillar, as he walked from one picture to the next concentrating on each of the images held out proudly by each student facing him.

'He's taking too long,' whispered Elena to Yioli on one side of her and Stella on the other. Elena got the giggles.

'He's going to choose me,' said Stella as he stopped and walked back in her direction.

The Principal stood back from the row of children and congratulated them for their beautiful art work. Andreas dropped his painting and it fluttered towards the Principal's black polished shoes. He made no move to retrieve it and left it there; Big Ben looking up at the Principal's nostrils. Niko then bent towards his sock which had concertinaed around his fat ankle and as he did so he farted. Elena stifled another giggle but Zacharias and Mirianthi chuckled loudly unable to contain their amusement. The Principle paused, a contorted expression across his face as he smelt the lingering odour. He ignored the incident and visibly shook the pained expression away. After a few moments he continued his speech with a simper.

'I would also like to extend my sincere thanks, and thanks on behalf of the class to *Kiria* Maria *and Kiria* Nitsa for giving the children the opportunity to explore their creativity. This is a wonderful liaison between teachers which will benefit the children's imagination when writing too.'

He then coughed to clear his throat. Elena was

overcome with mirth again which stopped no sooner than it commenced when the Principal looked straight at her. Stella laughed too. After a moment's hesitation, he announced the winner and rewarded the winning student with a blank sketch book and a set of colouring pencils. To the rest of the class he poured out a big bag of *lokmathes* into a bowl. They all tucked greedily into the deep fried doughnut balls coated in honey murmuring contentedly as the sticky honey stuck to their lips.

Going home at lunch time the children teased Elena calling her an 'English pillar box' because of her red hat but she didn't mind. She knew they were just being funny and she liked looking 'English' already.

'*Mama*, *mama*,' yelled Elena as she pushed open the door almost taking it off its hinges. She ran across the courtyard and into the tiny kitchen, holding her hat by the bobble.

'Yioli won the art competition but she gave me the prize because she said I'm much better at painting than she is and the Principal only gave her the prize because I kept laughing.'

'Slow down,' said her mother. 'You're going to swallow your tongue.'

'I'm so happy.'

'Well that's marvellous *agabi mou*,' said her *yiayia,* who stirred a pot of soup on the stove.

'And this is what I painted.' Elena carefully unrolled

her picture and held it up against her, spreading her fingers to stop the corners from curling inwards.

'It's beautiful, like you,' said her *yiayia*. 'You certainly deserved to win.'

'I hope you realise that's not all you're going to be doing in London,' said her mother.

'No. I know. But it's something I will be able to do every day!' she shrilled.

'Your smile always brightens our dark, dingy kitchen,' said her *yiayia*.

'Where's Andreas?' asked her mother.

'He's scraping snow off the *kafeneion* wall and putting it in his coat pockets.'

'Heaven help us.' Her mother rolled her eyes to heaven, smiling.

'He wants to save it. He's so silly,' said Elena in an amusing tone. 'He'll be able to see all the snow he wants in England!' Delirious with excitement she talked about the art lesson and the pictures cramming her mind.

***

'Gently Elena *mou*,' said her mother as Elena scooped the eggs and dropped them into the pan of bubbling orange water one by one.

'Why do we always do red?'

'Well, the colour signifies the blood of Christ, the colour of life.'

147

'But Yioli's mum says they can be any colour.'

'Red is traditional.'

It was Holy Thursday and the smell of the boiling onion skins and white vinegar filled Elena's lungs making her feel nauseous. However, she was excited about Easter knowing their travel to England was soon after. She was going to meet her father at last. So she didn't complain about fasting as she usually did and had even come to enjoy her diet of bread, olives, tomatoes, boiled beans and lentils drizzled with olive oil and lemon.

After half an hour, her mother strained the onions through a sieve, the orange juices filling a saucepan beneath it.

Elena stayed by the stove and watched as the water bubbled and the orange dye miraculously stained the shell of the eggs a dull cherry-red. Elena scooped them out with a slatted spoon into a bowl, careful not to break the outer shell.

'They don't look nice,' she said, disappointed her efforts had not produced the shining glowy red eggs her mother always made.

'Let them cool and then you can polish them with olive oil,' said her mother. 'That's what brightens them.'

Once they were cold to touch, Elena used a little cloth dipped in the thick green-tinged oil to give the eggs a beautiful shine. She heaped them into a basket which she carried over to the table and sat them in the middle taking pride of place alongside the *tsestos* filled with mounds of *flaounes,* baked early before sunrise. The smell was delicious and Elena licked her lips as her mouth watered, tempted to bite into one. Instead she re-arranged the Easter breads in the shallow basket made from palm leaves.

'Once we've eaten these we can gather the baskets and you can take them to Niko's mum. We can't take them with us.' Elena caught the sorrow in her voice. 'I'll start passing things on soon.' Elena didn't say anything.

'It won't be the same without our things,' said *yiayia* standing by the kitchen door.

'That's not like you to be worrying about things,' said Evangelia. 'But it's not about that is it? You don't want to come with us do you?'

'I'm fifty years old. No husband. This is the only life I've ever known Evangelia *mou.* What would a woman of my age do in a big city?'

'We will just carry on but in a different place. It will be the same.'

'Dear Evangelia *mou,* our hearts are Cypriot, we have culture and traditions. What do the British have? You've seen how they behave.'

'But you'll be with us. You'll see Panayiota again and all your other grandchildren,' said Evangelia reaching for her mother's arm, fighting back her tears.

'Yes there's that. And I want to go. But you will want to start fresh with your Kostas. You won't want me in the way.'

'Don't think like that. Of course we want you there. Elena and Andreas would be lost without you.'

'*Yiayia* you have to come.' Elena threw herself into her *yiayia's* arms, hugging her. 'You can't stay here *yiayia* on your own.' Her *yiayia* gave her a squeeze and walked out into the courtyard towards the old olive tree. Elena knew she was crying. Her mum was crying too even though her back was to Elena, she could see her shaking. Elena felt her heart squeeze in an odd way. She wasn't as sure about going as she was before either.

Elena brought her attention back to the eggs and how it wouldn't be long before they would be cracking one against the other after the Saturday midnight service. Their first meal would be the traditional Easter breads made with flour, eggs, *halloumi*, sultanas and fresh mint wrapped in sesame covered pastry. She couldn't wait and her stomach rumbled as she remembered she had not had any breakfast yet, too excited about making the *kokkina avga*.

***

On Holy Friday, Good Friday, the flags at the school and at the crossroads into the village were hung at half-mast and the church bells rang throughout the day in a slow mournful tone. Her mother cooked a simple dish of lentils in the morning ready for their evening meal. Together they walked to the church, taking with them flowers picked from their courtyard and fields along the way, to decorate the bier, a small canopied litter which represented the tomb of Christ,

which housed the *Epitaphio.*

The church was already a hub of activity when they arrived. *Pater* Vassilios was busying himself stocking up the candle boxes and flattening out the sand in the sand trays. A small group of women were individually decorating the window sills along the length of the church with little glass vases filled with perfumed flowers of pink, white and yellow hues. Four others were meticulously covering the bier transforming it into an organic sculpture of multi-coloured blooms at the front of the church. Scissors were snipping and fingers were bending and poking as the stalks of white and purple shimmering flowers were strung together with cotton and secured to the bier.

Elena and her mother joined the group at the front of the church and kindly offered to snip the stalks to the right length so the blooms could be secured to the wire netting. They worked in silence, a strained silence which felt like a taut elastic band about to ping.

Once finished, the bier, now wholly covered in the sweet smelling blooms, resembled a sculpture of flowers and only the small feet could be seen.

Three large jugs of rosewater sat on the deep stone window ledge. The sweet-smelling water would be sprinkled on the streets to purify the route as the

151

Epitaphio was carried around the village, followed by the congregants, each holding a tall lighted candle, and back to the church again in the evening.

'This is the last time we'll be doing this here,' said her mother, tears rolling down her face.

'Oh *mama*, don't be sad. We can go to church in London.'

'Yes, yes we can. And we will. But it won't be the same.'

'*Mama*, it will be better,' said Elena biting on her bottom lip.

'And your *yiayia* is more worried than she says, I can tell. I saw her stroking her bedstead yesterday and the day before she was in the courtyard staring; staring at the olive tree and the pomegranate tree. I called out to her from the kitchen but she didn't hear me, she seemed lost. She can't leave the home she's known all her life. What am I thinking?'

'*Mama*, please. We can't not go. I've told all my friends. *Baba* is waiting for us.'

Chapter Ten

Elena, 1958

ELENA TRIED TO lift her head from the pillow but it ached. She opened her eyes and thought she spied the black and white cows of her dream dancing on the cracked ceiling of the bedroom, smiling at her. It mustn't even be five o'clock, she thought, judging from the faint light seeping into the room through the closed shutters. Even the cockerels were silent. Her brother rolled over easily as she pushed him to the other side of the bed giving her room to stretch her long legs as she untangled herself from her nightdress which had wrapped tight around her. In London, she thought, I'll have my own bed.

She forced her eyes closed and tugged at the sheet. She thought of England, images faded in and out, soothing her fuzzy head, until she eventually dropped off again, the familiar roll of Andreas' snoring the last sound she was aware of.

***

In the street outside their house and in the courtyard too neighbours and friends and relations had gathered to wish them a fond farewell. It was an overwhelming sight with tears and hugs and kisses. Baskets of food and fruit and preserves were being pushed into her mother's hands but Evangelia had to refuse everyone's kind offerings.

'I have no room. But thank you. You eat them and remember us. God bless you my dear friends.'

'I'll have the *loukoumi*,' grinned Andreas as he gripped one of the little packages.

'You can have the *loukoumi*,' said their mother smiling.

'Travel safe. May God bless your new path. Go well. Send our best regards to Panayiota and her family. Go well. May God see you safely to London.' The well wishes kept coming as friends and neighbours hugged Evangelia and *yiayia* and kissed the children goodbye. Elena fought back her tears but cried saying goodbye to her school friends who had made her a card with a picture of Big Ben on the front and signed inside with their names written in English.

Elena, gripped onto her pink bag, crocheted as a gift by Niko's mum. Inside, her prized possessions rattled against each other; her Coronation Day mug, her rolled up picture, her small silver hairbrush and mirror, her father's worry beads and her doll. Despite her mother telling her to leave them to her friends she had insisted she bring them to London and in the end, her Mother had given up trying to persuade her.

In the midst of friends, bustling around her in the

overcrowded street, Elena laughed and cried and hugged. *Pater* Vassilios blessed them with a little prayer, wishing them a safe passage to England.

With heavy steps, Evangelia locked the gate to the courtyard for the last time and handed the key over to Zeno to keep an eye on things until the house was sold. She didn't speak. Elena noticed her mother as if for the first time. The chatter around her faded and for a few brief moments she was alone. Her mother was beautiful, even with sadness in her eyes. She saw her reach out to Zeno and how he gently squeezed Evangelia's hand without saying a word.

The bus hooted at the top of the village by the *kafeneion* and it continued up the steep path leading out of the village. Their school friends chased the bus waving and yelling goodbye, kicking clouds of dry earth behind them.

As the bus passed the sharp bend in the road Elena gave them one last wave and peered back across the beautiful bulk of mountains. She took in the rich pink earth and the silver olive trees. Standing beneath a lone, ancient pomegranate tree she spotted Manoli waving at her from the middle distance. The bouncing light of the morning sun aglow around him. She waved back smiling and then he disappeared in a cloud of dusty fumes as the bus trundled on its way.

The main road to Limassol was free of traffic most of the

journey but the bus slowed as they made their way from the outskirts of *Amathus* towards *Germassoia*.

They had been travelling for no more than an hour but the journey had already tired Elena. Her headache had cleared but her stomach churned, threatening her with sickness. Sweat prickled her body. She fingered the gold cross around her neck, stroking its smooth contours and feeling each rounded edge. It was the only piece of jewellery she owned. It was the cross her Godmother, long dead, had gifted to her when she was christened and which she wore always. As far as she was aware her mother didn't own much in the way of jewellery either. She wore her gold wedding band, her watch and a simple gold bracelet with three charms on it; a blue glass 'eye' to ward off evil, a filigree flower and a tiny cross. Andreas had a cross too but he had broken the chain and so it was kept in a little padded black box for safe-keeping until a time when the broken links could be repaired.

'It is in God's hands now,' her *yiayia* repeated as she watched Elena's fingers. 'We must trust in Him. This is the path He has chosen for us.' Elena stroked her *yiayia's* veiny hand and a lump in her throat threatened to bring on her tears as she thought of the little courtyard she might never sit in again. She thought about Manoli on the mountainside. How he was free but she would never talk or wave to him again.

Elena leant forward to look at her mother, red-eyed from saying her farewells. Saying goodbye to the villagers had been hard. She thought about them now. How they had come to the house bearing gifts and letters to pass onto their own relations already settled in London. Elena hadn't realised how many friends they had in the village and she knew too, how her mother, deep inside, was heartbroken to be leaving the place she had called home since her birth.

Elena was sitting in the opposite row across from her mother. Her mother yawned, scrunching her eyes and shaking her head to push the yawn out. She nodded towards Elena. Elena smiled back.

'Are we there, *mama?*'

'I think so. When we get off don't go anywhere until we collect all our luggage together and keep an eye on Andreas for me. And find somewhere for *yiayia* to sit while I make sure we have all our belongings.'

'I don't need keeping an eye on,' said Andreas, momentarily distracted from a piece of wood he chipped away at with his penknife.

'Then keep an eye on Elena Andreas *mou* and don't worry about me, I'm just fine,' said *yiayia*, diffusing the obvious argument before it erupted.

Andreas smiled at *yiayia* and puffed his chest out in a show of importance. Elena lowered her head to hide her smirk.

'We just need to stay together,' insisted her mother. 'It's going to be busy.'

Elena knew how nervous her mother was and leaned

across to hug her. She gave Elena a half smile as she pulled away. Her mother's shoulders were tight and almost touched her ears. Her hands, which gripped the top of her handbag balancing on her clenched knees, relaxed for an instant and her mother let out a sigh. She glanced over at Andreas gnawing at his fingernails.

As Elena sat back down, cigarette smoke wafted by filling her nostrils. Elena listened to Maria Kyriakides who sat tall with her shoulders back. She was graceful and her pretty low-cut top revealing her breasts. She talked throughout the whole journey, as she puffed like a film star on cigarette after cigarette. She must be nervous, thought Elena. No-one could talk for so long without stopping. Her husband Alexandros, with his neat grey beard and side-whiskers, intermittently made the right sounds to indicate he was listening. But Elena guessed he wasn't actively paying attention and every now and again he tapped his wife's hand as if placating a boisterous toddler. This small gesture between husband and wife alerted Elena as to how lonely her mother must have been without her father and how scared she must also be as she made the journey to London.

The two Kyriakides children, Marianna and Reno, about fifteen and nineteen years old, were sitting in front of their parents and hadn't said a word to each other the entire journey. Elena wondered what they were thinking. Were they excited? Were they nervous? What did they know about England, about London?

The squeal of screeching brakes flung the passengers forward and left a ringing in her ears like the scrape of chalk on the school blackboard. Out the window, clouds of dust billowed around the bus. Within seconds the bus filled with raised voices. Elena watched as some passengers stood up, straining to identify what was happening. Others walked to the front; raised voices became shouting. Women wailed and cradled their babies and children. Some of the younger children climbed out of their seats and ran to their parents, tears flowing. Panic suffocated the air on the bus now heavy with fear and panic.

As she continued to look, two armed police officers and three British soldiers pushed past those blocking the aisle. They slowed at each row of seats checking the faces of the passengers left, right, left right, making their way to the back of the bus. Women cowered as they passed them by and men protectively put their arms across the front of their wives and children.

They paced up the bus, their sturdy boots kicking over baskets of fruit over, sending figs and pomegranates rolling across the aisle and under the seats. Elena squeezed her crocheted bag between her knees, her fists white from gripping. She felt her shoulders tighten and her stomach knot.

'What's happening?' asked her mother.

'No questions,' answered one of the officers as two men from the back of the bus were dragged to the front of the bus.

'Leave us alone. You traitors. And you call yourselves Cypriots,' said one man, as he wrestled to free himself from the officer's grip.

'You're coming with us. We have questions you need to answer.'

'Leave him be,' said *Kirio* Kyriakides.

'Stay out of it or we'll arrest you too!'

'For God's sake, sit down,' said *Kiria* Kyriakides as she pulled at her husband's sleeve.

'Alright, alright,' he said, holding his hands palmside up, in surrender.

Elena didn't recognise the two men and wondered who they were. She wondered why the police wanted them and why the British soldiers wanted them. She wondered why no-one else was doing anything to stop them.

There were people shouting, some got off the bus and then there was a loud piercing bang. A gunshot.

There were gasps and prayers out loud and then the bus hushed to a heart-stopping silence, no-one dared to breathe. Elena's *yiayia* took Elena's hand in hers, crossing herself with the other, muttering to the Lord under her breath.

The gunshot was followed by another and Elena saw a gun being fired in the air. The two men from the back of the bus were lying with their faces to the ground, their arms stretched out. She bit down on her lip as a soldier yelled at the men still on the ground. Elena noticed how his lips twisted as he spoke.

The driver complained he had to get his passengers to the port on time to board their ship. However, this made no difference.

Outside, two other police officers were rummaging through the suitcases; one pulled luggage out of the hold and another clambered onto the roof of the bus throwing the baggage onto the ground. They opened a number of suitcases and it appeared as if they found something. More shouting and yelling. One officer barked orders. Elena caught a glimpse of the two men being pulled to their feet, handcuffed and pushed into the back of a British marked army jeep. She watched it speed off wondering where they would be taken.

The bus couldn't get as close to the port as her mother had hoped and prematurely pulled over at one of the bus stops opposite the beach some distance away. Their luggage was thrown off the top of the bus onto the gritty walkway. When someone recognised their own luggage in time they called out for it to be thrown towards, their arms outstretched to catch it. Complete chaos, thought Elena. Passengers called out and pointed for specific suitcases and boxes or called out to each other to stay together as they alighted the bus. The narrow stretch of pavement near the sea front became a pool of people.

'Sit on the wall and wait for our luggage to be handed

to us,' said Elena's mother, concern in her voice. 'We don't know who's going to be on the streets. Don't speak to anyone.'

Elena and Andreas did as they were told. The wall was warm from the beating sun and the base of it was crumbling, part of it half-collapsed with bits of scattered rubble on the ground. Andreas fidgeted, biting on his nails and kicked at the debris and broken bricks, scuffing his polished shoes. The odour around them was a pungent one with a sweet edge to it; car and bus fumes mixed with the salty sea air and a fragrant froth of hibiscus and wild-growing bougainvillea. Elena sat with controlled patience, focusing on the pink flowers of the bougainvillea, counting them, shutting out the noise of the crowded street. She took out her doll and stroked her face, her hair. A kitten lazed towards her and snuggled against her legs but as she bent to stroke it, it sprang away and disappeared behind a wooden cart selling cigarettes and sweets.

Each with their own suitcase Elena and her family walked towards the port. *Kirio* Kyriakides walked ahead of them, a suitcase in each hand, while his wife held onto a small vanity case. Elena realised how her mother struggled, as she passed the smaller suitcase to Andreas freeing her hand to carry the larger one, the weight of which was slowing her.

'Gosh, it's heavy,' said Elena, taking it from her.

'It is darling. Thank you.'

Elena walked along, the case bumping along her leg as she tried to keep the momentum of her pace going, but the case was too heavy and bulky for her, even with her mother carrying it with her. Her hand, before long, became sore and her arm throbbed. She stopped, annoying those walking behind her, who had to side-step to avoid knocking her over.

'Sorry,' she said to a woman who tutted.

Elena was about to swap hands when Reno stopped her in her tracks.

'I'll take that for you.'

'I am struggling a bit. Thank you,' Elena said. He took the case from her and slowed his pace to walk in time with her steps. He made the case look so light. It was as if he was carrying a bag of feathers, thought Elena, rubbing her sore, aching hand.

'So are you excited?' he asked.

'A bit, yes, I guess.'

'Well, I'm a bit scared to be honest,' he said winking at her.

'Me too,' she succumbed.

***

Once nearer the port hundreds more people filled the pavements and spilled into the docking area and to the main entry point marked for access to those travelling only; family members wished their loved ones a safe journey. Children cried, people hugged each other and made promises to write and to telephone. Others handed over gifts of fresh fruit and wrapped parcels tied with string; Elena imagined *paklava, galatoboureko, pitoues, daktila and kateifi,* the sweet filo and shortcrust pastries bursting with chopped pistachios, almonds and thick yellow custard sitting together in a warm goo of syrup. She rubbed her stomach, as it growled at her.

'That's the biggest thing I've ever seen!' said Elena. 'How will it keep afloat with all these people on it?' she asked out loud, to no-one in particular.

'It's doomed. It's doomed,' repeated her *yiayia* over and over under her breath but loud enough for Elena to catch. 'Doomed...like the journey of Odysseus...oh Lord be with us and keep us safe.' She pulled her black head scarf around her and crossed herself.

'Stop it,' said Evangelia. 'You're going to scare the children. Enough. This is hard enough as it is without you and your superstitions.'

Elena repeated the name of the ship, painted in black letters on its side, Mesabia, Mesabia, Mesabia inside her head over and over again. This calmed her and she decided, despite her *yiayia's* rambling, it was a lucky name. It was soft and gentle, an angel on water, she told herself just as much to convince herself as any.

'Look at all the cars driving onto the ship,' exclaimed Andreas.

'And all those people already on board,' said Elena as they filled the promenade deck, some shouting across the port and others waving scarves and sun hats in an effort to stand out from the milling crowds as they tried to attract their families left standing on solid Cyprus ground.

'One, two, three, four decks,' counted Elena out loud as she stared in awe at the huge rusty chains and worn cables dangling down the ship's sides, clanking as they pulled on a wooden beam near the ship's bow.

She bit on her lower lip and forced back the sudden urge to cry. She clasped her hands together and wrung them in and out of each other. Her heart was thumping in her ears and she wondered whether anyone else could hear it but no-one was giving her the slightest bit of attention, thank goodness. She stared ahead of her at the melee of white shirts and coloured summer dresses, the formal suits worn by some of the men and the pretty scarves worn by the women fluttering in the sea breeze.

Elena was wearing a yellow skirt and white blouse with butterflies on. The blouse stuck to her back as the sweat soaked through. It had been a parting gift from her classmates, chosen by her teacher. She had cried with delight when she opened the brown parcel tied with pink ribbon as she had been worrying about what to travel in.

They edged their way forward, the floating vessel looming above them, the sun beating down on Elena's head. The noises around her were unfamiliar. Chains clanged and scraped and sailors yelled instructions to each other. Cranes moved around like giant iron arms as they lifted and then lowered huge containers and bulging mail bags to the men working on the ship, their engines sending a monotonous, thundering growl across the air. There was a constant hub-bub of talking as passengers were ticked off a list and walked along the wooden gangway, waving and shouting back at those left on the port side.

As Elena and her family neared the head of the queue there was a delay with the family in front of them. The man from the ship seemed calm but he had the same curt manner the Principal at school. Elena peered at his white uniform; all he's missing are the wings and halo of an angel, she thought. She fixed her stare on the pretty gold stitching of the trim on the cuffs of his jacket and the shiny buttons glistening gold.

Elena fidgeted hopping from one foot to the other.

'Stop it Elena!' said her mother.

'Why are they talking so long?' asked Andreas, his fingers in his mouth again.

'There's a problem with their paperwork,' said *yiayia*. 'Have you checked ours Evangelia? Are you sure you've got everything?'

'Yes, I have,' said Evangelia but she took out the envelope from her handbag all the same and peered into the top of it, fingering through the folds of papers in it.

'Please stand to the side. You will not be travelling

today,' said the Purser to the family of seven. There were raised voices and some swearing and scuffling between the Purser and the man who appeared to be the father. The woman, she assumed the mother, cried as the children stood huddled close by; pale white, speechless.

Elena noticed her mother's face instantly colour. Elena knew she was panicking.

The Purser, who appeared calm given the continued barrage of raised voices around him, refocused on Evangelia.

'Passenger names please.'

'Surname Ellinas. Evangelia, Andreas, Elena. Surname Stefanides. Elena,' said Evangelia, as *yiayia* held onto her arm.

'Can I see your papers please?'

'Yes of course. They're here.' Evangelia, her hand shaking, slipped them out of the creased brown envelope she had kept safely on the shelf of her wardrobe for the past eight months. She handed him the now yellowed papers with worn corners, not making eye contact. Elena became aware of her mother holding her breath as the officer ticked off details from their passenger cards one by one, like *Kiria* Maria taking the register observed Elena. He checked the passports, finally exhaling as he passed the paperwork back to Evangelia. Elena felt the weight of waiting for him to respond around them.

'All checked and everything is in order,' he said. 'Welcome aboard the Mesabia. Please follow the directions of the Officer at the top there to your berth. We are scheduled to set sail at 3pm.'

'Thank you. God bless you,' said Evangelia.

'*Sto kalo,*' said the Purser dropping the official decorum for a second as he bid them a safe trip.

'Come on Elena,' urged her mother bringing Elena out of her reverie.

They waited on deck and Elena took in the noisy hum around her. There was a girl, not much older than her, crying, standing on her own and holding onto a canvas bag with a picture of Aphrodite on it. Three boys, about the same age, serenaded her, in an effort to cheer her up. One was tall with a floppy straight fringe falling across his dark almond-shaped eyes and wearing a pair of tight black trousers and a white shirt. Another was a little shorter, he had a birthmark on his left cheek and cherry red lips. He was wearing a navy blue cap with a picture of an eagle on it. The third boy was holding a cigarette in one hand and playing with a gold lighter with his other.

'Cry a little more, the tears suit you, the tears like diamonds, shining so bright, as bright as you.' The girl gave the boys a shy smile. This encouraged them to continue and this attracted the attention of the passengers milling around until eventually her weeping abated.

'Cry a little more, dear sweet thing, diamonds are precious, as are you, like you are to me.' The girl gave in to a smile as her mother reached for her hand. They walked along the deck, the boys still singing. Elena

168

thought she must like the attention. Elena considered she would like to be serenaded and was transfixed by the boy with the sweeping fringe. He caught her eye and she shied away.

***

Evangelia insisted they wait for the Kyriakides and after receiving directions to their cabin, waited on the open deck for them. Not far behind them, Reno was the first to ascend the ramp and he bundled towards them. He handed over the cumbersome suitcase to Elena, looking relieved as he shook his arm to bring back the circulation.

'We were saying how nice it would be if we could enjoy our first meal on the ship together,' said Maria, looking to her husband for approval as they appeared behind Reno.

'Thank you. We'd like that,' said Evangelia.

'Shall we say at 1pm?'

'Perfect. We'll see you then and thank you, that's thoughtful of you.'

'Don't mention it,' said Maria. For the first time Elena noticed the red spider-veins in *Kiria* Kyriakides' cheeks and her yellowed teeth when she smiled. Close up, she wasn't as beautiful or as glamorous as a real film star.

The inner cabin was small yet well-appointed with two sets of bunk beds opposite each other against each of the longer white painted walls. A round table with two chairs was placed between them and behind the cabin door was a wardrobe and a chest of drawers. A small wash basin was fitted in the opposite corner of the room with a mirror above it and a small cabinet below.

'Wow! I'm having the top bunk!' yelled Andreas, clambering the metal ladder like an orangutan.

'I'm having the top bunk,' said Elena, a stroppy expression crossing her face until she noticed the small wash basin in the corner.

'You can both occupy the top bunks,' said her mother. 'And *yiayia* and I can take the two bottom bunks.'

Elena rushed over to the basin. 'A basin with a tap in our room. Heaven!' she said as she splashed water over her face and washed her hands. She dried them on the small face cloth hanging on a hook and then wasted no time as she scrambled up the ladder and puffed up her pillow. She hid her face in its plump softness and exaggeratedly stretched across the starched white sheets and the pale blue blanket, like a star fish. 'A bed all for me,' and her laughter rang across the small space.

'Let's unpack and sort out our clothes,' said her mother, an impatient edge to her tone.

'Can we eat?' managed Elena, sitting up and pressing her stomach which felt empty. 'I'm so hungry.'

'We've still got an hour or so before we meet the Kyriakides for lunch.'

'Why are her teeth so yellow?' asked Elena.

'For goodness sake don't say anything like that in front of her.'

'But why?'

'She smokes too much and probably drinks too much,' said her mother, 'and I've probably said too much. Now...'

'Oh, however, will we find where we're going?' asked *yiayia.*

'The dining room is on A deck. I'm sure we'll find it, and if not, we can simply follow everyone else,' said her mother, already putting their clothes away in the wardrobe and filling the drawers with underwear and socks.

'I hope it's not too far,' said *yiayia,* as she pulled out a bag of *tiropites* from her handbag. Elena and Andreas jumped from their bunks and grabbed a couple of the baked mini cheese puffs, stuffing them into their ravenous mouths.

'I love these,' said Andreas talking with his mouth full, spitting bits of *loukoumi.* He took two, ignoring Elena who called him a big fat hog for not sharing the candied jellies with her.

'Well enjoy them. I doubt you'll be eating these again for a long time,' said their mother. 'And don't eat all the *loukoumi* Andreas *mou.* I doubt we'll be able to get it in England.' Elena watched her brother wrap the paper parcel up carefully, hiding it under his pillow.

Yiayia's shoes looked heavy and cumbersome on her slim feet. She bent to rub her ankles and Elena went and sat next to her on the lower bunk, cuddling into her.

'I s'pose we can't exactly get lost on a ship,' Elena said as she threw herself back onto the narrow mattress.

There was a knock at their door just before 1pm. Andreas answered it holding his belly. It was Reno, who had been sent, by his parents, to guide them back to the dining room.

'We would never have found it,' said Evangelia as they followed Reno up the companionway to the upper deck. Elena followed, noticing again how the vast azure sea sparkled against the brass rails and glossy white of the ship. She held onto the manrope wishing her friends Yioli and Niko and Stella and Mirianthi were with her. She felt small like a droplet in the middle of a vast ocean. She hadn't even realised the ship had started moving despite the loud horn and the smoke coming out of the gold funnel. She stood there momentarily overwhelmed; wanting to cry. Ahead of her the boy with the sweeping fringe appeared. He slowed his pace. Was he waiting for her to pass? Was he going to say something to her?

Reno noticed her looking at the boy.

'Don't pay any attention to him. He's a peasant boy. Up to no good I reckon.'

Elena flushed and lowered her eyes. How embarrassing she thought. But she couldn't help but

wonder if the boy liked her? She felt as excited as the day
the letter from England came.

In the dining hall the first thing Elena noticed was a huge
glass bowl full of red and green apples. She almost
jumped with joy, her anxiousness forgotten. Apples had
been too expensive to buy in Cyprus, at least for her
family, and she had grown up on a diet of carob, purple
figs, apricots, pomegranates, prickly pears and oranges;
fruits readily available and easy to pick from the trees
scattered in the many abandoned fields and orchards
around the perimeter of the village. She remembered the
many "fruit" trips she had taken to collect fruit in the little
basket which she had given to Yioli as a goodbye gift.
That sad, lost feeling surrounded her again for a moment.

It was a beautiful room with high ceilings and round
tables dressed with white table cloths and polished cutlery
and two different types of glasses, which she later
fathomed were glasses for wine and glasses for water.

But the initial joy of being on the ship soon waned.
The seas were rough, howling and hissing; life boats
whacked on the side of the ship like floating coffins. The
ship's hulk plunged across the open waters, sending salty
cold sprays into the air. Sea sickness struck most of the
passengers and the old and the young in particular were
doubled over buckets and even cooking pots. Clustered
children bent over the sides of the ship, the sound of their
retching filling Elena's ears, froth in the corner of their

mouths. She helped pass containers of various sorts around the deck as the acrid vomiting filled her nostrils.

Despite wanting to eat the spaghetti served at lunch and dinner time with a different sauce, she was also too ill. By the end of the third day she didn't make it to the dining room before she was doubled over. The boy with the sweeping fringe came to her rescue with a metal bowl. Once the sickness had eased he took her by the hand.

'I'll walk you back to your cabin,' he said, giving her a mock salute.

She soon became too ill to eat in the dining room again and she lay in her bunk bed for two days, wishing she were back home. She slept on and off. Blue smudges of exhaustion painted under her eyes as she curled on her bunk, images of boats and jetties, moorings and mud banks filling her restless mind.

Chapter Eleven

Christaki, 1958

'I KEEP TELLING you and keep telling you! No jumping off like that! Cheeky swines!'

The bus conductor, a tall slim man who wore a permanent pained expression, waved his arm at the Italians in mock anger. He yelled at the same group almost daily as they hopped from one bus to another avoiding paying the bus fare.

Christaki watched as they darted in and out of the London traffic and smiled. He recognised the young men, all of a similar age to him. A young woman who Christaki saw on his way to work every Tuesday sat opposite him and crossed her legs, one slim leg across the other. She adjusted her wool coat and placed her handbag on her lap. She wore a black beret and ruby red lipstick. She caught Christaki looking at her and smiled showing bright pearly teeth. Christaki listened to the machine churning out her ticket; an awful high decibel racket which he still hadn't got used to. He smiled back at her, as she winced at the sound and he gave her a shy smile back. The gentleman next to her, leaning on his tall umbrella, gave him a disapproving stare. Christaki wondered whether the man thought he was Turkish. There had been a huge demonstration by Turkish Cypriots at the weekend, with banners and signs saying "Cyprus is Turkish and Will Remain". Demonstrators, some in national costumes and waving the Turkish flag, marched to Downing Street with placards, expressing their dissatisfaction with the involvement of Britain's political action in Cyprus. Christaki wondered when the situation would ever end, ever be resolved. The news from their friends and family who continued to live in Cyprus only worsened.

The bus conductor helped an elderly lady onto the bus and dispensed a ticket to her. He walked away adjusting the wide straps across his back which held the ticket machine around his waist. He opened the machine and changed the paper roll, smiling at the joy on a child's face as he passed the surplus strip to the boy to play with.

Christaki peered out the window taking in the city; dirty, ruined, noisy. The bus trundled past derelict buildings and the bus journey, in contrast, was a colourful adventure. People hopped on and off, some eating, some talking, others laughing loudly while they bit into a bacon buttie. He smirked at the word buttie. It made him laugh and he remembered the first time someone had asked him if he wanted one. He thought they meant a bottom; his face flushed redder than the beetroot his mother boiled.

He thought of his mother, shrouded in black, and not wanting to upset her further he cried himself to sleep, away from her watchful eyes; tears of anguish and frustration soaking his pillow as he buried his head under its darkness. His mood pushed him further into a state of anxiety and hatred for a city he was now expected to call home. A city he struggled to love; a city where he didn't fit in.

Having quickly learnt where to find work from other Cypriot immigrants he leapt off the back of the bus just before Fenchurch Street. He had discovered an Irish building company recruiting labourers on a daily basis to clear roads, dig out trenches and run errands between building sites. Christaki was always selected. He was agile, strong and never shirked, rarely stopping for a break.

Christaki was aware both the guv'nor and the foreman, Mr O'Connolly, favoured him and he liked it. He missed *Kirio* Melis and the order and security numbers in columns had given him, but found comfort in the knowledge the foreman had his back. Mr O'Connolly stood over six feet tall and he was built like a brick-house with bulging muscles; a shamrock tattoo stretched across one and a Celtic cross with the names Bridget, Colleen, Tillie and Niamh adorned the other.

'I ain't messin' with your bloody foreign name. Chris is what I'll call ya. If you don't like it, you can sling your 'ook.' He punched Christaki on the arm playfully. His broad smile revealed cigarette stained teeth and a missing tooth giving the impression he was much older than Christaki guessed he was. 'But don't think you can call me what ya fancy!'

One February morning, with the fire in the hearth roaring, Christaki and his mother were having breakfast of boiled eggs and the white bread he hated.

'I miss the hot fresh bread you baked. This is cardboard. No flavour. No substance.'

'But less work for me, *agabi mou.*' But he understood his mother missed her baking and her little stone oven just as much as he missed his old life.

He chewed unenthusiastically on the bread as he peeled the shell off the brown egg. All the while he begged his mother to let him return to his father in Cyprus.

'*Mitera*, I want to continue my education. I want to be with *patera* amongst my friends and familiar surroundings, the village. I want to know what has become of Panteli and Yianni and Katerina.'

His mother sighed, her eyes full of dark pain and heartache. Christaki sensed she found life in London a challenge too, especially without his father.

'Things will improve Christaki *mou.*'

'But I don't want them to improve, *mama.* I don't want to be here.'

'*Ayios Tychonas* is not as you remember it. Things have changed there too with the fighting, fighting between all sides. The Turks are revolting against their Greek Cypriot neighbours and as much as I hate to admit to it, the other way around too. The Turks we lived in peace with have formed their own terrorist group *Turk*

178

Mukavemet Teskilati. Some Greeks are losing sight of what it is they are fighting for. Innocent people are being murdered in their beds. Your father says it is not as we remember it.'

'We should be there to fight for our country! This is no life! The weather is gloomy every day. There is no sun, there is no joy here at all. I can't swim. I can't ride a bike anywhere. The buildings are decrepit, crumbling.' He gave his mother a pleading look. She spoke, her voice cracking with emotion.

'Give it time. For me. I can't go back there Christaki *mou.* I cannot pass every day where your uncle was murdered and not be reminded of him. See his face. See a young life destroyed through jealousy and hatred,' she pleaded. He recognised how painful it was for her as tears stung her eyes. It was painful for him too remembering his uncle and his life so once full now snuffed, gone forever. 'And to risk losing you or your brother or sister. It's too dangerous now. We have to stay.'

'But we could make a difference in Cyprus. We could support our friends, our neighbours.'

'It's not how you remember it Christaki *mou.* Your father says there are 15,000 maybe even 20,000 British out there now. All those soldiers against 170 or so of our men, our boys, it's madness. The British are panicking, even attacking whole communities for sympathising with the EOKA effort.

'*Mama*, please. You're not listening to me. There are

179

no proper jobs here and as for doing accounts, my English isn't good enough.'

'But we are safe here *agabi mou.*'

'When the English smile it doesn't reach their eyes. They whisper and say things about the Indians, the Irish, that much I understand. They're so cold.'

'Your English will improve, son. Give it time. You will soon start your lessons again. Accounting is not out of the question. In the meantime, you must support mine and your father's decision.

'I'm sorry *mama*. I am trying. I am. But this is an impossible place.' Christaki ran his fingers through his thick dark hair.

'You're the oldest and you must show the way for your sister and brother. Your father and I have put all our faith in you. You are the head of the household until such time your father joins us.'

'*Mama.*'

'Now listen to me. Pavlo and Melani are finding life here difficult too living in such a big city, away from our family, those we love. Please Christaki try to like it for me.'

'I will try harder. But the cold is so cold.' The front door opened and then closed with a bang.

'Stop moaning.' Pavlo walked into the kitchen bringing in with him the stench of alcohol and a gust of icy air; a white hoar of frost dusted his head. He sloppily pulled out a chair and sat at the small Formica table. He grabbed an already cut piece of bread, buttered it thickly and ate it in two bites.

'Where have you been?' asked their mother.

'I was invited to a party, so I went.'

'You were out all night? What would your father say?' asked their mother.

'Well he's not here is he? And there's nothing else to do round here.'

'You could get a job.' Christaki's voice was heavy with sarcasm.

'Well I'm not working like a dog for a few shillings to come home with calloused hands and blistered feet.'

'You don't have to. You can do some training. My boss knows someone who's recruiting for an apprentice. It's in a hotel. In the kitchens. I'll come with you if you like, find out what it's all about.'

'That's wonderful isn't it Pavlo *mou?*' said their mother.

'Well, yes it is.'

'Anything else you want to say? To your brother?' Pavlo reluctantly thanked his brother and disappeared to get washed and changed into fresh clothes.

'Come and have some breakfast!' his mother called after him.

Christaki and his mother sat still for a few minutes; the only sound a clattering bang from Pavlo's bedroom. Christaki wondered whether working in a hotel with access to alcohol was a good idea, but he said nothing to his mother.

'The summer will come.' Christaki sighed deeply, resigning himself to a life of uncertainty and confusion. Similar story, different canvas, he thought as he remembered Pallikarides' poem and the young man who had given his life for the liberty of Cyprus from the British.

'The summer will come and we will fare well in this country of opportunity even if the English are as cold as their weather.' His mother laughed quietly reaching across and pinching his cheek. Christaki relaxed as he felt the mood between them lighten, at least for now.

Pavlo came back into the room, his face pale from a lack of sleep and no doubt food. His mother stood at the stove warming milk in a small pan to make him a glass of cinnamon milk. It had been Pavlo's favourite since being a child and she still often made it for him.

'So when can we go to meet this man?' asked Pavlo but Christaki wondered whether he was faking interest as a way to placate their mother.

'I'll meet you after I finish work one day this week and we can head off together. See what's on offer. One of the guys on the site last week said his son was doing the same thing. You could become friends.'

'Yeah, maybe. What about you?'

'What about me? The accounting? There's time for me to get into it once Father is here. Don't you worry about me little brother.' Christaki ruffled Pavlo's hair and slapped him playfully across the cheek.

The rest of the week passed with no further arguments or late nights from Pavlo. Christaki thought Melani was happy at school. She made friends with two local girls and willingly did her school work and helped around the house.

The following week, with the wind biting at their faces, making their cheeks pink and their lips hurt with cold, Christaki and Pavlo made their way to the St Ermin's Hotel. They walked to the front entrance and a tall man in a black overcoat and top hat bid them good evening.

'Good evening, Sir. We're here for a job in the kitchens.' Christaki spoke clearly proud of his English.

'You'll need to go out back. Red door marked staff entrance. Knock loudly. Someone'll let you in.'

'Thank you Sir.'

'Good luck, young man.'

Christaki and Pavlo made their way to the staff entrance and were let in by a young girl dressed in a blue dress and white apron. They followed her instructions to the kitchens meandering left and right along a warren of roughly painted narrow corridors.

The kitchen was a hive of activity; preparations for the dinner service. There were pots bubbling away, the ovens roared and a number of men and young boys dressed in their whites, chopped, stuffed and tossed ingredients at highly polished wooden and stainless steel surfaces. The noise was unbearable and it took Christaki a few seconds to adjust.

After a few moments, the Head Chef, Chef as he liked to be called, noticed them both standing inside the doorway and beckoned them over to the other side of the noisy kitchen.

'I don't know who you are but I'm busy here!' He was a towering hulk of a man and even more so with his tall white hat on his head. 'Concentrate on the soup!' he yelled at a younger boy in whites.

'It's about a job, for my brother. We'll wait Chef,' said Christaki.

Close to two hours later the Chef appeared in front of them as they waited in the cold, draughty warren of corridors. He had a gruff voice but a hearty laugh which softened his angular features and dark blue eyes. Within a few minutes of talking, mainly through Christaki who translated as best he could to his brother, the Head Chef offered Pavlo the job on a three-month trial basis.

'It don't bother me you not speaking English. In fact, it suits me.'

'Thank you,' Pavlo said.

'Thank you Chef.'

'Thank you Chef.' Pavlo looked at him through his dark lashes and gave him a nervous smile.

'You'll need to come in tomorrow morning at 5.30am. Dean'll show you your room now. You can come back tonight or tomorrow morning with your things. The room comes with the job and your meals are provided while you are on duty.'

Deaan, a slim boy, with long gangling legs and arms and a face full of pimples, stood to attention at the sound of his name being called and quickly nodded at Chef.

'How old you are?' asked Christaki.

'I'm fifteen next month. Hated school. Dad got me this job. He works in maintenance in the basement.'

'This is Pavlo. Paul.' Christaki corrected himself remembering what a fellow Cypriot had told him about anglicising their names so they didn't stand out so much. 'I'm Chris.' He remembered wondering whether it would make a difference, after all they both had strong accents.

'Pleased to meet you both.'

On their way home Christaki tried to remain chirpy. He hadn't realised the job would involve Pavlo moving out and living away from the family home.

'*Mama* will be happy. We'll just have to persuade her it's a good thing you living out. Explain the hours are long and you'll be better off living in, save you time in travel and the cost of the bus fare.'

'I'm not sure I'm going to like it brother.'

'Give it a chance. Chef was kind. He had kind eyes. He will take care of you. I will come and visit you as much as I can after work. I promise.'

'You'll become great friends, you'll see. You need to get serious Pavlo. *Mama* and *Baba* have made sacrifices...'

At home, while eating a bowl of hearty beef and onion stew, Christaki broke the news to their mother.

'Your father wanted us to stay together. As a family. This is not right. It's not right at all.'

'But *mama* this is normal for this type of job. It's a good job. A famous London hotel. Father will be proud of Pavlo just as you should be.'

'Of course I'm proud. I'm proud of the both of you.'

'Then don't take this opportunity away from him, *mama.*'

'*Mama*, I will do well,' said Pavlo, not sounding as sure as Christaki did. She didn't say anything else and sipped at her cup of warm milk.

'Then it's settled. I will get up early tomorrow and we can take your belongings to your new room before going to the building site.' Christaki tapped his brother on the shoulder and squeezed his arm.

'I'm still not sure about this. Shouldn't we at least wait and speak to your father when he calls this week?'

'Look, I think Father will be glad he has a job. I will still be at home and Melani too so you won't be alone *mama.*'

'Well, if you're sure.'

'Father has enough to worry about,' said Christaki.

That night his mother's crying sounded from her bedroom. He lay on his bed with his arms crossed above his head and wondered whether the job was right for

Pavlo. He didn't want to burden his mother with additional worries. He appreciated she was still mourning the loss of her brother and missing his father terribly. Having her sister, Alexandra living close by was a two-edged sword. She was with her sibling but it also exacerbated her grief for the loss of her brother.

He lay awake for a long time, listening to the barking of dogs and a yowling cat coming somewhere from behind the back yard. A chilly draught rose between the gaps in the floor boards and the wind came up in gusts around the house rattling the thin window panes. After a while the noise abated and he could hear nothing but the quiet hum of a motorbike in the distance and the roll of the late night buses on the high street. He drifted into a deep sleep and woke five hours later in the same position.

The early morning winter sun with its frosty shine came in through the gap in the thin curtains hitting him directly in the eyes. He sat up and rubbed his sleep-filled eyes; his head felt heavy. He could hear the local area awakening; the shuffling of the street cleaner with his wide broom and the clanking of the spade as he collected the debris and rubbish he piled by the road side. There was the thud of the coalman as he trudged heavily with the sack of black coal breaking his back. And then as if on cue the neighbour's cockerel crowed.

He padded down the hall, wrapped in the oversized blanket from his bed, and called to his brother to wake up. He waited and listened for signs his brother had awoken.

Within half an hour of waking they were both sitting on the top deck of the bus trundling towards Westminster and the St Ermin's Hotel. Pavlo held onto his suitcase as he balanced it across his knees. The morning sun had disappeared too quickly and the grey skies opened around them filling the bus with a moody crestfallen atmosphere.

'It's too early. I'm never going to get up this early every day.'

'You won't have to. You could roll out of bed ten minutes before your shift. You lucky bugger.'

'I don't feel lucky, bro.'

'You'll be fine. You'll meet the other trainee today too.'

'We're almost there. Come on.'

They both jumped off the bus and walked the short distance to the hotel's staff entrance. They made their way along the dark basement corridors and found themselves face to face with the Head Chef.

'Good morning. Organise your things and then come straight back. Dean here'll look after you. You'll be peeling potatoes today and preparing all the veg. It's a busy day…hurry up then!'

Christaki bid them goodbye, promising Pavlo to visit him after his own shift finished on the site. As he pulled the door open he stepped back to let a man in.

'Christaki *mou? Yioka mou* I am so pleased to see you.'

Christaki responded to the warm handshake and then

hug of *Kirio* Melis. 'It's so lovely to see you too, Sir. I had no idea you were in London.'

'Only a few weeks. I work in the Accounts Office here.'

'Pavlo's working in the kitchens. Three-month trial.'

'Well it's good to see you. You look well. I'm sure we'll see each other again.'

As Christaki stepped outside, he shielded his eyes from the glare of the morning sun peering above the old buildings of London. He was overwhelmed by the chance encounter with his accounting teacher. How big London felt one minute and then so small the next, he thought.

He walked the mile or so to the building site; it would save on the bus fare. The air was crisp. The streets here were still quiet. He wondered whether his brother was mature enough to take the job seriously. Hopefully the job would give him a focus. He'd been spending far too many nights out late and God only knew what he'd been getting up to. He was just thankful his mother hadn't realised how often he'd been staying out all night and if she had noticed he hadn't witnessed her reprimanding Pavlo. Perhaps she didn't have the energy.

He thought about his mother as he walked along the deserted streets with only the odd dustcart and milk cart rumbling along. He had come to realise she was a strong woman. A woman who stood by her ideals and did what she had to do to protect her family. His father was not the only one who had sacrificed a lot to get them to London safely. He only hoped they both had not sacrificed all they had.

The building site ahead of Christaki was cloaked in smog and whirling dust; it was like a ghost town. Another couple of labourers were hanging around the street and from a distance; the red tip of their cigarettes danced in the faint light of daybreak. Their hearty laughter rung in his ears. It reminded him of Panteli and Yianni. A wave of nostalgia came over him. Out of nowhere a loud hoot almost burst his eardrums and he felt someone tugging him from the arm, pulling him back. Before he realised it, he was on the floor, his trousers ripped, his hands red raw.

'Bloody hell mate. That was close.'

'I...I...'

'Didn't you see the feckin' bus coming straight for ya?'

'Uhh, no. Sorry.'

'Lucky you're wrapped up like an eskimo.'

'Thank you...you saved my life.'

'No need to be so dramatic. As long as you're not hurt.'

Christaki held onto the young man's outstretched hand and the blond youth pulled him up off the filthy pavement as he toppled over the kerb.

'No I'm fine. Thank you.'

'No worries mate. I'm Pete. Everyone calls me tricky Pete.'

'Hello Pete. I am Chris.' He wiped the front of his trousers and surveyed his open palms, scratched, bleeding. Pete offered him a cigarette and even though Christaki didn't smoke he took it, accepting the cigarette as a gesture of friendship.

'You'll live.' Pete laughed, revealing a mouth crammed with crooked teeth; his two upper front teeth both chipped. Christaki choked on the cigarette as he inhaled. 'You not a smoker?'

'No I'm not.'

'You'll soon get the hang of it. Never spoken to a foreigner before. Where's you from?'

'Cyprus.'

'My dad was stationed out there for about three years...a few months here and there. We never went. My mam didn't want to. Too 'ot she said.'

'It's hot there yes. Beautiful sea. Mountains. Olive trees, oranges, lemons.'

'Say the bells of St Clements,' sang Pete.

'St Clemen's?'

'Never mind. It's a nursery rhyme. A song for kids.'

They stood side by side in silence, Christaki took a couple more drags before they both stamped out their cigarettes on the road. A few other men gathered on the street with Christaki, aware it was time for his guv'nor to show. Having worked here for a few weeks he was no longer worried about not being selected.

The burly Irishman selected his labour for the day without delay.

'Damn it,' Pete said in a hoarse whisper.

'Sorry Pete,' Christaki said, disappointed Pete had not been picked. He wondered whether he would cross paths with him again.

'Not my day, mate.'

The day went slowly, too slowly. Christaki's knee was throbbing and had swollen; it felt hot to the touch and his hands were sore. He worked more slowly than usual.

'What's up Chris?'

'A bus nearly killed me today. This morning. That other boy, Pete, he saved me.'

'Lucky you. Here let me take a look at those hands.' Mr O'Connolly surveyed Christaki's hands and told him to go and get some gloves from the store bunker. 'And get some ice onto your knee tonight. Then iodine and Epsom salts should do the trick.'

At the end of his shift Christaki wanted to get home but remembering his promise to Pavlo he made his way to the St Ermin's Hotel. Pavlo had already finished his shift and was in his room. He was smiling and hugged his brother warmly when he saw him.

'*Ade re,* how did it go today? You look happy.' He felt glad speaking Greek. The English language was too difficult and he was struggling to interpret everyone around him. They each had different accents. Spoke too quickly.

'I didn't realise peeling potatoes would make me this happy. Chef is a good man. He's kind like you said he would be. When he's not shouting, he's laughing. But there's no time for talking and when anyone says anything to me I just say yes.'

'Well watch what you're saying yes to.'

'What happened to your hands? Your trousers are torn…'

It's nothing. I had a fight with a big red bus!' They both fell onto the small bed.

'Oh brother, we are going to be alright in this big city with the English,' Christaki said.

***

The next morning Christaki's knee felt better, less swollen. His mother had rubbed it with *zivania* and the whiff had wooed him into an instant sleep. He remembered falling asleep to the sound of his mother's cheery voice as she marvelled at how wonderful it was *Kirio* Melis was in London too.

Christaki arrived at the usual meeting point to discover Pete leaning casually against a lamp post. They smiled at each other as Pete walked over towards him.

'So you're alright then?'

'Yes. I am.'

'So d'you think the guv'nor might give me a chance today?' Pete laughed, a wide laugh which filled his eyes with light.

'He's a good man. If he's short of labour he's sure to pick you,' Christaki said, noticing one of the regular guys wasn't around. He always noticed him because he was the tallest amongst the men who stood waiting to be selected and had a shifty look about him; his eyes invariably downcast towards the ground, never looked anyone straight in the face. Christaki pulled Pete towards him and, as if Pete understood, he stayed close to him as the boss made his selection.

'No Kevin? Surprise bloody surprise!' asked the foreman.

'Not seen 'im,' mumbled another of the regular labourers.

'He might be ill. He wasn't feeling too good last night,' chipped in one of Kevin's mates.

'Probably half pissed. This is the last straw! I've had enough of him and anyone else who feels like shirking!' He straightened himself up. 'Guess it's your lucky day boy!' He slapped Pete on the arm and beckoned him to follow. Christaki smiled at Pete. He was glad his new friend had work today.

Pete was paired with Christaki. Today they had to carry piles of red bricks up the scaffolding ladders to the labourers on the platform four levels high. Pete was quick and even Christaki kept up with him with difficulty. They stopped for lunch at around mid-day, sharing what Christaki had with him; cheese sandwiches, a few tomatoes and the *kioftethes* Christaki's mum had rolled and fried the night before.

'Never 'ad meatballs like this afore now,' said Pete as he chewed. Both sat on the scaffolding platform, their heavy boots dangling over the side as they surveyed the London skyline partly camouflaged by the grey smog.

Around them the continuous clanging and banging penetrated the air around them. He listened to the sound of the site as it rose around him; heavy drilling, chains clanking, steel clashing with steel, incessant hammering and the piercing tinkle of the drills. Labourers called across to each other. It was not the peaceful sound of the lapping waves of the sea in Limassol. No, it was a different world, a noisy one.

Below, Christaki could make out the shiny black reflection of bankers in their bowler hats and long coats and smart suits with three-button jackets and pleated trousers. A world far removed from his own. He watched as they walked briskly along the pavements; some holding long dark umbrellas, a folded newspaper, a battered briefcase, their shiny black shoes in contrast with their crisp white shirts and the grime of the city. Christaki surveyed his dirty hands but there was nowhere to clean them so he wiped them on his overalls. He also noticed how Pete's hands looked like they hadn't been washed for days and his fingernails were little crescent moons of dirt.

Ten minutes before knocking off time there was a thud followed by a clatter of iron and steel. Christaki could hear shouts and a scream from the other side of the site. He went cold. The building site was a dangerous place to work and with little or no regard for regulations on health and safety there were sometimes as many as two or three injuries a month on the site. He saw someone lying on the orange clay ground.

Christaki and Pete scrambled the scaffolding and ran over. By the time they got there they couldn't glimpse much.

'Get back to work! The lotta you!' Mr O'Connolly was red in the face, his hands rubbing his face, his chin.

'Looks serious,' said Christaki.

'Well we can't do anything,' Pete said.

'Pint?' asked Pete as he downed his tools at the end of their shift.

'D'you think we should? It doesn't feel right after the accident.'

'We can drink to 'is health.'

They walked off in the direction of the Old Red Lion Pub. This was Christaki's first time in a pub having shied away from joining the other lads on the site before now. He had always been conscious of not spending his money on booze having seen and heard many a local drunk and raucous in the streets at night.

He marvelled at the high polish of the wooden bar and the gleaming handles of the draught beer along the top. He stood with his hands deep in his trouser pockets and surveyed the rest of the bar. Dark wood tables and low upholstered seats filled the area along the windows and taller tables were positioned at the end of the bar where a huge open fire was ablaze. On the open brickwork wall surrounding it hung bronze swords and shields and black and white photographs in dark frames. Pete ordered two pints of strong ale.

'Cheers mate.'

'Cheers Pete.'

They sat companionably at a table with sticky pint ring marks scattered over it and an array of empty glasses.

'Not sure where I'm sleeping tonight.'

'Sleeping Why?'

'Yeah. Nowhere to go.'

'Nowhere?'

'Yeah. Me mam's kicked us out. Says I'm good for nothing.'

'Why?'

'Long story mate.'

'Come home with me. My mother won't mind.'

'Really? Oh mate. You're too good.' Pete squeezed Christaki's arm. Christaki thought he saw tears welling in his eyes but Pete turned his head before he could be sure.

That night Christaki walked into the house with Pete close behind him. His mother was sitting by the hearth; bent over a pair of socks she was darning. She reached up to Christaki as he walked in, kissing him on both cheeks.

Noticing someone behind him, she craned her neck.

'This is my friend Pete.'

'He-llo Pete.'

'He's the one who saved me from getting run over. He needs to stay somewhere *mama.* He has nowhere to go. His mum has thrown him out of the house. He can't go back.'

'To throw your own child out onto the street. Dear Lord, unheard of.' Anastasia was mortified. She agreed to let him stay and said he could sleep in Pavlo's room.

Both boys ate. Melani stared at Pete from across the table all evening. Christaki noticed and kicked her under the table. She scowled back at him.

'So, Pete is it? How long are you staying?' Melani asked.

Christaki saw how Pete reddened at the question but he didn't kick him.

Pete ate every bit of food on his plate and finished off an entire second helping of liver with potatoes and onions.

***

Pete worked alongside Christaki on the building site for the next three months, staying over at his sporadically, a couple of nights a week. Christaki noticed Pete didn't want to outstay his welcome. Pete was a fast learner and always polite to the boss. He concentrated on the job and although he was a chatter box Christaki liked listening to his stories and even if he didn't always get the joke it helped improve Christaki's spoken English and his comprehension.

One Friday evening in May after a particularly long and physically exhausting day Pete rushed off saying he had to go to meet someone.

'What about the pub?' Christaki had got used to going to the pub with Pete; he felt grown up buying a round with the other lads and listening to their banter; often a combination of sex, women and what they were having for tea. Christaki was confused about tea until he realised they meant dinner.

'And tonight? Are you coming home with me?'

'I'll see you later.' Before Christaki could reply Pete had already sprinted towards the Old Red Lion.

Christaki wound his scarf tighter around his neck and lowered his head to avoid the rush of wind blustering around him. Even in the midst of winter he didn't remember Cyprus being this cold. He wondered how the other men didn't feel it like he did. He had three layers on and he still felt colder than being in the Troodos mountains in the depth of a snowy winter. His head was aching too. He wanted to get home. His stomach was rumbling having shared his lunch with Pete.

As soon as he had stepped into the house his mother called out to him to come into the sitting room, a shrill panic-like tone giving an edge to her voice.

'*Mama,* what's the matter? Is it *patera*?'

No, no…nothing like that. I went to the bottom drawer of the wardrobe to take some notes from the spending money your father gave me to tide us over until he joins us and…and…'

'What *mama*?'

'£5.00 is missing. I haven't spent it. I've been recording all our expenses meticulously in the notebook your father gave me.'

'That's a whole month's wages gone,' said Christaki.

'I've checked and checked again.'

'Have you asked Melani? Perhaps she borrowed some and forgot to put back what she didn't use.'

'She doesn't even know it's there.'

'Then who could have taken it?'

Chapter Twelve

Elena, 1958

THE MONTH OF June was three days away and Elena still wasn't used to the dark and dingy weather of London, always misty, foggy. She felt like she was always shrouded in grey; she could barely see the buildings, the streets, the sky, the landscape from a few hundred yards away.

The house her family now lived in on Copenhagen Street in Islington, a month and a half after arriving in England, wasn't much better than the one they had shared with *theia* Panayiota. Elena's only source of happiness was the roller skates her father had bought her and an old bike he had brought for Andreas, from a mate, he said. She spent hours in the street riding on the handlebars, Andreas pedalling far too fast, making her scream till she was blue in the face, breathless from exhilaration and the fear of being catapulted onto the pavement.

Elena lay on top of the lumpy mattress, trying not to think about the stains hidden under the blanket her mother had tightly tucked around it, the set of clean sheets over it smelling of washing soda. The sparse linoleum flooring, patchy with ingrained dirt, even after Elena had scrubbed it on her hands and knees, had frayed edges which curled around the perimeter of the room, like the rough tendrils of an octopus.

She remembered the first rambling house on Moray Road. Elena and her mother had spent the whole of their first day scrubbing and cleaning the rooms from one corner to the other despite *theia* Panayiota insisting the landlady had cleaned it in advance of their arrival.

It had been the tallest house she had ever seen, with crumbling layers of green paint clinging to the window frames and misaligned ledges. It depicted grimy dereliction, a war zone. Her mother's face had been one of resignation as they finally arrived after their exhausting tube journey from Victoria to Finsbury Park. Elena saw how her mother quickly re-compose herself, a smile set in stone across her face as she was greeted by her sister. Elena stood in awe of her aunt who was well-groomed, her hair in a beehive as she had seen in the magazines on the ship coming over. She wore a black dress with a full skirt which skimmed her knees, white polka dots all over it and cuffed sleeves which finished at her elbows. Her kitten heels were elegant.

Evangelia thanked Panayiota for organising the accommodation for them, hugging her tightly. The enormity of the reunion was too much for Elena as she noticed for the first time the dark circles around her mother's eyes and the flat light in her eyes. She watched her mother hug her big sister not having seen her for over three years and she couldn't help wondering why her mother had not been as emotional seeing her father after much longer.

Elena recalled the reunion at Victoria Station where her father met them as promised. She hated the noise and the throng of people moving at different speeds around them, alien conversations in loud voices drumming in her ears. She had walked close behind her mother dragging the suitcase along the concrete floor, her legs ready to buckle from the exhaustion of travelling through the night.

'There's your father.' Strangely it had been *yiayia* who pointed him out. A tall man, broad shoulders, long arms, wearing a grey suit, a shirt and tie. She kept staring at his black shiny shoes and an ache in her fought the urge to cry as she remembered her scuffed old school shoes. He was clean-shaven; a little red nick on his chin and had the bluest eyes. He scooped Andreas kissing him on the face over and over. Elena squirmed away from him as he reached for her, clutching her doll. She was suddenly shy in front of this man she knew was her father but did not recognise. He pulled out a knitted doll from a paper bag. He handed it to her saying, 'Now you have two.'

She took it from him whispering, 'Thank you, Father.'

'And this is for you.' He handed Andreas a dull yellow tin car. 'This is an Austin Saloon,' he said, his accent almost as English as the voices around them. Andreas's eyes sparkled like stars in the dark circles around his eyes.

He then changed his focus. 'My darling Evangelia, Mother, so good to see you...here let me take those cases.' Evangelia had stood motionless as he took the cases piled on the concourse. As he reached for the last one he leaned in and kissed Evangelia on the lips. Her mother did not look like she enjoyed the kiss and she pulled away from him; her pink lipstick across her lips like smudged rose petals.

'Evangelia *mou*, my darling. You're here. Life will be different for you but in time you'll love it as I do.' After hugging *yiayia* too he indicated for the family to follow him. He was assertive, strong and it was reassuring to discover her father knew where to go, what to do. Elena felt the tightness in her chest alleviate as she walked between her mother and *yiayia* holding them tightly by the hand. Andreas walked ahead with his father. Elena noticed how he walked with his chin tilted high and his shoulders back pushing out his chest. She smirked, he's wants to impress Dad she thought.

The taxi ride left Elena nauseous. *Theia* Panayiota covered Elena's face with lots of little wet kisses and Elena thought how she closely resembled her mother but different. She quickly came to realise their mannerisms and expressions were similar rather than their physical features although they were both tall and slim. Andreas shied away from his aunt's kisses, nibbling at his finger nails. Elena could see how he felt out of his depth amongst the hospitable, noisy family who were but strangers to them. *Theia* Panayiota's husband, Uncle Thomas, pinched one of his chubby cheeks and ruffled his hair, making a grizzly bear sound. Andreas gave him a surly stare which gave way to a half smile.

Their cousins, Harry, Petros and Emilia, a few years older than Elena and Andreas, spilled out into the street to welcome them. Uncle Thomas bundled them inside, instructing his children to help with the luggage. He had a gruff voice and a dark moustache which jiggled when he spoke. His eyes were hidden behind thick, black spectacles, only his thick eyebrows visible above the rims. He wore a dark grey flannel suit with pleated trousers and a white shirt. His shoes were shiny. Elena peered at her own shoes, a thin film of dust dulled their sparkle.

The house was dark and unwelcoming, damp seeped through the bulging patches on the walls and ceilings and the smell of urine and cooking odours penetrated the stale air. There was an instant chatter and joviality, as if to mask the pungent odour. Tears and hugs were commonplace the entire afternoon as they were welcomed and shown around the rooms reserved for them.

The three rooms Elena's family occupied were dingy and desperately cold despite the two bar electric fire *theia* Panayiota had lent them. The accommodation was bare, with nothing 'homely' about it apart from the odd trinkets her mother had brought over from Cyprus. The furniture provided was basic, shoddy. Each room, lit by a single naked light bulb hanging in the centre, felt heartless.

Two rooms were used as bedrooms, one with two single beds and the other with a double mattress on the floor which her mother shared with *yiayia*. A heavy mirror, speckled with black stains, hung by a tarnished chain from the picture rail in the sitting room above the threadbare sofa, a dark purple rug covered part of the floor. The paint peeled off the skirting boards and the doors were grimy with dirt marks and smudges from the traffic of former occupants. The smell of damp permeated everything, stifled the air. Elena was devastated. This was not what she had imagined all those months of waiting to come to England. Her stomach plummeted with dread and fear and homesickness.

The many rooms were spread over four floors and everyone used the same front door. It became evident to Elena there were as many families living there as there were rooms. She lost count of the different faces she saw and the voices that filtered through the thin, damp walls and sagging ceilings. The Irish landlady, although initially friendly and welcoming, quickly disseminated a long written list of rules: No use of the WC before 7am or after 10pm. No visitors after 5pm. No dogs or cats. Rent had to be paid weekly in advance by 9am of the Monday each week, cash only.

There were many mix-ups as her mother couldn't

read what she was being issued with and the rules differed to those being followed by *theia* Panayiota and her family. Uncle Thomas intervened, trying to reason with Mrs O'Flaherty, but she remained stoic and unreasonable in her demands. Irritated by the constraints, Elena's increasing frustration strangled her. She was used to being free and having lots of outdoor space. She felt restricted, imprisoned.

Despite people everywhere, Elena was lonely and the alienation swamped her. She cried into her pillow at night until her eyes were red and sore. She twitched and flinched at the unfamiliar sounds; the clank and banging of the latrine door, which hung precariously from one hinge, the wind rattling the bedroom window's thin panes, the drunken shouts of men returning home from the pubs. She missed her friends and her simple, uncomplicated life of *Kato Lefkara*. She missed the scraping of the goats, the humming of the cicadas, the hushed tones of the old men walking home, from the *kafeneion*, as the sky departed from day to night.

Elena remembered seeing a man, maybe a bit younger than her mother, smoking on the landing between the second floor, where they'd resided and the third floor occupied by her aunt and cousins.

She'd stood inside the bedroom door, mesmerised, her eyes fixed on his filthy fingers, as he flicked his cigarette lighter. He pulled his quivering bony knees, protruding through his dirty jeans like bent twigs, towards his chest. He sat on the floor, oblivious to her watching him, inhaling deeply on the roll-up, slumped against the grimy, stained wall. His face was grey and pasty, his eyes sunken. His greasy lank hair shone in the shaft of light coming from Elena's open bedroom door. She remembered her disgust as he leant over and spewed all over the floor, the acrid smell making her gag. She never opened her door, onto the landing, on her own again after that. She often wondered if the man was still living there and why he appeared to have no family.

**

'Why can't we go to school?' argued Elena one morning during those early weeks. She slurped at her cup of warm milk and ate her toast hungrily. 'We've been here for nearly six weeks.'

'Be quiet!' Andreas scolded. 'Who needs school?'

'Well how do you plan to learn English you idiot?'

'You can learn and then teach me. I'm not going!'

'You'll both go soon enough!' interrupted her mother as she buttered some toast for Andreas.

'I'm so bored at home,' whined Elena.

'Go and help your *theia* Panayiota.'

'Cleaning. That's all I've done since I got here. This house is horrid!'

'As soon as we are settled in a place of our own we'll get you into a school close by. I promise Elena *mou*.'

'Be patient, Elena *mou*,' her *yiayia* said.

'And Father? Will he come and live with us?' asked Elena.

'Yes I would think so.'

'Well, can we go out and buy a uniform so we're ready?' she asked.

Elena didn't miss her father at first, being used to not having him around. But as time went on she did wonder, however, why he rarely spent any time with them. What was the point of them moving here? Where was the better life her mother had painted for her?

'Where's *baba*?' she asked that same evening as she dished up the mashed potato she had made all on her own.

Her mother took the meat filled shortcrust pasties, her aunt had encouraged her mother to make, out of the oven. 'He's working.'

'But why does he work so late? And all the time?'

'To make money to feed us all. Now be quiet and eat up. This looks lovely Elena *mou*,' her mother said taking a forkful of the fluffy mash as she blew onto it to cool it. Mashed potato had quickly become one of Elena's favourite foods after her *theia* Panayiota introduced her to it. Elena had never eaten mashed potato before coming to England. She savoured the light fluffy texture and the sunny yellow created by the butter she melted into it.

'Then why do we keep searching for shillings for the meter?' asked Andreas who hadn't touched his mash or his pie. His voice was innocent, unsure.

'Why don't the lights work?' asked Elena.

'The candle in the window isn't bright enough,' complained Andreas.

'Well, he hasn't been paid yet,' said Evangelia, repeating what her husband had said to her two nights before. Elena already knew the whole conversation. She had been woken by their hushed but agitated tones and listened hidden in her bedroom. He had sneaked into the house and Evangelia had caught him going through her purse. He had taken what little money she had even though she had begged him not to.

Her mother's hushed tones relayed her pleas for housekeeping from her father but he said he couldn't give her any. Elena had only caught a part of what her mother had said to her father in response. She re-called the fragment of the conversation…playing cards again with your so-called friends… to the early hours.

Eventually her father moved to their current rented accommodation on Copenhagen Street with them. He had not joined them at *theia* Panayiota's and stayed away for a while saying he had his rent paid up for another six weeks in a house he already had lodgings in. Elena wondered why her mother didn't insist he move in with them but she daren't ask her. She could see how upset she was and how strained things were between her mother and father. They rarely hugged or kissed like she'd seen other couples do.

But she now noticed her mother had hung up their *stefana*, wedding wreaths, on the wall above the double bed in their new bedroom. She recalled the symbolism of this; the bride and the bridegroom promising a sweet coexistence to each other. She secretly soared at this and accepted it as a sign of her parents' commitment to each other and their happiness.

The second house, spread over three floors, was in a slightly better condition externally and internally than the first. It had a red brick façade across the ground floor and the rest of the front was painted chalky white. It had a solid front door painted black with a brass knocker and huge, square sash windows which Elena quickly discovered were draughty and let all the cold in. Elena and her family occupied the second floor which was converted into a separate flat. It had a separate inner entrance door at the bottom of the staircase leading up to a square landing. Two bedrooms and a small make-shift kitchen opened onto this area. The toilet facilities were outside in the concreted yard; a brick-built lean to at the back of the house. Although everyone still entered by the same front door being at the top of the house meant it was a little quieter and the second door offered Elena greater security.

The only downside to the move was there was no room for *yiayia* to come with them and so it was agreed she would continue to live with *theia* Panayiota until such time larger lodgings to accommodate her too were secured. Elena missed her *yiayia* dreadfully and she knew her mother did too.

The journey by bus was too expensive to see her more than once a week and too far to walk there and back. Elena continued to cry at night, soaking her lumpy pillow with hot, salty tears. She missed the smell of her *yiayia's* skin, whose aroma of sweet rosewater filled her with warmth and wrapped around her like a blanket. This wasn't how it was supposed to be.

It felt strange not having a house of their own even though renting homes, her father reassured her, was commonplace. Elena was often woken by the hubbub of different people coming and going at all hours as they wandered up and down the stairs. She often lay awake fierce confrontations invading her dreamy sleep and she wondered whether her mother was woken by the shouting too. The scurrying and pitter-patter of cockroaches and beetles echoing in the night woke her too. She wondered what they were doing in the middle of the night but she and her mother never spoke about it. At least this house was less crowded.

***

'You're Cypriot!' said the woman delightedly standing behind them in the queue; the sense of comradeship instantly obvious in her beaming face. Andreas and Elena were talking Greek in the grocery store. 'I'm Georgette, originally from *Pano Lefkara*,' she said to Evangelia, tapping her gently on the shoulder.

'Oh how lovely to hear another Greek voice!' A smile creased Evangelia's tired face.

'That's how I feel when I hear our Mother tongue!'

'So lovely not to have to try and figure out what's being said. Sorry, I'm Evangelia. Lovely to meet you. I'm from *Kato Lefkara*, fancy meeting someone from the same village.' Elena watched her mother's face light up as she relaxed being around a fellow Cypriot. Her mother had never been warmly open towards strangers and seeing her mother smile and chatty made her happy.

'Oh I have friends in *Kato Lefkara*... Maroulla and Zeno. You probably know them being such a small community.'

'Oh yes, I do,' said Evangelia, reddening slightly. 'Their son Niko was in the same class as my two.'

'I hear they're planning to come to England too.'

'Really? I haven't heard.'

'There are so many moving across with the troubles getting worse. Soon we will have our own piece of Cyprus here in the middle of London,' said Georgette.

'I would certainly welcome that.'

'So you're new round here?'

'Yes, a couple of weeks in this area,' Evangelia said, composing herself. 'My husband's been here a lot longer though.'

'Well welcome, truly,' said Georgette with warmth.

'Thank you. We're still finding our way around. The language and weather is the hardest thing for me. It's grey, it's dull, so little light. And of course I miss my things, my pots and pans, my cutlery. We couldn't bring it all with us. I even miss the donkeys braying and the cockerel.'

'Oh, I've been here for nearly two years and still miss my things from home. And I can't speak English too well. There are a lot more Cypriots round this way though so I don't have to make as much effort as I used to. But what choice do we have? You'll get used to it in time just as I have,' she laughed. 'Apart from the weather!'

'God willing. Lovely to meet you Georgette,' said Evangelia paying for the shopping. 'Hopefully see you again.'

'Actually before you go, I hope you don't mind me saying but, I've got a hot water bottle I don't use anymore. You're welcome to borrow it for the children for as long as you need,' she offered. 'I couldn't help overhearing your son complain about the cold. It takes getting used to.'

'The bedroom Elena and Andreas share is freezing. There's a film of ice across the window panes last thing at night and first thing in the morning. Andreas is constantly complaining about the ice box chill every opportunity he has. It's the first week of June and yet the cold continues to bite at our skin.'

Evangelia, hesitantly agreed to use it temporarily and

was most grateful when one of Georgette's sons, a strapping lad of about eighteen years old with jet black hair and eyes to match, dropped it over a couple of hours later. The earthenware device was eagerly passed between Andreas and Elena to warm up their beds. They both whooped with joy as their hot mattresses enveloped them as they settled for the night. With jumpers and coats piled over their blankets too Elena was cosy and warm as was her brother who said he loved the hot water bottle more than anything.

'What a nice lady,' Elena said, as she got into her warm bed. 'She had lovely hair as well didn't she *mama?* Like a film star,' she said dreamily, remembering her soft black curls pinned into place.

'Yes, lovely,' said her mother fingering her dull, brown hair which hung limply round her shoulders.

'And her blue coat was so pretty. All those folds across the back…it was lovely.'

'I didn't notice her coat but I'm so grateful I've met someone who I can speak Greek to, a new friend, someone who understands what it's like to be in England.'

'You can be happy here now *mama*. It won't always be like this,' she said delighted her mother had made a new friend. 'And the summer will come, it just has to.'

As Elena said the words an ache in her stomach reminded her of the pain she used to get from eating too many sweet figs straight off the trees. No figs here, she thought, and no jingly bells to alert her to the return of Manoli's herd at the end of his long shepherding day in the mountains.

***

As time went on Elena was desperate to join the neatly uniformed children walking to school in the mornings; girls with their grey pinafores and white knee high socks and the boys in grey shorts and matching long socks. She briefly remembered the hand-me-downs in the village and was glad she wasn't forced to wear other children's clothes any more. Out of the grimy pane of glass in the sagging window, framed with thin floral curtains, she watched the children run along Copenhagen Street and past their house on the opposite side of the road.

'Catch!' called out a boy of about eleven to another as he threw his grey school cap across to him, his blond hair flopping over his eyes in the light summer breeze.

'Bleeding 'ell Charlie, what sort of throw was that?' he called out momentarily losing his balance as he reached for the cap. Flying way off course, he only just grabbed it. He took two steps forward and threw it back, scuffing his black shoes on the cobbles.

'You daft beggars,' called out the woman with them, as she scurried to keep up, the rushing threatening to mess up her perfectly back-combed hair. She pushed a navy and white pram with huge spoked wheels with force. The thin tyres got caught in the uneven pavement as did her fire orange pumps with pointed toes and slender, stiletto heels.

'Is that the best you can do? You're joking!' shouted back Charlie as he missed the cap flying towards him and it fell into the street.

'Your mam'll kill me if you lose that cap! Charlie! Alan!' Charlie ran out into the street. There was a screech of brakes. 'Charlie!' yelled the woman, her hand on her chest as she called out in panic.

'Oi! Watch out! You little blighter!' yelled a man on a bike. He swerved awkwardly around Charlie, narrowly missing him, shaking a fist wildly in Charlie's direction. The man, in a dark brown coat and cap, his flannel trouser bottoms flapping, recomposed himself. Panic over, he wobbled dangerously from left to right and righted his bike, one hand holding onto his cap while the other gripped the handlebars.

Charlie appeared to be oblivious to the danger he'd been in. He ignored the shouts of the man, laughing loudly. He scooped up the cap, and not bothering to dust it placed it on his head.

'Little pillock!' he yelled at Alan.

'No I'm not!' shouted back Charlie. They both laughed loudly as they lolled down the street, their leather satchels banging against their thighs. Elena listened not sure what they were saying, unfamiliar with their accents. She watched them wrap their arms over each other's shoulders. An overwhelming desire to cry came over her as she realised how much she missed Niko and Yioli. She gazed at the sun as it peaked weakly through the wispy clouds and imagined her friends were saying hello from another world but looking at the same sky.

'You lot enough!' yelled the woman, as she stomped across the street. Elena saw them disappear through the school gates. They mingled in the throng of pupils in the playground dwarfed by the huge, red brick building situated on the opposite side of the road. An eye-sore compared to school in Cyprus, she thought, as she sat on her bed. How she wanted to fit in, to be in the playground, despite its ugliness.

'What are you doing?' asked her mother, interrupting her day dreaming as Elena sat cross-legged drawing in the pad she brought with her from Cyprus. Her mother placed the pile of ironed clothes on the top of the wobbly chest of drawers.

'I'm breathing through my mouth so I don't have to smell the Dettol.'

'Well it's better than the whiff of urine and sweaty bodies,' said her mother, as she sat heavily on the bed next to her. 'I know it's not much better than the house we moved into when we first arrived but it's a bit quieter.'

'Yeah, I know. People in and out,' replied Elena.

'It will get better. This is only temporary Elena *mou*.'

'I know *mama*,' she said as she squeezed her mother's hands, folded together in her floral aproned lap.

'I leeve Copen-ha-gen Strit Is-ling-tone,' practised Elena in English, her diction clear but crude. 'I come Cyproos.'

'What are you drawing?' asked her mother, changing the subject.

'Dresses and shoes,' she said proudly, turning her book round to show off her sketches.

Her mother gave her a little smile and said, 'Beautiful. And Elena *mou,* all will be well, I pray every night.'

Elena regarded her uniform drooping limply on the metal hanger on the outside of the broken wardrobe. It had a door missing, but it had a full length mirror on the inside of the one door which hung precariously from its rusty hinges. 'I think school will be great. The English children look nice,' she said as she re-called the boys playing catch in the street.

'And don't forget to look out for your brother when you start school on Monday,' reminded her mother.

***

Tudor School on Essex Road was a thirty-minute walk from home. Her mother couldn't afford the bus fare there and back daily and so Elena and Andreas strolled along, keeping pace with their mother as she crossed Upper Street and continued into Essex Road.

The school was a maze of long corridors and

staircases, classrooms and a library. It was much bigger than the village school they had gone to and there were many pupils. Each classroom door was labelled 1A, 1B, 1C, 1D up to 4A, 4B, 4C, 4D. Elena and Andreas were welcomed into 4B with Miss Fisher. They were the eldest in the class but Elena didn't mind and Andreas, she thought, didn't even notice.

Miss Fisher, their class teacher, walked with a determined stride and every morning she stood at the front of the room, welcoming each pupil by name as they came in and took their seats. She stood in front of the black board, tall and erect, smoothing down her plain blouse and tugging at the ends of her flicked hair. Elena couldn't figure out why she was a Miss and not a Mrs; she looked far too old to be a Miss.

Elena quickly made friends with pupils in her class; Susan Pollard, Caroline White, Janet Simmons, Alan Churchill, Edward Barnes and Judith Varady from Hungary. The school day was much longer than they were used to, starting at 8.45am and finishing at 3.20pm. Elena and Andreas stayed in school for their lunch, the dinner hall a bustling hubbub of laughter and relaxation although Andreas complained about the food and the strict dinner ladies to Elena. Elena quickly learned to find her way around the building but Andreas continued to struggle.

'Where were you?' asked Elena as he skulked towards her after getting rapped on the knuckles with the ruler for being late.

'I got lost,' Andreas hissed.

'For God's sake. It's not difficult. The doors are all numbered. They go in order around the corridors.'

'Be quiet. Clever clogs!' Andreas sulked for the rest of the history lesson. He didn't perk up until after lunch time where he beat Alan at marbles. He walked home with Elena and his bulging trouser pockets, full of glass marbles, jiggled noisily all the way home.

***

In class Janet and Elena initially shared a double desk with an ink well in each and Andreas shared the same with Edward. As the term progressed the children moved around depending on how well they did in their test papers and so Elena ended up sharing with Susan, Alan and Judith at different times in the school year. Janet, however, wilfully remained her most loyal and best friend. Andreas and Edward didn't get on well and unfortunately for Andreas he remained seated with Edward throughout the whole school year despite begging Miss Fisher to be seated away from him.

'What sort of accent is that?' Edward mocked, vapid hostility in his voice when Andreas spoke. Andreas ignored him.

'Shut it,' Janet retorted glaring at him with her piercing blue eyes as she bit on her already bitten fingernails. She flicked her long blond hair over her shoulder and ignored the boys' sniggering and exclamations from the back of the room. Her dusting of freckles seemed to dance across her snub nose as she held her serious stare.

Elena and Janet volunteered to be milk monitors and dinner monitors. Janet shared her packed lunch with Elena; cheese and pickle sandwiches and gherkins and on the days she ate school dinners she would let Elena eat her pudding.

The girls and boys would play marbles on the hard surface of the playground and slide around the playground when it was icy, despite the teachers on duty shouting at them.

Andreas quickly became interested in girls and used to lean up against the wall at morning break ogling the girls skipping, their school skirts tucked into their knickers.

'As it's the last week of term we have two certificates for Most Improved Spoken English,' announced the Head Teacher, Mr Bainbridge, in the weekly assembly. 'Elena Ellina and Judith Varady. Let's give them a huge round of applause.'

Alan and Edward whistled loudly with their fingers and all the other children clapped and cheered as the two pupils weaved their way up to the stage to collect their certificates. Miss Fisher, their class teacher, beamed and clapped loudly over the noise. The other teachers congratulated Miss Fisher and Elena gave her teacher a wave as she stepped off the stage to sit back in her place amongst her classmates.

'You're my honeysuckle,' said Janet, her chubby arms wobbling like spam as she cuddled Elena. 'My honey bunch.' Janet was Elena's best friend at school and she gave her a huge hug as they filed back into the classroom to begin the day's lessons. They got on so well and found the same things amusing. They chatted together endlessly at play times and hung back after school to giggle and flirt with the boys. They were inseparable.

'I have to go,' pleaded Elena. 'My mum's waiting.'

'Five minutes,' begged Janet. 'The new boy, Andy, is looking at you.'

Elena blushed as she caught Andy's eye. She pulled away from her friend, who was hanging onto her sleeve, and fixed Janet with an expression fizzing with laughter.

'I'll see you tomorrow,' Elena trilled and tapping Andreas on the shoulder she ran off ahead of him her long plaits dangling behind her. 'Last one home's a loser!' she teased.

***

Money was still tight and Elena and Andreas always found new ways of being entrepreneurial. Elena, capitalised on her drawing skills and would cover a page with lots of crossing lines and different shapes. Colouring them in beautifully she sold them to her friends to make a bit of pocket money. She spent the money on sweets on the way home from school knowing her mother didn't have the money for confectionary.

Elena didn't complain although she did ask why they didn't own a house of their own.

'You find me £2000 odd to buy a house and I'll buy one,' complained her father. Although Elena also knew their rent was extortionate.

The best parts of Elena's day were breakfast and then her snack at bed time. She relished how light and soft the bread was and toasting it on both sides under the grill she spread it thickly with lashings of butter. In the evenings, before she went to bed her mother would warm a cup of milk for her and stir in brown sugar to sweeten it. Elena would sip it slowly, savouring every gulp.

Over the coming months she became better acquainted with her father. One Saturday afternoon he came home and called out to them as they played in the street with their friends. They both rushed to him. Andreas threw himself into his father's arms and he ruffled Andreas' hair.

'*Baba*, stop,' he said.

'Come on princess,' he called out as he dropped Andreas to the ground and took Elena's hands in his, dancing with her in the street while they all cheered.

'I'm taking you out for lunch. Call your mother.'

Elena called her mother from the front door and a few minutes later Evangelia appeared in the doorway, her apron floury.

'What's all the fuss?'

'*Baba* is taking us out to eat,' the children chimed together.

'I'm making bread, she said. Give me a minute.'

Ten minutes later Kostas extended his arm and Evangelia linked her arm through it. The children ambled alongside them and Andreas kicked a ball of scrunched up newspaper across the road to the others who were messing around on the street.

'I know it's been hard,' Kostas said to Evangelia. 'It will get better.'

'Only if you stop the gambling.'

'It's not that bad. Don't worry.' Elena eyed her father quizzically who gave her a little nod.

'You don't have to make do Kostas. It's not easy when there's rent to pay, the meter to operate, the children to feed and clothe and my mother to look after.'

'Let's think about today, Evangelia *agabi mou.*' Kostas extended his big hand out to Elena who took it in her slender one. 'Today we will feast like the Greek Gods.'

'Yippeee!' yelled Andreas, jumping up and punching the air excitedly.

Evangelia smiled at her husband. He smiled back and the creases around his eyes deepened. They strolled arm in arm towards Islington High Street. A Rag and Bone man in his cart trundled past them, his call 'Any old iron? Any old iron?' cutting into Elena's thoughts; why couldn't it always be like this? All of them together, smiling, happy.

Her father stopped at the Newsagents, half way along the street towards the café, to buy a 5-pack of *Embassy Filter* cigarettes. They continued past Lockwood's Bakeries, the irresistible smell of fresh bread and doughnuts causing Elena's stomach to rumble loudly. Set between Western's Laundry and Islington Furniture Rooms the café windows were tall and wide and misty with condensation. As they entered, the odour of grease and cigarette smoke filled Elena's lungs. She tried to acclimatise to the noisy garrulous chatter of the diners who were seated at the many cream tables, with red edging, set in rows.

They took the table nearest the front; the majority of the others already taken with punters. It was noisy; a constant pinging of the till drawer opening and then banging shut added to the sound of chatter. Elena marvelled at the array of people.

She had never been to a café before although she had often passed the one nearest to where they lived. She flicked a few crumbs off the plastic table and twiddled her fingers under the table to drop the few still clinging to her onto the floor. The stickiness of the linoleum pulled at the soles of her shoes and she kicked away what appeared to be a piece of pastry and a squashed chip with her foot. She wondered whether all English people were dirty and felt a bit disgusted with the lack of cleanliness she witnessed around her. She glanced at the white and blue tiled walls, grimy with oil and grease, a stack of manhandled newspapers piled haphazardly on a chair by the counter.

She gazed out of the curtainless window, making a small clear circle in the condensation with her finger. The expanse of grey sky draped the buildings in its cloak of gloom, a few white clouds at its periphery. For a brief moment nostalgia enveloped her and she wished she was in Cyprus with its blue skies, fresh mountain air and the quiet of the village.

Her father studied the menu and pointed to the black board which had other dishes scribbled in white chalk over it. Andreas fidgeted around with the salt and pepper pots and oohed and ahhed with a cocktail of joy, excitement and pride. Her mother, seated opposite Kostas, glanced at the menu card and listened to some of the translations Kostas made.

'What can I get ya?' asked the waitress, her stained red apron taut around her big middle and her bosoms drooping to her waist. Elena got a whiff of flower fragrances as she held up her pad and pencil at the ready, a warm smile lighting up her round face. 'The specials are on the board.'

Having already decided, Kostas ordered for the four

of them. Elena was happy her father could speak such good English and she couldn't help but smile as she took her mother's warm hand and held it under the table.

'Two pies and mash and peas, chips, fried egg and bacon and chips and saveloy.'

'Anything to drink?'

'Two teas, one milky coffee and a glass of milk,' ordered her father competently.

'Coming right up,' she replied in a sing-song voice.

The food was surprisingly delicious and Elena ate slowly, savouring the ketchup which she had squirted generously over her chips, greasy and golden. Andreas ate too quickly dribbling his egg yolk and then smearing it across his face with the thin serviette he'd balled up as he tried to clean his chin. Her mother moistened a hanky with saliva and rubbed the warm sticky yellow away, leaving a red mark from all the rubbing. Andreas leaned back uncomfortably in the plastic chair trying to dislodge the big meal he ate. He rubbed his tummy in circular motions.

'I'm so full,' he said.

'Well, you ate too quickly,' said his mother.

'So lovely. Thank you, *baba*,' said Elena, glaring at Andreas.

'Thank you, *baba*,' said Andreas, although he didn't look happy.

The same waitress came over to clear the empty plates. 'Anything else I can get ya? Stewed apple and custard for all?'

Evangelia said in a hushed whisper, 'We don't need to go overboard.'

'Yeah it's a treat *mama*,' said Andreas but before he said anything else Elena kicked him under the table. Andreas sat with his arms crossed.

'No, you're right Evangelia *mou*. And thank you for putting up with me.'

Elena looked at her mother's expression. Her lips were closed tight and a sweaty sheen appeared on her forehead. Elena knew her mother was upset but wasn't sure why.

They sat another few minutes in silence. Kostas lit up a cigarette and after paying the bill they left the café.

Walking back home a parked ice cream van boomed 'oranges and lemons' above the noise of the intermittent traffic; a Ford Popular, a mini, a couple of lorries and the odd bus and many horse drawn carts. A queue of noisy children and parents wiggled its way along the pavement. As they passed by Elena looked up at the pictures of the 'cornet' and the 'brick'. The cornet had a huge dollop of vanilla ice cream on it and the brick, made up of two rectangular wafers, was filled with a vanilla slab of ice cream. 'The drink on the stick' showed a picture of a Lyon's Maid 'orange maid'.

'No!' yelled a boy of about six years old as he stared at the wafer cornet he'd dropped, spattering his shoes and the front of his father's trousers with melted, gooey ice cream.

'You daft beggar,' said his father as the boy blubbered at the blob of vanilla seeping into the cracks of the pavement.

'Stop with your crying. We'll get another one,' said his mother and she proceeded to wipe the boy's shoes with a yellow handkerchief and then wiped his snotty nose. 'Ugh that's sticky,' the boy said pulling a face.

'You can get washed properly at home,' she said.

Two boys waiting in the line had witnessed what happened and smirked.

'Cheeky twats,' the boy's father muttered in their direction. They instantly twisted away but Elena knew they were still sniggering; their shaking shoulders giving them away. A woman standing behind them, clouted one round the head.

'Stop it!' she admonished. 'I won't tell you again.'

'Ouch!' yelled the boy. 'It's not funny,' he said to the other who was doubled over chuckling loudly.

Elena looked towards her father hoping he'd offer to get them one but he didn't even so much as notice the vendor. Elena thought about all the times she had day dreamed of being in London with her father and how it had been a good day today yet her mother still looked sad. The smirking boys reminded her of her old Cypriot classmates and how they sniggered at Andreas's obvious slowness. At the time the laughter had addled her but now she missed the giggles.

Elena carried on walking more slowly now, her parents walking two paces ahead of her and her brother even further ahead, his hands in his trouser pockets and his hair sticking up at the back like the tail of a bird from the way he had slept. She marvelled at the shop displays as they weaved in and out of the crowded pavement; the fabric shop with all its rolls of materials, the newsagents with a huge sign for a paper boy stuck on its door, the off-Licence with wooden crates of bottled beers stacked high. Her eye caught the sign for the betting office. Her mother's pace quickened but then she stopped suddenly.

'You go on ahead,' Kostas said, halting outside a shop Elena had seen men going in and out of and once an old lady in a pink knitted beret. 'I won't be a minute.' He disentangled his arm from her mother's and pecked her on the lips.

Elena turned from her father to her mother and back again. Her mother didn't say anything but her lips tightened and she gripped the side of her handbag. Elena wondered why her father was going into the shop she knew Alan had told her his own dad went into and 'wasted his money'. The three of them made the twenty-minute walk home in silence and Elena slowly realised her father must suffer the same problem as Alan's dad. He was a gambler. Gambling, according to Miss Fisher, was not a clever thing to do. An underworld of cheats and liars, is what she said.

Her father's gambling explained a lot; his late night "entertaining" friends and the lie-ins where he only surfaced in time to "nip out" and his notes, tucked here and there, which Elena came to realise had to be his form book and his log of bets. Elena knew now he went out to put his bets on and his gatherings were when he played cards, gambling away not only his own money but the money her mother worked hard for too.

As they arrived home a fracas broke out two doors away from them. Her mother searched frantically for the front door key.

'You filthy animals!' yelled one of their Scottish neighbours. She pushed a group of teenagers out the house but not quite in time, so one of the girls vomited over her gleaming door step.

'Don't have a cow,' said one and they all burst out laughing and jeering. 'Haven't you had a hangover before?'

The spew smelt like vinegar and permeated the air as the sick clung to the girl's long hair. She started to cry, bits of sick clung onto her hairband like some sort of exploded science experiment. She coughed and a bubble of snot came out of her nose.

'One of ya hold 'er 'air,' said another girl with two bushy bunches, ginger orange, and freckles sprinkled across her face.

'Ye better pack it in!' the woman cried as she banged

the door in their faces only to open it a few minutes later splashing their feet and lower legs with soapy water as she chucked a bucket over the step; the sick and water mixture trickled towards the road and over the kerb as it left a trail of bits behind it on the pavement. She threw the hard-bristled brush at them. 'Clean it up. I want it sparkling!' The yelling and hurling of abuse continued.

'Stop staring,' said Elena's mum as she continued to rummage for the key. 'Oh, your dad has it,' she remembered.

'I'll run back,' offered Elena.

'Don't bother, here he comes,' said her mother. 'I don't want you wandering off when there's trouble brewing.'

'There's *baba*,' called out Andreas. Elena saw her father walking briskly towards them, a big smile on his face. She hoped this meant he had won some money and crossed her fingers behind her back but somehow she saw her hope soaked in red.

***

Whenever she was at home, Elena helped her mother with the washing which still had to be done manually, much as it was in Cyprus. The main difference was they couldn't rely on the hot sunshine to dry the clothes, which came in weak splashes, and wringing the garments was hard work. Elena's hands were dry and sore from all the scrunching and squeezing and from rotating the heavy iron mangle's arm in the yard.

Andreas and her father sat in the kitchen to keep warm by the stove. He was counting his winnings.

'This,' he said, 'is the equivalent of three months' wages.'

He was a chef in a hotel in London and did the breakfasts and lunches although recently Elena noticed how he was still in bed as late as 8 am when Elena and Andreas left for school.

A few weeks later Kostas' gambling habit and late nights back fired on him and he lost his job for being unreliable.

'It's because they can pay those Indians less,' he complained.

'Well, what are we to do now?' asked Evangelia.

'I'll find something. But in the meantime you may have to take in some extra work, do machining from home. You'll get paid piece work. I'll sort it.'

'Well, if you think that's the only way...'

'I could help too,' said Elena sensing her mother's disappointment. Elena's sewing skills had not gone unnoticed in school and she got an A+ on her report card for the detailed needlework embellishing her tea towel and the teapot cosy she had knitted, although sadly both samples of work remained at school as her father had no money to pay for them.

Her teacher, however, delighted in using them as

examples in class.

After school on Monday of the following week, Janet bought a 'brick' and shared the last bit with Elena. They simultaneously wiped the dribbling ice cream from their faces as they walked back through the school gates.

'One day I'll buy you a whole one,' said Elena.

'Don't be silly. You're my honeysuckle!'

'You're my English rose,' giggled Elena, as she licked her lips and then her sticky fingers one by one.

Elena enjoyed having a close friend and it made missing Yioli and Stella easier to bear. She often thought about them as she lay in her freezing bed, trying to warm up under the layers of covers and prayed to God they were well. She had written to Yioli when they first arrived but had yet to receive a letter back. Perhaps Yioli had a new best friend now like she did. She would ask her when she wrote to her.

Edward sauntered across the playground, one hand in his trouser pocket, an evil glint crossed his eyes. Elena wondered what he was up to. Then, in a flash, she saw him swipe Andreas across the back of the head as he was huddled in a group with some other boys, bent over a drain, playing marbles.

'You English pig!' screamed Andreas as he sprung to his feet and threw a punch which landed bang on Edward's nose.

'You bloody foreigner!' yelled Edward momentarily

stunned. He tried to stem the blood pouring into his mouth. The collar of his shirt became a patch of red.

'Fight, fight, fight!' chorused the five other pupils as they encircled the two opponents as if in a boxing ring. Edward and Andreas glared at each other.

'What is going on?' commanded Mr Collins, the Music teacher as he ran across the playground from his end-of-day duty post by the side exit gates.

'He started it!' said Andreas, his head bowed.

'Let's see what the Head master has to say.'

Elena ran over and tried to intervene but Mr Collins wasn't having any of it. Janet tried too but couldn't persuade him either of Edward's teasing of Andreas.

'All the time in class. Ask Mrs Fisher!' But both girls' comments were ignored. Mr Collins, losing his patience, grabbed Andreas and Edward by the scruff of the neck and hauled them up the steps of the school's main entrance.

'The rest of you get home!'

'Mum's going to go mad,' said Elena, tears stinging her eyes.

'I'll tell her what happened,' said Janet, trying to be helpful. 'Please don't cry my honeysuckle,' she said as she hugged Elena tightly.

At home that evening, it was Kostas who was furious with Andreas. Home for a change, he blasted Andreas with all his anger and thrashed him with the belt on the back of his chubby legs. Andreas froze, momentarily stunned. Tears stung his eyes. An expression Elena had never seen before crossed his face. He grabbed his father's wrist, glaring at him. Andreas did not take his eyes off him. His father shook off Andreas' grasp, raised his arm ready to thump Andreas with his open hand.

'Leave me alone. This is your fault!'

'Don't you dare speak to me like that!'

'It's true! We're stuck in this stupid country, no money for the stupid meter, no money for treats, no proper home.'

'Enough!' Kostas glared at Andreas.

'No! That's just it. Nothing is enough here. It's Mum I feel most sorry for!'

'That's enough,' begged Evangelia.

'No *mama*, what's all this for?'

She sat heavily on the wobbly kitchen chair, her bottom lip trembling, fighting back the tears.

'I'm old enough to understand what's going on!' he ranted. His mother took him in her arms. Elena stood by the kitchen door, watching the scene in front of her. She was shaking with shock. Her brother had never stood up for himself in the same way before. It disconcerted her. She felt as though she was losing her place as the responsible one. She watched as her mother burst into tears; Andreas clenched and unclenched his fist. Her father, speechless stood over them. His face was blackened with an anger Elena had ever seen but before anything else happened Kostas grabbed his jacket from the back of the chair.

'I've had enough! I'm off out!' He pushed past Elena.

'Don't go Dad,' Elena said as she fought against her.

***

For the next seven weeks, the whole of the summer holidays and the first week back at school, her father didn't come home, not once. They had no word from him and she knew her mother was worried he'd never come back. But strangely the seven weeks were calmer, peaceful although quietly sad.

Her mother's home machining brought in good money. Evangelia was quick and accurate with her stitching. Her boss, a tall wiry man with a grey pallor and yellow teeth, was a kind, friendly man. Elena however recoiled from the odour of stale cigarette smoke he brought in the with him whenever he visited to collect his bundles of blouses. Her mother was responsible for attaching the collars and cuffs. He told her mother she was his best machinist and would often add a bit extra in her little brown envelope at the end of each week. Whatever money she made she used to pay the rent and feed the electricity meter.

Being used to counting the pennies Elena could see her mother didn't fritter her money away but Andreas and she enjoyed a few treats – Sherbet, bubblegum, the odd comic and a wireless which her mother rented from Radio Rentals.

Elena obediently visited the local store to pay their grocery 'bill' and finally Elena also paid for her textiles and brought them home. Georgette discovered they could afford to buy olive oil from the chemist and they all celebrated one evening with a proper Cypriot salad and grilled pork chops for dinner as they ate together crammed in the small kitchen, the windows wide open to let in the summer breeze.

Elena and Andreas were warmer as they fed the coin-operated meter more regularly. Elena was allowed to visit Janet for dinner one day after school for sausages, mash and baked beans much to Elena's delight whose taste buds were becoming more adventurous since school dinners.

At home though, Elena still worried about her mother's health. She looked more tired than ever as she bent over the sewing machine. The intermittent whirring droned on and on as as she pressed the foot pedal. Elena wondered whether this was the life her mother wanted and an ache in her heart took her back to *Kato Lefkara*; tears stinging her eyes. Maybe they should never have come...her mother looked old.

Chapter Thirteen

Christaki, 1958

CHRISTAKI SAT UP until past midnight listening for Pete's rat-a-tat at the front door. He fought against the rhythmic ticking of the clock on his bedside table pulling him into sleep. The knock at the door never came. The following morning dawned with a dull lifeless grey sky. He rose early, throwing on his clothes and shaking as the cold, sodden material hugged his skin. He called out good bye to his mother and left for work without breakfast. His mother's words of upset banged against the front door as he pulled it closed with a thud. His stomach churned not from hunger this time but from a bad feeling; a sensation which made him uneasy, almost sick. There was a lump in his chest and he put his hand on his thumping heart to ease the ache.

He willed the bus to move faster as he peered out of the grimy windowpane at the tall brick buildings; office blocks, warehouses, factories. The journey was slow; the road being dug up at one point caused impatient drivers to hoot in frustration, the noise of the traffic unbearably invasive.

When Christaki finally arrived Pete was not at the meeting point and he wasn't in line for the morning's selection either. For the rest of the day Christaki was like a rabbit in the headlights of a car; jumpy, easily startled, wide-eyed every time someone called his name or dropped a tool. Pete did not appear for the whole day. £5.00 was a lot of money. What could Pete have wanted it for? If he took it at all, wondered Christaki, but then who else could have taken it?

The day went by painfully slowly. Christaki had no company and was no longer used to working in isolation. He missed Pete's idle chatter. He wanted the day to end so he could go and find Pete. He wanted some answers and somewhere deep inside he went from feeling foolish for trusting Pete to being worried for him. Had Pete conned him? Was he not a friend after all?

***

Battling against the grey May drizzle, which had begun to thicken and fall in cold sheets, Christaki searched the warren of back streets. After two solid hours of searching every alleyway, every side street and three of the local pubs he knew Pete often drank in Christaki almost gave up hope of finding him. In the quickly fading sunlight the burnished bricks of the buildings looked warm and burnished. But he was soaked to the skin. Suddenly shivering he realised how cold and wet he was.

Eventually, as twilight closed in, when he could hardly make out what was two feet ahead of him in the pitch darkness, a moaning caught his attention. He strained his ears; the darkness thick in the alley. A stumbling figure came out from the shadowy obscurity. He tripped on the uneven paving stones.

Out of the shadows, on all fours, crawling like a wild creature, an amorphous shape appeared. As he moved out of the penumbra he clumsily fell to the floor in the pool of light from the street lamp. Christaki saw his face first; covered in bruises and cuts and dried blood. Was it Pete? Christaki's mind fuzzed over, incapable of taking in what his eyes were showing him. Had it not been for Pete's scarf, albeit covered in brown blood stains, he would not have recognised him.

'Pete!' Christaki lunged towards him, his arms outstretched to catch Pete as he dragged himself up and then fell forward again. 'What's happened?'

Pete flopped into Christaki's arms like a rag doll, his breathing laboured. Christaki couldn't make sense of his words. Pete's mouth twisted in pain as he tried to speak, pain visibly casting a shadow across his battered face. His eye opened a crack, a tear escaped. Christaki realised how obscured his vision must be. A mood of despair enveloped Christaki as he held Pete. Pete took Christaki's hand and brought it palm down to his chest. He held it there and stared at Christaki speechless. Christaki sat there helpless and watched as his friend disintegrated before him; silent tears streaked Pete's bloodstained face. Christaki bit hard on his lower lip to stop himself from crying. He had to hold it together. He found Pete's other hand and closed his warm hand over it; Pete's was cold. He was unconscious.

Panic rose in Christaki's chest and threatened to burst him open. He shifted Pete and slapped his hand, called his name over and over. After what felt like an eternity Pete came to and Christaki found the strength to lift Pete into a semi-upright position. He let out a cry of pain like a wounded animal and held onto his side.

'We need to get you warm and dry. The hotel. It's not too far. Clean you up a bit. Then you can tell me what happened.'

Christaki hooked his arm around Pete and Pete leaned into him. They stumbled through the misty sprinkling of rain twice almost falling over as Pete dragged his left leg awkwardly along the cobbled streets. Eventually at the St Ermin's Hotel, Christaki left him slumped up against the wall by the rubbish bins adjacent to the staff entrance.

'Don't move. I need to check it's all clear.' Pete's chin tipped forward, resting on his chest.

The air, thick with the smell of rancid food, sewers and stale waste spiked his nostrils as he disappeared into the building.

Christaki and Pavlo slinked Pete to Pavlo's room without passing anyone in the corridors. Pavlo came back from the outside lavvies with a bucket of water and a dishcloth.

Between them the two brothers cleaned Pete up and managed to bandage his leg. Pavlo sneaked in a bowl of soup from the staff canteen and after a few sips Pete fell into a semi-conscious sleep.

'He'll have to stay here tonight brother. He's not strong enough to go home. Mother will be frightened seeing him like this. It will bring back too many memories of her brother, the attack, his death…what shall we do?'

'Leave him here. I'll sleep in with Dean next door.' Christaki pulled the blanket over Pete.

They both agreed Christaki would return before sunrise to get him out of the hotel before anyone realised he was there.

Their plan worked. The following morning Christaki left home early on the pretext he said he would do an extra early shift for Mr O'Connolly and needed to pick up some materials for him. His mother, not yet risen from her bed, patted him on the cheek and snuggled back under the covers to go back to sleep.

Pavlo's hotel room smelt of antiseptic and stale breath and sweat.

'So Pete, my friend, how are you?' he asked wishing there was a window to open, to let some fresh air into the cramped room; instead he propped the bedroom door open a few inches.

'Better thank you, to both of you.' Pete shifted himself into a semi-upright position in the small bed which he was pouring out of.

'What happened? Why haven't you been home?'

'I'm sorry. I had to sort something out. I promised.'

'Is that what got you beaten? To death's door?'

'Yeah. It is. Look I was just trying to help someone.'
Christaki sighed.

'A girl. She needed my help. She was pregnant.'

'You got a girl pregnant? And then she beat you up?'
Christaki's eyes were wide. 'What help did she need?'

'Well, you know…'

'No, I don't know. I don't understand this.'

'She needed an abortion.'

'You gave her money for an abortion?'

'No. Not me. Someone else she didn't want to tell him.'

'So what's it got to do with you?'

'I promised Janet's older brother I would always look out for 'er. He died of pneumonia a couple of years back.'
Christaki struggled to keep up with what Pete was saying, his words strangled and twisted, hoarse.

'So you took, no stole, money from my mother's house to pay for an abortion.'

'I'm sorry. I'll pay it back. All of it. I was short. I've been saving up every penny to 'elp 'er.'

'You should've told me. Instead you steal from my mother. And now what am I supposed to do? How can I tell her this? This would be too much for her.'

'Please don't tell 'er. I don't want 'er to think bad of me. I'll pay you back.'

245

'What happened to the girl?'

'Her old man saw me creeping out the house after passing on the money. He assumed I was messing with 'er. I managed to get away but, well he caught up with me. Found me. Half wasted he was, with two mates. You know the rest.'

'And is she alright? The girl?'

'I don't know. I can't go back there can I?'

'We have to make sure she's alright. Abortions are dangerous…illegal Pete.'

'Mate I know. It's a big mess, it is.'

Christaki, despite the turmoil inside him about the girl's predicament, was relieved Pete was alive and recovering quickly. He went via the hotel every evening after work to check on his friend until on the fourth day he found him sitting up in bed and laughing.

'Thank God you are well.'

'I am. Thank you mate. I owe you. And your brother.'

***

The following morning, with a little pleading from Christaki, Mr O'Connolly took Pete back on.

'No disappearin' again lad. Last chance. And why're ya limping?'

'Accident, Sir. But it's fixed now.'

'I've got a job needs finishing here so no slacking!' Christaki winked at Pete and Pete smiled back. 'I don't want trouble on site! Get on with the work and we'll get on just fine.' He had his job back.

Every passing day Pete's physical health improved and he became more determined than ever to work hard.

'I'll pay you back Chris. Every penny.' Christaki kept a close eye on him and they became close again but something in Christaki had changed towards Pete. His guard was up and it would take more than the return of the money for Christaki to trust his friend again. Christaki hoped the feeling would pass.

***

After three months of working on the site Mr O'Connolly was waiting for Christaki by the main exit gates at the end of the day.

'Eh, Chris. The guv'nor's been keeping an eye on you. He says you're doing well.'

'Thank you, Sir.'

'So I've got something I wanna discuss with ya.'

'Yes, Sir.' Christaki moved to the side to let the other labourers by.

'I'd like you to go on the electrician training course. You're trustworthy. You're 'ard working. You're a quick learner, clever. You're a good lad. What d'you say Chris? There'd be a few extra bob in it for you too.'

'Thank you, Mr O'Connolly, Sir. I like this very much.'

'No need to be so formal, you fecking eejit. Get off with you now.'

'Thank you Mr O'Connolly. My mother will be happy.'

'I'll talk to you about it next week. Have a good weekend!'

'I will. You too!'

Christaki walked towards the bus stop imagining the joy his mother would feel when he told her his good news. He was a few steps away when he heard someone calling.

'Oi! You!'

Christaki carried on walking.

'I'm talking to you! You hitch up from some foreign country and take our jobs, our opportunities…'

Christaki found himself face to face with Kevin.

'Kevin right?'

'And what's it to you?'

'Nothing.' Christaki took a step back, the alcohol and tobacco coming off Kevin's breath pungent, stale.

'That apprenticeship should've been mine. Been grafting there for that O'Connlly for months, longer than you, pal!'

'I don't know anything about that. He came to me. I'm sorry.' Kevin raised his hand, his fist clenched, his jaw tight. Christaki raised his arm across his face to protect himself. He felt a rumble of fear in the pit of his stomach. Kevin was twice his size and tanked up. It wouldn't take much to flatten Christaki. Christaki flinched.

'That's enough lad!' It was the foreman. 'Kev you got a problem with the guv'nor's decision you take it up with him!'

'Wanker!' he said as he spat at Christaki's feet and walked off. 'You ain't heard the last o' this!'

On the bus journey home Christaki thought about Mr Connolly's offer all the way home. The excitement he had originally felt now crushed by Kevin's poisonous animosity towards him.

He mulled it over all the way home. It wasn't accounting he admitted but it would give him a specialist skill and he knew with all the building work going on he would never be without work. He prayed Kevin would back off otherwise he'd no choice but to decline the offer. He didn't want to bring bad luck to his mother's door even though he knew his mother and father would be pleased his hard work was being recognised and rewarded. His mother had always said having a practical skill would never leave you hungry. Despite his doubts, he proudly pushed his chest out and shoulders back, a small smile danced at the corner of his mouth, as the bus trundled along the patchwork of pot-holes on the road home.

***

'*Agabi mou.* What did I tell you? I've been praying to St Fanourios and he has brought me good news. My prayers have been answered. Praise be his name.' His mother crossed herself and raised her eyes to heaven. She hugged and kissed him; pinching his cheek until it tinged red under the pressure of her fingertips.

As she took the roast potatoes out of the oven she sang an old traditional song Christaki had not enjoyed from her lips in a long time. The words poured out of her; words of courage and determination. Christaki recognised it; she used to sing it at home in *Ayios Tychonas*. She was jubilant; for the first time since the death of her brother his mother was not only smiling but singing too. Maybe it would all be alright, after all.

'We just have to find Pete now.' She dropped the heavy pan onto the scrubbed table and dished out their evening meal. 'Melani, dinner is ready *agabi mou.*'

Christaki wanted to tell his mother about Pete, about the money and the girl but instead he said, 'Pete's a tough guy. He will be working on some other site and will surely show himself again mother. Don't you worry about him.'

'When's he coming back?' asked Melani as she pushed her long hair out of her eyes. She took a mouthful of food and winced at the heat as it scalded her mouth.

'Hopefully soon. Anyway how's work going?'

'I'm learning something new all the time. The girls are all lovely.'

'Well don't go making friends with everyone,' said Christaki. 'The English are not all like us.'

'Oh big brother. You're such a cynic,' she teased.

'I mean it Melani. Keep yourself to yourself. There's stuff you need to keep away from. Watch yourself.'

'I work as a telephone operator not in the secret service,' she laughed.

'Enough now. She's a good girl. Let's eat.' His mother interrupted. She didn't want another argument at the table. That's all we seem to be doing recently, thought Christaki and with only him and Melani at home he knew his mum wanted harmony around her, love not war.

They ate their meal in silence until a knock at the door with a rhythm Christaki recognised echoed down the narrow hallway. He got up to answer it and seconds later walked back into the room. Pete hung back a few steps behind him.

'Who was it?' asked Melani.

'Good evening. I am so sorry to be disturbing your meal.'

'Pete!' Melani became so excited she knocked over her glass of water and then her fork fell into her lap. Christaki looked at her and realised what was different about his sister; she was growing up and she liked Pete; she liked him a lot.

'Good evening Pete, *agabi mou*.' Christaki watched his mother as she remained calm and waited for Pete to speak.

'I wanted to apologise for my behaviour. To say sorry.' Pete was hovering at the kitchen door.

Christaki's mum and Melani looked confusedly from one to the other and then back at Pete. Christaki realised they had both not understood what he was apologising for.

'The missing money, I took it. I'm ashamed.'

'You must have needed it for something important,' Anastasia said matter-of-factly. Christaki hoped Pete wouldn't tell her the real reason, wouldn't be that honest about it.

'I did but I should've asked. Please forgive me.'

'Well you're here now and you've apologised. Sit and eat dinner with us.'

'Are you sure?'

'Who am I to reject you when you come to me with an open heart looking for forgiveness? Forgiveness will come from God.'

Pete sat down with tears in his eyes and wiped them away with the back of his hand. He placed the scrunched notes from his pocket on the table. He placed his hand on Anastasia's.

Christaki was overwhelmed with the scene before him and relieved the real reason for taking the money hadn't been revealed. But, his friend was sitting at the table again and his mother was calm and forgiving. He thought his heart would burst with love and admiration. She was an incredible woman. In his eyes she was an angel.

Pete chattered away throughout the meal, Christaki translating some of his stories for his mother who listened intently, smiling all the while.

'Nothing gives me greater pleasure than seeing my table full of food and people to eat it.'

Chapter Fourteen

Loizos, 1958

IN MAY, DESPITE the sagging slate-coloured sky, the first signs of Spring kissed the trees with tight rose blossom buds.

Standing on the concourse at Victoria Station Loizos stared around him searching the crowds for Anastasia and his children. He pulled his black wool coat around him tighter as the cold air playfully seeped under it and made him shiver. His breath came out in hot gusts in front of him and dissipated into the damp chill. The hype of activity around him, the frenetic pace and the noise, amplified by the hollow hulk of the station, was almost too much to bear. Shouts, guffaws and excited screams echoed around him before the great glass dome overhead swallowed them up. The long journey threatened to ambush his consciousness. He fought against the twisting pain in his stomach; exhaustion and sudden worry invading his usually level-headed composure.

Village life seemed a long way away from this noisy urban cocoon. Close by, two women in matching coats with brown fur around the collar, searched for their tickets or travel documents. Two suitcases with a hat box balanced on the top stood at their stockinged feet. A porter, his uniform soaked through, shuffled by huffing like a village donkey as he pushed a trolley heavily laden with two trunks, a suitcase and several packages towards Platform 3.

'Excuse me, Sir. Mind your back, Sir.' Loizos took a step to the side to avoid him but stepped instead onto the feet of a gentleman in a black suit who wasn't watching where he was going.

'Bloody fool! Watch your step!'

Loizos stood there apologising in Greek. The English word for sorry lost in his head. He eventually found the word written on his notepad but the man had long gone; the word disappeared from Loizos' lips into the hub-bub around him. He held open the page with his thumb and carefully translated words; thank you, hello, please, yes, no, way out, sorry, my name. A screech from a whistle cut across his concentration. He reached into his coat pocket and shook out the last cigarette from the scrunched paper packet.

Where are all these people going, he wondered. He continued to gaze around the busy station and up at the signs. Even Limassol on market day had never been this hectic.

He continued to wait; a lost boy at the school gates. He peered up at the signage and advertisement boards fathoming their meaning from the images; cigarettes, newspapers, coffee, food.

A crowd of people emerged all at once from an

adjacent platform with Gatwick Railway Station marked above it. Further along the guard pulled the metal grille across another platform's entrance a few seconds after a man and woman raced through waving their tickets.

He picked up his luggage afraid of getting separated from it in the increasing throng and withdrew into the shadows near a tobacconist. Two queues meandered their way across the concourse as passengers shuffled towards the ticket windows. There were people of all colours. He had never seen a black man before or an Indian. He thought how the black man would have done the work of two or three men during the carob harvest and marvelled at the size of him. He stood two feet above the rest in the queue. As the crowd eventually thinned the sound of running footsteps filled his ears; he recognised the rhythm of the pitter-patter.

He caught sight of Anastasia and Christaki. Within seconds Anastasia saw him too and she ran to him. Tears pricked his eyes, his throat congested, emotions washed in and out. She hesitated for a second then gripped his hands and fell into his arms.

'I never thought I'd see this day. Thank God you are here. Safe and in my arms.'

'*Agabi mou* I was always coming.'

'I've missed you. The children have missed you.'

'Welcome *patera.*' Loizos sensed how emotional Christaki was; guilt smothered him as he realised what a responsibility had been put upon him in Loizos' absence.

He surveyed his son who not only appeared older but who had filled out; his chest broad and his muscles strong.

'*Yioka mou*, Christaki *mou*, good to see you. Where are Pavlo and Malanie?'

'Both at work. You'll see them at home,' said Christaki.

'And they are both well?'

'Yes. London has been cold and dark and wet. I've been so alone without you.' She fumbled with the gold clasp on her bag.

Loizos felt a stab of guilt as he took in his wife's attire; she still dressed in black, still mourning the loss of her brother and he admonished himself for not having been here to support her. Support her as a husband should support his wife.

'I'm here now. We won't ever be apart again. Not until the day I die.' As Anastasia slumped against his chest Loizos sensed her relief. The enormity of what his wife had coped with on her own dawned on him more acutely as he held her frail body, thinner than he remembered it, in his arms for a few more seconds before pulling away from her.

***

Outside the station a truck blasted by throwing fumes and dirt up Loizos' nostrils and he struggled to breathe; a foul mess of bird droppings splattered the pavement as raindrops plinked in the puddles, the spring sky a blanket of angry clouds and fragments of pellucid blue.

A siren wailed in the distance somewhere. A group of porters were huddled together against the grimy red brick wall; a mass of leaden grey in the harsh light of the morning sun. A man was having his shoes shined outside the Tea Room; the boy polishing with vigour and energy, his swift movements controlled. He must have been no older than nine or ten. Further along from him a man was selling newspapers calling out the headlines in a gruff deep voice. People snatched these from him as they rushed past not even glancing in the man's direction.

Loizos noticed how those around him seemed to be in a hurry to get somewhere; a complete contrast to life in Cyprus, or at least life as it used to be before the Cyprus tragedy, with trundling buses, slow donkeys and hours spent in the *kafeneion*. He fought the urge to criticise and instead followed Christaki and the others to a taxi.

He barely said a word during the ride home; Christaki filled him in on the news, about Pavlo's work in the kitchens and about Melani's job as a telephonist. He sat back and his heart swelled with pride. His family had coped without him. He had taught them well the importance of working hard and caring for each other.

Loizos was welcomed by the whole family including cousins who he had tucked away from his conscious mind after months of separation, and in some cases years.

Anastasia cooked a feast of roasted lamb, *kleftiko* with potatoes and onions and there were pickles and even fresh bread she had baked herself the night before.

'Welcome home Loizos.' They all toasted him with clinks and chinks of their glasses, filled generously with the *zivania* Loizos had brought over with him. The table, like an overstuffed market stall, overflowed with jars of black olives, green olives, fresh leaves from the vines to make *koubebia*, stuffed vine leaves, and olive oil; all sent over by family and friends from the village.

'You can only get olive oil in the pharmacies here. Tiny little bottles.' His cousin smiled and he raised his glass. '*Stin iyeia mas.*'

'To our health,' they all repeated and downed their drinks in one.

After dinner Loizos sat quietly and watched Anastasia with a relief so big he wanted to reach out and never let her go. He had missed her. She busied herself in the small room. He watched as the sun set orange and yellow and pink through the window, casting warm shadows across her until it became a smudge of inky blue; all the while Loizos sat still, scratching intermittently at his unshaven chin with his thumb, mesmerised by her beauty, despite her sad eyes and pale face.

Loizos made love to his wife, as if for the first time, tentatively touching and caressing her, learning her body all over again. He was gentle at first but then the urgency, and the want of all those months without her, engulfed him and he took her with a clumsy, uncontrollable force. He held her in his arms and hiding behind the mask of darkness in their bedroom he opened his heart up to her; an alien act to a man who had always found it difficult to show his love openly.

'You're a strong woman Anastasia *mou*. Being united with you and our children is what kept me going in these darkest of times. I've seen things a man should never see. Every day I thanked God you were not there to witness the blood and grief twisted on people's faces. Every day I prayed I would be by your side. We will never be apart again.'

Loizos marvelled at the high riding moon through the slit in the curtains, he was comforted by the curves of his wife's warm body certain he would do anything to keep his family from being apart ever again. That night he fell asleep with love and hope for his future etched on his heart; for his family's future; for their new life. That night he fell asleep with tears stinging his eyes; emotions pulling his heartstrings.

***

As time went by Loizos adapted. He noticed how Anastasia competently made decisions without seeking his advice or approval and at first this worried him. But he quickly came to realise she had simply become so as a way to survive without him, in this huge city of hustle and people and noise. He also didn't fail to notice how Anastasia's sad eyes and sallow skin slowly appeared more radiant. He hoped it was because of him but also wondered whether it was the approach of summer and the longing for warmer days.

And one morning, to his delight, he woke early to the sound of her beautiful voice. Standing in the kitchen door, Loizos' heart raced as he watched her sing and sway her body to the sweet melody as she prepared breakfast in the cramped kitchen. This was his wife as he remembered her before her brother's murder. He was relieved to finally say goodbye to the image of the desperately unhappy woman ingrained in his mind and heavy in his heart all the time they were apart. He knew acceptance was the only way forward and he had to open his heart and his mind to a new future. He knew too things were never going to be as they had been in his beautiful village of *Ayios Tychonas.*

Loizos wasted no time in setting himself up in business. As luck would have it a villager from *Ayios Tychonas* had recently bought a house a few miles away and had told Loizos about an old cobbler wanting to retire.

Within a few weeks and after several meetings, Loizos negotiated the rent on the tiny shop in East Finchley; a rural area, with few houses but he had vision and knew London would be expanding and growing.

'One day, East Finchley will no longer be

countryside. I'm telling you, there will be homes and shops and bus routes and life as busy there as it is where we are now. All the immigrants need houses to live in and they can only be built where there are no houses already.'

Loizos was ready to trade immediately since the tools and equipment in the cobblers was similar to his own. His business quickly thrived. His workmanship didn't go unnoticed and before long there were gentlemen from the City sending their shoes for repairs and requests for shoes to be made to measure.

'Business is strong, *agabi mou*,' he told Anastasia one morning.

'That's wonderful news. We must give thanks to God.' She crossed herself and offered up a little prayer.

'And thanks to Him for bringing us back together,' he said as they both got ready to go to church for the Sunday Service of the Great Martyr *Panteleimonas*. Loizos hoped life would continue to be good to them in England after all.

Chapter Fifteen

Elena, 1959

ELENA, DESPITE HER art teacher wanting her to sign up for Art College, worked on the sewing machine at the factory where her mother now worked. Elena's education was secondary to any chance to earn a living due to the family's sporadic income.

Working at the clothes factory meant she was always being watched and criticised by her mother who worked at the sewing machine next to her. Sometimes the constraint stifled her breathing. With her father gone again her mother was clingy and relied on her too much.

As much as Elena loved her it was overwhelming at times. The strain swallowed her all too often. She wanted to have some fun, to live a little but declined every invitation from the other girls she worked with so many times they hardly bothered to ask her out anymore. Her mother seemed insouciant to her daughter's plight which made it worse for Elena.

Her only consolation was having the opportunity to talk to the pattern cutters and designers so she could learn as much as she could about the fashion industry. She asked questions and even helped out when she had finished her batch of machining. The pattern cutter often gave her the "cabbage"; leftover fabric after the sample patterns were cut. Elena used them to sew her own clothes at home. She sewed scarves and blouses and even a pair of shorts which she couldn't wear in front of her mother but she loved them. She still dreamed of being a fashion designer and every opportunity she had she would be at the designer's side taking everything in.

Elena slipped from one outfit into another, clothes strewn all over her bedroom as she tried to find something different from her practical work clothes to wear. She shivered against the cold seeping through the thin walls as she discarded a tunic dress. Since working she had begun to choose the sort of clothes she wanted to wear; one's she had observed in magazines lying around the factory floor and where she couldn't afford them she made her own improvising, tweaking, using the fabric remnants she had.

A feeling of ill-ease shrouded her otherwise excitement to be going out and was further exacerbated by her mother's complaining.

'You know I don't like you going out,' called Elena's mother from the sitting room.

'Oh come on *mama*. I've not seen Janet in six months and you don't need me tonight. All the washing's done. The ironing's done.'

'But it's so cold. You'll freeze when the wind's up your skirt.'

'I promised we'd keep in touch after we left school.

She's my best friend!'

'It's too cold.'

'I'll put my coat on. And my scarf.' Elena bit on her lip to stop her from raising her voice as she became increasingly agitated.

'And who will I talk to? Your brother's nowhere to be seen.'

'I'm sure he'll be home soon. Please *mama*. Just this once. I never go out and I've got my own money.'

'Well if you're happy to leave your poor old mum at home on her own while you go off with your friend.'

'I won't be late. I promise.' She gave her mum a kiss on both cheeks. She snatched her jacket hanging in the hallway and slammed the door behind her. She was free! She shook off the guilt and took a purposeful stride in her new boots. She invariably always stayed home with her mum and she was beginning to feel old before her time. She wanted to be out, having fun. There was no point in being in London if she couldn't enjoy herself, she thought.

Elena walked quickly. The biting February wind tugged at the scarf threatening to carry it away even though it was wound tightly around her neck. The house had been unusually stuffy and a niggling headache pressed around her temples. She breathed in the cold air deep into her lungs and the pressure in her head alleviated slightly. Her kitten heels click-clacked along the pavement as she sprinted with joy to the café her father once took her to…it felt like a long time ago.

'Good evening Mrs Berts.' Elena smiled at the post office clerk as she walked past.

'Good evening.'

She took in the whole street and wondered how she had ever not liked it here.

'Catch me!'

'You're going too high!'

She recognised a group of six or seven children playing on the street corner. A boy in a pair of shorts and black sturdy shoes swung from a rope suspended from the boughs of a tall oak. He was swinging back and forth higher and higher getting ready to jump. He sang with all his heart, screaming as he belted out a rhyme.

'When I went to Dover, saw a birdie flying over, up, up, up and over, when I went to Dover.' Two other boys joined in as they watched on, while a smaller boy and a girl were crouched in the dirt collecting stones and sticks. She shivered as she noticed they too were in short socks; their bare legs red raw from the sharp wind.

Further along the road still two boys were kicking a ball back and forth to each other while two older girls, perhaps twelve, did handstands up against the front of the house and cartwheels across the street.

A few minutes later she burst through the door of the café, knocking into a burly builder coming out at the same time. Giggling she sat opposite Janet.

'I thought you weren't going to come.'

266

'I said I would, didn't I? Hey what's the matter?' Janet had a look of panic about her; there were dark circles around her eyes and she had no makeup on. Janet always wore makeup; thick dark eyeliner, dazzling blue or green eyeshadow, layers upon layers of thick black mascara and the brightest cherry red lipstick.

'Sorry,' Janet said, nibbling on her thumb nail.

'Sorry? What d'you mean?'

'I...' Tears threatened to fall. Elena didn't like to see her friend in such turmoil.

'Let's get out of here. Come on.' Elena pulled her out of her seat and they both ran out of the café. They ran in tandem, Elena holding Janet's hand until Janet pulled free of Elena's grip and slowed down. Elena stopped a few paces ahead of her, doubled over, gasping. Janet winced, holding onto the stitch in her side.

'What are we escaping from?'

'Nothing. Everything.'

'What d'you mean?'

'I've got something to tell you.' They both took a few moments to compose themselves and then clinging onto each other walked to the Wimpy Bar, which had opened a few days before Christmas on the high street.

The waitress took Elena's coat and scarf and then waited for Janet to remove hers.

'Come on, slow coach,' teased Elena.

Janet took her coat off and squeezed behind the plastic red table. Elena gawped at her bulging tummy and then back at her incapable of hiding her utter shock.

'Before you say anything. I'm not fat. I'm pregnant. Almost nine months pregnant actually.'

Elena quickly found her voice. 'I had no idea.'

'Well neither did I till it was nearly too late.'

'I don't know what to say.'

'And before you ask, I didn't know I was pregnant when I last saw you. You going to say congratulations?'

'You didn't have a wedding without me did you?'

'No. No wedding. No husband. No ring.' She wiggled her empty wedding ring finger at her and sighed.

'Oh, Janet. What happened? I can't believe I didn't know. I can't believe you've done it. I can't believe you're not married. My mum would kill me.'

'Oh Elena. My sweet honeysuckle. Everything is a mess. A big mess.' Janet burst into tears. Elena got up and walked round the table. She shoved Janet up a bit and sat next to her, held her hand and stopped herself from commenting on her bitten down nails. She didn't say anything. Finally, Janet's tears stopped and after trumpeting her nose into a paper serviette she spoke again.

'His name was Graham. I met him one night in the pub. It was one of the girl's birthdays and she invited us all for a drink. I wouldn't normally have gone but she's a quiet girl and I felt a bit sorry for her. There was only four of us in the end.'

'And?'

'Well it was a blast! She sprayed a bottle of pop everywhere, soaked me.'

'And where does Graham fit in?'

'He said we could go out to dry off and well I don't need to spell it out do I?'

'You, you know, with him?'

'Yes. We clicked. You know. We went out to talk in the alley and it happened.'

'And was it worth it?'

'At the time yes. I don't know. He had the kindest eyes. Big soft hands.'

'But he didn't hang around when you told him you were pregnant?'

'I haven't told him. I've been too scared and then I tried to have an abortion.'

'An abortion?' Elena looked around the restaurant hoping nobody had caught what she'd said. Thankfully everyone was too engaged in either their own conversations or eating to notice her and Janet. She swallowed hard to steady her panic. 'An abortion? Oh Janet…'

'I couldn't do it. A friend of my brother's helped me get the money together but in the end I couldn't go through with it.'

'Oh my God, Janet, you poor thing.'

'I don't remember much. The woman was kind. I did whatever she asked of me. I went for a wee, even took my knickers off. I followed her to the kitchen.

'The kitchen? Oh my God Janet!'

'I got up onto the table covered in a white sheet. She helped me get into the right position, on my back. I remember the Geyser gurgling away as she washed her hands with hot water at the sink.' Janet's eyes watered.

'It's fine. She was lovely. Kind. She even brought me a pillow and put it under my head.'

'Oh my darling.' Elena fought back her own tears.

'But lying on the stained sheet with the doctor asking me questions I was scared rigid. I remember being so cold. So bloody cold.'

'I wish you'd told me. Oh Janet to have suffered on your own.'

'Well I didn't,' Janet said.

'I'm glad you didn't go through with it. You could've been seriously hurt. Damaged for life.'

'But now I'm here. Pregnant as can be. Mum won't speak to me. Dad's worse…won't even look at me. I've been staying at my aunt's on the other side of the river.'

'So that's why I haven't seen you around.'

'Yeah…I'm sorry.'

'No, I'm sorry. I should've realised something was wrong. I should've tried to find you.'

'I doubt Mum would've told you where I was.'

'The main thing is you're well. You're going to keep the baby aren't you?'

'We'll see. I want to keep it. I do. But Mum's being pressurised by Dad,' said Janet.

'Your dad'll come round. He's a softie under all his shouting and yelling. When are you due?'

'Within the next two weeks according to the midwife.'

'Oh Janet. Are you scared?'

'Too late to be scared. I want it to happen now. And I'm getting too fat.'

The waitress walked over and threw two menus onto the table.

'Let me know when you're ready to order,' she said in a clipped voice as she walked to the back of the restaurant towards the service hatch.

'Stroppy cow!' Janet fell about laughing as soon as the comment left her lips and Elena quickly joined in. It felt good to laugh. Elena hadn't laughed like this in a long time. Wiping the laughter tears from her eyes Elena picked up the menu. Janet stroked the top of her rotund stomach and eased back in her seat in an effort to move away from the table's edge which was digging into her.

'Too fat to even sit comfortably,' she half-heartedly complained.

'You're just a darling. Look at you. I still can't believe it.'

They ordered a Wimpy Grill each. Janet still fussy as ever, without the grilled tomato. They both ordered a strawberry milkshake.

They chatted about this and that; the latest fashions, the ups and downs of being a telephone operator, boyfriends, of which there weren't any, life as a machinist.

'No boyfriend? You can tell me you know,' said Janet as she sucked up the last of her milkshake through the straw.

'No, there isn't, Janet. I wouldn't be allowed. It's not how things are done in our culture. Mum's ever so strict and so is Dad.'

'But you live here now. Things are different.'

'Not in my house.'

'We need to see more of each other, though once the baby's here, I'm not sure how that's going to work.'

'You'll be fine. And yes, we will see more of each other. I promise.'

They finished eating the rest of their burger meal in relative silence. Elena couldn't eat all of it. Janet picked the fries off Elena's plate with her fingers. She pronged the curled saveloy sausage too and scooped it into her mouth chewing loudly.

'You're hungry.'

'Eating for two Els.' She patted her stomach and wiped the dribble of ketchup from her mouth with her folded serviette.

'It's dark. It's cold. I can't come all the way home with you but I can walk you to the station,' said Elena.

They walked arm in arm along the darkened street, the occasional pool of light from the street lamps guiding them. Fog cloaked the road ahead and Elena couldn't make out the houses on the other side. She snuggled up to Janet as they walked. She wondered what it would be like to have a baby growing inside of you. She liked the idea of having a baby. A little boy or girl to love and give kisses and cuddles to. Her own mother wasn't demonstrative, and Elena blamed her own father for that. Unless Elena gave her mother a kiss goodnight and a hug she rarely gave her one any more. She gave Janet a tight squeeze at the underground entrance before walking her short ten-minute journey home. She picked up her pace, realising the time.

As soon as Elena took a step inside the door her mother's slap stung her.

'What time d'you call this?' Her mother grabbed at her arm, wagging her finger in Elena's face.

'Mama! What's wrong with you?' Elena rubbed at her cheek, the sting hot under her fingers, the prickling sensation lingering.

'What would your father say?

'Well he's not here *mama* so there's nothing he can say.'

'Don't you answer me back. Where were you?'

'Out. With Janet.' Elena watched as her mother's eyes widened.

'Janet, Janet! She's a bad influence on you. I don't want you going out with her again.'

'She's not even the one who wanted to go out. I

wanted to go out. Yes, me.'

'Why? That's not how you should be behaving.'

'I'm sixteen, nearly seventeen and all I do is go to work…clean the house, cook, sleep.'

'What else is a girl's life about? A woman's life?'

'I want to get dressed up and put on make-up and laugh and…live! I want to live *mama*. And you should want to live too.' She looked into her mother's sad eyes, what she saw tore at her heart. 'All you do is hide in this house waiting for *baba*. But he doesn't care about you or me or Andreas. He's got another woman you know.' The second she said it, Elena regretted it. She flinched in anticipation of another slap but it never came. A stinging sensation on the backs of her legs reminded her of the slaps she used to get when she was younger, running around the courtyard of their home in *Kato Lefkara*. She would laugh and giggle, the giggling evolving into tears as her mother rained the slaps down on her bare legs. There was no giggling now though.

Her mother slumped onto the top stair.

'Don't you think I know? Don't you think I've seen them together?'

'What? Seen them?'

'From far away and beloved rather than close by and arguing.'

'Oh stop using proverbs to conceal what you really feel *mama*.'

'Don't tell me what I feel! That woman even

approached me at the bus stop one morning and introduced herself as a friend of my husband's. Plastered in make-up, devil red lips. Smelt like a *boudana* in a brothel. I remember exactly the feeling, it strangled me.'

'And you never said anything? You never mentioned it to me?' Elena's eyes stretched open to the point it pained her. She continued staring in disbelief at her mother. 'Why didn't you tell me? Why haven't you forced *baba* to stop?'

'Because the relationship between a husband and wife is no-one else's business.'

'Well Dad doesn't think that does he? He's making it her business and God knows how many others there are. No wonder he doesn't come home. He's like a dirty stray tom, roaming for a cat in heat…it's disgusting.'

'Don't talk about your father like that.'

'Oh *mama* pleaeease. I can't listen to you defending him. He's disgusting and I would never allow my husband to treat me like that. Never!'

Elena, with tears streaming down her flushed face, ran to the bathroom and slammed the door. She leaned over the sink, gripping onto the sides, her knuckles gleaming white with anger. She washed her face to take the heat out of her but an incensed irritation still flamed through her.

Her brother came in. The quiet of the night with only the cats screeching told her it was late. He pushed the bedroom door ajar and whispered her name, but Elena pretended to be asleep. She kept her eyes shut tight, held her breath, and when his footsteps receded along the hallway, she gently exhaled.

She was too tired and sad to talk to him. He was allowed to go out and enjoy himself while she was chained to her mother's side; at work, at home. This was no life. She wanted to be free. She wanted to escape the confines of her mother's small mind and unbending rules and reference to her culture and what was right and what was wrong. She wanted to find a man who would love her and cherish her and hold her hand. She had to find a way to make a life of her own away from her mother. She had to do it soon before she lost her mind.

***

A few weeks later, after a particularly tiring day at the factory, Elena ignored her mother's pleas to go straight home after work. Out in the unusually bright sunshine Elena decided to take a stroll around the park. Ahead of her padded a child, a stick in her hand, her golden curls circled by the sun's rays, like a halo. A woman shrieked as she stretched her arms ready to catch the child who toddled off balance.

As Elena entered Cherry Tree Wood, a man sat in a heap on the bare ground, leaning against the tree trunk of an old oak. His coat, threadbare in places with no buttons was secured around him with a piece of fraying string. He was playing the violin beautifully. The high shine of the instrument contrasted with his filthy fingers and dirt-ingrained nails. The sweet sounds echoed within the tree-filled space and heralded Elena's ears.

In front of him his upturned flat cap, placed on a folded newspaper, held three coins. They sparkled reflecting the light; mocking Elena's inner turmoil, mocking the bedraggled outer appearance of the man. She looked at him and he looked straight at her. She quickly turned away, embarrassed he had caught her staring.

'It's almost like being in love,' he sang to her.

Elena smiled shyly and carried on walking sorry she had no coins to give him. What sort of a life did he have? She wondered. And the thought took her to her father who she hadn't seen for nine weeks.

The last time she had seen him was before he visited the house while she and her mother were at work. He had raided the jam jar in which her mother put aside money for the rent. They found it capsized and empty on the kitchen table next to a plate of burnt toast and half a mug of milk. Since then he hadn't been back; had made no effort to contact her mother or any of them.

She wandered around the park taking in the fresh blooms and the green grassy banks, the violin's melody still dancing in her ears like fairy whispers. After a while, feeling calmer she decided to head off home. She didn't want another row with her mother.

As she rounded the corner to her street she saw a

police car; it was parked in front of her house. She gripped the shoulder strap of her handbag and ran.

'What's going on?' she asked just as her mother opened the front door.

'We have a warrant to search these premises.' The officer thrust a piece of paper into Elena's hand.

'Why? What's going on?'

'We believe Mr Kostas Ellinas lives here. We've been tipped off he's been dealing in fraudulent and stolen national insurance stamps. We're here to search the premises, love.'

'He's not here.'

'When's he likely to be back?'

'He doesn't…' She realised in time telling them her father didn't live with them would be a mistake. The police evidently were not aware of this and if they guessed it would have tipped them off to search elsewhere for the stolen stamps. Elena was in no doubt they would find her father guilty of the crime they suspected him of.

'But he doesn't know anything about this!' she said instead, focusing on her mother whose face was full of utter confusion.

The police officer and three others behind him pushed their way past Elena and her mother. They moved around the property with determination, organised and regimental; in their dark uniforms they reminded Elena of the infestation of black ants they once had in Cyprus; one went upstairs, one into the kitchen, one into the front room and the other into the back yard.

Elena glanced at the warrant wide-eyed. She couldn't believe her father's name was on it. Elena tried to console her mother who sat broken on the edge of the sofa, the stuffing escaping from the cushion under her bruising weight like a foam of sea; matching the anger in both their eyes, the hurt.

'I could absolutely kill him! What is he doing? Ruining our lives! Why did we ever come to this God forsaken place?' said Evangelia.

Elena sat with her holding her hand. The officer in the room downright ignored them as he emptied the drawers, pulled up the rug, pulled back the curtains, opened the small chest they used as a coffee table. Elena sat there and watched while cutlery, letters from Cyprus, her mother's Bible were tipped out onto the top of the cabinet. Two glasses smashed as they toppled onto the floor from the cabinet; shattered glass like shrapnel sparkled tauntingly in the harsh winter sun.

'Be careful with that! Elena snatched a vase from him.' He looked at her blankly and carried on sifting through the contents of an emptied cupboard over the floor.

Elena hugged the vase as if it were a newborn in her arms, stroking the curved sides absently as she leaned in towards her mother who held the Bible in her lap. The noise of their belongings being thrown out of place echoed throughout the house. She focused on the simultaneous ticking of the clock in the kitchen and in the sitting room; a comforting regular beat.

'Nothing upstairs,' announced one of the police officers from the bottom of the stairs. Elena noticed him looking at the hanging wall clock. He made as if to remove it from the wall but was distracted by another call from the kitchen.

'Nothing here either. The kitchen's clear.'

Within half an hour they began to concede. They loomed momentarily over Elena and her mother and filed out of the room one by one. Elena sighed. She could have told them they'd find nothing at the start.

'Sorry to have troubled you. Good evening.' The officer who had handed her the warrant tipped his hat and walked towards the front door.

The four police officers left to the neighbours' twitching curtains and their sudden frantic scrubbing of their front door steps. Elena watched the tail lights of the police car disappear. She closed the front door behind her but not before throwing the neighbours a dirty look; something she had mastered from Janet.

'Nosey old bats.' She laughed at the saying which Janet had taught her.

'*Mama*, it's fine. They didn't find anything. He won't go to prison.'

'I don't care about him going to prison. Not anymore. He's ruined me. Ruined all our chances of happiness.'

Evangelia stormed out and into her bedroom. Elena

followed her.

'Please *mama* enough.'

Elena watched as her mother snatched the *stefana* from the nail on the wall and threw them onto the bed. She then collapsed on top of them as the tears came. Her mother was inconsolable.

Elena disappeared into the kitchen. She set the metal kettle on the stove and waited patiently for the whistle to drown out her mother's sobs. As the shrill whistle cut across the silence of the house Elena wondered where her brother was.

The seriousness of what had just happened hit her. The police. The discarded *stefana*. Uncontrollable floods swamped her; tears of utter desperation. Tears for her mother, for her friend, for her, even her scoundrel of a father.

Chapter Sixteen

Evangelia, 1959

'TELL MR WASSERMAN I'll be in as soon as I can.' She was going to be late for work which had never happened before but her insides were rolling like a ship on a wild sea.

'Let me stay with you, *mama.*'

'No…you go…I don't want to give him an excuse to have a go at the both of us.'

'He's always having a go even when there's nothing for him to moan about.'

Evangelia huddled under a mound of blankets shivering; she exposed only her hands as she held onto the cup of tea made by Elena.

Evangelia heard the click of the latch as Elena left for the factory and within the hour she forced herself out of bed. She washed and dressed and taking her coat and handbag made her way carefully downstairs to the front door. She ignored the drift of uncollected mail on the mat.

Outside the air was biting and nausea engulfed Evangelia. She leaned on the front wall forcing herself to stay conscious. It must be something I ate, she thought. After a few minutes of slowly inhaling and exhaling, she quickened her pace towards the bus stop. She maneuvered

round three workmen who were shoveling thick clumps
of heavy clay back into a wide trench.

'Alright darlin',' spat one of them, his lips greasy
with butter as he chewed noisily on a doorstop sandwich.
She ignored him. Red-faced with embarrassment she
stared straight ahead and kept walking.

'Too posh to talk eh? Bloody foreigners!' He called
after her but she didn't glance back.

It was nearly half past ten by the time she alighted at
the other end; three hours late for her shift. She watched
as the grimy red double-decker revved and clumsily
plundered off along the busy road; the light of day glowed
dimly through the leaves of a huge chestnut. She shielded
her eyes against the harsh winter brightness and made
kissy sounds in the direction of a cat who sat in the tree's
shade licking its paws. She walked past the Jewish bakery
and the smell of freshly baked bagels followed her up the
street. Her stomach churned in response to the bready,
yeasty aroma. She felt her mood lifting and gave a weak
half smile at two nurses who walked past chatting to each
other distractedly.

As she walked across the cobbled courtyard of the
factory unit, the tall building cast dark shadows across the
paving slabs. She shook off a shiver; a dull heaviness
pulled at her limbs. She craned her neck and caught a
glimpse of her boss's face at his office window. He waved
to her, she could feel him following her with his eyes, but
she pretended to not have seen him.

As soon as she took off her coat and hung it on the rusty wall rack her boss strolled over.

'You can report to me at the end of your shift.' He stood over her, the whirr of the twenty or so sewing machines drowning his voice. She saw Elena glance over, gesturing at her mother to tell him to shut up. He obviously wasn't pleased and she dare not do anything to irk him further.

'Yes of course.' She stayed at her machine and worked through the next three hours not stopping even for a glass of water; she couldn't stomach anything.

'Lunch time!' Elena called as the old tin wall clock struck exactly 1.30pm.

'I'm not hungry. I need to get on. The boss isn't happy with me.'

'I don't care about him. He's a bully. You need to eat.'

'I'll eat at home later.'

'You're white as a ghost, *mama*...you have to eat something...drink something...' pleaded Elena. As Evangelia pushed and pulled the fabric through the foot of her machine the floorboards creaked and sighed under her weight in unison with her own sighs of exhaustion. The wooden box mounted on legs at the end of her machine quickly filled with the cuffed sleeves she was working on as she worked as fast as she could without compromising the quality of her stitching.

Elena however was persistent and eventually

Evangelia took a slice of bread and a chunk of cheese and placed it on the table of her machine. 'Thank you. But I'm going to work through.'

'Your daughter's right. He's a nasty piece of work. Wish I could tell him where to go...' said another Greek Cypriot woman who worked two machines away from Evangelia.

The afternoon passed with not so much as another word from the boss who would normally come out and yell at the girls for talking too much or for working too slowly. Five o'clock came around and Elena prompted her mum to stop machining.

'The boss wants a word so you go ahead and get dinner prepared. I'll be on the next bus,' said Evangelia.

'I'll wait for you.'

'No you go. He already thinks you're too big for your boots.'

Slowly the girls said goodnight and wandered off site leaving Evangelia at her machine. She felt duty bound to continue working even though she had never taken a day off sick or been late since taking employment at Ely's Dress Manufacturers.

Her boss eventually came out of the office slamming the door behind him, rubbing his big hairy hands together.

'So you think you can be late now you've been working for me a while, eh?'

'No not at all...I wasn't well.'

'Well you look well enough to me.' A combination

of halitosis and acrid sweat made her heave and she visibly recoiled.

'Sorry. It won't happen again.'

'No it won't. Or that daughter of yours and you will be outta here.' He moved a step closer towards her and she felt his thigh against her arm. She shivered. 'Anyway enough about work. I wanted to spend some time with you. You're a fine woman and you're never here alone.'

'Well I have to go now if that's all. Dinner won't cook itself.'

'Talking of dinner, I'm rather hungry...'

'My husband will be home soon so I can't be late.'

'Oh I know all about your husband...he's not even around is he?'

Evangelia peered at him. His pupils, menacingly black, pierced her. She pushed back her chair and made to get up from behind the sewing machine. She stumbled slightly as the chair tipped back and she tripped on the front leg. He reached out for her; his grip tighter than was necessary.

'Thank you,' she said, her head spinning worse than ever.

'If you really want to thank me, there's something else you can do.' Before Evangelia took in the situation he pushed her round and forced her over the sewing table. He pulled at her skirt and ripped her knickers down below her knees. He held onto her hair and pulled her head back as his urgent rough thrusting burned her. Her head thumped as she struggled to focus, her vision blurred. Her legs took root to the cheap linoleum floor, stiff with pain. It was over within a few minutes. She didn't stop him. She didn't scream out. She couldn't find her voice.

'Didn't realise you'd make it this easy.' He stood close, too close. His words grazed her cheek as sharply as if a knife edge scraped over it. She didn't look at him. She didn't move. She heard him pull the zipper on his trousers. The sound invasive, physically painful. She followed his footsteps across the factory floor to the office.

Terrified he would return she still didn't move. She didn't know how long she stayed there for but eventually her legs gave way; she dropped to the floor. Shaking, she pulled at her skirt to cover herself. A burning sensation gripped at her. Her insides tangled, twisted, knotted. There was blood running down the inside of her leg. She watched it, mesmerised by its lucid vigour. Then it trickled dry and into nothing, staining her leg a smudgy brown. She edged her knickers over her feet and scrunched them in her hand. Her knuckles white with anger.

A loud banging at the main doors startled her. She recoiled. Conscious of her state of undress; not wanting to be seen. She crouched behind the sewing machine gripping the back of the chair for support. Her legs still trembled beneath her, threatening to give up on her.

'No, I'm still here.'

'Well move aside. Let me in.' She heard a man's voice. She didn't recognise it.

'Not now. You know how it is, extra perks of the job.'

'You dirty dog.'

'Don't tell the wife.'

'Nothing to do with me. Leave you to it.'

'Thanks mate.'

'Will call back tomorrow. Want all the money you owe me.'

'Yeah sure. Counted out on my desk already.' She listened, too scared to breathe, as the door slammed shut and seconds later a car back fired outside in the courtyard before noisily screeching off. The engine noise echoed around the four walls of the inner courtyard and rang around in her ears bringing on the nausea again. She heard her employer cough, clear his throat. He called over to Evangelia.

'Call it a night luv. See you on Monday. Oh and this is our little secret.' Acid bile strangled her throat and she gagged, retching over the floor. Sick spattered two rolls of fabric and a bundle of zippers dumped next to her machine.

She wiped the back of her hand across her mouth. She pulled herself up holding onto the iron base of the sewing machine. She steadied herself and walked as a newborn lamb does towards the door gripping onto her handbag; her knickers stuffed into the bottom of it. As she approached him he sneered at her; looked her up and over; his brown teeth and comb-over crooked. He turned to go back into the office, dismissing her as if she was nothing.

Something in her snapped. Before he had time to spin round she snatched the iron reel holder from the stash outside the office and lunged at his back. He lay on the floor; groaning. She didn't expect the crack and his haunting gasp as blood seeped from the side of his head. His ear hung there; a baby bat, open, raw. He forced himself round, his face contorted into an ugly grimace. But she didn't see him. She didn't see a man. She saw an animal.

She dropped the reel holder. The clanking made her jump. He opened his eyes, tried to speak. She swore at him and then spat in his face. Cursing him in Greek. She walked towards the main doors. As she passed the office she saw the wad of notes on the desk. Without a moment's thought, she dashed in and grabbed it.

She slammed the door behind her. She remembered her coat. She couldn't go back now. She ran, her feet barely touching the dark concrete stairs to the ground floor. She pressed her open palm to her side to ease the growing ache and ran as fast as she could to the bus stop. She sat at the back of the bus wanting to hide away from the other passengers. The whole time she held onto her handbag with one hand, the other gripped the scrunched notes stuffed inside her cardigan pocket. As she tightened her hand she felt a searing heat run up her arm. That's my punishment, she thought.

***

'Dinner's ready *mama.*' Elena called across the long narrow hallway from the kitchen.

'Sorry I'm late. I just need to have a wash.' Evangelia called back as she disappeared into the bathroom. She locked the door behind her. She sat on the bathroom floor and cried her heart out.

'*Mama*, come on. Elena said dinner is ready.' Andreas sounded irritable.

'I'm coming Andreas *mou.* I'm feeling sick again, go ahead without me.'

When she eventually came through Elena and Andreas had already finished eating and she could see the back of Elena as she stood at the stone Butler sink washing some dishes.

'You don't look well, *mama*,' said Elena as she turned towards her, dripping soap suds onto the linoleum floor. 'Let me make you a cup of chamomile.'

'Thank you *agabi mou.* It's been a long day and this sickness has exhausted me.' She avoided Elena's eyes and sat at the kitchen table with her back to Elena on purpose; she didn't want her to recognise the pain she knew was etched across her features. She pushed her hand between her legs and could feel the heat coming off her;

the bruising hurt like hell. Oh the shame of it. She thanked God tomorrow was a Saturday. She would be alright by Monday. She had to be.

At 7.30pm Elena entered her mother's bedroom to check on her.

'Why're your clothes bundled like that?' she asked, pointing to the garments squashed into the corner by the dressing table.

'They're old…the cardigan's got holes in it.'

'But it's your favourite. *Theia* Panayiota sent it years ago.' She took a step towards the clothes.

'Don't Elena *mou.* Don't touch them. Something awful has happened. Call your brother.'

Elena and Andreas listened to their mother. Elena held onto Evangelia's hand and stroked it the whole time as her mother's tears continued to come. '*Mama*, we should call the police. He attacked you, he hurt you.' Elena bit on her lower lip. Evangelia knew Elena was afraid.

'Too right! He's an animal!' Andreas was raging, pacing the small bedroom.

Evangelia bit hard on her bottom lip as she recalled the version of events relayed to them; she omitted the rape. If they knew the truth. Oh, she felt so ashamed.

'*Mama*, are you listening? We should call the police.'

'No. It's not necessary. I'm fine. He's a businessman. He has a reputation. The police have already been here enquiring after your father. If they are here again we will be branded with a bad name. No. This stays between us. Promise me.' She grabbed Andreas and pulled Elena closer to her. 'No police.'

'Why?'

'Because,' she said as she pulled a pillowcase from under her and shaking it open showed them the crumpled notes.

'Where did you get all this?' asked Elena.

'I've never seen so much money,' said Andreas as he tried to hide his elation.

'I took it, from his desk.'

'You stole it?' Elena's eyes widened in disbelief.

'She didn't steal it. It was there.'

'However you justify it, Andreas, I shouldn't have taken it.'

'Well we can't take it back now. We risk getting caught with it.'

'We should hide it and use it when we need it. We mustn't tell Father,' said Elena.

'And I shall go to the factory and see what's happening,' said Andreas.

'I'm coming with you.' Elena gave her brother a defiant look.

'No, you stay here.'

'I'm coming. You won't find your way in; it's all doors and gates,' said Elena.

'What if he's still on the floor, dead?' Evangelia asked.

'Well let's be sure first. Then we can decide what to do.'

Andreas called for Georgette. It was Georgette who had heard about the flat above the launderette and put in a good word with the landlord who owned the launderette for Evangelia. Within a week Evangelia had moved her few belongings into the two bedroom flat; without Kostas.

Georgette bathed Evangelia. Evangelia could tell her friend had guessed what had happened to her but she said nothing. Both women held onto each other and Georgette allowed Evangelia's tears to flow freely. Evangelia was grateful but no words could comfort her. They sat mostly in silence. Before Georgette left the house Evangelia took her friend's hand in hers and asked to swear not to ever tell. With tears stinging her eyes Georgette swore on her life and left.

Evangelia sat up for the rest of the night waiting for Elena and Andreas to return home. Despite the Panadol and salt bath she was aching and on edge and uncomfortable; she could neither sit for long or lie for long; each position causing her to focus on the sensation between her legs.

The hands on the wind up clock next to her bed seemed to move more slowly as each hour passed. She flinched at the slightest sound, her body tense with fear; tense with the pain she felt. She doused herself with warm salted water to ease the pain but the stinging was unbearable as she dabbed herself. She heard the clattering of a dust bin lid and then the screeching of stray cats. The image echoed how she felt inside; dirty, unloved, abandoned.

She thought of *Kato Lefkara* and the tears fell unchecked as she made herself a cup of tea and took more Panadol to numb the pain. She heard voices.

'You should have stayed outside,' said Andreas.

'Why? Because I'm a girl. I wanted to come in. I need to do this for *mama*.'

'Elena *mou*, Andreas *mou*, thank God you are home safe.'

'Why are you out of bed? Where's Aunt Georgette?' asked Elena.

'She stayed as long as she could. Well, did you find him? Is he? Is he dead?' Evangelia felt the strain on her heart and in her head as she asked the unthinkable.

'No. I mean I don't know. He wasn't there.' Elena followed her mother back into the bedroom. The thud of Andreas' boots seemed to thump against Evangelia's head as he toed them off in the hallway. Moments later, he bundled into the room too, closed the door behind him.

'We went in. The door was unlocked. The light in the office was still on,'said Andreas.

'He never leaves the door unlocked.' Evangelia whitened, her hands shook. 'Oh dear Lord, what have I done? I have murdered a man...'

'Please *mama*, don't say that. He wasn't a man. He was a monster. A bully. If he's dead, I'll be glad!' Evangelia recognised Elena's tone sounded calmer than Elena must have felt inside.

'Oh dear Lord, what will we do?' Evangelia asked.

'We can't do anything,' said Andreas. 'He wasn't there.'

'Wasn't there?' Evangelia's eyes opened wide in horror.

'There was blood on the floor outside the office but no body. We cleaned the blood up… found bleach and cloths in the kitchen area. We wiped everything clean. Everything has been left looking normal. We cleaned around your machine too.'

'Elena *mou*, you went in despite promising not to? Oh dear Lord save us from our sins.'

'I had to get your coat. Andreas wouldn't have recognised it.' Evangelia recognised her excuse but said nothing more.

They both promised and Elena reluctantly agreed she and her mother would go back to work on Monday as usual.

'It's the only way we will find out if he's still alive and …if he is, whether he has reported me to the police…we'll get a knock at our door before then.'

That night Elena slept with her mother. Evangelia slept fitfully. Her eyes barely closed. Sleep evaded her. She woke drenched in sweat her heart beating so hard she thought it would escape from her chest.

'*Mama* I'm here. Don't be afraid.'

'Elena *mou?*'

'You've had a bad dream. You called out.' Evangelia hoped she hadn't called out anything to reveal her true torment.

'What did I say?'

'I couldn't make it out. But I'm here. You're dripping. Let's get you changed into another night dress.' Evangelia was glad it was still dark afraid Elena would see the truth of her attack revealed in her bruising.

And so her restless, haunted sleep continued for three nights. Monday morning came too quickly. Emotionally delicate and physically weakened after her ordeal, Evangelia coped too with the pain of the black and purple bruises between her legs reminding her of what had in fact happened. She had been spotting all weekend too but for that she was thankful. At least I know I'm not pregnant, she thought.

'We don't have to go in today if you're not well enough.'

'No *agabi mou*, I'm fine. We need the money.'

'I can find a job somewhere else, with better pay, until you're fit and well again.'

'I'm fine.'

Evangelia walked to the bus stop, more slowly than usual on Monday morning, the bruises on the inside of her legs more painful than ever. Elena held onto her by the arm and walked at her mother's pace.

Evangelia wobbled mid-step as she walked across the factory building courtyard; her feet already aching in her kitten heel shoes. She held onto the splintered banister as she climbed the concrete stairs to the workroom; she felt hollow with exhaustion. Her heart raced and she wiped a sweaty brow with the back of her hand.

The women bent over their machines worked as usual as Evangelia and Elena walked in. A few bid them good morning as they walked by them to their own sewing machines. The atmosphere no different as it normally would be after the weekend. A couple of the younger girls chatted to each other in Hungarian as they helped each other thread their machines. The boss was not on the factory floor. Evangelia noticed the office door was still ajar but she could not make out his silhouette behind the tinted pane of glass in the dividing wall.

She straightened her chair, still upturned where she'd left it on Friday. She settled at her machine and waited for the supervisor Josie, to bring her allotted bundle of garments to her. She felt Elena staring over at her. Evangelia glanced at Elena for a split second afraid she would cry if she locked eyes with her daughter for too long. She had to get a grip, no-one knows anything, she told herself as she switched on her machine.

'Looks like the boss had a party on Friday. Half a bottle of whiskey on his desk and papers strewn everywhere,' said Josie as she placed the bundle onto

Evangelia's sewing table. Evangelia gave her a watery smile, not trusting herself to speak.

The morning passed for Evangelia as sombrely as a funeral service.

The girls stopped for lunch at half past one. As the last machine silenced two policemen walked in. One was a foot taller than the other and automatically took out his notebook as they both stood by the entrance doors. Josie got up and walked over to them. Slowly the girls stopped talking one by one, curious as to what the police might want.

'We're looking for Mr Ely Wasserman.'

'I've not seen him this morning although he must've been in earlier. The factory was open when I got here at half past seven.'

'Would he normally be here now?'

'Yes he would. He likes to make sure the girls arrive promptly. He's a stickler for punctuality.'

'Do you know if he has any business in Kentish Town?'

'No. Why?'

'We found his car. There appears to have been an accident. There's blood over the dash, steering wheel and head rest.'

'Is he alright?'

'We have as yet been unable to locate him. We wondered if he might have made his way back here after the accident. His car is less than half a mile away.'

Evangelia listened carefully but her English failed her and she didn't grasp everything being said. She tried to remain calm and continued turning cuffs with a knitting needle on the dress sleeves stitched earlier.

'When did you last see him?'

'On Friday evening. At about half past six. I left him to lock up.'

'Can we search his office?'

'Of course. Go ahead. It's open.'

'Is that usual? For it to be unlocked in his absence?'

'It's always locked unless he's here.'

Evangelia watched, wide eyed, as the two policemen entered Mr Wasserman's office and rummaged around; opening the filing cabinets, drawers and file after file. The girls got up from their machines and making their way towards the kitchen area for lunch they slowed their pace outside the office to peer in. Some of them speculated about the whereabouts of their boss and whether he was dead.

'No point in gossiping,' said Elena. Evangelia remained silent. Her face as white as the wash on the village houses back home.

The police came out of the office and told Josie they may have to come back at a later date. They asked her to call them if she heard from him or remembered anything. They left as quickly as they arrived and didn't ask to speak to any of the other staff. Evangelia sighed in relief.

The rest of the afternoon passed by too quickly and

when it was finally time to clock off Evangelia was one of the first to leave her work station.

She walked in silence with Elena next to her. She didn't say anything to Elena until they were a few paces from home.

'The police can't find him. Oh Lord I am in so much trouble Elena *mou*.'

'*Mama* listen to me. The police don't suspect a thing. It sounds like they believe he was in a car accident. End of. Don't volunteer any information at all. To anyone. Josie included. Did she see you still at the factory on Friday when she left?'

'I don't think so. She would have said goodbye to me had she known I was still there.'

'Don't say anything,' said Elena.

***

The following morning the police were back, one of the police officers from the day before and a different one. This time they wanted to interview each member of staff.

'So you left the factory at what time?'

'At half past six. She was ill in the morning, so she stayed late to make up the time.' Elena translated for her mum.

'And did you see or hear anyone? Anyone hanging around? Did anyone come to the factory?'

Evangelia shook her head from side to side. 'No,' she

answered.

The younger of the two police officers noted her address and asked her to come back to him if she thought of anything else. Evangelia and Elena left the factory. Outside Evangelia crumpled. She couldn't bear it any longer. The lies, her daughter lying for her, the rape; it was all too much for her; she felt crushed.

The days and weeks passed and slowly the girls got used to working in a happier more jovial atmosphere. None of them had ever particularly liked Mr Wasserman. Josie rose to the challenge, especially when she was offered more money and kept things running as agreed with Mr Wasserman's brother who persuaded her to 'keep things ticking over'. No-one caught up with the man who had come to collect his money. Elena told her mum it was likely to do with something illegal and so it was unlikely he would come forward even to say Mr Wasserman had company on the night he disappeared. The safe had not been broken into and so no-one was aware any money had been taken.

Weeks later, the first crocuses pushed through the hard ground and the gossip had quietened. The new routine without Mr Wasserman became the new norm. At that moment one of the Hungarian girls rushed in waving a newspaper. All the machinists, apart from Evangelia, sprung from their sewing machines to marvel at the headline somewhere in the middle of the front page. "Factory owner found dead" read the header.

There were oohs and ahhs and a few cries of horror but generally the girls were used to him not being around now. They had all found themselves at the end of his tongue-thrashing or sarcasm at least once. He was unlikely to be missed. Evangelia fought hard against the tears which sprung to her eyes. She disappeared to the toilets and cried into a handful of toilet paper. She was relieved and yet on edge. This would now be a murder enquiry.

Chapter Seventeen

Elena, 1959

IT ALL HAPPENED so quickly and Elena found herself on a train to Blackpool. It was a long journey. Her mum huffed and puffed complaining about the noise, the air, the people on the train. Elena in contrast was excited to be going somewhere new; it was an adventure. Getting away from London locked the nightmare of the attack on her mother in a fortress, with high walls and barred windows.

***

In Blackpool they were welcomed with open arms and big generous hearts and although they were there to work, and the work was tiring, Elena's spirit was light and carefree; every day felt like a new beginning, a new adventure. She had heard so much about the cousin she didn't know, she felt she knew her already, and was sure they would get on.

In contrast to her life in London, where she was always at work with her mum, or at home with her mum, here she felt unrestricted, like a caged bird set free. She instantly liked her cousin Margarida and her playful, fun nature and it brought out Elena's cheeky side, which Evangelia didn't encourage.

The work in the chippy was hard. It was physical and the hours were long as well as the amount of preparation needed in advance of each day. But Elena and her mother soon found their rhythm, whereas Andreas seemed to take off and use his time as he saw fit. Elena wondered where he disappeared to. Why didn't their mother ever question him?

Elena's aunt gave Elena's pay envelope directly to her and so for the first time in her life, Elena had her own money. She gave most of it to her mother knowing how much they needed it to pay what they owed back in London but the little she kept gave her a sense of freedom and she relished in it. She bought ice cream cones, a scarf from the market and encouraged by her cousin, she even bought herself a pair of ruby red kitten heels.

Three weeks into their seven week stay, Elena finally persuaded her mum to take an afternoon off. She could see how exhausted she was and wondered how her mind was too.

Elena couldn't wait to get to the beach which was filled with holiday makers from one end to the other. It was the first time she had seen the sea since Cyprus and the first time she was on an English beach. paper streamers and flags and bunting cheered from all directions; all-singing and all-waving arms welcoming her. The sand was sticky, big fat granules a dull yellow, the sea a disappointing murky green reflecting the grey-blue sky and weak slices of sunshine.

However, despite the cold sand and the dull crashing waves of the sea she looked around her full of excitement taking in the vivid cacophony of colours in everything; rows of striped deckchairs, flapping windbreakers pushed into the sand, buckets and spades discarded by children as they sat licking at their ice lollies, the sticky juice staining their chins.

Elena marvelled at the many people still on the beach, fully clothed, since there was more cloud than sunshine in the dirty grey-blue sky above. Some had their skirts and dresses hitched high over their knees while others lounged with shoes and tights, men in long trousers still in their shoes and socks, flat caps shading their eyes from the sun. It was a funny sight!

'Look at everyone in their clothes, even their shoes,' remarked Elena.

'Well it's hardly warm enough to take off our cardigans let alone get our feet out. We'll catch our death.'

'Come on Elena! Margarida!' called Elena's mum. Elena didn't utter another word as she followed her mum who stomped ahead.

'He was a toffee apple and candy floss rolled into one,' drawled Margarida.

'You're mad.'

'I'm going to show you what Blackpool's all about

chuck if I can get you away from your mum!'

'Good luck with that one, Mags.'

'Never say never,' she said winking with one eye and then the other.

'Show off.'

'But don't you just lo-o-ve me?' she sang in a ting-a-ling voice. Elena shook her head in mock denial. This was the most fun she'd had since leaving school and Janet.

Andreas walked ahead of them and found a spot amongst the sprawling holiday crowd and laid out a blanket and two bath towels on the sand eventually pegging the corners with the two bags and his shoes as she fought against the breeze coming off the cold-looking sea. Elena threw herself onto the sand and kicked off her shoes, toeing them off as she lay back feeling the weak sun on her face. It wasn't the heat of the Cyprus sun but it was warm all the same and she smiled as she closed her eyes, humming a little tune out loud.

A family of seven sat next to them; the leftovers of an earlier picnic still strewn across a stained tablecloth. The dad had a knotted handkerchief on his head and he was leaning all the way back in his deckchair reading a newspaper, holding its flapping pages at an angle to block the sun from his eyes. The woman lounged in the deck chair next to him, her legs stretched out over his; her bare feet sandy, her trousers rolled up around her knees. She was in her bra; pale pink silk with wide elasticated straps which were cutting into her fleshy upper arms where she had lowered them to avoid getting strap marks. She had her eyes screwed tight against the sun and her face was shiny with sweat; Elena could see beads of perspiration sitting in her hairline around her forehead. Both adults, seemed oblivious to the arguments around them between the five fair-haired children; Elena guessed they were between the ages of six and fifteen, maybe sixteen.

'You ate three sandwiches, you liar!'

'No I didn't.'

'So what if he did?' said one of the older girls.

'You can shut up you scrawny thing.'

'I'm not. Muuuum…'

'Leave Mum alone. She's sleeping.'

'No she's not. Mum never sleeps in the day.'

'Well she is today.'

'Muuuum…'

Elena listened to the conversation back and forth between them and it reminded her of times gone by playing games in the school playground in Cyprus. Everyone talking, joining in, no-one listening to anyone in particular…they had been happy-go-lucky days she hadn't appreciated at the time. She should have treasured them more, she thought, and she wondered about Yioli and Stella and Mirianthi. And Niko too.

A couple walked past holding hands. Elena looked across at them and envied the girl. She was wearing shorts and a matching bra top, her slim midriff showing. She had her hair scooped in a soft beehive, her eyes hidden behind sunglasses. Her tan sandals matched her handbag; its strap was wrapped around her wrist. She laughed, openly flirty, at something her boyfriend said and he laughed too. Elena noticed his loose blue shirt, buttons undone to his waist, a pair of cream coloured shorts underneath. His hair was swept into a quiff and flopped over his forehead. He was carrying a striped canvas bag and a beach towel over one arm, his other arm was around the girl's waist as they walked across the sand, clumsy and awkward as their feet sunk deeper, the girl's sandals filling with sand. The girl stopped, and leaned onto him shaking the sand granules out. Behind them another couple were following close by.

'I wish Janet could've come with us,' said Elena.

'This isn't a holiday Elena. We're here to help out your aunt and uncle and to get some money together to pay the overdue rent.'

'Well she deserves a holiday Mum. She's been through a lot.'

'Enough. Stop dreaming girl and remember why we're here.'

'Bit difficult to forget mum when it's all you keep going on about.' Elena regretted saying it as soon as she did. She knew how much stress her mum had been under the past few weeks with her dad going AWOL again and the rent falling into arrears. She thought about her dad and for a second she hated him. She hated him so much she didn't even want to call him her dad any more. He was no good for them. She could see that and she hated herself for it but she wished her mum would meet someone else, someone who would love them all.

She closed her eyes again and thought about the sort of life she would have if her dad had provided for his family like the head of the household should. She wouldn't have to be working in the poxy fish and chip shop and she would be at art college surrounded by lovely arty people and friends. She still dreamed of going to art school and although she didn't have much time for drawing she often sketched her ideas on the backs of used envelopes and even paper napkins from the fish bar.

Her mum settled on the blanket and Andreas sat next to her, arms clasping his knees drawn up against him as he openly admired the girls going by. Evangelia smacked him on the arm telling him to show some respect but he simply laughed at her and pinched her nose between his thumb and two fingers, twisting it, his playful mood matching the fun, beach atmosphere.

'Look the blackbird's got your nose, Mum,' he teased. Evangelia tutted.

'If your father were here…'

'Well he's not Mum so stop going on about him. You said yourself, we only have each other to rely on so why are you even mentioning his name?'

'Well what do you want me to do? Pretend he doesn't exist? I can't and anyway be quiet. I don't want your cousin knowing our business.'

Elena felt her mum's pain and her shame; she had felt the same too over the years and realised too it must be worse for her. Being here was making them all a bit tetchy and she cursed her dad under her breath, but quickly bit her tongue to stop the curse from coming true.

Andreas opened his mouth to say something and Elena shook her head to tell him to stop. He diverted his attention to three girls walking past. One rubbed her bottom to shake off the sand from the back of her red shorts. The beach was noisy; children chasing each other, toddlers begging for donkey rides, babies crying in the heat; their little lungs raw from screeching. The sound of the promenade fair in the background blasted its tunes across the open air, muffling the screams from the roller-coaster log flume, as the riders dipped into the first drop of the ride. Above it all, much closer, the bell of the ice cream vans parked along the beach front tinkled. Elena could just make out the Derby racer with its white horses; the outside horses seemingly moving faster than the inner ones as those riders held on with all their strength.

Two haphazard rows in front of them, two girls crept up behind a man sleeping in a deck chair, his trousers pulled to his knees and his bare feet resting in his shoes. They stifled their giggles as they stuck flags on little cocktail sticks between his toes and behind his ears. He flinched a little and the girls jerked back shocked by his sudden movement, but he settled without delay, scratching one of his elbows before crossing both his arms across his belly.

***

A few hours later, emptying sand from their shoes on the road side by the top of the beach, a young woman balanced herself on the iron railings at the top of the beach. She looked out into the road, her dark blue dress with a full skirt and white polka dots all over it. Her head was thrown back in merriment as she tried to hold her skirt over her legs which had been lifted by the sudden wind creating a balloon around her thighs. A little girl sat on the pavement in front of her playing with a bucket of sand and her spade. She scooped the sand out bit by bit and piled it on the ground and next scooped it back in again. Elena was about to point the little girl out to her mother when Evangelia called out.

'Koulla? Koulla!'

The woman in the dotty dress stopped laughing.

'Evangelia? I can't believe it's you. What are you doing here?'

'Koulla I'm so glad you're well. I kept going over that dreadful day again and a...' Koulla shook her head from side to side and interrupted her.

Elena saw a look of bewilderment cross her mother's face and wondered what had caused it.

'These must be your twins. Lovely to meet you both.' Elena couldn't take her eyes off Koulla. She looked like a model; porcelain skin, shiny hair and a figure to die for. She felt guilty for comparing Koulla to her mother who made little effort when it came to her appearance and wondered whether it was lack of money or lack of self-esteem. She often tried to persuade her to buy something a bit more modern but she always insisted on wearing the same clothes over and over again.

'We're at the Sea Blue Chippy overlooking the promenade. Come by and we'll talk. I'm so happy to see you Koulla. Glad to see you are safe.'

'I'll do that, thank you Evangelia. It's lonely here on my own and the work here is coming to an end. I can't rely on my family forever.'

'I'm here for another month or so, so don't miss us. Come soon.'

'I will. I promise. I may even come to London for work.' Elena wondered who she was too because she didn't recognise her from Cyprus.

'I'm here for the summer, helping out, that's all. If you decide to come to London perhaps you can travel back down with us.'

'Really? Oh Evangelia *mou*. You're too kind,' she said jumping from her perch and taking the little girl by the hand.

'See you soon, then, Koulla,' her mother waved goodbye and the child smiled, revealing two top teeth missing.

'God willing,' said Koulla.

Two nights later Elena was serving in the Fish and Chip Shop; her mother had taken poorly and had finished early so Elena and Margarida not only served and cleared tables but also fried the fish and chips.

'Get me some more newspapers from out the back. I'm running out,' said Margarida to Elena. She wiped her hands on her faded flowery pinafore and put the metal tongs back on the shelf above the fryers. The air was stifling; the smell of fish and oil and greasy brown vinegar.

'Let me finish this batch of cod and I'll go.' Elena gave a big sigh as she wiped her brow with the back of her hand, the heat from the hot oil rising around her like a steam bath. She looked towards the outside of the shop, beyond the punters queuing, grease-streaked windows and oil-marked walls; this was surely a prison and if it hadn't been for her cousin and the banter with the tourists, she would have gone mad.

'The usual?' asked Elena as she smiled at Old Man Bob. She took the newspaper sports pages she had put to the side for him and laid out his cod and chips, throwing in a gherkin and a pickled onion. She smothered the food with salt and vinegar and wrapped the meal in newspaper. She knew it would be his only hot meal of the day. He came into the shop every day at half past five; not a second earlier and not a second later and as a local, he was well known and respected. She had heard the stories of how he lost the sight in one eye in the Second World

War and was a local hero for saving the lives of two lads, twins, who lived a few miles further along the coast.

Elena knew he was lonely and she saved the sports pages for him so he would have something to read in the evening. She winked at him and as she handed the warm parcel to him he gave her a toothless grin back.

'You're a pretty one you are. If only I was twenty years younger.'

'And the rest,' called out Margarida as a mischievous grin spread across her face.

'Cheeky mare,' he said. His spirit was unbroken and he always had time for a natter. Some days he would lean against the counter and tell them of his lady friends and the loves of his life; he'd had many but he had never married. 'Not after losing my Mavis. I couldn't marry anyone after her,' he would tell them often with a pool of tears behind his eyes.

As Elena peered over the fish and chip fryers and warming trays she saw Little Pete and his brother Tommy standing by the door. She gave them a smile. Mrs Abott, a widow with five young children lived three streets away. Elena had taken pity on her and had dropped in the leftovers during her break one afternoon and ever since it became their understanding she could have the scraps.

Elena unlocked the back gate and let the boys into the yard. 'Give me a minute. We're so busy I'll be as quick as I can.'

She served another six regulars before she managed

to run back to them. She found them sitting on the cold floor; both jumped to attention when they saw her come out. 'There's a couple of pies in there too but don't tell anyone about those. And say hello to your mum from me.'

Little Pete took the two newspaper bundles from her and ran off with Tommy in tow; neither one of them said a word.

'If I see another gherkin I'll be sick,' Margarida said as she rolled three portions of oily skate and an extra scoop of chips in the last of the newspaper.

'Oh Mags if I see another pickled onion I'll be sick,' said Elena and although she was exhausted, the backs of her lower legs aching from her high heels, she was still smiling.

Margarida fell into a plastic chairs as the last of the punters walked out. The hours passed without Elena hardly realising and it was past eleven o'clock when she finally turned round the fish-shaped "CLOSED" sign on the door. Her aunt and uncle left for the night leaving them to clean up. Both girls stunk of fish and deep fryer fat and they still had at least another half hour of work to do before being able to call it a night.

'D'you fancy going out?' asked Margarida, mischievousness spreading across her face, as she pulled herself up from the chair. She dismissively brushed the bits of batter leftovers from the warming trays.

'Where?' Elena's spirit perked up straight away. She stopped mopping and leaned on the mop; the steamy pine of *ZAL* hung in the air.

'My old school friend runs a pub, he'll let us in for a night cap if we hurry. He's always up late with his groupies.' Margarida threw the scoops, shovels and scrapers into the deep sink in the back corner of the shop and the clanking against the porcelain of the sink echoed around the empty shop. 'They can soak overnight with the fish trays,' she said.

'Gosh, Mags it sounds like fun but won't we get caught?' Elena was wiping over the metal plaque on the wall. Her cloth dragged across the embossed words "RESPECT AND LOVE GETS THINGS DONE", tacky as it clung to the grease. She rubbed with vigour until it wiped clean.

'We won't,' said Maragarida.

They disappeared into Elena's room above the shop and got changed; there wasn't enough time to wash their hair but at least they changed their clothes. Elena put her ear flat against her mum's bedroom door checking she couldn't hear any movement. She crept out in stockinged feet as quiet as a mouse, her shoes in her hand.

Outside, Elena leaned into Margarida as she squeezed into the shoes Maragarida had lent her. With their arms interlocked, they walked down the street, both smoking. Elena's ankle kept going over as she tottered in the high heels which were at least two sizes too small. But she was glad to be out in the open air. They sneaked to the back of the bar and rapped on the door with their knuckles.

'Mick, it's me Mags. Let me in.' Margarida let out a sigh of relief as she heard someone unbolt the door. It opened revealing, in contrast to the dull exterior, a shiny, spacious bar.

'This is Elena. My posh cousin all the way from London.'

'Well, hello. Pleased to meet you,' said Mick taking Elena's hand and kissing it gently twice before straightening up; he was over six feet tall and despite his long roman nose and thin lips, Elena found him attractive.

'Pleased to meet you too,' said Elena stifling a giggle, unsure whether his affectionate gesture was genuine or a showy act. Behind him she saw three angelic-like girls, all with blond hair, sitting in the amber light of the cracked wall lamp. A couple of lads threw crisps across the table at each other sending potato crisps in all directions.

'I finally meet the mysterious cousin from London,' said Mick.

'I am?'

'Yep! What music d'you like?'

'Oh, umm, Cliff Richard, Buddy Holly, Shirley Bassey.'

'I'll see what I can do for you.' Mick walked over to the Juke Box with a swagger Elena wanted to laugh at.

'You're my living doll,' he said turning back to her, as the popular Cliff Richard tune blasted out. Two of the girls sprung to their feet to dance.

'Come on,' they both said to Elena and Margarida, but Mick had already taken Elena by the hand and pulling her gently was moving to the beat.

At first shy, Elena gingerly hopped from one foot to the other but as she gained her confidence she swung her hips and twirled in towards Mick and out again as he held her by the hand. She pirouetted like a ballerina. The music draped her like silken swathes. She loved listening to music and now she realised how much she liked dancing to it. They danced together through Eddie Cochran's *C'mon Everybody* and Elena drank Coca-Cola with something in it, but she wasn't sure what.

Elena kicked off her shoes in the middle of the song, glad to be able to wriggle her toes free. She danced with Margarida and Mick and even laughed at her stockings now snagged from the rough wooden flooring, sticky with spilt drink.

'We gotta go, Els,' said Margarida eventually, pointing at the clock behind the bar. She pulled Elena from the seat she was slumped in.

'I wanna stay. I'm having such a good time. I feel alive!'

'You most certainly are,' said Mick, slurring his words and leaning in to kiss her. Elena moved towards Margarida's outstretched hand and Mick's kiss landed half way between her lips and her left cheek.

'Guess we gotta go then,' said Elena, her smile radiating her otherwise tired, now pale face.

'See you tomorrow?' asked Mick.

'Not a chance,' said Margarida as she fiddled with the lock on the door.

'Night night, Mick. It was lovely to meet you,' said Elena and she blew him a kiss.

Mick caught it, put his fingers to his lips and pretended to faint as he fell back onto the banquette.

'If we get caught...' said Margarida as they walked home like baby deer taking their first steps.

'If we do, it was worth it and...' Elena didn't finish her sentence as she threw up on the pavement and all over her cousin's shoes.

'Oops,' she giggled.

'Let's get you home.'

***

Not getting found out emboldened the girls. Both nervous, they had promised each other there was no changing their minds, and they entered the Blackpool Bathing Beauty Competition.

Elena didn't have a bathing suit of her own and so she borrowed one of Margarida's which was a bit big round the hips and a bit tight round the bust but it was the best she was going to get.

They hatched a plan to get out of work the day of the competition. From the night before they both complained of stomach cramps running in and out of the outside lavvy. They grumbled about being sick each time, to make it as authentic as they could.

'You've caught something. A bug. I can't have you working in the restaurant if you're ill there's no knowing who might catch it and they'll blame our fish and chips,' said Elena's aunt.

The next morning, after Elena was sure her mother would be busy downstairs with the lunch time trade, she and Margarida got ready for the bathing competition.

'If we get caught,' said Elena.

'We won't El,' said Margarida, applying her thick black eyeliner and mascara and an hour later they were on the promenade with a group of eighteen other girls.

'Ooh, fourteen's my lucky number,' said Margarida slipping the white cardboard plaque around her wrists so it faced upwards.

'Well I don't have a lucky number but if I had to have one I'd say fifteen was the one,' said Elena as she was handed the number fifteen. She positioned the band on her wrist and, warming to the clicking cameras of the local reporters, she gave them her biggest smile. After a strut up and down the make-shift cat walk, with crowds of holiday makers watching and cheering, it was time for the winners to be announced.

'Number fifteen,' yelled Mick as he waved his arms at Elena. He promised he'd come to watch and he had. Elena smiled back at him. She remembered the sneaky kiss they'd had behind the fish shop two nights before. Her first proper kiss.

'And in reverse order the Blackpool Beauty Queens are...' Elena and Margarida gripped onto each other. Elena's heart thumped with nerves.

A scream rose around them every time a winner was announced. There were tears of joy and disappointment. The contestants kissed each other and hugged and the onlookers dispersed along the promenade and onto the sandy beach. There were tears of joy, tears of disappointment.

The winners posed, sashes and bunches of flowers with parched petals in their arms, sitting on two wooden boats, stranded on the beach, the Blackpool Tower and a fluttering Union Jack visible behind them.

***

'Oh gosh, Mags if we'd won there would've been hell to pay. We lied about our age, we would've been in the paper and my mum would've killed me for sure!'

'There's a chance we might still be in the paper.'

'You're a winner in my book,' said Mick as he kissed Elena on the cheek.

'Hopefully I'll be home by then and your mum will

be too busy wrapping fish and chips to read the pages!' said Elena as she wriggled free of Mick. 'Stop it, Mick, please, someone'll see us.'

'I don't care,' he said, pulling Elena towards him again as she giggled.

'We really are prettier than the others,' said Margarida, giving him a look.

'Well it was fun and I'm glad we did it. Now we have to sneak back in. Without you Mick!'

'Not yet. Let's go and get an ice cream. Walk along the beach. Did you see some of those guys?'

'They were nice I suppose,' said Elena.

'Nice? My *yiayia's* dress is nice! They were so handsome.'

'We're sure to get into trouble with you carrying on like that,' said Elena.

'Better make it worth your while then,' Mick said, winking at her.

***

Walking back towards the fish and chip shop Elena's stomach churned with hunger and nerves.

'My mum's sure to notice something. Oh Mags.'

'We've washed our make-up off, we've messed up our hair, so let's say we went for a walk to get some air. To shake off feeling sick.'

'If she says anything, you do the talking. She'll know

I'm lying to her.'

They approached the fish shop and Elena's mum was brushing around the front door step. 'Don't even think about lying to me, Elena. I know where you've been. All afternoon we've had customers saying how pretty you both looked and how you should've won the competition.' She threw a bucket of soapy water over the step and scrubbed with the brush again.

'Mum, I'm sorry.'

'Don't lie to me. You're not sorry. Here I am struggling to make ends meet and you're off prancing around half naked. It's shameful, That's what it is.'

'It was my fault, *theia.*'

'It's not your fault Margarida. I blame my daughter who's become a liar. Shows no respect for me or our traditions anymore.'

'Mum, please don't say that. You know it's not like that.'

'Then tell me what it's like Elena because I don't know what's happened to you!'

Elena tried to console her mother but she shook off her hug and refused to speak to her for the rest of the day.

Elena worked the evening shift with Margarida, in silence, until Old Man Bob came in and brought a smile to their faces.

Night fell and as Elena lay in bed, she deciphered her feelings. She loved her mother dearly but she was beginning to love the life England enticed her with more. Mick had awakened something in her. Blackpool had injected light and hope.

She fell asleep, not with a heavy heart but, with a fluttering, new excitement in her and dreamt of sandy donkey rides and vanilla ice cream and polka dot bikinis and hot kisses.

Chapter Eighteen

Christaki, 1959

PETE PULLED CHRISTAKI to the side of the yard.

'I saw Janet from across the street a few weeks ago,' he whispered.

'A few weeks ago?'

'I didn't speak to 'er. Just saw 'er like. Kept me distance.'

'And?'

'And nothing.'

'Did she look well?'

'Yeah. Looked fit and 'ealthy like. She'd just come out of the Wimpy with another girl. I didn't exactly stare at 'er.'

'Why didn't you tell me before?'

'I don't know. I didn't hang around. Didn't want to get beaten again by 'er old man. He coulda been watchin',' said Pete.

Christaki though was relieved to discover Janet was alive and well. He wondered what sort of a girl she was? How scared she must have been going through an illegal abortion on her own.

***

As the months passed by Christaki was becoming more comfortable living in London. He adapted to the pace, the noise and even the pubs and the thought of going out one evening excited him.

He had arranged to meet Pete and four other lads from the site at The Sir George Robey pub in Finsbury Park. He had avoided going to the pub since the incident with Kevin and he wouldn't normally have gone out on a Monday but Cliff Richard and The Drifters were live at The Empire. Pete had persuaded him to go. Their boss had even allowed them to clock off fifteen minutes before the end of their shift.

'Look at you!' cajoled Pete, as Christaki walked into the pub.

He knew he stood out in his winkle-pickers, slim cut un-pleated trousers and polo shirt with lime zig zags across it. Christaki walked over to the group sitting under the sloped timber ceiling.

'Hello,' he said noticing two new faces; girls he'd not met before.

'Is that you Chris?' Pete looked at him as if seeing him for the first time.

'You said make an effort.'

'And you certainly did that,' said Janet introducing herself. 'Nice to meet you. This is my best friend in all the world, Elena.'

'Oh, hello.' So this was Janet. Christaki's mind clouded with panic on seeing Janet and other feelings charged at him as he stared at Elena. An overwhelming excitement and a sudden giddiness came over him. Elena had a modern, adventurous vibe about her; nothing like any of the girls he remembered from the village.

'Bloody 'ell Chris, cat got your tongue?' Pete shrugged at Janet and Elena. 'This is my mate Chris. He's from Cyprus too.'

'I would never have guessed,' Elena said. She smiled and he suddenly felt hot and bothered. He took his jacket off and threw it across the back of one of the velour chairs; stained and pot-marked with cigarette burns. *I Need Your Love Tonight* by Elvis Presley blasted out from the Juke Box.

'Right. Let's get the drinks in now we're all here. The show opens in under an hour so we have to get moving,' said Pete.

Pete and Christaki both made their way to the bar. Pete ordered the drinks, spouting them off one after the other with no problem.

Christaki sighed with relief since his mind was clouded with the image of Elena; she was absolutely beautiful with big almond eyes and kissable lips. He looked back over his shoulder and took in the soft waves of her hair styled in a fashionable beehive; wispy tresses straggling her slender neck, teased him seductively. He couldn't believe he was feeling like this. But for now, he had to get a grip.

'Am I right in thinking that's Janet? The one

SOULLA CHRISTODOULOU

who…What are you doing inviting her? What if her father sees her with you? He's sure to kill you this time.' Christaki blurted out to Pete, glad he hadn't noticed him going quiet around Elena. Christaki battled to hide his bubbling feelings.

'I didn't invite her. She was here already. How can I tell her to go? To not talk to me?'

'So it's the same girl?'

'She has no idea what her old man did to me, Christaki. She's innocent in all this.'

'She can't be innocent if she got pregnant, Pete. For God's sake!'

'Look, she seems okay. Isn't that the main thing?' Ignoring him, Christaki grabbed a metal tray from the end of the bar and, balancing the array of glasses on it, he walked back across the pub to the others. His shoes pulled against the tacky stickiness of the floor and, as he handed out the drinks, he fought off his mixed feelings.

Christaki pulled a chair over to the group, the legs scraping across the floor. He squeezed into the circle between Pete and Elena. She shifted her seat over slightly to give him a bit of extra leg room and as she held onto the side of her chair, Christaki felt her hand graze his arm. Electricity ran through him and he almost bounced with the joy of it. His anger abated and something else took over. An unfamiliar sensation filled him; a feeling he liked.

He noticed Elena was smoking and found himself

wondering whether her parents knew. He wondered too whether she enjoyed the break with conventions and knew his parents would be most disappointed if Melani smoked; something a good Greek girl didn't do. But strangely, as he watched Elena pucker her full lips around the cigarette, full of confidence, he was drawn to her like a dancing honeybee to a fragrant flower. A tiny beauty spot above her upper lip caught his eye. She noticed him staring and exhaled slowly. The motion excited him. It was as if her eyes held secrets; secrets he wanted to be a part of. The juke box, playing *Smoke Gets In Your Eyes* by the Platters, teased him.

Christaki focused on the brown ceramic ashtray advertising John Bull Bitter. It threw him into a nostalgia, back to the village and the plastic *Keo* ashtrays at the *kafeneion*. He lent across the table to stub out his cigarette. As he did, Elena reached across and their hands brushed lightly against each others; like flowers in the breeze gently leaning into each other. Their eyes met again for a second but it felt like an eternity. She smiled, revealing perfect white teeth.

Pete's voice broke into his reverie as he nattered on, talking for them all. Christaki didn't join in the merriment of conversation lost in the wonder of Elena.

When it was time to make their way to The Empire Christaki hadn't even tasted his drink.

'Not drinking that?' Pete picked up the glass and drained it in one, smacking his lips and wiping his mouth with the back of his hand. 'Come on everyone. Let's go and dance with Cliff Richard!'

'Oh we're not coming in. We don't have tickets and we have to be home soon. We're hoping to see him as he arrives in his big car. Elena's mum is real strict so we can't stay long.'

'That's a shame. Isn't it Christaki?' Pete playfully jibed him in the ribs and Christaki pretended to fall to the floor, feeling a flutter dance across his chest. He was conscious of Elena's hazel eyes on him.

'So excited, if we see him, we'll be so lucky. It's been a rush getting here straight from work,' said Elena. Christaki thought how lovely she looked in her everyday work clothes. Her English was clear, fluent and he suddenly felt embarrassed of his Greek Cypriot accent.

They bundled out into the fresh air; Christaki pleased to be out of the stuffy hot pub as he shook off a baffled, perplexed sensation which gripped him.

They walked towards the music hall and joined the crowd of fans already outside the building. There was a thrill in the air. A sudden high pitched sound made by one of the girl's screaming alerted them to the street behind them. Cliff Richard was climbing out of the car and suddenly there was a swarm of girls around the car and hands and arms reaching out for him. Elena and Janet were in the middle of the throng having been pushed along with the wave of people.

Christaki could see the top of Elena's head and a

moment later she was swallowed up by the crowd as they parted momentarily. Police were blowing their whistles and shouting commands to move back away from the car. It was bedlam. The noise was ear crashing and for a second Christaki panicked as he too was pushed into the melee. The excitement around him was something he had never experienced before and he was drawn into the charged atmosphere in the air. He found himself behind Elena. Someone from behind jutted up against him and his face was pushed forwards.

He inhaled the familiar smell of Vosene, the sweet citronella making him heady, and suddenly he wanted to touch the silk strands loose around the back of her neck.

'Sorry. Everyone's pushing,' he said as he saw her twitch in reaction to his touch.

'You're telling me,' she said as she focused on the street again.

'Alright pal?' Christaki felt his blood freeze in his veins. It was Kevin and he was shoving into him real hard. 'Your girl, is she?'

'You leave her alone!' Christaki tried to turn round but he was packed in tight between the hundreds of fans.

'Or what?' asked Kevin as he kicked Christaki. Momentarily stunned Christaki felt his legs buckle from the sheer force of the kicks as greedy gravity pulled him down. Then the kicks stopped.

'He's there. I can see him. I can touch him!' Janet pushed forward, screamed and promptly fainted. She collapsed between the crowd and only the bodies around her wedged Janet's body up. Christaki urgently pushed forward and managed to grab onto her.

'Help! A girl's fainted!' Christaki called out. Two policemen pushed towards him as the crowd separated around her. They grabbed Janet just as she slumped forwards.

'Thank you,' said Elena. 'She could have been trampled.'

'You're welcome. I hope she's alright.' Christaki frantically continued to scan the crowd for Kevin. He watched as two policemen dragged a man, struggling viciously against them, towards a police vehicle. He broke loose of their grasp and swung at one of the officers, blood pouring from his face. Three other officers bounded in and restrained him as he shouted obscenities at them, his flailing arm hitting one of them in the face. Christaki recognised the menacing voice; it was Kevin's. He realised he would have no problems from him for a while. Instant relief flooded him, pushing away his fear.

'She'll be fine. I will look after her. Christaki?'

'Sorry, I…' Christaki forced his attention back to what she was saying reluctantly.

'You don't have to wait with us.'

'No, I will. Of course I will. I'll walk you home. Both of you.'

'What about the show?'

'I can give Cliff Richard and The Drifters a miss. It

was Pete's idea to come.' He couldn't admit he didn't want to stay now, not after Kevin's physical attack on him and his implied threat to Elena.

They shuffled through the thinning crowd, Christaki glancing towards where Kevin was now being pushed into a police car. Janet slouched on a wooden bench, a green uniformed medic by her side.

The doors of The Empire were open and floods of fans were pushing their way into the building. Christaki couldn't see Pete or any of the others.

Janet was fine apart from a grazed knee and elbow and she had no concussion. Janet held onto Elena's arm and Christaki's and the three of them walked slowly towards her house. She lived within ten minutes of The Empire and although it took them twice as long to walk the short distance, they made it.

'Gosh. Chris I'm so embarrassed. First time you've met me and I faint. What must you think of me?'

'It's alright. You're fine.'

'And my mam's going to bloody kill me. I'm late and Sarah'll be getting tired. I need to get her to bed soon.'

'You have a little sister?' asked Christaki.

'Yeah, I do. You?'

'Yes, and a brother. Melani and Pavlo.'

'Melani? Oh I work with a Melly. She's so funny.'

'My brother works in the kitchens of a London hotel and my sister's a Telephone Operator. I didn't know she used the name Melly.'

'It must be her. It's our pet name for her. Easier for us all to say Melly,'said Janet.

'Oh, I suppose it could be her. But there are many Cypriots in London.'

'Well, yes you're right. I work with all sorts there, but Melly's great.'

'And your sister, Sarah works there too?'

'No. Sarah's my baby. She's three months. Jenny's my sister. She's still at school.'

'Your baby?' Christaki's mind was running away with him. Janet can't have had the abortion. She obviously went through with the pregnancy. He had to find Pete and tell him.

'Yes.' She tilted her chin defiantly.

'Anyway she won't sleep without me. She needs to drop off in my arms.'

'Pete, does he know about Sarah?' Janet, confused for a moment, realised Christaki knew about Pete's involvement in the planned abortion.

'No, he doesn't.'

On the door step Elena hugged her friend good night. Christaki watched Elena as she squeezed her friend tight and found himself wishing to be held like that by a woman, by Elena. Elena caught him staring and he looked away awkwardly.

'See you soon. Next time I'll come in to meet Sarah.'

***

Christaki could sense how nervous Elena was as they walked alone, in tandem. His heart raced faster than a wild hare, conscious of his thigh knocking gently against hers.

'My mum would kill me if she knew I was walking out with you, with a man.'

'Well, we're not walking out. I'm walking you home. There's a difference.' Confidence filled him.

'Not in her eyes.'

'So your mum is stricter than your dad?'

'Dad's not around much. You know, with work and other commitments.'

'Oh, right.'

They didn't say anything else until they arrived the top of Elena's road and she insisted she walked the rest of the way on her own.

'I don't want a row. I know my mum. But thank you for walking me.'

'I will. What a coincidence you meeting him.'

'It was a quick hello really,' said Elena suddenly not wanting to create the wrong impression of herself. 'Well, good night. It was lovely to meet you.'

'And you. Good night then.' He took four paces and stopped. He turned around and watched her walking away from him. He knew he shouldn't but he couldn't let her slip away from him. He wanted her like he'd never wanted anything or anyone before. Could this feeling be so wrong? His vision blurred as his mind became cloudy with his jumbled thoughts. Something in him snapped. He pushed past a woman carrying two bags of groceries. Kevin's words rang in his ears.

He ran up behind her, taking in her soapy scent. For a moment he was back on the open stretch of mountainside overlooking *Ayios Tychonas*, the air filled with the light floral smell of cyclamen.

'Elena.' He grabbed her around the waist and pulling her towards him planted a kiss on her lips. She didn't say anything. He put his finger on her lips to shush her not wanting the magical moment to be spoilt. For a second he thought she was going to cry. Her eyes sparkled and he felt a sensual heat coming from her. He held her gaze for a second more.

He stood watching her until she stopped outside a doorway between the shops and disappeared inside. The noise in his ears was deafening and he realised it was the sound of his thrumming heart.

Christaki made his way back to The Empire by bus where the street was much quieter now although there were still a few people milling around the entrance of the building. He knew there was another show later the same evening and more people would be lining the street again before long. He decided to catch the bus home; he could update Pete tomorrow.

'I met one of your work friends, Melly,' he said as he walked into the sitting room to see Melani running the electric vacuum cleaner over the new carpet. She switched it off. The television was humming in the background.

'It's easier to be Melly at work. Anyway, who did you meet?'

'Janet and her friend Elena.'

'Before you say anything she's a good girl. She just got herself into a bit of bother...'

'Hey I'm not saying anything against her. But did you know she's the girl Pete helped, why he took the money from Mother's savings.'

'No. I didn't know.' Christaki watched her face drain of colour. In that second he thought he understood why. Melani thought Janet's baby was Pete's.

'You like Pete don't you?'

'You don't know what you're talking about!'

'Well you keep away from him. He's not like us. Don't you dare go getting into any trouble. I mean it.'

'I don't go out to get into trouble dear brother. You and Pavlo and Mother and Father make sure of that.' She stomped out of the room and slammed the door behind her.

The following morning, he sprinted to work from the bus stop. Out of breath, he called out to Pete in the distance.

Pete waved.

'Alright mate? You missed a real banger of a concert! What happened? One minute you was there and then you was gone.'

'Janet, she fainted, the ambulance crew helped her. Then I walked her home safely. And Elena.'

'Oh right. Is Janet alright? Is she hurt?'

'No. Yes. I mean she's alright. Pete, she didn't have the abortion.'

'What you talking about? I took her there myself.'

'She has a baby girl called Sarah.'

'Oh my God! Mate! That's the best news. I kept waiting for the holy Jesus and Mary to strike me down for my sins.'

'Well the story has a happy ending.'

'Can't believe it, mate.' Pete ran his fingers through his hair over and over.

Christaki watched his friend closely and realised the perplexed expression on Pete's face was one of deep satisfaction and relief.

***

'You will all need to think about marriage,' Loizos announced one day while they were all seated around the table having Sunday lunch. It was one of those rare afternoons when Pavlo was at home and the statement was met with stunned silence.

'We have to think about Christaki first,' said Anastasia. 'He is earning good money and with our help will have the deposit for a house too. He has much to offer a future wife. Do you have anyone in mind?'

'Well one of my customers, a Greek Cypriot, Georgette, has mentioned a young woman called Elena. She describes her as beautiful, caring, well-raised and hard-working. Son, what do you say?'

Christaki's mind was reeling. Could this be the same Elena he'd met in the pub only a few nights before? Could he be that lucky? Dare he ask his father more about the Elena he mentioned? Should he tell him he's met a girl already who he liked and who he was sure liked him? His mind raced, turmoil churning his stomach over and over.

'I don't know, *patera*. I haven't thought about it. I will take my guidance from you and *mitera*,' Christaki eventually said.

'When she next comes in, which probably won't be for another few weeks or so, I will ask her to arrange a meeting between our two families. We can meet the parents and see how you like the girl. If you don't there are plenty of Cypriots over here now so our traditions can be upheld.'

'We live in London! You can't expect him to marry through *proxenia*, an introduction! That's not how things are done here!' Christaki saw how his sister realised her mistake, of being too vocal, and tried to calm herself, biting on her bottom lip, but he couldn't help but wonder why the arrangement would upset her so much. After all, she knew the way things worked. He wondered whether she had met anyone through her work. She had certainly seemed more cheery than ever; and complained less about being in London.

'It's the way we do things. The way our parents taught us things are done. We will not turn our backs on our traditions, our culture because we now live in London, Melani.' Loizos looked her straight in the eye but she turned away, pretending to arrange the fruit in the glass bowl on the mahogany side cabinet and wondered whether their father had noticed. Christaki and Pavlo said nothing but looked at each other, both holding their breath.

'Well I want to marry someone I fall in love with. Someone who knows me and understands me,' she said, her back still to her father. Christaki knew she was being insolent.

'A good man will love you and empathise with you. Love and understanding comes over time,' said Anastasia.

'And if it doesn't?'

'Enough, Melani. Look at me when I'm speaking to you. You will do as I ask and when the time is right you, too, will be introduced to a suitable man.' Melani turned around and stared defiantly for a few seconds before walking out of the room.

'Is that how you feel Christaki *mou?* Pavlo *mou?*' asked Anastasia as she folded a tea towel and placed it on the table.

'I don't know. I suppose an introduction is a good

place to start.' Christaki wanted to please him; he knew disagreeing with his father would have been disrespectful. He knew how his father was both proud and confident that, of all his children, Christaki remained respectful.

Loizos expressed his contentment that Christaki had successfully qualified as an electrician.

Christaki was painfully aware of his father's expectations and the pressure on him to follow the Greek Cypriot culture and traditions his parents believed in. He knew his roots were important and he admitted they were important to him too. Living in London had been a huge life choice, forced in more ways than one, for his parents, one they hadn't anticipated ever having to make. And now he too was faced with a dilemma of a different kind.

Chapter Nineteen

Elena, 1959

ELENA BANGED AT the clasp of the sash window with the heel of her shoe until it gave way. The evening carried a biting chill; it filled her lungs. Her head ached. She shook a cigarette out of the scrunched packet hidden amongst her undies drawer and lit it. She realised she missed Blackpool with its fresh sea air and also missed the female company of her cousin. She reluctantly thought about the attention Mick had shown her. London felt smoggy and looked greyer than ever after the blue skies of the coast. She thought about Janet too and the fun they had until she'd fainted.

As she perched on the window sill, she took a long drag and then evenly exhaled; she watched how the smoke disappeared into nothingness as it evaporated into the outside air. Her heart pounded and she understood her mother was hurt, felt let down by her behavior. That her mother tried her best. They both did.

The dingy back yard mirrored the heavy sky; the gate banged in time with her escalating headache. A puddle of mud glistened in the last light of day. Her mind raced as she went over past family times, as if analysing a series of paintings for the first time, trying to figure out why they now looked different; was the colour of her memories darker now? She went over her thoughts in bright hues but smudges of sooty black, stormy grey and dirty brown smeared the picture in her mind; now tarnished, blurred, unclear.

Ducking her head out of the window, Elena stubbed out the cigarette on the wall below it careful not to catch herself on the splintered ledge. She pushed the butt into the bottom of the cigarette pack, wedging the packet behind her underwear at the back of the drawer. If her mother suspected she smoked, she never said anything, but all the same, Elena would never smoke in front of her; it seemed disrespectful.

She sighed a deep sigh and remembered Christaki and how his tall, slim frame bumped against her as they walked, sending electric ripples through her. She imagined running her hands through his thick black hair which fell in a wave across his forehead and oh those eyes; serious, solemn. She remembered his voice; how he spoke with careful thought. He had been the first man she had ever been alone with, without a chaperone; without an aunt or her mother or a work colleague. She wondered whether she would see him again, and her mother's harsh words came crashing in on her.

A slow dread came over her, followed by a quiet excitement as she pushed the words out of her mind. She wondered if he thought about her. Giddiness overcame her. Was this love?

She found her mother in the kitchen making *avgolemoni;* she could smell the lemons and see the milky yellow of the eggs coloring the otherwise clear liquid in the soup pot.

'You sit down *mama*, I'll make us a cup of tea until dinner's ready.' Evangelia reluctantly stepped away from the stove.

'I'm…I'm…' Elena discerned her mother was still trying to apologise but she was interrupted by the bang of the front door. Andreas' footsteps echoed up the stairs. She waited for the key in the lock.

'What's for dinner?' he called from the hallway.

'Can't you work it out? Your nose is big enough to smell it!' teased Elena, relieved her brother was home to lighten the atmosphere.

'Come here sis! You might be taller than me but I'm stronger!' He swept her up and twirled her round the small sitting room which lead into the boxy kitchen. Elena's feet kicked a picture frame which crashed to the floor; the glass splintered.

'Enough you two!'

They both stopped squealing at their mother's raised voice. They looked over at her, her crying silhouette in the doorway between the kitchen and the sitting room.

'*Mama* stop it. What's wrong? Is it that other woman?'

'What woman?' asked Andreas.

'Shall I tell him or will you?' asked Elena.

***

Over the next few weeks, Elena kept an especially close eye on her mother and coaxed her to go for walks in the park and to meet with her friend Georgette for coffee and Koulla who had made the move to London.

'Come on *mama* we've spent so long saying things will get better, that the summer will come and now it's finally here we need to relish it...before we find ourselves saying those words again, sitting here in the dull light of day yearning for summer all over again.'

'Very well. But only for an hour. I promised to visit *theia* Panayiota and *yiayia.* And there's the washing and those collars need turning before Monday. The new boss wants them finished. I can't let him down.'

'One hour it is,' said Elena.

They walked to Cherry Tree Wood, arm in arm, and followed the meandering path under the thick canopy of ancient oak, hornbeam and silver birch; fortresses of the umber-brown forest. Weak shafts of milky light seamed through the rustling foliage and snapping branches.

Their silence enveloped them for a few moments as they slowed their pace; twigs crunched under their feet, the sound cushioned by the moss-veiled trail. Her mother broke the silence, pointing out different birds as they flew between the branches. A flash of brown caught their attention as a rabbit scampered amongst the hedgerow and scurrying squirrels chased each other through the reaching horse chestnuts. But Elena sensed her mother's discomfort.

'What is it *mama*?'

'I shouldn't be out. People will talk. What if someone sees me and tells your father?'

'*Mama* for goodness sake. You're going for a walk with your daughter. And as for Father, he's the one who should be worried.'

'Not that again…'

'Yes that again. He's off with that woman. Don't people talk about him? Don't people wonder what's going on?'

'People mind their own business.'

'When it comes to men's infidelities but not when a woman is out walking with her daughter?'

They came out onto the open banks of soft green grass and the sunlight's intensity hurt Elena's eyes. She raised one hand to her eyes and with the other she pulled at the loose knot of her neck scarf. She pulled it off and scrunched it into a tight ball before stuffing it into her handbag. Two children on tricycles wobbled past them followed by the parents who stayed close in case they fell off, thought Elena.

A wave of melancholy came over her and she missed the moments she didn't ever have with her dad and she missed the moments she still wouldn't have. Her thoughts were punctuated by shouts and yelps of joy coming from the play area.

A huge number of children played happily; the witch's hat merry-go-round was full of little bodies climbing, and jumping and swinging from the higher bars; the solid wooden rocking horse moved up and down at a terrible speed sending girls' plaits into the air whipping their faces and flying behind them; the swings were quieter, two of them sitting idly as the other two were pushed higher and higher by two girls standing on the wooden seat and bending their knees in an effort to push themselves higher as they flew forward each time.

A gold clasp on a red handbag caught Elena's eye. A woman smoking a cigarette looked over at a little boy in a blue pair of trousers and blue collared jacket standing at the top of the metal slide. A man waited at the bottom of it, calling to the boy to come to him. Elena couldn't make out the man's face but something about him looked familiar. The toddler whooshed the length of the metal run and the man caught him before he fell off the end. The man scooped him up in his arms and waved to the woman who laughed and waved back.

'It's *baba*...but who's the little boy?' But Elena had already formed an answer; his bastard child and she was his fancy piece.

'Let's go Elena *mou*,' said her mother.

'No! I want to know what's going on? Is Dad living with her and her son or is that his son and his other woman?'

Her mother put out her arm to stop her but Elena

pushed her away. She walked right up to him before he even became aware of her.

'Dad?'

'Oh Elena *mou?* Are you on your own? Is your mother with you?'

'Is that all you can say? Well at least that's something!'

'Well, I…'

'Why come here? To our local park! To rub Mum's face in it!' Elena said.

'I'm sorry…I didn't…'

'Didn't what Dad? Think? You never do! And who is he?'

'No…yes. Sorry this is little Kostas.'

'What are you doing here?'

'Uh…um…He's my friend's son, Andriana…'

'And is he yours? And who exactly is Andriana? Like I haven't worked it out!'

'Not here Elena and don't you dare speak to me in this way! I will talk to you later!'

'Later? Dad you never come home. We haven't seen you for weeks, months…do you even know what happened to Mum?' Evangelia approached and stood next to Elena.

'Elena, enough. Let's go. We can talk to your father at home. Not here. With everyone watching.' The pleading in her mother's eyes crumbled Elena.

'*Mama*, please, let's not walk away. Let's do this

now. Look at him!' Tears poured. Elena wiped her cheeks, her hands streaked with smudges of black mascara; black tears fell onto the front of her white blouse. Elena dabbed at her eyes with a hankie aware her face would be a smudge of black eyeliner and green eyeshadow and pink lipstick. But she didn't care. She didn't want to walk away from the situation. She wanted to face things head on but in the end her mother's pleading forced her to reluctantly walk away.

***

At home, impatient for her dad to come home, Elena told her mother she was going for a walk. Her mother didn't argue.

Elena came out onto the high street. She squeezed her eyes against the yellow cheerfulness of the sun, dodging the mums with prams and the dads carrying their sons on their shoulders. An old lady hobbled along with a metal walking frame and a painter and decorator whistled as he carried two pots of paint, brushes sticking out of the pockets of his overalls. Her mood, in contrast was one of thunder; everything in her screamed to confront him.

As she approached the end of the high street the ominous shadow of the railway bridge at East Finchley Station cast a patchwork of melancholy ahead of her. It seemed to engulf her, accentuating the deep wretchedness and frustration within her, the building heat oppressive.

She surveyed the gravel grey paving stones, methodically laid in perfect symmetry with each other. If only life was like that, she thought.

'Sorry.'

'No sorry, I wasn't looking, Christaki?'

'Hello.'

'Hello.'

'Don't worry. My foot will survive…I have two you know…'

'What are you doing round here?'

'My father's opened a cobblers a couple of streets up…Lincoln Road.'

'How wonderful. Good for him.'

'Where are you going?'

'Nowhere really. Anywhere but home again.'

'Has something happened?' Christaki asked. She bit on her lower lip nervously wondering whether she could trust him with her father's infidelity but she chose not to.

'No. I needed a bit of fresh air.'

'I'm too early to meet my father. Can I buy you a cup of tea?'

'A cup of tea?' she mimicked him; a posh British accent leaving her lips with a smile.

'You have a lovely smile Elena.'

'Thank you Christaki.'

Elena walked back, nervous she might bump into one of the nosey neighbours but equally excited to be with Christaki.

They halted outside the Bite To Eat café with its Typhoo Tea advertisement across the entire left-hand wall by the door way.

'I'll take you somewhere a lot nicer next time.'

'Next time?' She preceded Christaki into the café.

'Well, yes, if you'd like me to.'

'I would need to ask my mum and I doubt she'd agree to it Christaki. I shouldn't be here now.' She sat opposite him with her back towards the front window and the door in an effort to conceal herself from any prying eyes.

'There's no harm is there? We're not doing anything wrong.'

'Maybe not in our eyes but in the eyes of our parents. I'm sure yours would be the same wouldn't they?'

'I admit yes. But I don't see why we can't just talk to each other.'

'Nor me. So let's talk.'

Christaki ordered mugs of tea and a teacake each for them. Elena tried not to slurp her tea, which she habitually did, and took tiny bites from her teacake. She would normally have ravished it in one mouthful but her appetite had refused to relish the sweetness. Sugary foods were her favourite and her mother rarely had the money to spend on puddings and desserts so this should have been a treat. She thought back to the last time.

Christaki leaned back in the metal chair. Elena drank in the soft contours of his face and the way his lips moved as he chewed. She was about to say something when she saw a brown mass of fur scuttle across the floor. She startled, sending her teacake onto the floor with the saucer and her tea slopping over the scratched top of the table. Her screams were instantaneously followed by the screams and yells of panic from other patrons.

'It's a rat,' said Christaki. 'Come on, let's get out of here!' He grabbed her hand and pulled her out of her seat as she snatched up her handbag. They made a dash for the door. They ran for a few hundred yards before they finally both stopped.

'Oh my…I can't believe I just saw a rat for real. I've heard them scratching in the back yard at night…urgh…they're horrid…ugly,' Elena said laughing, overcome with nerves all over again. He quickly joined in and the two of them doubled over in the street; Elena not caring they were being stared at.

As the summer breeze blew a strand of hair across her face she went to pull it over her ear. Christaki reached up at the same time and their hands brushed. It was electric. He pulled away. She tugged at her hair nervously, composed herself after wiping her eyes. She continued to play with her hair.

She realised her dark mood of earlier had vanished; completely lost in him, she was hot and her hands were sticky. The summer heat suffocated her, or was it Christaki too? She suddenly became conscious of her sweaty upper lip.

Christaki looked deep into her eyes and leaned in for

a kiss. She turned her head away so his lips scraped the side of her cheek awkwardly. The action reminded her of Mick and she felt guilty.

'Why don't you come and meet my father. I'm sure he'd like you.'

'Really? Without my mum knowing about you first?'

'Just to say hello.'

'I suppose it can't harm anybody.'

They crossed over and into Lincoln Road. Elena's nerves turned to a quiet excitement humming through her chest. She took a couple of deep breaths.

'How do I look?'

'Beautiful,' he said.

He pushed the door to the small shop and a silver bell above the door rang across the small dark interior. Elena followed him in and noticed how the droning machinery swallowed the jingle of the bell.

From the shadowy corner, a man of average height sat bent over the bench, nails held between his lips as he tacked away at the sole of a shoe. He wore once white overalls and a pair of spectacles sat on the top of his head.

Glue and old leather smothered Elena's senses, the sound of a quiet whirring filled the small space. There were chalk sticks, a pot of different sized brushes and a number of shoe moulds lay haphazardly across the battered wooden bench. Elena looked at the polishing and grinding machines, the shoe clamps of varying sizes and the shoes tied in pairs with a numbered ticket attached to

353

them piled high against the back wall, filling three deep shelves.

'Hello, *patera*.' Christaki called out over the hum–drum of the machinery and crackle of the radio.

'Hello *yioka mou*. I thought you were getting here later?' Loizos spat out the nails into his hand and switching off the machine turned to face his son.

'That was the plan but the journey didn't take as long as I thought.'

'Oh hello young lady. Can I help you?'

'*Patera*, this is Elena. A friend of mine. A friend of one of Pete's friends.'

'Hello Elena. You must be from Cyprus with such a beautiful name.'

'Yes. My family came over here a few years ago.' Elena answered in Greek.

'You live locally?'

'Not far. Further along the high street with my mum and brother...and my dad.'

'Pleased to make your acquaintance Elena. I'm Loizos, Christaki's father.' Loizos extended his blackened hand, after wiping it on the front of his overalls. Elena shook it and thought of her own father's hands, soft and flabby. These were the hands of someone who worked hard, she thought. Someone who looks after their family.

'I'm going to walk Elena home. I'll be straight back *patera*.'

His father gave him a stern nod.

'See you again Elena,' said Loizos, with soft severity.

***

Elena drifted home as if in a dream. Her dad lounged languorously on the single seater, his feet crossed at the ankles on the coffee table. His shoes, unceremoniously thrown in the corner of the room, looked out of place and an empty glass tumbler sat on the cheap wooden console table beside him. A newspaper, open at the horse races, lay across his lap. His shirt buttons, undone to his waist, revealed a whisper of hair peeking out from the scoop neck of the vest he wore underneath.

'Where's *mama*?'

'Where were you, is the question that needs answering right now!'

'Out. I went to look for you.'

'*Mama, mama*?' Elena called out.

'She's washing some of my shirts.'

'She's doing what?'

'She's doing my laundry.'

'I don't believe it. Dad! For goodness sake. You can't slide back in like, like…'

Elena stormed out and called out for her mother. She raced through the kitchen, noticing the lit candle sitting on the peeling faded red window ledge; it reminded her

355

of their tiny kitchen in *Kato Lefkara* and for a moment paused.

Seconds later she ran down the stone steps where she found her mother hanging out her Kostas' shirts. The shared washing line already heavy with the wet laundry slumped too close to the dirty earth of the small flower bed. Sweat beads collated across her mother's neck and forehead and there were patches under the arms of her thin blouse. She looked exhausted; dark rings around her eyes.

'*Mama* please. Don't let him do this to you anymore. We don't need him. He does nothing for us. He uses this house like it's a boarding house, not a home.'

'I can't ask him to leave.'

'Why? Why not?'

'Because we made promises, in God's eyes, in church.'

'That's not it *mama*. He's broken those promises.'

'Leave it Elena.'

'No, I won't. I'm sick of all this. This life. It's no life for any of us.'

'It's the life God has sent us. We must be grateful.'

'You don't believe that. Not really. What are you afraid of?

Her mother rested her hands on her belly. She held Elena's gaze. Said nothing.

'No!' Elena said, a strangled animal-like cry filling her ears as the realisation hit her.

'I am. I know it,' Evangelia said, almost inaudibly.

'Pregnant? How?' Elena gasped, staring in disbelief.

'I feel it…'

'*Mama*. No you can't be. How can you be?' Her mother looked at her, pain streaked across her features contorting her face into something ugly, unrecognisable.

'I am and it's your father's. That's the only way forward.' Elena shivered even though the sun, still burning down into the shabby square of a yard, bounced off the crumbling brick walls. Her eyes filled with tears, her heart constricted and released as it pounded loudly in her chest. She fell to the ground and sat on the grimy dusty concrete. Her mother knelt beside her. They cradled each other. They both cried together. Elena repeated the words 'no *mama* no' over and over until she was snivelling and incoherent. Her words came out muffled by her crying as the mucusy discharge from her nose ran into her mouth.

Elena sat there aware her father didn't bother to come and find them. The sun dipped behind the tall brick wall separating their yard from the one of the flat above theirs, and Elena shivered with cold. Eventually they both pulled away from each other; stiff and aching from the tight position they had sat in and from the hard uncomfortable ground beneath them.

'Please Elena *mou* you mustn't say anything to your dad. Promise me. Swear on Jesus' name.'

'But how can you ask me to lie *mama*? How can you

go on knowing all this is a lie? That man raped you and now you're pregnant with a dead man's child.'

The slap came out of nowhere. Elena reeled back from its force and landed on her back, the crack of her skull on the brick edging of the path echoed in her ears, before she passed out.

'Oh, thank God you're awake.' Her mother moved slowly out of the battered Lloyd Loom chair, crossing herself and giving thanks to God.

'*Mama*?'

'Don't speak now *agabi mou*. Here, drink slowly, slowly. Sit up if you can, you don't want to choke.' She lifted a glass to Elena's lips with care. 'Elena, *agabi mou*. Please I'm so sorry, I never meant to hurt you.'

Elena blinked against the fading light of day.

It was obvious how Evangelia struggled to find the words of comfort she could not deny Elena deserved. Her mother's actions had shocked her.

'I didn't mean to lash out, but I couldn't hold it in any longer. I didn't mean…'

'*Mama* I know. It was an accident. Dad should be apologising. Not you. It should be that horrid man who…who…'

'Stop it now, please. Your dad's outside the door and Andreas. They can't know…not yet.' Elena winced as the back of her head rubbed against the pillow.

'Shall we let them in for a bit? You've been out for a

few hours.'

Her father and Andreas bundled into the small bedroom; their bulky forms blocking out the dimming light from the window.

'You gave us a right fright,' said her brother squeezing her hand gently

'Glad you're alright my girl.' Her father appeared inconvenienced by her accident. Or was it something else? Did he look guilty?

'I'll go and bring you some soup. Warm you up a bit.' Andreas followed his mother out of the room as she shuffled out ahead of him. Elena sensed his impatience to get out, guessing the emotional charge weighed too much for him.

Left alone with her father, Elena, although still groggy, seized the opportunity to speak to him about Andriana.

'Who's that woman to you Dad? And don't tell me she's a friend. I'm not a child. I'm a woman. A woman who has eyes and understands life.'

'When did you grow up so quickly?'

'While you were sleeping around. While you left Mum to fend for us on her own. While you were gambling. While you were looking after your bastard son. Shall I carry on Dad?' She harnessed her instinct to shout at him and instead spoke in a whisper. He raised his hand to slap her. He held it in the air like an eagle suspended in flight.

His arm shook from anger. He held it there, trembling. Holding his stare, defiance raged through her. She tilted her head, wincing in pain. Eventually he lowered his arm and said one word.

'Sorry.'

Her mother never mentioned what had happened again and neither did Elena. It became one of those family secrets buried under layers of superficial conversation, painful smiles, unsaid words which hung on the lips like sour buttermilk, the beat of a song which never quite works.

Chapter Twenty

Evangelia, 1959

SHE THANKED GOD every day Elena hadn't got hurt any worse than she had. Kostas had stayed with them for a few days after the accident. He spoilt them all with fancy cakes and gifts and gave Elena lots of attention but Evangelia could see how her daughter was not going to be won over with grand showy gestures. Slowly he tired and on one of the hottest July days on record, on the pretext he was going to buy some groceries, he disappeared for three days. After that his stay at the house was even more sporadic.

Part of her made excuses for his behavior; she should have joined him sooner; she should have made more effort to tell him she loved him. Perhaps the fault lay with her that he found love in the arms of another woman, a man has needs after all. If she had been here, by his side, he would have loved her as a husband should love his wife. But then he did love her, but he was weak and had given in to his vices.

***

Evangelia had begun to tire more easily. The fluttering of

a baby growing inside her reminded her of the blessing of new life, above all else whizzing in her head. Conscious of her changing shape, she wore clothes more loose in their style and shape, but knew her family would soon notice the full curved contours of her pregnant belly before long, and she had yet to tell Kostas. She worked from home at the weekends to supplement the income from the factory she now worked in, having left the other factory; struggling to face being there every day after what happened had become too much for her. Elena had changed jobs with her. They were good machinists, both of them.

She arrived early at work and knocked to be let in before the work force poured in. She made herself comfortable and stayed hidden behind her machine and swathes of fabric all day, running to use the toilet like a scared rabbit when she could hold her bladder no more.

She clocked out later too; this avoided anyone seeing her and also meant she got a seat on the later bus and avoided standing all the way home on the earlier crowded, noisier buses.

Elena often waited with her but after a particularly hot day, she ran ahead of her mum, promising to make a start on dinner. Evangelia, relieved, was left with her thoughts, alone, after the suffocating noise of the machines all day at work. Her dress was sticking to her and the sweat soaked her back and trickled between her breasts. She wished she had money to make a dress out of some lighter, cooler fabric but she knew that would be indulgent. She had never said it, but she was happy Elena sewed her own clothes from the fragments she salvaged from the factory and preferred she used the material to create clothes for herself than for her mother. She was in no real need for pretty clothes; after all who did she have to look nice for?

She wiped her brow with a wet paper towel from the toilets. Her mind focused on getting home and telling Kostas about the baby, if he was home. She hadn't spent any time with him at all since those few days after Elena's fall and, although she wished over and over she had told him that night, she knew it was pointless chastising herself. Nothing could be changed now, nothing at all.

She sat on her own at the front of the bus, downstairs away from the open back to avoid the dusty hot July air whirling around the lower deck, lost in her own jumbled notions. She focused on the scuffed plastic of the step and the blotched face of the woman sitting further along from her.

Evangelia, along with so many other Londoners, struggled to cope with the increasing temperatures. She peered across the bus staring ahead of her. She let her apathy wash over her, her fatigued bones as heavy as the weight of a net of olives. Opposite her a woman was stuffing her toddler with broken chunks of a doorstop white bread sandwich. Evangelia tried to breathe through her mouth; the whiff of the spam making her gag along with the irregular bumpy ride.

At first she didn't take in the softly spoken yet urgent words of the passenger as he walked towards her.

'Evangelia, Evangelia. Is that really you?'

She recognised the voice as it echoed in her ears; suddenly a warm rush came over her as she focused on his face.

'Zeno?'

'Yes it's me.'

'I'm sorry…I was…what are you doing here?' Her face flushed instantly and she gripped onto her handbag. He looked older than she remembered him, older than thirty-five, as if life had beaten him.

'I came a month ago with Niko.'

'I had no idea. Sorry…I didn't expect to ever see you again.' The words were out before she could stop herself.

'I didn't mean to shout out, to shock you, but to see you again…'

'How are you all? Maroulla?' Evangelia let the words tumble out while her heart did somersaults in her chest and she forgot to breathe.

He sat next to her and took her hand in his. She didn't pull away. She saw something cross his eyes; his demeanour changed. Awkward at the openness of his physical expression, she focused on the warmth of his hands, the soft skin of his fingers reassuring her.

'She was killed. Two months ago…an explosion a couple of kilometres outside Larnaca.' Evangelia's eyes widened with horror. She couldn't take in what he was saying. She realised what she saw in his face was grief, a black, heartfelt grief.

'I can't believe it, no. No, may God rest her soul. I am so sorry Zeno. I keep up with the news through friends and their relatives still in Cyprus.' She babbled on but couldn't stop herself, her voice shaking, her hands suddenly cold despite the claustrophobic heat on the slow-moving bus. Someone pushed against her legs and she tried to move them over without appearing rude, her legs sticking to the seat.

He sat so close the warmth of his breath and the scent of his aftershave kissed her face. Too scared to speak, to show her emotions, Evangelia stroked his hand but avoided his eyes. A slow burning came upon her, her heart raced and she became acutely conscious of a fresh sheen of sweat breaking out across her forehead. The silence hung between them for a moment.

'Can you move along a bit mate?' interrupted an old man as he puffed on his cigarette, oblivious to the smoke going into their faces. Zeno shuffled closer to Evangelia. She tucked her elbow into her, but they were still so close.

'We read about the troubles growing worse. It doesn't seem real our beloved Cyprus is suffering such hate and violence.' She tried to keep her voice measured.

'It's been a worry every day. People in villages complaining about the curfews they're under.' He lowered his voice, 'the British. People are desperate, and in desperate times people take risks they otherwise would not.'

'How sad,' Evangelia said as she wiped her brow.

'Tempers have risen over time and there are still many who love England and don't want trouble with the English; not everyone wanted *Enosis* either. It's a mess. We all want peace, we will welcome independence. It will come soon. We love our country,' whispered Zeno.

'Hating people takes too much energy, destroys your soul.'

'Nobody wants to see their own people murdered, imprisoned, yet they fight on. Too much bitterness and too many regrets. But how have you been, Evangelia *mou?*'

'It's been hard here too Zeno. It's so different to Cyprus; the cold, the people, the work. There's no blue sea, no beautiful mountains. How I miss those green Lefkara mountains. But Elena and Andreas have settled and they are both working. We go to church most Sundays. It's a routine of sorts.'

'I'm glad they're well. They were always such good children, a credit to you,' said Zeno.

'But ignore me, going on, with all your grief.'

'I'm coping Evangelia. I have to deal with what God has sent me with what strength and belief in Him I have.'

'We all do, yes. Yes, that's all we can do.'

'How's Kostas?'

She hesitated. She didn't want to lie to her friend but

at the same time she didn't want to betray her husband. 'He is well.'

'Something tells me otherwise. What is it?'

'It's nothing. I am well. All is well. How is Niko?'

'He's seen too much, heard too much. He's getting on as best he can. We both are.' He cleared his throat and looked directly at her. 'It's so good to see you.' In his eyes she saw the same warmth and affection she had carried with her from all those months ago in Limassol.

'This is my stop.'

'I'll get off the bus with you.'

'No. Thank you. It's not necessary.'

'Can I see you again?'

'Zeno, I'm still a married woman. Nothing has changed.'

'But...I'm sorry. Please, Evangelia.'

'Zeno, this is impossible. You know it, as I know it.' Her voice caught. She held onto the grab handle, as the bus came to an abrupt stop.

She walked to the open exit at the back of the bus, following the other passengers. Afraid her emotions would come tumbling out she didn't look back. The chaos in her mind was eased yet intensified by his presence. His steps scraped the bus's rubber floor behind her and the sound caught in her ears.

On the street, when he called her name, she walked on; life was complicated enough. But she couldn't ignore the skipping in her chest. She shook her head, shocked at how her heart somersaulted the way she imagined a young teenager's in love would. Poor Maroulla, but thank God Zeno was safe. The moment she thought it she felt her heart tighten. Was she a bad person to reason like that? She knew nothing could become of her and Zeno. She was married. She was pregnant. She kept walking with dragging strides, slow and lethargic, one hand wedged under her belly.

***

At home, her mind in turmoil, she forced herself to focus on her immediate issue. She knew what she had to do. She had to tell Kostas about the baby and convince him the child was his. She knew if this didn't convince him to stay with her then nothing would. She composed herself. She let herself in and climbed the stairs to her front door, her feet as heavy as lead. As she put the key in the lock she knew without calling out Kostas was home. The smell of his tobacco lingered on the staircase.

Leaving her shoes in the hallway she padded into the living room, the floorboards creaked and complained, under her heavy, tired steps. She continued the conversation she had been dreading all this time and yet felt lighter as the words left her.

'I cannot believe you have been this irresponsible Evangelia!'

'It's a gift from God.'

'Gift from God?'

'Yes.'

'For God's sake. How could this happen? I can't afford to raise another child. Not now.' Evangelia bit her tongue 'til it bled. His words cutting her like a razor shell. She looked at him reproachfully. Frustration surged through her but she held her emotions intact.

'You didn't raise our first two Kostas,' she said quietly.

'Well don't expect me to live here with a screaming baby.' Kostas pulled himself up from the sofa, stubbed out his cigarette in the ashtray and pushed past her, nearly knocking her off balance.

'I don't expect anything from you. Not anymore,' she said, holding onto the door frame for support with one hand as her other rested across her belly protectively. All she wanted was to shout at him about Andriana, about his other child, about how desperately unhappy she was. But instead she listened to her own heartbeat in time to the ticking of the clock as he put on his shoes and left the room without glancing in her direction.

Evangelia should have been angry but instead she was relieved, numb even. She ran her hand gently over her belly to soothe the ache from his shove. He hadn't questioned her about being pregnant in the first place; they had only slept together a few times since being reunited. She sat heavily and looked to heaven and then across to her icon of Mary holding the baby Jesus in her arms. She crossed herself as silent tears came from deep inside her; a place where frustration, rejection and disappointment had lain dormant for so long it finally had to escape.

Later, as she sat at the bare table with Andreas and Elena, that same heart swelled with love for them.

'Why aren't you eating *mama*?' asked Elena.

'I'm tired *agabi mou.*'

'Eat a little. I'll make you a fresh camomile. Like you used to have back home. Warm you up.' Evangelia realised how cold she was as Elena's warm hands enveloped hers.

'No, I'm fine.' Exhausted, Evangelia took to her bed early. She didn't want to be around Elena and Andreas; she didn't want them noticing how frail and sad she was. As she lay on the lumpy mattress she tossed and turned to ease the niggling pain in her lower back. She struggled to keep warm and alone she listened to the unsettled climate; thundery summer rain lashed and the wind howled as the thin panes rattled against their force.

Every time the floorboards creaked she stiffened, listening for Kostas' footsteps but deep down she knew he wouldn't be back. Not tonight. Maybe not ever.

Unable to get comfortable she stayed in bed, tense and wakeful, shaking with cold despite the heat coming off her. Her back ache worsened, spreading across the whole of her lower back, yet eventually she must have fallen asleep.

Some hours later she woke with an unbearable ache across her lower abdomen. She reached between her legs and felt an ooze of something damp, instantly warm and then cold within a few seconds. She lay there transfixed. She knew what was happening, recognised the feelings, the aches and the moisture still coming, for what they were. It's God's punishment, she thought, as she played with the stickiness until the blood congealed on her fingers.

She lay in the dark, the storm thrashing around outside, and Evangelia cried all the tears she never imagined she had. That night she lost the baby. That night she yearned not for Kostas' arms around her but Zeno's.

Chapter Twenty-One

Elena, 1959

THE WEEK PASSED painfully slowly, but the day Elena had arranged to meet Christaki finally came round.

'You haven't forgotten I'm going to meet Janet have you Mum?' She had slowly begun to use Mum instead of *mama* now her English was fluent and her mum no longer corrected her use of the word mum, like she did at first.

'No I haven't forgotten as long as you're here for when *theia* Panayiota comes. She should be here soon. And where's your father?'

'Dad? Why would he be here?' The bell cut the conversation short and Elena, high spirited, took the stairs two at a time and jumped the last four almost crashing into the main door into the house.

'Hello *theia*.' Elena stood aside to let her aunt in and was taken aback with the presence of another three people she did not recognise; one of them a young man and two older people; obviously his parents. Her heart dropped as soon as she realised what was going on. She quietly followed the group to the door of the flat where her mum was waiting to greet them. She wasn't surprised at all and Elena realised this had been a pre-arranged meeting; *proxenia*.

After an hour of polite chatter, Elena excused herself. Her mum followed her into the narrow hallway.

'Where are you going?'

'You know where I'm going. Mum how could you do this to me? You knew *theia* wasn't coming alone. Why didn't you tell me?'

'I didn't want you to be nervous. This way it's more natural.'

'There's nothing natural about being pushed into a corner Mum and you know it.'

'Come back in and we'll talk later.'

'I'm not coming back in. I'm going out. Please make my excuses,' said Elena.

'What will I say?'

'The same excuse you made for Dad. I have other commitments I need to attend to. Isn't that what you told them?'

'Elena…'

'Whatever you think of. I'm not sitting in there a moment longer. I'm sorry…I just can't.'

Elena grabbed her scarf and handbag from the metal coat rack and quietly shut the front door behind her.

Three quarters of an hour later she arrived and waited impatiently for the waiter to seat her. She gazed around at the plush brasserie style restaurant, adjusting her eyes to the dim interior and pools of yellow candle light. She thought how lucky she was to be dining in a place like this. A tinkle of a laugh cut across the restaurant and she strained slightly in the dim light. At the far end of the room Christaki, with his back to her, a pretty young girl leaning over the table towards him; were they holding hands? She wasn't even an hour late and yet here he was bold as brass.

Tears of hurt and frustration coursed through her. She made for the door and then snapped round. Taking long strides to Christaki, she tapped him on the shoulder.

'Hello,' he said but her slap hit him across the face. She rubbed the sting in her hand and watched Christaki's expression change as it dawned on him what Elena had thought she'd witnessed. She became conscious of the hushed conversation around her and humiliation threatened to deplete her nerve completely.

'It's not what you think…'

'Don't deny it. You're all the same. How could you?'

'Elena please let me explain. Let me introduce…' But Elena wasn't listening. She pivoted and purposefully walked out without another word, her head held high.

Elena caught the bus to Janet's house. She knocked on the pane of the front room quietly not wanting to wake Sarah. As Janet swung the door open Elena fell into her arms crying.

Sitting cross legged on the kitchen chair Janet listened to Elena's rambling through her tears and endless blowing of her nose.

'So basically you didn't wait to hear what he had to

say so you don't actually know who the other girl was.'

'Well, no, but...'

'There could be a perfect explanation.'

'Oh yeah. Of course. So it's totally coincidental he's with a pretty dark haired girl with a pointy little nose and eyes far too big for her tiny face.' Janet's face contorted into an expression Elena couldn't fathom.

'That's Melly! His sister! Oh you're so silly Els, but I do love you my honeysuckle!'

'I've been such a fool. What will he think of me now?'

***

Another week went by and although Elena made a diversion on the way home from work anticipating she would bump into Christaki she didn't and then she had an idea. On Saturday, after finishing the weekly chores at home she left her mum sewing and walked with purpose and determination towards the cobblers. She was afraid of what his father may say to her and indeed what he may deem of her coming to seek Christaki unannounced. It wasn't the done thing, but she had no other way of making contact with Christaki and she was willing to take a chance. She had to. She had ruined everything. And that's not what she wanted.

As she neared Lincoln Road she slowed, nerves getting the better of her. She wiped her sweaty palms together and rounded the corner.

'Where are you off to *agabi mou?*' It was her dad. Damn she thought, that's all I need.

'What's it got to do with you?'

'Don't be like that. I'm still your father. Come here. Give me a hug,' said Kostas.

'You disappear for months and now you want a hug?'

'I don't want to fight.'

'What are you doing here? You better not be after money. Mum's been through enough.'

'Oh your mum can take care of herself,' said Kostas.

'You really don't care do you? She lost the baby. She was devastated!'

'We can't talk here on the street.'

'I'm busy. I'm…picking up my shoes…from the cobblers.'

'I'll come with you.'

'No it's not necessary.'

'Come on Elena give me a chance to make things better. I'm still your father.'

'I'll meet you in the café in five minutes. Order me a cup of tea.'

'Good idea,' he chuckled. 'I'll get you one of your favourite sticky buns too.' She smiled at him if only to placate him.

She waited a few seconds to make sure he was not going to change his mind about accompanying her and then strode towards the tiny shop.

Twenty minutes later she pushed the door open to the café, the greasy steam hitting her as she sat opposite her dad. The conversation between them was stilted but civil. She over-stirred her mug of tea finding solace in the clinking of the spoon on the china; anything but to look at her father.

She consciously slowed her chatter in order to prolong her time spent in the café with him. He appeared exceedingly happy at how she seemed to want to spend more than a few minutes with him.

'Where's the shoes?'

'The shoes?'

'The ones you were getting mended.'

'Oh, they weren't ready yet. He said he'll have them ready for me next week.'

'He must be busy if he's letting customers down.'

'Yeah, there're shoes everywhere in there I don't know how he keeps track of where they all are and who they belong to. Heaven help any customer who loses their collection ticket.'

'I heard he's from Cyprus, the owner.'

'Yeah he is. But he speaks English quite well, heavy accent but he can communicate well.'

'He's got two sons, about your age. One's training as an electrician, the other a cook.' Elena said nothing. She took a slurp of her tea, grateful it had cooled and taking a bite of her treat she forced the unpalatable mouthful down into her churning stomach. Her eyes darted around the now crowded café; she felt like time was lingering and she couldn't move forward.

'I don't know them.'

'Really? I thought you knew Christaki?' He leant back in his seat and lit a cigarette, blowing the smoke away from her. She forced her lips to stop trembling. She removed a cigarette from the packet on the table. Kostas gave her a disapproving look but instantly Elena saw him slump back in his seat; a man defeated.

'And if I do? You can't tell me to live my life one way, when you live yours another.'

'Elena *mou*. You'll understand one day. It's been hard and yes, I've been weak, but I've tried, I honestly have.'

'How have you tried Dad?' Elena blew smoke in the direction of the table next to them.

'I've been lonely. I wanted you to come here with a home waiting for you. It didn't work out and the longer I left it the harder it became to get sorted...'

'Why didn't it work out?'

'Because I needed to make a life for myself. I missed your mum. I missed you and Andreas. I became addicted to the gambling, got in a bad crowd...'

'Dad, you're not a teenager...'

'No, no I'm not. But I was young. In a foreign country. On my own here for nine years. I've made mistakes but I'm not the tyrant you think I am.'

'What are you doing round here? Has Andriana

thrown you out? You want to come back home, is that it?'

'Don't you talk to me like that.'

'I'm only asking Dad. It's not fair on Mum. She deserves better than the life she has. All she does is work. You never take her out. You're never around.'

Elena waited for him to say he had needs because Janet's dad had said those same words when he was rowing with his wife. The tension radiated from both of them. She had overstepped the mark. A hush descended between them which accentuated the clatter of cutlery against crockery around them as the other diners indulged in eating.

'All I'm saying is be careful. That lad seems a nice boy. So does his father.'

'What are you saying?'

'I'm saying London is big, it's new and exciting for you and it's easy to forget our traditions here. If you like him and he likes you, we have to do things the right way.'

***

Elena dutifully kissed her dad on both cheeks and watched him amble off towards the betting shop another lit cigarette already in his hand. That's where his money still goes, thought Elena sadly, squandering it all on gambling, cigarettes and booze. She rolled her eyes and then scuttled towards the cobblers after her dad's back retreated into his betting haunt. She hesitated for a split second before making her way towards the shop. Her mind racing with her Dad's words.

Determined, she walked slowly, in an effort to calm her growing nerves still unsure of what she was going to say to Christaki if he was there. Footsteps drew near before his voice. She turned to face him, the words already spilling out of her, jumbled, incoherent, inadequate.

'I am so sorry. Please forgive me.'

'For your lateness, your rudeness or your wild mind running to conclusions?'

'All of it.' It was then she became aware of the girl standing at a distance behind him.

'I'm sorry to you too. You must be Melani? Melly.'

'There's nothing to apologise for on my part. I thought it was hilarious.' Elena's eyes darted from Melani to Christaki. Melani's contagious laugh burst forth and within seconds had them both laughing too.

'So?' Christaki said eventually, his eyes glistening from laughing too much.

'So nothing,' said Melani. 'You two like each other. A lot from what I can see. So we now have to work on Mum and Dad.'

Elena wanted to hug her right there on the street. She wanted to kiss her and jump with joy. Instead she smiled and said, 'Thank you.'

'So what happens now?' asked Christaki.

'We let the love in the air work its magic and get you

two together.' Melani smiled, throwing her arms around her brother and hugging him tight.

Chapter Twenty-Two

Christaki, 1959

'I DON'T WANT anything. I'm bored and planning a wedding would be fun. I like Elena too. Your face when she slapped you.'

'Yes enough of that night.' Christaki stretched to swat her on the arm but too quick on her feet, she ducked his swipe.

'Looks like there might be many more "nights",' she said giggling as he grabbed her around the waist and swung her round and round.

'Put me down you donkey!'

'So what's the plan?'

'Not sure yet, but I can guarantee it'll win you the love of your dreams and you'll live happily ever after.'

Over the next few days Christaki begged Melani to hatch a plan. 'I miss her. I want to be with her. She might meet someone else. I can't miss my chance.'

'Don't be so silly. If her family were considering marrying her off they would've done it by now. Her dad not being around is going to weigh in your favour. Her mum won't want her to marry in a hurry, leave her on her own.'

'You really are the Duchess aren't you?'

'So does that make you Dick?' They laughed together about the TV series they both watched but even that was a rarity these days. Since being in England Christaki had felt his family's unity unravel. London was a big city taking them in all directions in the day. Their jobs had taken each of them on a different journey. They no longer held hands to go to school, to go to church and when at home they were rarely all together. At dinner time Pavlo wasn't always with them and Melani spent more hours at the Telephone Exchange.

Christaki looked at his sister. She had become a beautiful young woman and he wondered whether she had any admirers. After all, if Elena had admirers why wouldn't Melani? He thought about the extra shifts she had taken on at work and wondered whether there was a reason for her to be so willing. It's not like she needed the money. Their parents were financially secure, supportive and generous with money.

Could there be a secret boyfriend? She seemed happier recently; not so surly and argumentative. Was she maturing or was there another influence on her behaviour? He hoped her interest in getting him and Elena together would mean she would open up to him if there was someone. Time would tell and Christaki tucked the thought away, at least for now.

Christaki met with Elena clandestinely; they met for an hour for a cuddle and a kiss or to catch up on the week's news. They both enjoyed the flicks and this was one of their favourite date nights and it only cost a few pennies. They went to the Warner pictures in Leicester Square avoiding the Gaumont cinema at Tally Ho Corner It was too close to where Elena lived and Christaki's father's cobblers. They did not want to bump into anyone who may pass on gossip to their parents.

Christaki had never felt happier and was sure his family would love Elena as much as he did. His love for her grew with each moment he spent with her; she was not only an absolute beauty but had a warm, jovial personality which counter-balanced her serious, mature attitude towards work and earning a living to improve her circumstances. Although Christaki's family were wealthy he had ambitions and dreams of his own which took him beyond the family's attitude towards wealth and money. He wanted money to change his life; to give him something more. With Elena by his side he was certain they would achieve everything they both dreamed and wished for.

One evening, while sitting in the back row waiting for the Cliff Richard film *Expresso Bongo* to start, Christaki took Elena's hand and placed it between his legs. He felt the tremor of excitement run through her as she felt his arousal pushing through his tight trousers.

'This is what you do to me Elena.'

'How?'

'Because you're you,' he whispered in her ear before leaning in to kiss her. She wriggled as he nuzzled her neck.

'You're tickling me.' Aware of her uncertainty he loved her even more for it and he felt his own excited trembling fill him. He was as new to this loving thing as she was yet he couldn't slow down. His head became fumbled; a fish caught in a net. He wrestled with a wild, craving for her, a real physical desire, which pumped through his heart.

She left her hand there, between his legs, throughout the entire film. Christaki understood how awkward it must have been for her, but he liked it; liked the way it felt; the way it fitted there.

She didn't move it even when they kissed, more urgently this time. Their kissing became more and more fervent, fired up. Each time they kissed it was like she was stoking a fire within him. The feelings Christaki felt were like none he had ever felt before and he loved Elena all the more for making him feel that way. Everything about her was pure beauty and she oozed sexy...not a word he had used before, ever, but it was the only way to describe her delicious full lips on his, her big pert breasts as he lost himself in their buxomness, and her smooth long legs. He ran his hands over her legs and stopped at her ankles, so slim he could close each hand around them.

When he was with her, it was as if, the rest of the world did not exist. He was lost in her; her smell, her touch, her taste and although he only smoked tobacco he imagined even smoking pot wouldn't make him feel like this.

'You're my living doll,' he sang to her. 'Gotta do my best to please you. You satisfy my soul,' he sang Cliff Richard's words to her.

'You sound just like him.'

'I want to spend the night with you,' he said. He kissed her, devouring her lips and tongue.

'The night?' Her voice caught in her throat as she pulled away from him.

'I'm going to find a way. I can't keep stopping like this. Controlling myself around you is impossible.' And he broke into song again, 'My living doll. You satisfy my soul.'

Elena was playful and laughed and giggled which he recognised as nerves. She shied away when he gave her a compliment. He loved the way she held back from him; her long mascaraed lashes sweeping across her hazel eyes. Yet he could tell she was like a bird, set free, when she was with him.

***

'Someone at work was due to have two days off,' said Melani as she came in from work a few days later.

'And?' asked Christaki.

'She's booked a room at the seaside to visit his friend's sister; she's a nurse at the local hospital.'

'And?'Christaki's impatience was getting the better

of him.

'She's not going now, something about an extra shift her husband can't get out of, but it's too late to cancel the room. I've told her you'll take it and pay her over and above what she's paid.'

'You are genius. But I don't think Elena be allowed to go, to stay out all night.' Maybe Melani didn't have someone secretly hiding somewhere otherwise she would have found a way to take the room herself he thought.

'One step ahead of you. She can say Janet's parents are going to visit family in wherever and Janet's asked Elena to keep her company while she's gone.'

'Do you think Elena will go for that? And her mum be persuaded?'

'There's only one way to find out.'

***

Two weeks later Christaki and Elena boarded a crowded Brighton Belle at Victoria Station. A previous train had been cancelled and so passengers were travelling on the later train.

Elena and Christaki's journey was uncomfortable. Elena giggled and laughed at the situation while Christaki was irritated by it; the carriage was overcrowded and noisy. It was as romantic or intimate as he would have liked it to be. While Elena chatted with an old lady travelling to visit her niece in Brighton, Christaki was being poked in the ribs by a large gentleman invading his personal space and taking up at least a third of his seat. All he wanted to do was sit next to Elena. To feel her warm body next to his, to hold her hand, to look into those beautiful eyes. Instead he was being ambushed by a grizzly bear.

He tried to pass his time, by looking out of the window at the scenery, which he would normally have found inspiring. The train passed through tunnels and carved out crevices in the mountains, rocky terrain, woodland scattered with farms and villages and rolling chalk cliffs. But he was itching to get to Brighton and although he noticed the landscape, he didn't appreciate it and it passed in a blur. Thoughts only of Elena and being with her crowded his mind.

Eventually, the overweight gentleman alighted the train and Elena moved next to Christaki. But their closeness was short-lived; an elderly lady carrying two oversized bags looked at Elena pityingly and Elena gave up her seat for her so she could sit comfortably with her luggage next to her in the gangway.

***

Once they alighted the train at Brighton, Christaki felt his anxiety and frustrations pass. He took Elena's small suitcase, threw his bag over his shoulder and reached for her hand. He held onto it tightly. After traipsing around for half an hour, and after asking three different people for directions, they stumbled across the hotel set back along a side street off the sea front. A tall picturesque building, it was painted blue, with window boxes full of geraniums and pansies at the windows.

The landlady welcomed them with a hearty cheer and showed them to their room tucked away on the top floor; hidden in the gabled roof of the tall town house. It was perfect. The bed was a double with a pretty flowery bedspread and fresh white pillowcases. A small ceramic jug of pansies sat on the dressing table and there was a sink in the corner of the room.

'Finally here,' said Christaki throwing himself onto the bed and kicking off his shoes.

'We are.'

'Come here then.'

'Let me unpack first. I don't want my clothes to crease.' Christaki sensed her nervousness and didn't persist.

He watched, with patience and control he was unaware he possessed until now. She shook out her dress and hung it up. She put her underwear in the drawer of the dresser and pushed the suitcase behind the armchair in the corner of the room. He marvelled at the make-up and toiletries she had with her and wondered whether Melani had that much. He'd never noticed.

'So,' she said.

'So,' he teased.

He pulled her onto the bed. Lying next to him he planted a long, deep kiss on her lips.

'Wow,' she said licking her lips, her eyes sparkling like nuggets of gold in the day's dusky light.

***

After a walk along the pier and a simple dinner of fish and chips, straight out of the newspaper wrapping and drenched in vinegar, he loved Elena with a passion he never realised he had in him. He kissed her, enjoyed their caresses and then finally he made love to her; sweet, innocent and then hungry, hot.

He didn't want the night to end. He watched her sleep as she curled into him. He was sure he loved her with all of his heart. Nothing was going to stop him from marrying this girl.

Chapter Twenty-Three

Christaki, 1959

BACK IN LONDON, Christaki focused on his work and threw himself into his training with more vigour and energy than ever. He had to make money to save up for a house. He would need a home to offer Elena if they were to get married. He understood her family were not well off and calculated how him being able to offer her a home and a stable life style with love and security would help to win her parents over.

He continued to meet Elena once a week and although they never spent the night together again it had a lasting effect on him and kept him close to her as well as pushed him ever closer to his dream, of being husband and wife, one day. Melani seemed to soften over time. She threatened to tell his parents about his liaison with Elena only once and had since not mentioned saying anything again. Christaki silenced her by giving her money and although he hated giving in to her the thought of losing Elena was far worse than his hurt pride.

'You're so lucky you've met Elena,' said Melani as they were laying the table for dinner one evening.

'Yes I am and you will be too one day.'

'Somehow I don't imagine my life will be so simple

dear brother.'

'Course it will be. Why wouldn't it?'

'Because…nothing. Forget it.'

'Tell me. What is it?'

'It's nothing. Just that life would've been simpler if we'd all stayed in the village. Cyprus was simple. We all knew how to behave, what to do, what was expected and there were no distractions, nothing to take us off course.'

'Well you didn't do a good job of it, that strike and all.'

'I mean love and relationships.'

'You'll meet someone too Melani. You'll be happy. Mother and Father will soon be introducing eligible men to you.'

'So, you're still keen to marry her?' she asked changing the subject.

'You know I am. Why?'

'You know. I just need to know what's going on.'

'Well you do know. And don't you have your own life to think about?'

'You won't have one though if I tell Mother and Father what's been going on!'

'Melani I know it's hard sometimes. I feel it too. Go and have some fun,' he said.

'I will. On Friday,' she smiled at him as she took the money he handed to her.

***

Christaki thought about his sister as he lay in his bed that night. How well did he know her? She had a fair amount of freedom since working, more so than she would have had in Cyprus. She worked away from her mother's prying eyes and away from home which he knew was unusual for a Greek girl. As he lay in the semi-darkness, the hooting of an owl piercing the night's silence, he wondered what was going on with her. He recalled how she flirted with Pete; his sister was a young woman, a manipulative, clever woman yet she could be kind and loving too. What man wouldn't want to be with her?

His thoughts continued to plague him into the early hours. Did she have a boyfriend? He wondered who it would be if she did and why she hadn't told him. Was he English? Was he Irish? He was sure that, if it had been a boy from Cyprus, she would have told him. He was suddenly annoyed with himself for taking his eye off the ball. His parents relied on him to keep an eye on her and to keep her from mischief, more so than on Pavlo who still lived at the hotel. He remembered her involvement in the school strikes back home and shuddered. She could so easily have been arrested that day.

***

One Friday afternoon, a few weeks later, Christaki decided to follow Melani. He knew she clocked out at half past five. He stood by the bus stop waiting for her to emerge from the staff entrance.

At a minute past the half hour, Melani bundled out just as he had anticipated and tied a brightly coloured scarf around her head. She leaned against the wall and lit a cigarette. Shocked, Christaki wanted to confront her about smoking but knew he would then have to explain why he was there in the first place. He watched as she puffed deeply on the cigarette, smoke curling and rising into the air away from her. After three or four drags she threw it to the ground and stepped on it, twisting on her toes as she did so. She looked confident away from home. She looked more sure of herself than the seventeen-year old she was and wondered when she had become so self-assured.

He waited to see which direction she would take and then followed her keeping his distance a few paces behind her; a woman and two young boys walking between them, camouflaged him if she were to look back.

After walking at a steady pace for about ten minutes, weaving in and out of the growing pedestrian traffic and end of the day commuters, he saw her stop outside a small community hall. He wondered what she would be doing there. He watched her face break into a smile as a small child, a girl, of maybe five or six, came out of the main doors towards her. Melani stooped and hugged the child in her arms.

Taking her by the hand, together they walked back towards the main road. Who was the little girl? How did

Melani know her?

On the high street they resembled any mother and daughter walking together hand in hand, chatting, laughing. They disappeared into the Wimpy and at this point Christaki decided, without a second thought, to follow them in a few minutes later.

'Melani! What are you doing here?'

'Oh, Christaki. This is Rose. This is my brother Chris.' She used the short English version of her brother's name to introduce him.

'Hello Chris,' said Rose.

Christaki sat next to Rose. He was unsure of what the situation was and knew this was not the time to confront his sister, especially in front of the little girl who had her hair in bunches and a face dotted with brown freckles.

'So what brings you here?' asked Melani.

'I was, you know, just passing and saw you.'

'You mean you were spying on me.' An awkward silence fell across the table, interrupted by the waitress who brought over two milkshakes.

'Anything for you?' the waitress asked pushing out her buxom bosoms stretching the fabric of her outfit as it strained against the popping buttons.

'Oh yes, a tea please. Thank you,' said Christaki.

'So who's Rose?'

'She's John's daughter, one of the managers at the Telephone Exchange. We're good friends. I help him out by looking after her.'

'Oh right. And Rose's mum?'

'She's no longer around. It's the two of them, Rose and her dad. Isn't that right sweet heart?'

'Me and you against the world!' Rose sing-sang in a shrill voice.

'That's right.' Melani leaned in and tickled Rose under the arms until she begged her to stop.

'Oh right. So you look after Rose as a favour?'

'No not exactly. Now's not the time to discuss this.'

'Discuss what?' A tall fair-haired man, with long legs and a dark suit loomed over them.

'John. This is John. John O'Brien. This is my brother Chris.'

'Daddy!' cried Rose nearly knocking over her milkshake.

'Hello my angel. Have you been a good girl for Melly?'

'As always,' said Melani, her face tinging crimson red as she spoke.

John pulled over a chair from the adjacent table and ordered a milkshake too from the passing waitress.

'Pleased to meet you Chris. Nice to meet a member of the family at last. I was beginning to imagine you all had red horns or fangs or something. Anyway sorry to interrupt.'

'No it's fine. I was telling Chris it's the two of you, you and Rose.'

'Yeah. Her mum buggered off with some bloke and

disappeared to Cork.'

'Oh, I'm sorry.'

'No don't be. Best thing that could've happened, otherwise I wouldn't have changed jobs and wouldn't have met your wonderful sister.' There was an awkward silence as John pulled back from Melly realising too late his kiss was inappropriate in front of her brother.

'Anyway what do you do Chris?'

'Apprentice electrician. Close to finishing.'

'Good for you. There will always be a call for electricians.'

The rest of the half hour was filled with small talk and when John left with Rose, Melani and Christaki stayed behind to talk.

'So?'

'I know what you're going to say so don't say it.'

'What? I was going to say he seems like a great guy and his daughter is lovely but do you really want to be involved with a man who has been married, has a daughter and who isn't Greek?'

'It's too late Christaki. I'm already involved. Mum and Dad will kill me but I love him. And he loves me. He wants to get married.'

'Well good luck with that one. Mum and Dad won't have it.'

'I don't care. I'm going to do whatever makes me happy. And this is it. John makes me happy. I'll run away if I have to. I don't care.'

'You will break their hearts. You know that don't you?'

'And what about mine?'

He looked across at her; the defiance of her chin, her steely eyes, pouty lips.

'You'll have to tell them both how you feel. You can't go on sneaking around.'

'I'm not sneaking around. I see him whenever I want.'

'You know what I mean. Before someone sees you and tells them. That's what they'll never forgive Melani.'

'I know. Will you tell them with me?'

'Yes I'll try but I'm not sure I agree with what you're doing.'

'You don't have to agree. I'm doing it anyway.'

That same evening, after they finished eating and the plates were cleared, Melani broached the subject. Her father sat with the newspaper open on his lap in the sitting room and her mother was darning a pile of socks, her hands working methodically as she pulled the needle through the wool and neatened the ends off.

'Father, Mother I wanted to speak to you about something. Something important.'

'What is it?' Loizos asked, his concentration momentarily distracted from his reading. Christaki knew he had detected the quiver in his daughter's voice.

'I've met a man and we want to be married.' Melani

spoke with a slow and deliberate tone, her shoulders pushed back. She stood tall her body ready for the verbal attack she clearly anticipated.

'A man? Where did you meet him? Who introduced you?' asked Loizos, his body suddenly rigid, tension straining his features.

'Why this is a surprise,' said Anastasia as equally shocked as her husband.

'I work with him at the exchange. His name's John and he has a daughter called Rose.'

'A daughter? No Melani, please don't tell me he's already married.'

'He's not married any more. His wife left him. His daughter's an angel. You'll both love her.'

'Don't you dare to presume this is acceptable!' her father stood up, throwing his newspaper across the room. 'How dare you see a man, a married man behind our backs! How dare you disregard and disrespect our way of doing things!'

'Loizos calm yourself. Please,' begged Anastasia.

'And you knew about this?' Loizos addressed Christaki, his voice thunder, spittle on his lips, bubbling in the corners of his mouth as he spat the words out.

'I only found out tonight. A few hours ago.'

Loizos paced the room. He kicked the side table; its contents flying across the room, a broken glass and debris covered the carpet.

'I'm furious. I'm disgusted!' Before anyone could

say anything else he struck Melani across the face and pulling her by the hair dragged her through the door, along the hallway and to the front door. 'Don't come back! Ever!' He pushed her out into the street, slammed the front door shut, the glass panes shaking.

'Loizos, no.' But Anastasia, Christaki could see, was talking to a deaf man. His father went upstairs and stayed there the rest of the evening.

Downstairs, Anastasia quietly let Melani in after hearing her sobbing outside the front door. Melani unusually offered to make some tea and the three of them sat, at first, without a word between them, the merry chink of the china mocking them.

'So what happens now?' asked Melani eventually.

'I don't know. You really have shocked us though. How could you do this?'

'I haven't done anything. I've fallen in love. I'm happy.'

'But he's not even Cypriot. He has a child.'

'Yes mother, a child! Not a devil.'

'I'm disappointed Melani and I can't make any promises but I will try to speak to your father. In the meantime, you must promise me not to see John again until we sort out where to go from here. Your father and I will need to meet this man. We must do things properly from this moment forward…if we are to meet him at all.'

'But…'

'No! Don't argue Melani. I'm on your side but you have to be patient now. You have to trust me.'

'Do as Mother says Melani,' urged Christaki.

They finished their tea and after Melani took the cups into the kitchen they all retired to bed. There were no more conversations that night. His mother's heavy footsteps shuffled as she climbed the stairs, followed by the muffled sounds of talking behind the closed bedroom door. He gave Melani a hug and even though he disagreed with what she was doing, the situation she found herself in wasn't all that different to his, as he knew he was deceiving his parents too. He went to bed with a heavy heart.

***

After a night of broken sleep Christaki woke early, as the yellow sun rose above the rooftops, casting a glow into his bedroom through the gap in the curtain. He rubbed at the corners of his eyes and for a second was sure he could hear the hiss of the sea. He dressed and, grabbing a cold pie left over from dinner the night before, made his way to work.

All day he was on edge. He wondered what his parents' final decision would be and whether he too should be open and come clean about seeing Elena. The thought of disappointing his parents hurt him physically and he felt his heart pushing hard in his chest. He worked through lunch, sweat mingling with the dirt, his shirt clinging to his skin like a dusty damp sheet. He was meant to be meeting Elena in the evening briefly after work but something in him squashed his excitement and he felt sick at the betrayal.

'What's wrong Christaki?' asked Elena as they sat in the far corner of the restaurant, hidden from view by the dark oak partition.

'It's Melani. She's been seeing someone. He's got a daughter and she's told my parents she wants to marry him. They are reeling from the betrayal and the lack of respect for our traditions. It's made me think I'm just as bad. They deserve better. They have always raised us to do the right thing and yet here we are, lying to them.'

'Then let's tell them together and then I can tell my parents too or at least my mum.'

'I will tell my father first. I can tell him at the shop when I visit him. It's a good place to have a conversation.'

***

Later that week he broached the subject with his father.

'Father do you remember the young girl I introduced you to a few weeks ago? Elena.'

'Yes, I do. Pretty girl. Hazel-brown eyes.'

'Father. Please don't be disappointed in me but I've fallen in love with her. I want to marry her.'

'You're telling me this because of Melani?'

402

'No, yes. I didn't want any more secrets.'

'Secrets?'

'I've been seeing her and I know that's wrong in your eyes Father but we are close. She is respectable and loving and kind and hard-working.'

'I understand Christaki *mou*. But will her parents?'

'Well I want to tell them. I want us to tell them together. You and Mother too.'

'How will we arrange the meeting?'

'There must be a way of doing it so she does not lose her respect.'

'Respect? You should've thought of that before my boy,' Loizos said with a slight growl in his voice, 'But I do agree with you, she's a lovely girl.'

***

As coincidence would have it, Georgette was in the cobblers two weeks later and saw Christaki there too. He busied himself stacking some newly delivered boxes of shoes on the higher shelves for his father. She mentioned a young woman called Elena, the daughter of her friend, and wondered whether the family would be interested in a *proxenia*. And so it was organised.

***

The situation with Melani, however, did not pan out so

well and daily arguments filled the house every time the family found themselves together until one day completely unannounced and out of the blue Melani arrived home with John in tow.

'Pleased to meet you Mr and Mrs Dionysiou,' said John.

Loizos shook the young man by the hand formally; Christaki could see how his father fought with his inner emotions, the tension across his eyes, but he was not a rude man and his daughter's poor behaviour was not going to let him forget that. Anastasia looked across at her husband before saying hello to John.

They all took a seat, Melani sat next to John on the couch, Christaki pulled over a chair from the dining room table and Loizos sat opposite them all, in his single seater.

'I'll make coffee,' said Anastasia as she scuttled out of the room, her slippers slapping the floor as she went; the sound warm, comforting in the otherwise austere silence.

'So you work at the Telephone Exchange.'

'Yes, Sir. I am a manager there. Oversee a team of twenty-two.'

'And you have a daughter?'

'Rose. She's five years old.'

'And your wife is no longer in your life?'

'No, Sir. She is somewhere in Ireland. She has no claim on Rose...or me.'

'Well it seems as though you are doing a fine job

caring for your daughter on your own. It's not easy bringing up a family, working...it takes energy, commitment, guts.'

'Thank you, Sir.'

'And now you want to marry my daughter and you think I should let her, with no ties, no messy background, an honourable background and upbringing, marry you?'

'Sir, I would be most honoured. She is a wonderful woman and Rose loves her...'

'Oh and I love her so much. She's such a lovely little girl. You would all love her too. I just know it,' Melani said with passion and excitement in her voice; Christaki knew she was running ahead of herself.

'We have become a family,' said John reaching over to take Melani's hand and then pulling it back when he noticed disapproval cloud Loizos' face.

'Well now is not the time to discuss this. This is not our way.'

'But Sir, I love her.'

'I need to consider this thoroughly. But I appreciate you making the effort to come here.' Christaki knew these words were not easy to say for his father, and his heart filled with pride to be his son.

Anastasia bustled in with a large tray tinkering with not only her best crockery but a platter piled high with *shamishi*; deep fried doughy folds covered in a thick layer of icing sugar. She passed round the little cups filled to the brim with the thick Greek coffee and offered a sweet pastry to John. Christaki admired his mother's resolve to be polite and to remain hospitable.

***

Over the next few months there was much discussion, many arguments and a lot of door slamming on Melani's part. Melani went from being openly disobedient to a shadow of herself, losing weight, hardly eating. It was as if the silver moon of hope had faded, taking with it Melani's gleaming light.

Chapter Twenty-Four

Elena, 1959

'YOU SAW *THEIO* Zeno on the bus? When? Why didn't you tell me? Was Niko with him?' Elena's questions came pouring out as the bus trundled along.

'A few days ago. Yes, Niko's here too but I didn't see him.'

'That's wonderful. Andreas will be so pleased to see our old friend. What other news did *theio* have? How is everyone?' Elena saw her mum's hesitation. 'What is it? What's wrong?'

'*Theia* Maroulla was killed in an explosion. *Theio* Zeno is here on his own with Niko. They're living fairly locally, apparently. I didn't ask. I was so shocked to see him, to hear his terrible news.'

'*Theia's* dead? Oh my God, that's awful. I can't believe it.' Elena struggled to swallow as bubbling grief rose within her.

Evangelia said nothing more and Elena reached for her hand. The sun blinded Elena's eyes and she averted them to avoid its glare. The bus was surprisingly full but she remembered it was the school summer holidays; the usual crowd of mothers with their prams and pupil-age children were out enjoying the unusually hot weather. She stretched her legs out in an effort to cool herself and kicked someone. Ready to apologise, she found herself staring into the eyes of Christaki.

'Hello,' said Christaki.

'Oh hello.' Elena could feel her mother's eyes on her and realised instantly she would be wondering who the young man was. Before she had time to articulate an answer Christaki was introducing himself.

'I'm Christaki.'

'Oh yes. And how are you acquainted with my daughter?'

'We met briefly one afternoon. My sister Melani works with Janet, Elena's friend, and Janet knows a friend of my brother's too. They work in a hotel, in the kitchens.' Elena felt herself cringing at how Christaki was evidently trying to justify their acquaintance.

'That's nice. Well pleased to meet you, Christaki you said?'

'Christaki, yes. Chris in English,' he said as Elena stifled a giggle at his response, before they all, rather awkwardly, got off at the same stop.

'I'm going to see my father. He owns the cobblers on Lincoln Road. It's been nice meeting you *Kiria* Evangelia,' said Christaki. Elena gave him a cheeky smile which was returned. Oh how he made her giddy! For a moment she forgot the sad news about her *theia*.

***

Walking home her mum strode ahead, taking long, determined steps.

'Wait *mama*. I can't keep up with you.'

'No, but it seems you can keep up with everybody else. I cannot believe you've been out with that boy behind my back.'

'I've not been out with him. He's been at the same place as me and Janet. That's all. I can't avoid men all my life Mum. Because Dad's a bad one it doesn't mean all men are like that.'

She saw how her mum's shoulders softened and her pace slowed a little. 'No, you're right. There are some good men out there. But you mustn't be seen Elena *mou*. People will talk, say things about you and then no one will want to marry you if you're unpure.'

'Oh *mama*. What people? We're all the same. Who's going to see me talking to a boy? A man? And think it's wrong?'

'Greek people talk. And two things spread quickly; gossip and a forest fire!' said her mother.

Elena rolled her eyes.

'We mustn't forget our roots and the way things ought to be done. I will have to speak to your dad about this. I can't have you talking to that boy without his parents' permission or your father's for that matter.'

'Well it's too late. I've met his dad. And Dad knows too.' As soon as the words were out she regretted them.

'What? When? How?' Her mother's voice caught in

the back of her throat.

'He worked it out the day I saw him on the high street and I couldn't deny it. I couldn't lie to him. That would've made me as bad as him.'

'And the boy?'

'Christaki walked me home. And he took me to meet his dad at his shop.'

'This is a disaster.'

'Oh *mama* it isn't anything. We walked and talked.' But deep inside Elena couldn't deny how she felt about Christaki and wondered whether she should tell her mum of her true feelings before Christaki met anyone else and she lost her chance with him.

At home, she watched as her mum lit a candle by her icon of Mary holding baby Jesus and her mouth moved in prayer, Oh, Holy Mother…she watched as her mother crossed herself and kissed the icon, desperation on her face. Elena wondered whether she was praying for her *theia* Maroulla or for Elena and she silently crossed herself too hoping for some sort of comfort, reassurance from above that all would be well. The tears welled and stung the back of her eyes.

***

'Please come for a cup of coffee Evangelia. Bring Elena,' said Georgette as she loaded the washer in the launderette.

'Thank you for the invitation Georgette, but I wouldn't want to impose.'

'Not at all. We're friends after all. Come next week on Tuesday after work.'

'I don't much feel like it. We had bad news about a friend. Well you would have heard of course.'

'Maroulla? Yes, I did. God rest her soul. But our lives go on.'

***

The following week Elena and her mum walked into Georgette's house only to find another family there too. Elena couldn't believe her eyes.

'These are our good friends,' said Georgette as she introduced everyone. '*Kirio* Loizos, his wife *Kiria* Anastasia and their three children; Christaki, Pavlo and Melani.'

Elena sat on the edge of her seat praying Christaki's father didn't say anything about meeting her previously.

Christaki smirked a couple of times in her direction; a silly smile which made her heart leap like rabbits in spring.

Her mum appeared awkward; perched on the arm of the sofa, her arms crossed, her lips tightly clamped. Elena felt her mum's discomfort and knew it was because she already knew of Elena and Christaki's acquaintance.

They sat and had their Greek coffee; the chatter

between them, although mainly one-sided, was of pleasant happy memories of home; the smell of pine in the air after a rainfall, the wake-up call of the cockerel, and the vines heavy with grapes, their scent filling the air. They talked too about their serious concern over the continuing conflict back home and the stories of more and more arrests in the middle of the night, of casualties for both the Cypriots and the Turks and of course the young British soldiers too.

***

Two days later, again in the laundrette Elena and her mother bumped into Georgette.

She took Evangelia's hand and said, 'Christaki is a lovely boy. He's a good match for your Elena, no? He's expressed an interest in her Evangelia *mou*. He'd like your permission to meet again.'

Elena's eyes widened. She said nothing but felt her palms become sweaty with nerves and excitement.

***

It was arranged the two families meet again at Elena's home; this time Elena's father was to be present. Her mother insisted they create the right impression.

Elena's nerves ate away at her. She could relate to how forced hospitality, in the *proxenia* situation, was hugely embarrassing; her cousin Emilia had been introduced to a man ten years older than her and she had locked herself in the outside lavvy for nearly an hour. Even Elena had not been successful in coaxing her back into the house until eventually the family left with their son having been convinced Emilia had a poor tummy. Elena had giggled until she was doubled over, holding her aching side.

Elena ate nothing of nutritional value the entire day, but demolished a whole bag of Sherbet Lemons and Raspberry Drops. She tried various outfits, clothes spilled over the bed and onto the floor and her wardrobe doors hung open like a gaping mouth full of chewed food. Finally, she settled on a sky blue dress with golden yellow flowers printed over it. It was tight-fitting, gently hugging the curve of her hips and small waist. The scooped neckline not revealing any of her ample bust and the short sleeves had a button detail. Her neat kitten heels in a matching blue finished off her outfit. She spent over an hour setting and backcombing her hair into a tall but soft beehive. She applied her make-up with a shaking hand but in her heart sensed this was going to be easy. She knew Christaki liked her and could find no reason why her father would disapprove of him.

Her dad didn't let her down and a stunned swell of pride filled her heart. He was clean shaven and put on his grey flannel trousers; his shirt was starched and his shoes, which Elena had polished the night before, shone like a sheet of glass in the sun.

Her mother wore a navy dress and a white scarf around her neck. Elena noted how she was playing with it; nervous she thought.

Elena heard her mother's pleas from her bedroom at the end of the hall. 'Andreas, don't go out tonight.'

'It won't make any difference me being here *mama*.'

'It will show we are a united, supportive family.'

'But we're not are we...Dad's hardly ever here.' said Andreas, losing his temper.

Elena stood in the doorway and watched him grab his leather jacket and a packet of cigarettes from the coffee table.

'Stop arguing, show some respect. Andreas...don't be late. This is important and I want you here.' Kostas spoke with authority.

At exactly half past six the doorbell rang and Kostas went downstairs to let their guests in. The flat looked immaculate; Elena spent all of Friday evening after work and Saturday morning scrubbing, sweeping and wiping from corner to corner. The open windows let in what little summer breeze there was and the starched white nets fluttered freely. She stared across at her mother who was crossing herself and re-arranging one of the icons on the mantelpiece alongside the one photograph they had of their home in Cyprus. She knew her mother would be praying for the right outcome from the meeting.

Everyone warmly kissed and shook hands. The small front room soon overflowed with conversation.

Evangelia, wearing the one good dress she owned, showed Anastasia her embroidered table cloths.

'How beautiful, you sew *Kiria* Evangelia, with such precision. You must have the patience of a saint. I sew too, mainly on the machine, though I hand finish hems and sew buttons by hand,' said Anastasia.

'Oh I do machining too. I take in blouses and skirts and I do finishing too, but that doesn't bring me the same joy as my *Lefkaritika.*'

'Well I can see why, it's beautiful. And your thread is as soft as silk.'

'My friend sends it, bless her, otherwise I couldn't sew here. The cottons are not the same from the haberdashery.'

'Yes, there are so many things I miss too from our beloved homeland. I miss my stone oven the most. I used to bake bread every week and even for my neighbours too. I miss the smell of the carob leaves. I used to bake the bread on the leaves, oh what a smell. The bread here is tasteless. Christaki still complains about it.'

'What do I complain about?' asked Christaki, hearing the mention of his name.

'The bread, the weather, the people. What don't you complain about?' smiled his mother as if to soften her accusation.

'I only speak the truth. But I've made some good

friends here too,' he said looking towards Elena.

'Yes Cyprus is a wonderful country but we have to face facts, it's in the midst of a civil war and there seems to be no solution in sight. Archbishop Makarios may be elected as President now that he's back in Cyprus. His deportment must've lasted, what three years? But still what hope will that bring?' Loizos' voice trailed off.

'Everyone believes in him but he may be a wolf in sheep's clothing, hiding behind religion.'

'Who knows? It's still a mess whatever anybody reports.'

'I heard about the looting and burning buildings. Civilians killed daily on all sides, it's a dreadful situation. The bomb at the cinema in Larnaca and the two men killed in their own *kafeneion*…another bomb on the outskirts of Paphos' said Kostas.

'Well, we must pray for peace again soon,' said Evangelia.

Eventually the conversation fizzled out and Kostas stubbed out his half-smoked cigarette.

'Now we have drunk our coffee let's speak of the reason we are here.' Kostas' voice echoed around the room as he spoke a little too loudly. He must be nervous too, thought Elena.

'We don't need to ask anything. We are already informed and we are sure.' Loizos spoke in a hushed grainy voice, but not with the assurance Elena had heard him speak before.

Elena didn't expect such a definitive answer so early on in the gathering. She had still been dreading their meeting, at the cobblers with Christaki, being mentioned. She tried to appear composed but on the inside the blood was pushing its way around her body so hard and fast she thought she would burst.

'Elena bring some olives, some food from the kitchen,' said her dad. Elena noticed how he appeared overly excited and wondered whether she had missed something. She walked past Christaki who was sitting on a chair near the door and tripped over the edge of the rug. He reached out to stop her from losing her balance. She felt her full cheeks redden like round fat beetroots.

'What's happening out there? I can hear talking, lots of it,' said her mother bustling in the kitchen over the plates of food she had prepared.

'They say they're sure *mama*.'

'So soon. No other meetings? Darling how wonderful. How blessed you are to have found such a decent man. I know he will love you and I pray to God he will look after you always.'

'It's got nothing to do with love,' interrupted her dad as he walked in. 'He looks like a good, hard-working boy and he seems to be a one-woman man. He has no idea about the clubs in the West End. I prompted him and he stared blankly at me…even seemed a little embarrassed at being unable to respond.' He hesitated and then carried on with a catch in his voice. 'The family are well off. I believe they may be able to help us.'

'So you're hedging your bets on help? What sort of help?' asked Elena.

'Whatever I need,' said Kostas.

'What does that mean?'

'Never you mind,' he stumbled on. 'The family have not questioned what I do or what sort of a man I am. Their only interest is in Elena. For that we must be thankful. So we will wait and see how this plays out.'

'Plays out?' Elena felt her eyes widen like full moons.

'I know I could be a better husband, a better father to you. Just let me deal with this.'

Overcome with emotion, Elena hugged her father with a mixture of love, pity and loathing for all he had put them through. Despite all his faults, she shook off the bad feeling she had in the pit of her stomach. She knew despite his weaknesses, his mistakes, he was a loving man. He hugged her back, stroking her shoulders and arms affectionately.

'Whatever you believe is the right thing, Kostas,' said her mother. Elena knew her mum was rooting for her father to agree to the union.

They all walked back into the sitting room and placed the small plates of typical Cypriot delicacies on the table. The smell of mint sprinkled over the *spanakopites,* filled the air with a fresh light scent and black olives gleamed in spirals of pastry. The fried halloumi chunks, all the way from Cyprus, were gifted to them by Georgette to celebrate the meeting. The salty smell reminded Elena of the sea the day they boarded the ship. There were salted and roasted almonds from the trees in *Kato Lefkara*, apricots and peaches preserved in syrup, dried figs and freshly sliced apples.

Elena carried in side plates and the linen napkins they had so carefully brought from Cyprus so long ago. Embroidered by Elena's great, great grandmother, she could not remember ever seeing them being used before.

'We're not looking for money and a dowry. We can see you're a good honest young woman Elena,' said Loizos.

'So?' asked her dad. 'If you're keen to agree to the *loyiasma*, future betrothal, I want your word that you are committed to Christaki and Elena getting engaged,' Kostas said to Loizos.

'You have my word,' said Loizos.

'What have I missed?' Andreas asked as he walked in.

The flow of the proceedings was interrupted with introductions and Christaki edged over towards Elena.

'May we have our health and happiness always,' he whispered to her.

'Let's drink to their union.' Kostas opened a bottle of *zivania,* brought over from Cyprus and kept in the back of the pantry for such an occasion. He poured the clear liquid into tumblers, too generously, and stood to make a toast; the raised glasses chinking loudly as they touched in unison.

'To our children's union.'

'To Christaki and Elena,' said Loizos. 'And a peaceful Cyprus once more.'

The mention of Cyprus took hold of Elena's feelings and they swirled around her like fizzy pop; she missed Niko and all the others too; Stella, Yioli, Petro, Sofia, Stella and wished she could have shared her good news with them face to face, other than in the affectionate letters she wrote less and less often as time had gone on. She thought of their little open courtyard with its fruit trees and warm stone floor, a deliberate exercise in nostalgia, and she wished her happiness could be magically transferred back home and she allowed herself to be cocooned in sadness.

***

Two nights later the doorbell rang. Elena ran down the stairs, her hair still damp, and loose around her shoulders, after washing it.

'Christaki.'

'Elena. How are you?'

'I'm good thank you. You?'

'I couldn't wait to see you. These are for you.' He handed her twelve long stemmed crimson red roses, and as she took the bunch from him her fingers touched his.

Her whole body felt a shot of electricity.

'No-one has ever bought me flowers before,' she gasped, elated and excited about the future.

'And no-one else ever will. You're mine. I'm yours.' His face shone like a dazzlingly lit mirror. He leaned in towards her and kissed her on the lips. She leaned in towards him; the flowers gently dropping to the floor. Her heart raced. It was the most delicious kiss she thought she would ever have. Pure happiness charged through her veins and she imagined her blood was the brightest red it would ever be.

'Father sealed the deal with yours, but believe me when I say I want this.'

'What are you talking about? What deal?' Elena lowered her voice, fearing to be overheard.

'Your father's debts, I'm going to pay them off in return for his blessing.'

'You're going to do what?'

'Elena, I thought you knew. It's to avoid any discredit to you or me.'

'Discredit? Discredit? And you think that 'buying' me doesn't do that?'

'It's not like that, trust me.'

'Trust is a big word,' said Elena.

Christaki held her gaze. The shriek of a cat broke the moment between them. He was determined not to pressurise her into committing herself to him now her father's indiscretion was out.

Dusk began to settle with a shiver and Elena, too afraid to say something she may regret, watched the sky darken behind him. She cut their conversation short, making excuses she had sewing to do. She harnessed her instinct to shout and pushed away her feeling of profound irritation. She closed the door, careful not to slam it in Christaki's face which is what she felt like doing. She hung on the latch and then leaned back against the door, hugging herself, tears flooding her face, a pulsing pain in her temples. How could her father do this? How could he tarnish even something as beautiful, and as innocent, as this for her?

'Dad, we need to talk,' Elena said as calmly as she could muster as she grabbed her coat from the hallway stand.

'Talk? About what?'

'Not here. I don't want Mum hearing this,' she said. 'Mum? I'm popping out with Dad to Radio Rentals...pay the TV and radio for next month,' she called to her mum, who was pottering in the kitchen.

'Okay *agabi mou*. Ask how many payments we still have left too.'

'See you soon. We won't be long.'

Her father pulled on his jacket over his turtleneck and slicked back his hair.

They walked along the busy street. Elena pulled away from her father as he tried to lock her arm into his. She looked straight ahead, conscious she had hurt his feelings, but she was seething. In her jacket pocket, she fingered the glass *mati* one of the women at work had given her when she had heard about her union to be married. She played with the smooth rounded edges of the blue bead, a talisman against the evil eye, and trusted it would protect her.

Elena pulled out one of the plastic seats in the café, brushing a few crumbs off it before she lowered herself into the seat. Her father sat opposite her, calling across to the waitress for two mugs of tea. The café's stillness accentuated his booming voice as it cut across the quiet. The clink of cutlery and the sizzling of a grill the only sounds, the lingering smell of grease and coffee.

'Dad, what's going on with Christaki?'

'What d'you mean? He's marrying you.'

'I mean with your debts!'

'You haven't said anything to your mother have you?'

'No. D'you think I want her to be humiliated, again, by you?'

'It's a perfectly fair arrangement. He loves you. He wants to be with you and I've agreed. He doesn't want you worrying about debt so he agreed to help me out, that's all.'

'That's all? How does he even know about your debts?'

'I happened to mention something and he offered to help me,' Kostas said.

'Offered or felt pressurised?' She felt a wave of sympathy cross her face and she shook her head.

Elena walked home alone. Her father told her he was meeting a friend about a possible new job but she knew he would be going straight to the betting shop. Her father, she knew, was a weak man and she could see this clearly now. Whatever help Christaki gave him he would always end up in debt. It was a familiar pattern. She knew what she had to do but had to win her mum round.

She took the stairs two at a time and let herself into the flat. She could smell the sweetness of fried onions. Her mum was still in the kitchen, bent over the stove, her hair hanging loosely around her shoulders.

'Oh hello, *agabi mou*. I didn't hear you come in.'

'Mum, there's something I need to talk to you about and it's serious.' She watched as her mum's face paled to match the ashen wall behind her.

Chapter Twenty-Five

Evangelia, 1960

EVANGELIA KNEW IT was wrong but as the months passed she found herself reflecting on Zeno and his predicament and her own life's path. With Elena's betrothal confirmed it only highlighted her own poor plight and lack of a proper relationship with Kostas. Elena had revealed her father's underhand and manipulative plan to use Elena's betrothal to settle his debts and this had sickened her and embarrassed her more than his infidelities.

It was hard to know, to be sure, what God planned for her but she knew in her heart Zeno was a good man and he would care for her; he cared for her already. So to this end she planned to pay off Kostas herself and to end their relationship once and for all. Divorce would be out of the question but she felt confident God would guide her and show her the way through this mess. She would put her trust in Him.

She had not spoken to anyone about her emotions and she tried desperately to untangle the knots twisted inside her. The only person she would be able to talk to would be Zeno, if she dared, and after seeing him on the bus, she had not seen him again.

Instead she focused on running her home, keeping it clean and tidy and paying the bills; the bills that grew and came at her like crashing waves, each time stronger than before and more forceful. Kostas' arrest and imprisonment for fraud had made no diference to her financially and in fact, meant that she was able to keep track of her own finances without him sneaking in and taking what she had.

Sitting in Evangelia's front room drinking their Greek coffee and sharing a plate of freshly fried *lokmathes*, Evangelia and Georgette enjoyed each other's company, despite the thrashing rain rattling the thin window panes.

'Don't you miss Cyprus?' asked Evangelia. She bit into the deep fried dough ball drenched in honey and blew through her mouth to evaporate the steam from it.

'Sometimes yes. But then I read about the horrors of what's gone on and how Cyprus isn't how it used to be and wonder whether I miss something that's not there anymore. I'm not how I used to be either.'

'I suppose we all change. And who knows what independence from Britain will bring with it for our beloved Cyprus.'

'Things will change again Evangelia *mou*. We have to accept that. You have to accept that. The Treaty is just a piece of paper. Britain, Turkey and Greece still have the right to intervene. It's no Treaty of Guarantee at all.'

'Yes, you're right. I must admit I've not given it

426

much thought.'

'Well, you've had other things on your mind,' said Georgette.

'My husband, as much as it hurts me to admit it, to say it out loud, is a good for nothing man easily swayed by gambling and the swinging hips of other women with painted faces and high heels.'

'But you have Elena and Andreas. Elena is such a good girl, Evangelia.'

'She will leave me soon too. The *proxenia* has been a success.'

'I know. And that's wonderful.'

'It is, it really is. She's growing into a young woman with a mind of her own and despite living in London, with influences all around her; music and fashion and bars and parties, our Cypriot traditions haven't totally been forgotten.'

'But?'

'But I fear more for myself than for her. I know I can't keep her prisoner at home. I know I'm strict. That I may be pushing her away even before she marries.'

'She will never leave you. Daughters never do. She loves you. But yes, she'll marry and hopefully be happy. Is that not what you want for her?'

'It's what every mother wants for her child,' Evangelia said.

'Then stop worrying. Or is there something else?' Evangelia, aware of her friend's intuition, hesitated.

'I'm lonely and I'm tired. Tired of fighting and fighting for what? And so ashamed. My husband being thrown into prison. For fraud.' There she said it. It was out now and she couldn't take the words back. She looked at her hands in her lap, her long slim fingers entwined, and sighed. She felt as though she was betraying her husband even as she spoke the words but deep down she knew Kostas could never take her loneliness away.

Inside Evangelia fought her demons; she too was being influenced by her new London life, full of a multicultural kaleidoscope of different people. She thought about the woman who lived across from her and how he always drunk, layabout of a husband was nowhere to be seen recently. Her neighbour now had a smile on her face for the first time since Evangelia had met her. Evangelia was sure the woman had told him to get out. She knew too she would be better off without Kostas.

***

Two weeks on, Evangelia, feeling low, decided to leave the confines of the house. She missed being outside, surrounded by the plucky aromas of fresh herbs and zesty fruit in her little courtyard.

She turned right out of her front door and walked in the direction of the park. Its tranquility had been taken away from her since seeing Kostas there with his love child and mistress and at the last minute, and without a thought, something took her in the opposite direction towards Tally Ho Corner.

She walked at a brisk pace for about half an hour, not allowing the tearing wind to slow her. Above, the trees' fall leaves clung to the boughs as they shook from the chill. Golden leaves of ochre yellow and rusty orange, littered the street and flew high in the air, caught on the edge of the wind's breath.

The sound of squeaky brakes made her grimace as a double-decker pulled up at the bus stop ahead. Passengers hopped and vaulted off the bus creating a bottle-neck across the pavement and she eased her pace as she approached, to give them time to disperse.

As the crowd dissipated, a man stood alone, one hand tugging on his cap and the other pulling something out of his pocket. The wind caught it and but it tore itself free and fell to the ground. He bent to pick it up and it was blown further along behind him, threatening to fly into the road. He moved with a skip and a jump and just caught the piece of paper. He straightened up, relief etched on his face and Evangelia recognised him at exactly the same moment he recognised her.

'Evangelia. What a pleasure to see you.'

'And you Zeno. How are you?' She held the scarf around her neck, catching the tied corners to stop them fluttering across her face. She hoped he didn't see her cheeks burning.

'Apart from out of breath chasing my receipt I'm

healthy and that's all I can ask for.'

'That's good to hear. How's Niko?'

'He's doing an extra shift at work.'

'He was always a hard-working boy. I remember him in the village, his head always stuck in a book.'

'I'm going home. I've dropped my shoes in to the cobbler in East Finchley. A Greek Cypriot by the name of Loizos. You might know him.'

'I have met him, yes. His son is to be wed to Elena.'

'Congratulations. What lovely news.'

'It is indeed, Zeno.'

'And where are you heading?'

'I don't know. That's a good question but one which I will fail miserably to answer.' Evangelia lowered her head in an effort to hide the pain she knew was etched across her face, deep in her eyes.

'Well you must come for a cup of coffee...or tea...please say you'll come. I live close by. It's only a short walk.'

'Oh I don't know Zeno.'

'Niko will be home soon and he will be so happy to see you. You'll see for yourself how happy he is to be here and of course how animated he is about Cyprus' long awaited independence.'

'What will the neighbours say?'

'They're Irish. They do not care whether I live or die. They're too busy shouting obscenities at the black family who have moved in across the street to notice me anymore.'

'Well if you're sure, I will come for a cup of coffee and to see Niko. I'm sure he has grown into a fine young man.'

***

Zeno's house on Sylvester Road had a garden and a wooden gate and a path leading to the front door. Evangelia noticed the path had been freshly swept and a paper bag of soggy leaves stood in the corner behind a neatly trimmed holly bush.

Inside, it was well-proportioned and furnished beautifully with pieces of furniture she recognised from his house in Cyprus.

Sitting in the warmth of the electric fire in the front room Evangelia sipped at her frothy Greek coffee careful not to spill it as she balanced the demitasse and saucer on her shaking knees. She wondered what she was thinking coming into a man's home when she was a married woman.

'You've a lovely home Zeno,' she said, to break the spell she felt was contorting around her like a swirling rain.

'It doesn't feel like a home. Without a woman it is simply a house.'

'You'll meet someone one day Zeno, give yourself time.'

'Time stands still when your heart is broken.'

'You're a lovely man, caring, kind. I will never forget the way you came to my rescue in Limassol.' She leant over and patted his hand with deep affection.

'That was a sad day. That was the beginning.'

'Oh, I'm so sorry. I shouldn't have said anything. How thoughtless of me.'

'No, not at all. At least now our homeland can hope for a new start, hope for a happier, safer future. Independence after what? It must be eighty odd years.'

'And to think the British flag came down for the last time on 15th August; the day of St Mary. It's as if she has looked after us, in the end.'

'Yes, there's that too, of course,' said Zeno.

'I'm not too good at the maths but yes, it must be eighty years.'

Zeno seemed a little agitated and fidgeted in the single seater opposite her. He jumped up quite suddenly and before she knew it he was kneeling in front of her. 'Evangelia mou, forgive me for interrupting. I know I shouldn't say this but I have often thought about you. About you, as a woman. I've fallen in love with you. In fact, I've always loved you.'

'Zeno, please, you're grieving for your wife. You're confused.'

'Do not dare to tell me what I'm feeling Evangelia *mou*. I am a man. I am sure of my feelings and I am sure of them for you. Please don't push me away.'

'Zeno, please. I am a married woman.'

'In name only. I see how unhappy you are. I saw it seaming furrow after furrow across your forehead year on year in Cyprus and I see it now.'

'I'm okay. I have Elena and Andreas. Our little flat is simple but it's a home.'

'It's not okay. Nothing has changed. Tell me you feel the same way.'

'I'd better go before we both say things we come to regret.'

'I cannot regret how I feel for you. I cannot apologise for the words I say because they are the truth.' Zeno's voice pleaded, heavy with emotion.

Evangelia got to her feet.

'No please, sit a while longer. Let's talk. I'm sorry. I've been saying these words in my head to you for months. I have to tell you how I feel.'

'My husband and I are married. He is well and he is here,' she said lowering herself back onto the brown velour sofa.

'But you haven't answered my question. Tell me you feel the same as I do.'

'I'm a married woman,' she repeated lamely, her cup rattling on the saucer as her knees trembled.

'But he is not your husband in the way that it counts. Admit it. He is no longer in your heart, your home, your bed.' His words were gentle; no sting, no criticism. Evangelia knew what he said was true. She had no husband. He was never around. Her heart felt like it was going to break. She didn't trust herself to speak.

They sat in mutual silence for a few minutes, the only sound the erratic beating of her heart echoing in her ears. Evangelia sipped the last of her coffee. She placed the cup and saucer back on the bamboo tray on the coffee table. She sighed and then broke the constricting silence.

'I'd better go. Thank you for the coffee.'

'Please don't be so formal. Please say you'll come again. Can't we at least be friends?'

'Of course we can Zeno. Friends. We'll always be friends.' He leaned in and gave her a kiss on each cheek; she felt his soft stubble against her skin and the resolve in her melted. She took his face in her hands and kissed him gently on the lips. He held her around the waist and pulled her closer for a second. She could feel his heart swell for her and she became woozy with excitement and the pit of her stomach was on fire. They stood holding each other's gaze.

'Evangelia *mou*. Is this how friends feel? Is this so terribly wrong?' She said nothing before pulling away from him, untangling his arms from around her. Her unsaid words remained between them like a shield.

Outside the wind had abated and Evangelia welcomed the fresh chill as it touched her face. She felt light-headed and blundered her way to the end of the path. She wondered whether the feelings between Zeno and her could indeed be true. She reeled at her boldness, her forthrightness, and wondered whether living in London had given her a sense of daring she had never before had the courage to explore.

She knew no other emotions other than those she had for her husband but reluctantly she had to admit they were gone. They were feelings of habit, of fear, of not wanting to be alone. But she had to admit she was alone and Zeno stirred a yearning in her; one she thought she would never feel again. She was still a woman with needs, still relatively young at only thirty-six and yet this life had aged her beyond her years and she knew now she wanted to break free.

As she walked back towards home, her mind filled with pictures of Zeno and her, and she wasn't sure whether to smile or cry.

***

At home her nervous energy found an exit in the familiar rhythms of cooking and baking; *kioftethes, lokmathes* and Andreas' favourite *eliopites.*

Her hands busied rolling and kneading and frying and turning. The repetitive movements soothed her and although initially her mind could not be calmed she felt herself relax eventually. The breeze from the open kitchen door seemed to blow away her doubts and her guilt.

She eventually allowed her thoughts to go back to the

kiss. She shuddered at her forthrightness. She had never done anything like that in her life. She admonished herself and yet felt liberated by her act at the same time. Like a bolt of lightning bringing light to the darkness, she knew what she had to do, especially with the news of Kostas' plan to clear his debts.

By the time Elena and Andreas got home from visiting *theia* Panayiota and their *yiayia* the meatballs had been browned off beautifully and sat heaped in a bowl in the middle of the kitchen table. The baby doughnut balls, drenched in syrup, sat shimmering like nuggets of gold on an oval platter and the olive pastries still smoked hot from the oven.

'You've been busy,' said Elena, popping a meatball straight into her mouth.

'Well there's no point in sitting idle. And I want to talk to you both about something. Something I've thought a great deal about...a decision I've come to.' Evangelia felt the misty coils of fog lift as her words poured out and she accepted it had all got a bit too much for her.

'I've decided once you're married next year Elena *mou,* I'm going to tell your father to leave. I cannot live this half-life. This lie any longer. I want to start again on my terms. It will be my chance to do things differently. To put myself first.'

'I didn't know you felt like that. You've never said anything,' said Elena.

Andreas remained silent. His eyes brimming with

436

suspicion, he leaned back in his seat.

'I didn't want to burden you and I didn't know until today that's how I felt, that this will be the right thing to do. For all of us.'

'Does Dad have any idea?' asked Andreas.

'No, he doesn't but I'm going to tell him immediately after the wedding. I cannot put my happiness over Elena's, I can't jeopardise your union with Christaki.'

'What will Dad say?' asked Andreas.

'He'll probably be relieved of the responsibility of being married, of having two women in his life. And having his debts cleared.' said Evangelia.

'Mum, I love you.' Elena leaned in and hugged her.

'Have you met someone else?' asked Andreas.

'No one new. It feels like the right time.'

'But there is someone?' asked Andreas.

'I'm fond of Zeno, Niko's dad, and he's fond of me.'

'So you've been seeing him?' Andreas asked, his tone accusatory.

'No I haven't. I've seen him twice since he's come to England. But we know how we feel about each other.'

'Well what does that mean? How can you know?' asked Andreas.

'Because how I feel about your dad is not the way I feel when I think about Zeno, how we feel about each other. We can't pretend and we shouldn't have to any more. Your dad clearly wants to live a different life, separate to the one I imagined we'd have together. That pains me. But I'm still only in my thirties and I want to be loved again.' Her heart pounded in her chest, but she spoke with a level voice. She remembered the saying "a heart that loves is always young.". And she felt eighteen again when she thought of Zeno.

She had never spoken so openly, but knew she had to be honest with the children. As grown up as they now were she didn't want her mistakes to thwart them emotionally. She didn't want her humiliation over the years to tarnish their own relationships; to think that what she had, or indeed not had, was normal.

'Well good for you Mum. Dad's been such a fool,' said Andreas. 'He's weak and selfish. You deserve someone who'll look after you.' His voice mellowed; like warm honey thought Evangelia. 'Someone who doesn't deceive and lie and spend his days in prison. And I'll say it to his face when he dares to show up.'

As Evangelia tidied up after their meal she felt a weight lift; she had been dreading telling them but now that she had she was glad. And she realised they were both young adults with thoughts and dreams of their own. She thought about the old proverb her grandmother used to say to her as a child; "when one door closes behind you another opens.".

This was going to be a new beginning for her. For all of them. No more looking back, only forward. Her daughter's words came to her, the summer will come, the same words of Pallikarides who had given his life for what he believed in. The words held such pain and such hope. Yet finally Evangelia felt her heart fill with the warmth of summer; the warmth of Zeno's loving declaration.

Chapter Twenty-Six

Christaki, 1961

TO AVOID A scandal, Christaki's family dressed and went to church as usual. Its heavy doors welcomed them into the rich shadowy interior. The arched recesses glowed with lit icons and sand trays overflowed with amber-coloured candles, wax spilling like hot honey pools across the bed of sand granules.

Christaki heard his mother, when questioned, tell her fellow parishioners Melani was helping an elderly neighbour who was unwell and in bed. He knew it was lie having found her bed cold and empty that morning. He knew the lie would sit heavily on her conscience but also understood she had no choice but to conceal the truth, whatever that might be. Christaki caught his aunt's disbelieving stare and those of the other parishioners. He couldn't wait for the sermon to finish so he could find Melani, find John.

At the end of the service he walked out of the church, ahead of his parents, the stained glass window splashing the flagstone floor with a blur of colours as he pushed his way through the melee. The bright hues gave him encouragement; a good sign, like sunshine after rain, and his heart leapt with the hope of finding her, and making things right between them all.

His search took him first to the café he had initially seen her in with Rose. It was closed. Of course it was; it was a Sunday. He paced the neighbouring streets not truly believing he would find her. He wandered for nearly three hours; his feet ached in his leather shoes and the cold made him shiver as sweat soaked through his shirt. He walked back in the direction of home, cutting through the park. He needed the open space and fresh air.

As he walked along the gravel path, he thought about his life, and how far he had come from the young man he had been when he left Cyprus. This new life had taken its toll on the whole family; bathed them with positive experiences but scarred them with others. He fought the prickle of tears as he remembered the white-washed, tumble-down village houses, the tiny winding streets with no pavements, the carob trees with their red flesh and the smile of *Pater* Spyrithon as he walked around the village, always with open arms and a listening ear.

The path opened up into a wide children's play area, empty apart from a little girl and two adults. The child was running ahead of them in a red coat, excitement colouring her face rosy pink.

'Rose, Rose!' Christaki called.

But as he approached, running towards her, the man and woman scooped up the child. They swore at him, before walking quickly away.

'I'm sorry. I'm sorry. I made a mistake,' he said, running his hand through his hair in agitation, fighting his frustration, breathless.

He sat on a wooden bench and buried his face in his hands. He wanted to cry. To scream.

He had no idea how long he'd been sitting there when a tympanic rhythm of footsteps came up behind him. A giggling tickled his ears followed by a joyous screech.

'Are you crying?' A child's sweet voice filled his ears.

'No, no. I'm happy. I'm so happy,' said Christaki as his gaze settled on Rose's face. A few feet behind her John walked towards him. Melani smiled and laughed playfully, squirming in John's embrace, as he walked with Melani scooped in his arms.

'Melani. For goodness sake…what were you thinking?'

'Hello to you too dear brother!' she planted her feet on the ground with a thud and walked towards him.

'Melani! Please. There has to be a better way than running away,' he said embracing her tightly.

'The other way hasn't worked. I've been patient. I've tried.' Melanie pulled away.

'Father and Mother are so worried. And here you are laughing and enjoying yourself.'

'I'm not enjoying myself. John forced me out of the house. I've been miserable.'

'She really has Chris. She's been full of tears, inconsolable,' said John.

'Not that you'd care. You're taking sides, you're doing things right and you're too in love with Elena to care about me,' said Melani.

'Oh come on, Melly, they do care. Your family love you. Christaki loves you.'

Melani collapsed into the arms of John. Her sobbing attracted the attention of an elderly couple walking by and Rose hugged Melani's legs.

'You must come home. This isn't the way,' pleaded Christaki.

'I've said that all along but she won't listen,' said John.

'You must come home, show them what you have, convince them. Make them see this is what you want, but that you want them in your life too,' said Christaki.

'No, they don't understand…'

'Please,' said Christaki, his voice strained, tired.

'It's what I want more than anything, but Father is adamant. He's blind to what I see. What I feel.'

'Let's go back…together…let's sit and talk…he'll listen.'

'Go Melly. I'll wait to hear from you. It will be alright. I promise,' said John.

'He's not understood so far. How's it going to be alright? He's ignored my feelings; the life I want. He keeps dragging me back to "if we were in the village".

Well we're not in the village. We're here now. And I love John.'

'Let's go back and make him see. I think he'll listen. He'll listen for Mother's sake if for nothing else. She's miserable and sick with worry. He can't allow himself to be the cause of more pain for her.'

'Not now, Christaki. But soon. I promise.'

***

The ongoing disagreement over Melani's wishes to marry John continued to overshadow the wedding merriment that should have prevailed for Elena and Christaki. Loizos growled and thumped and stomped. He let out big sighs. No-one, not even Pavlo with his silly hotel stories, could bring a smile to their father's face.

Two days later Melani came home. She walked in and their father glared at her as he sat in front of the television in the living room. Their mother wept with joy and crossed herself as she took Melani in her arms and promised John and Rose were welcome to be a part of their family.

'Nothing is worth the heartache of not knowing where you are,' said their mother. Anastasia gave Loizos one of her looks; the one none of the children ever argued with, and surprisingly neither did their father. Instead he left the room. His silence spoke to them more clearly than any words.

444

The next few days passed without any conversation between Melani and Loizos. He left for work early, he returned late. He clearly had no intention of forgiving Melani what he believed was insolence.

One evening, Loizos returned home much later than usual and Melani threw herself into his arms.

'*Patera*, where have you been? We've all been so worried. Your dinner has dried up warming in the oven and...'

'Is everything well?' asked Christaki and Anastasia, their voices a duet.

Loizos took Melani's face in his rough hands and kissed her on each cheek.

'Be happy my child,' he said.

'You've forgiven her? Oh thanks to God,' said Anastasia crossing herself.

'I am Father. I'll never let you down. I promise,' said Melani, the words tumbling out of her in relief, in excitement, as tears stung her eyes.

'If the last few months has taught me one thing it's this. We haven't come this far to lose each other. Keeping my family together has been and always will be my priority.'

'Oh, Loizos *mou*,' said Anastasia.

'We have one life. One chance. Take it Melani,'said her father.

Christaki welled up as their father hugged his daughter. He looked away, not wanting to intrude on this private moment, a rare demonstration of paternal love. This was the side of their father they rarely witnessed; a softer man hidden behind discipline, strength and formality.

Christaki's thoughts filled with Elena and he knew, more than anything in the world, he wanted her. He knew he would stop at nothing to be with her and he empathised with his sister. This energised him and gave him a sudden burst of Herculean strength to face whichever life unfolded before him.

***

With four weeks to go until his wedding day, Christaki experienced a strange, fluctuating barrage, of thoughts; Cyprus' troubles past and present, friends and family left behind, fogged him. His emotions yo-yoed from sadness to elation though he made every effort to hide these. He knew, too, how they had battled with their own emotions and pulls towards their culture and traditions, to accept Melani's future marriage to John. Accepting the marriage, of course, eased tensions externally but he knew the turmoil they still felt inside. But his love and respect for his parents was evermore stronger because of their acceptance of change.

He also longed for their mother to come out of mourning for her brother. It pained Christaki to see her dressed in black from head to foot.

He knew his father felt the same; his mother smiled one minute and appeared deep in thought the next, she barely spoke a word at dinner, a glazed expression shrouding her face like the sheer black scarf she wore at her brother's funeral.

His father worked later than usual and Christaki recognised this as his way of keeping out of Anastasia's way, not wanting to overcrowd her. When he was at home he was gentler, less opinionated and his hand would uncharacteristically find its way to hers, and taking it he would hold her hand in his.

Chapter Twenty-Seven

Elena, 1961

WITH TWO WEEKS to go until her wedding day Elena was fired up with more energy and drive than she had felt in a long time. She was excited about her big day, overwhelmed with the constant well-wishes from the neighbours and Greek community and most of all the unwavering love from Christaki and his family. She quietly worried about her father and his reaction to her mother's news after the wedding but pushed this to the back of her mind, refusing to let the negative thoughts take away her joy.

When she wasn't working at the factory she was designing and piecing together her wedding dress. Her future mother-in-law had bought the material for her as an engagement gift and it was the most beautiful snowy white silk she had ever touched.

She had squeezed a sewing machine into her bedroom and every surface groaned under piles of fabric, rolls of lace, strings of beading and loose ribbons. She even had her *yiayia* hemming and stitching for her.

Elena filled her time with sewing and making *bonbonnières* for the reception. Koulla made the flower corsages and pretty sky blue bow decorations for the church using scraps of fabric left over from the material Elena used for the bridesmaids' sashes. All that sewing in Cyprus had served Elena well and her heart warmed with happy thoughts.

She daydreamed of the splendour of the Greek Orthodox Church; its serenity and tradition. She wished for the day to go well for her mother more than for herself. She hoped her mother would have her day of showing to the world her daughter was marrying well and was happy. She knew how her mother prayed the union to be a success, to be something her own marriage never was.

Her mother perched on the end of Elena's bed; swathes of fabric drowning her.

'You will make a good wife, Elena *mou*. You will be happy for sure with Christaki by your side and your children will be blessed to have the support of such a loving, hard-working and supportive family.'

'Children? Oh *mama,* there's plenty of time for children. I want to design, have my own fashion label, get in with a designer, I want to do so much before then.'

'God will see to it you are blessed, I know it. I pray for it each and every day,' said her mother as she crossed herself three times.

'Now, what do you think of this?'

'It's beautiful,' said her mother comparing the wedding dress made up of pinned fabric pieces against the drawing Elena held up.

She sensed her mother was a little agitated and, not

449

sure whether to broach the subject of her intention to tell their father to leave, she left her thoughts unsaid, the words, stuck in her throat.

Her father continued to come and go, at his own will and with no explanation as to where he was going and it took all of her strength and determination to refrain from telling him of her mother's plans. Andreas on the other hand was furious.

'Who does he think he is? No financial contribution, without so much as a by your leave and Mum puts up with it. Makes me so mad!'

'It's not for long now. You can't say anything Andreas. We both made a promise to Mum.'

'You made the promise. Not me.'

'Well promise me now. Don't you dare go ruining everything. And you won't just be ruining it for me and Christaki…but for Mum as well. She wants nothing more in the world than for me to get married without any drama, no upset. Then she will settle into a new life, a new life only she can carve out for herself.'

'Oh alright. Stop going on. But if he has one more moan, about anything, I don't know what I'll do.' Andreas stormed out, the door's slam causing the glass in the door to shake.

Chapter Twenty-Eight

Elena and Christaki 1961

IN HIS BEDROOM, Christaki pulled on his new crisp white shirt, the coolness of the fabric enveloped him reminding him of the early spring Limassol sea. It seemed so long ago since he bathed in it. Today his heart burst with happiness and a deep sorrow. He thought about his uncle, killed in cold blood and how his family had left Cyprus, their home, the only life they had ever known. What was it all for? Had it been worth it? He often found himself wondering whether his parents were happy with their decision. It was hard to tell. They did not complain, at least not to him, and they worked every day as hard as they could. Their morals and ethics as strong as ever. He wondered about Cyprus left in tatters, Cypriots and Turkish people still living in fear despite gaining independence, from the British, only a few months before.

Downstairs he could hear family members arriving to wish him well and to see him as a groom before his bride did. There was much talking and laughter, the sounds rising through the floorboards and thin walls of the house.

He buttoned his shirt and tucked it in. He shook off

his melancholy. Standing in front of the mirror, he knotted his tie, the way his father had taught him and pushed his hair back. This was it. The first day of his life as a married man.

**

'Hey! Here he is!' called out Pavlo as Christaki walked into the crowded sitting room.

'My handsome boy, *agabi mou*,' said Anastasia. Pulling him towards her she kissed both his cheeks. '*Theio* Michael would be proud of you.' Tears filled her eyes and she quickly looked away. Christaki knew how difficult today would be for her and felt a lump in his throat.

'Let the music begin,' Loizos called out. The lone violinist playing a couple of practice notes across the strings now broke into the traditional *stolisma* tune to welcome the groom.

Family members, young and old, clapped in time to the music and clicked their fingers as they watched Christaki experience the tradition of having the red scarf, *zoni*, tied and untied around his waist three times by his mother, father, sister and brother and his aunts, uncles and cousins. Each time they kissed him on both cheeks. The violinist continued playing his tune, the soft notes closing in around Christaki's ears, making him tremble. He shook his head and exhaled sharply in an effort to keep them in check. He had not anticipated the custom would make him feel this way. His stomach rolled and churned with an overpowering passion, and he wanted to cry. He fought back the tears as he caught *Kirio* Melis, his accounting teacher, clapping in time to the beat, clearly fighting his own emotions.

Their mother moved around the room with a light step, almost as if she was floating. She looked different. Christaki stared at her as if seeing her for the first time. Then he realised what was different about her. She wore a simple navy shift dress with a touch of delicate pink lace around the neck line and cuffs. In her hair, she wore a pink rose. She had disowned the traditional all black of mourning for her brother. His heart swelled but before he could make a comment the guests were toasting his happiness and a long life full of good fortune and many children.

'You look beautiful *mama*,' said Christaki and Melani in unison a few moments later. He knew this was a huge consideration for their mother and recognised how adding the splash of bright pink to her outfit was her way of showing her love, support and commitment to Christaki on his special day, of being wholly present and demonstrating her happiness at the union.

'I made it specially,'she said beaming, almost the same pink as the trim of her outfit.

Their mother passed the *kapnistiri,* a delicate silver receptacle which held the small piece of charcoal and burning olive leaves, three times over his head, whispering prayers as she blessed him with wishes for his new married life. The air filled with wisps of silver grey smoke and a sharp fragrant scent, from the *kapnistiri's* burning ashes, wafted still. It reminded him of the church in the village…the smell never changed whatever time of day you entered it.

'Come on brother!' called Pavlo, shaking Christaki out of his reverie. He grabbed Christaki by the arm and pulled him into the tiny open space in the middle of the room. They elbowed family out of the way and they stepped back to form a circle around the two brothers.

They danced together; Christaki's confidence growing with every step; his reminiscing dissipating as the atmosphere filled him with warmth, love and hope. Loizos joined them and they stepped from side to side, kicking out their legs, careful not to kick anyone in the crowded space. The atmosphere was one of ecstatic delight and merriment. The *zivania* flowed and the music carried on; bouncing off the walls of the room and escaping out of the open windows. Clapping, cheers of joy and jubilation eminent.

Melani clapped to the beat and shuffled on the spot; she sparkled with joy. The pencil skirt of her blush pink wedding outfit, accentuated her slim hips and the button detail on the jacket complemented her pretty pillbox hat with its spotted veil.

Christaki winked at her. He knew the huge sacrifice

their parents were making by accepting John's future marriage to Melani, but he could also see how this had brought Melani the greatest happiness. He knew, after everything, it was about happiness, health and good fortune. They had said for so long the summer will come and it was finally here for all of them.

The room filled with sunlight and drenched the pale walls with a soft yellow glow. The hub-bub of celebration filled the room; aunts passed around plates of homemade sweet and savoury pastries, olives, sesame and fennel bread and little dishes of syrupy drenched fruits. Bottles of red wine and *zivania* filled the glasses of those guests still milling around to watch the groom leave his home as a single man for the last time.

***

Elena's wedding morning was quiet and serene. She woke early and washed. She ate a breakfast of a boiled egg and a thick slice of toast, before any of her family had risen. She relished the silence and lost in her thoughts as she played with her father's worry beads. She sat with the black and white photograph which had once sat proudly in her little bedroom in Cyprus and ran her fingers over the faded image. She remembered how she had yearned to come to the land of green fields and fat cows; remembered her dream. It felt so long ago now and yet she wanted those same feelings of excitement and promised happiness to cover her again and engulf her with nostalgia and warmth. She smiled at the memory, realising that despite the highs and lows she was winning. She was getting married and this would be the beginning of her new life; one with Christaki that would bring new opportunities, experiences and happier times.

Her mind trailed off to her mother and father, and inside she knew their relationship had come to the end of whatever had been holding them together. She hoped they would both find some peace and contentment in whatever life they now chose for themselves. She wondered how her father would really cope without his Evangelia and how her mother would actually cope with the blight of a broken marriage. She hoped that Zeno would take care of her and bring her the security and love she knew her mother deserved.

She believed that this would be the start of their new life in London; one that would bring the traditions of Cyprus and the different way of life here crashing together but in a positive way. This was her life now; this was all their lives now.

The bell rang and she ran downstairs to open the door.

'You're early,' she said to Janet.

'Look, I'm no expert and I want to give you the best hairstyle ever. Even Vogue will want to feature you on their front cover! Oh my God! You're getting married!' she screeched as she followed Elena into the flat.

'I know! It's like a dream come true! It's really happening.'

They disappeared into Elena's bedroom and Elena pulled back the thin curtains to reveal a weak, watery light as the sun rose above the tree tops.

'I've brought every clip and grip imaginable, just in case.'

'I've got that picture of how I want to look. Kept it in case you forgot.' said Elena. She leant across and pulled a magazine cutting from the dressing table drawer.

'You're going to look beautiful. You are beautiful. Oh Els, I'm so happy for you. I'm going to cry.'

'No crying Janet. Not today. Between us we've shared too many tears. Today's going to be about laughing and dancing and hugging!'

'And kissing...don't forget the kissing...'

'And kissing...' said Elena as she felt her face burn crimson with the excited anticipation of kissing her husband.

***

From across the road Christaki could make out the huge white columns of the church's main entrance and portico; it stood proudly against the weak cloud streaked sky and today it seemed to look grander, bigger, and prouder than usual. At least six hundred guests filled the wide stone courtyard from wall to wall. Christaki could only describe it as a frenzy.

He not so much walked as was pushed and shimmied along the grand courtyard of the All Saint's Church in Camden. It proved a challenge to reach the main steps leading to the grand oak entrance. The excitement all round him was thrilling and he couldn't help but smile from ear to ear. He spotted Pavlo standing at the top of the wide curved steps leading to the main entrance of the church and waved at him. As he made his way over to him, cousins and uncles patted him on the back warmly while aunts grabbed him and kissed him on both cheeks. A wave of noisy choruses rose around him and carried him towards his brother. The crowd swept him along, as did his absolute joy. The outpouring of love enveloped him; family and new friends from their Greek Cypriot community, business associates of his father and work colleagues; these people proved how their lives had moved on. There were many in the sea of faces he didn't recognise but knew they would be connected to Elena's side of the family. Children of all ages, dressed in their Sunday best, watched in awe.

In a few hours he would be married to the most beautiful girl in the world.

***

Inside the church it was more subdued, even though the guests pushed their way in to secure their seats nearest the front. Christaki stood waiting for Elena to arrive, at the back of the church, as was the tradition in the Greek Orthodox faith. Something caught his eye, a shadow by the altar, and he shuddered. He could have sworn it was his *theio* Michael. But when he looked again there was no one there.

'This is the day you become a man. A husband and God willing, a father very soon,' said Loizos.

'I hope I don't let her down, Father. I love her, truly I do.'

'And she loves you.'

A hush descended upon the church as whispers, that the bride had arrived, echoed around the sombre interior, and a hush descended. Although dim there was a glow as ochre candles, like light-tipping wax fingers, shone in the sandboxes, highlighting the dark icons; their gold embellishments glowing serenely in the flickering candle light.

There was a sudden bustle of excitement and then he saw Elena arrive.

***

Elena steadied herself as her dad, with nervous, clumsy fingers, fiddled with his tie and pulled at his shirtsleeves. She was about to take her first step into the church when he hesitated.

'Christaki's a good man, *agabi mou*, and I want you

to know I've made many mistakes and have made many wrong decisions, and judgements in my time, but this is right. And, if there's a God, I wish you everything good He offers.'

'I know Dad, I know,' she said, fighting the prickle of emotion threatening to form tears, as her voice quivered.

'I love you.'

'And I love you too.'

As she climbed the last step, hitching up the sweeping trail of her figure-hugging dress, she saw the back of Christaki as he waited for her inside the heavy arched doors. She knew how he must be feeling; that he must be as excited and nervous as she was; she could see it in the stiff slope of his shoulders under his suit jacket and the twitching of his feet as he swayed slightly back and forth from his toes to his heels.

She approached, moving almost silently, and as if he sensed her close he turned round. His smile said it all and she relaxed, shaking the tension from her shoulders. Her father gave her a kiss on each cheek and took his place ahead of her at the front of the church.

Christaki, holding her bouquet until now, handed it to her. She took it in her left hand and took slow, even steps with him. The aisle opened up ahead of her reminding her of the yellow brick road in *The Wizard of Oz*, and she was aware of her heart racing. She willed herself to remember the faces looking at her, the smiles, the well-wishes being whispered and mouthed across the rows of pews and sea of faces. She wanted to remember every second of walking down the aisle with her husband-to-be.

Conscious of her feet moving, her small, purposeful steps took her to the front of the church as she held onto Christaki's arm; his closeness making her heady with excitement.

Ahead of her she could see Janet and Melani in the dresses she had sewn for them standing to the left of the aisle. Her father took his position next to her mother to the left of the altar; opposite them stood Loizos and Anastasia, her new parents.

She thought about how their strong respectful marriage was something to adhere to. She had seen how Loizos ruled the roost with a strong hand but yet he had a heart full of love and understanding. She knew her mother-in-law, like her own mother, would guide her and give her advice.

As they approached, the grave-looking priest hushed everyone without raising his voice and he commenced the first part of the service. Goose bumps pricked at her skin like pins as she realised this was it; her chance to live her life on her terms with a man who loved her.

A gush of love filled her as she looked over towards her mother and her father. However, she chose to look at it, they had both brought her to where she was now, and for that, she was thankful.

Christaki couldn't take his eyes off Elena and he kept glancing to the side. She looked utterly radiant. He wanted to kiss her.

He tried to focus on the ceremony and the words of the priest, but they washed over him. He watched the flickering flames of the two tall wedding candles positioned either side of the altar and was momentarily mesmerised by their warm amber glow.

The Service of the Betrothal continued and the priest offered prayers as he asked for God's blessings upon their wedding rings, handed over to him by Pavlo, who had carefully wrapped them in a white handkerchief and placed them in his inside jacket pocket. The priest, in the Name of the Father and the Son and the Holy Spirit, held the rings in his hand and blessed the couple, touching Christaki's bowed head and then Elena's. He then placed their wedding band on each of their ring fingers.

Pavlo and Janet stepped forward. Pavlo slipped the ring off Christaki's finger and Janet took the wedding ring from Elena's finger. They swapped rings and then Pavlo and Janet each put the swapped ring back on the ring finger of the other. They carefully repeated the action another two times, three in total.

Christaki fought an overwhelming feeling. He knew the exchange of the rings signified how in their married life the weakness of one partner would be compensated by the strength of the other and he hoped he would always be strong for Elena. The priest's words continued to reverberate around the church and the three *psalti*, chanters, sang in unison as their low voices filled the church with a sombre, heavier feel. This marked the service moving into the Sacrament of Marriage.

The priest handed Elena and Christaki a lit white candle each, symbolising the couple's spiritual willingness to receive Christ in their life; the "Light of the World". For Elena, this was a huge moment in the ceremony and reminded her of how as a young girl she imagined getting married one day. She also knew in her heart how God had brought her here and that she had nothing to fear. She trusted Him and trusted Christaki and their new life together. She glanced towards her parents and wondered how this part of the ceremony made them feel. Did they feel let down by Him or by one another? She didn't recall her mother ever blaming God for her failed marriage. Her mother's face however, looked angelic in the candle light and, at one point, Elena saw her *yiayia* give Evangelia a little nod and she wanted to run over and reassure them both all would be well.

The priest moved to the other side of the altar and, facing the congregation, took the two wedding crowns, *stefana*. Standing before Christaki and Elena he blessed them both in the name of the Father, and the Son, and the Holy Spirit as he gently touched the crowns on their heads. Once finished, he carefully placed the crowns upon their heads and Janet and Pavlo interchanged the crowns, from one to the other, three times as witness to the sealing of Elena and Christaki's union to each other.

The rest of the service, including taking their Holy Communion from the Common Cup, continued in a blur as Christaki flitted in and out of focus, his mind already on the wedding reception and dancing with his bride.

Elena, in contrast, concentrated on every aspect of the service. She noticed the melting wax of the wedding candelabra as it trickled in riverlets, she looked at her father's stoic pose which she knew hid the guilt he felt at failing her, failing her mother.

Melani, Janet, a few other girls from the telephone exchange and Pavlo, Andreas and Niko together with the families lined the steps outside. As Christaki and Elena walked out of the church, hand in hand, the crowd showered the couple with confetti shouting Mr and Mrs at the tops of their voices.

'I never thought I could ever be this happy,' said Christaki to Elena.

'And you've awakened such joy in me. A joy I thought I'd left somewhere in Cyprus with my childhood.'

'Me too,' he said.

'It hasn't ended, it's just begun *agabi mou*,' said Anastasia, dabbing her tears as she threw a handful of rice over them. Christaki smiled as he remembered his mother insisting on the tradition of rice throwing.

The hundreds of guests organised themselves as best

they could and photos were painstakingly taken on the steps of the church. Looking around, Christaki took in the mish-mash of family and friends and children sitting across the front steps in a row, fresh smiles and cheeky grins. His heart swelled with happiness and he gripped Elena's hand tightly.

Elena tightened her grip too. She instantly felt strength and assurance. She knew this man would look after her always; she felt a sting of tears behind her eyes.

The photographer interrupted her thoughts as he called out instructions but few guests listened. Everyone already in the party mood, they continued to chat and laugh. The noise was almost deafening. The photographer clicked away, joining in with the flow of the occasion.

***

In the back of the wedding car, a cream Rolls Royce, that Elena's *theio* Thomas had paid for, Christaki took out a black box from his suit pocket.

'This is for you. A wedding gift from me.'

'But I haven't got you anything,' Elena exclaimed as she took a hairpin of sparkling blue sapphires set into a delicate yellow gold filigree flower from the velvet cushion.

'I don't need anything but you. This belonged to my great grandmother. It was amongst my uncle Michael's belongings. My mum said he always said he would give it to his wife one day. Mum said she's certain he would have given it to you, had he been here today.'

Elena, bit on her bottom lip to stop her emotions from tumbling out. She knew how much Christaki and her mother-in-law had loved Michael. 'It's beautiful. I will treasure it.'

'Here, let me put it in your hair,' he said, and with trembling fingers he slid the jeweled hairpin into her heaped tresses and kissed Elena on the lips. 'It can be your something blue.'

***

Elena's wedding day unfolded into the most beautiful fairytale she could have ever imagined.

The days of cooking by aunts and cousins and neighbours meant each table overflowed with homemade authentic Greek Cypriot dishes. Piles of wrapped *kourabiethes* filled boxes stacked against the wall by the main doors of the hall. The entire day reminded her of the Queen's Coronation when she was only a small girl. The celebratory tone filled every part of her as the live music bounced off the walls and the hall bustled with all her friends and family. Even Stella and Mirianthi had made it and she felt happier than ever to see her old childhood friends.

There was an abundance of merriment, dancing and singing till late evening. Elena twirled and smiled, moving around the hall like a queen. As she danced the traditional money dance, her dress became covered in one pound notes. Her dress could barely be seen under the layers and chains of notes pinned to her. Christaki looked like the ancient God Hermes as he mirrored her steps wearing a crown made of notes.

She watched as Melani and John admired a pirouetting Rose on the edge of the dance floor and behind them she could see Janet and Pete leaning into each other, looking relaxed and close. Koulla and Leon sat on the sidelines with their sleeping daughter lying across their laps. Her *yiayia* sat chatting to Georgette, *theia* Panayiota and *theio* Thomas. Her cousins were dancing and her new in-laws were holding hands as they watched on.

Her own mother watched as *yiayia* leaned into Evangelia; a picture of strength and resilience. Evangelia's expression seemed one of relief and Elena understood why. She knew after the wedding her mother too would be starting her new life. She searched the crowded hall for her father but she couldn't see him. She turned round as if sensing someone looking at her. It was her father. He gave her a little wave, turned away and left her watching his back retreating through the main doors. She felt a pang of guilt and then relief. She had to at least love him for not wanting to be the cause of any ill-feeling or surge of emotional outburst that may have tarnished her otherwise wonderful day.

The guests continued to dance until the last few left were ushered out into the dusky evening by the caretaker. Reluctantly they hugged and kissed Christaki and Elena in turn, wishing them well and promising to see them soon.

Elena handed out the last of the *kourabiethes* wrapped in coloured tissue and tied with white ribbon.

Elena watched her new husband's face glowing. 'We're really married,' she said.

'And this marriage, I promise you will be built on love and understanding, making decisions together, supporting each other.'

Elena took Christaki's hands in hers and facing him she swallowed.

'What is it Elena *mou?*'

'Let's go home,' she said.

The End

Glossary

Ade	come on
Agabi mou	my love
Avgolemoni	a clear soup made with rice, eggs and lemons.
Baba	dad (informal)
Bandoboulion	market place where mainly fruit, vegetables and other fresh and processed food is sold as well as other general wares
Bourekia	little parcels of deep fried pastry filled with a creamy cinnamon sweetened cheese, dusted with icing sugar
Boutana	whore
Bouzouki	a long-necked plucked lute of Greece. Resembling a mandolin, the *bouzouki* has a round wooden body, with metal strings
Bravo	well done, good job.
Daktila	light shortcrust pastry fingers filled with chopped almonds, deep fried, soaked in syrup or dusted with icing sugar
Efharisto	thank you
Ela	come, come here
Eleftheria H Thanatos	Freedom or death
Eliopita (s) Eliopites (pl)	a bread or rolled pastries made with pitted black olives and chopped onions.
Enosis	unity (with Greece)

Epitaphio	The Epitaphios is a Christian religious icon, typically consisting of a large, embroidered and often richly adorned cloth, bearing an image of the dead body of Christ, often accompanied by his mother and other figures, following the Gospel account.
Ethniki Organosis Kypriou Agoniston	
	the National Organisation of Cypriot Fighters (EOKA)
Fanouropita	a traditional sweet-bread baked in the name of Saint Fanourios
Flaounes	Cypriot Easter traditional Sweet & Savoury cheese-filled pastries
Fournaki	traditional domed stone or clay oven built outdoors
Galatoboureko	is a traditional dessert made with layers of golden brown crispy phyllo, filled with a milk or semolina custard and bathed in rose-scented syrup.
Gazi	a simple embroidery stitch used when making Lefkara lace
Halloumi	a traditional Cypriot cheese made of cows' and goats' milk, can be eaten cold or grilled, fried or barbequed
Kalikanzari	make-believe, fairy tale imps
Kalimera	good morning
Kalinichta	good night
Kalispera	good evening
Kapnistiri	a small silver ornate holder used during the wedding ceremony to burn dried olive leaves.

Kateifi	An dessert made with roughly chopped walnuts, scented with ground cloves and cinnamon, wrapped into buttered crispy shredded filo pastry and bathed in scented syrup.
Kafeneion	traditional coffee shop found in Greek Cypriot villages, where the men of the village collate and drink coffee, play backgammon, chat and generally put the world to rights.
Keo	KEO is a Cypriot beer. It is a light straw-colored lager with a thick head. The beer has been brewed in Limassol, in Cyprus, since 1949.
Kioftethes	deep-fried meatballs made from pork, potatoes, onions, parsley. Can be eaten hot or cold.
Kiria	Mrs (and can be followed by the surname or first name of the person)
Kirio	Mr (and can be followed by the surname or first name of the person)
Kleftiko	traditional meal of lamb pieces on the bone marinated in garlic, olive oil and lemon juice cooked in a clay oven with potatoes, bay leaves, carrots and onions
Kokkina avga	hard boiled eggs dyed red for Easter
Kolokithaki	courgette
Koubebia	stuffed vine leaves (or spinach leaves) usually filled with pork mince, rice, tomatoes and fresh parsley
Kourabiethes	rich, golden domed crumbly cookies covered in layers of icing sugar traditionally served at weddings and on saint's days.

Lefkaritika	tradition of lace-making in the village of Lefkara, key characteristics are the hemstitch, satin stitch fillings, needlepoint edgings, white, brown, ecru colours and geometric intricate designs.
Lingri	a game played by children in the school playground using sticks and flicking them to see which goes the furthest
Loukoumi	This is the Greek name for Turkish delight. It is a rubbery-textured candy, extremely popular throughout Cyprus and Greece, but its origins are Turkish. It is made from gelatin or cornstarch, sugar, honey and fruit juice or jelly, and is often tinted pink or green. It is cut into bite-size cubes and can contains chopped almonds or pistachio nuts. It is often served with coffee or as a sweet nibble with a drink after dinner.
Lokmathes	deep fried doughnut balls coated in honey
Louvi	black-eyed beans traditionally boiled with spinach or slices of courgette and drizzled with olive oil and freshly squeezed lemon
Loyiasma	the permission given by parents for their son and daughter to be betrothed in marriage
Mati	a circular glass charm that shows a curious blue eye. It is the Greek evil eye symbol - the *matiasma*. The "eye's" main purpose serves the function of warding off the effects of the evil eye (someone's bad intentions towards another person)
Mama	mum

Mitera	mother
Na	a word uttered alongside a hand gesture of the hand held palm up towards the face of another meaning generally stupid
O theos na mas voithisei	may God help us
Opas	a word called out by dancers and those watching the dancing
Paklava	a sweet dessert pastry made of layers of filo filled with chopped nuts, sugar and cinnamon, drenched with syrup or honey.
Panigiri	a street festival usually to celebrate a special occasion or a Feast Day or celebration day on the Greek Orthodox calendar
Pastelaki	a sticky concoction of sesame seeds, almonds and pistachios bound together with honey and cut into bite size chunks
Pater	Father (as in a priest in the Greek Orthodox church)
Patera	father
Paximathia	crunchy dry-baked bread sticks
Pitoues	any small bite-size pastries, sweet or savoury
Proxenia	Greek tradition of match-making
Psomi	bread
Re	colloquial term used which means friend, mate, mostly used between male friends and close male family member, terms of endearment
Sas	you (plural) when it comes after a greeting

Shamishi	deep fried doughy folds dusted in icing sugar
Spanakopita	a bread or rolled pastry made with spinach and chopped onions.
Stifado	rabbit baked with onions in a traditional clay or stone oven or in a modern-day oven
Stin iyeia sas	to your health, cheers
Sto kalo	go safely
Stolisma	the traditional music and fanfare surrounding the dressing of the groom in his home and the bride in her home on the wedding day
Tavli	backgammon (most commonly played by men in their own homes and in the village coffee shop)
Theia	aunt, aunty
Theio	uncle
Tiropites	cheese and egg savouries
Tomates	tomatoes
Toumbeleki	a hand drum
Tsestos	shallow basket made from palm leaves used for bread or fruit
Turk Mukavemet Teskilati	Turkish Resistance Organisation TMT. Turkish-Cypriots sought to defend themselves against the Greek-Cypriot terrorist organisation EOKA by forming this group, though they mainly relied on British defence
Vasilea	hop scotch (a game played by jumping and hopping along a grid of number from one to ten normally chalked out on the ground or pavement)

Vasilopita	a New Year's Day/Christmas cake which has a coin hidden inside it which represents good fortune to the person who receives it in their piece of the cake when it is cut.
Yiayia	grandma
Yioka mou	my son, term of endearment
Zhto H Hellas	Hail Greece or God Bless Greece
Zivania	an alcoholic drink made from the remainder of the pressed grapes used to make wine. Drank from small shot glasses it's the local firewater of Cyprus.
Zoni	a red silk or cotton scarf used as part of the *stolisma* and represents fertility

Author Bio

Born in London to Greek Cypriot parents Soulla
Christodoulou spent much of her childhood living
carefree days full of family, school and friends. She was
the first in her family to go to university and studied BA
Hotel & Catering Management at Portsmouth University.
Years later, after having a family of her own she studied
again at Middlesex University and has a PGCE in
Business Studies and an MA in Education.

Soulla is a Fiction author and wrote her first novel Broken
Pieces of Tomorrow over a few months while working
full time in secondary education. The novel has been
nominated for the 2017 Reader's Choice Awards. She is
a mother of three boys.

She is a compassionate and empathetic supporter of
young people. Her passion for teaching continues through
private tuition of English Language and Children's
Creative Writing Classes.

Her writing has also connected her with a charity in
California which she is very much involved in as a
contributor of handwritten letters every month to support
and give hope to women diagnosed with breast cancer.
One of her letters is featured in a book 'Dear Friend',
released on Amazon in September 2017.

She also has a poetry collection, Sunshine after Rain, published on Amazon. The Summer Will Come is her second novel which has received an endorsement from William Mallinson, Author and Historian. Her current work in progress, for now, is titled Trust is a Big Word and will be her third fiction novel.

When asked, she will tell you she has always, somewhere on a subconscious level, wanted to write and her life's experiences both personal and professional have played a huge part in bringing her to where she was always meant to be; writing books and drinking lots of cinnamon and clove tea!

Thank you!

It is with a grateful heart I thank you for reading my book. I would love it if you would keep in touch and invite you to connect through any of my social media platforms.

I look forward very much to welcoming you and hope you continue to support me on my writing journey as I will support you too in any way I can.

The world is a big place and there's room for all of us to be successful, so join me and let's enjoy future happiness and success together as we celebrate achievement hand in hand.

With much love, Soulla xxx

Other books

Broken Pieces of Tomorrow

(Fiction)

Georgia, a second generation Greek Cypriot woman, faces an uncertain future after her marriage breaks down leaving her with three young sons.

Along the way, through tears and heartache, she pieces her life together after having lost herself for too long in motherhood and matrimony.

A journey of emotional and spiritual self-discovery, female friendship, love lost and love found.

5* Amazon Reader Reviews

A heart-warming journey of emotional self-discovery. The novel gives the reader an insight into the experience of the modern London Greek Cypriot community and is also an open and honest account of losing and finding true love…I thoroughly enjoyed it.

- LJ

Heart Felt and Heart tearing; to use a cliché it's a Rollercoaster of emotions…struggling to come to terms with infidelity and marital breakup, fighting to keep her family together…She awakens to a new her as she comes out of the trauma and pain of what's happened to her and her children…Incredibly well written; I couldn't put it down. Coming to terms with life problems against a backdrop of North London Greek Orthodox family life; if nothing else you'll love the descriptions of Greek Cypriot cooking.

- Andrew

…amazing book and truly couldn't put it down. I could feel what the characters felt, the pain the laugher and the determination. The storyline engulfed me with lots of peaks throughout. Highly recommended.

- AS

Sunshine after Rain

(Poetry)

A collection of thirty poems inspired by old sayings and phrases. Many of us have grown up listening to our parents and grandparents saying them, our teachers and friends.

Included in the collection are poems written around a number of different themes and ideas including: hope, love, happiness, disappointment, beauty, struggle, resignation, joy, life, nature and of course that most British of all things, the weather!

Social Media

soulla-author.com
soulla-author.com/blog
twitter.com/schristodoulou2
instagram.com/soullasays
facebook.com/soullabookauthor
uk.pinterest.com/asceducational
scriggler.com/Profile/soulla_christodoulou_anastasia_loizou

Book Club Guide

A Book Club Guide for Broken Pieces of Tomorrow is available via my website so please take a look.

soulla-author.com

I hope you enjoy discussing the story with your friends and family.

Book Review

All reviews are welcome so please take a few minutes to leave yours.

If you're not sure what to include in a book review then you can look at some helpful tips, available on my website.

soulla-author.com

Thanks again for taking the time to read and review my book.

Printed in Great Britain
by Amazon

69329498R00293